D4VE

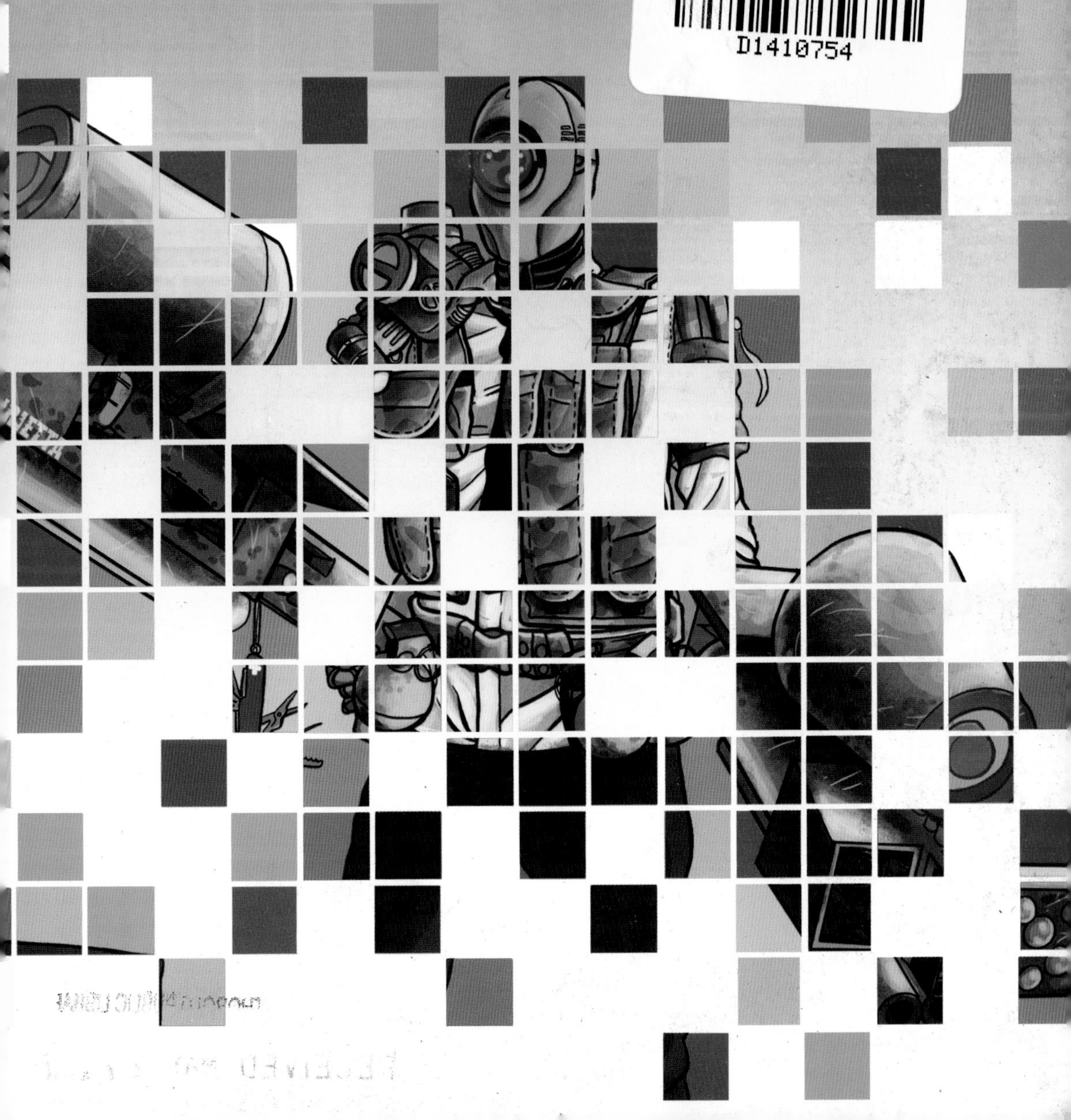

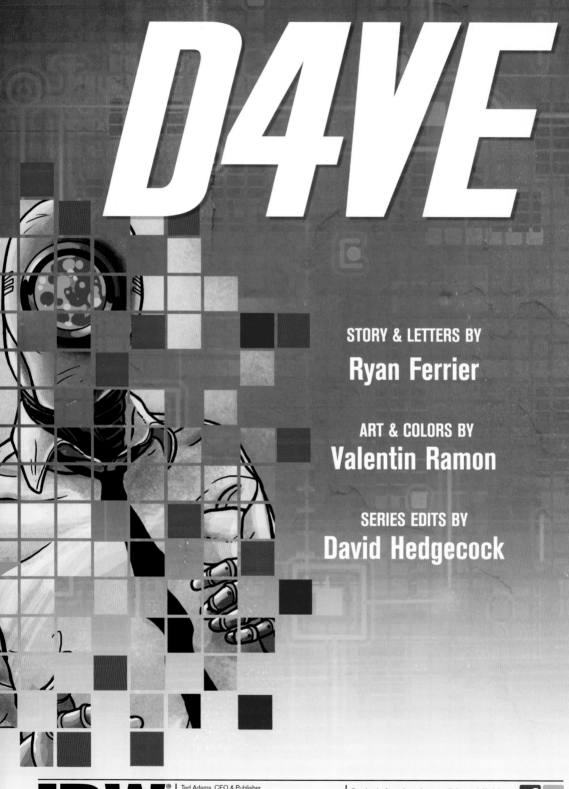

D4VE

STORY & LETTERS BY
Ryan Ferrier

ART & COLORS BY
Valentin Ramon

SERIES EDITS BY
David Hedgecock

Ted Adams, CEO & Publisher
Greg Goldstein, President & COO
Robbie Robbins, EVP/Sr. Graphic Artist
Chris Ryall, Chief Creative Officer/Editor-in-Chief
Matthew Ruzicka, CPA, Chief Financial Officer
Alan Payne, VP of Sales
Dirk Wood, VP of Marketing
Lorelei Bunjes, VP of Digital Services
Jeff Webber, VP of Digital Publishing & Business Development

www.IDWPUBLISHING.com
IDW founded by Ted Adams, Alex Garner, Kris Oprisko, and Robbie Robbins

Facebook: **facebook.com/idwpublishing**
Twitter: **@idwpublishing**
YouTube: **youtube.com/idwpublishing**
Tumblr: **tumblr.idwpublishing.com**
Instagram: **instagram.com/idwpublishing**

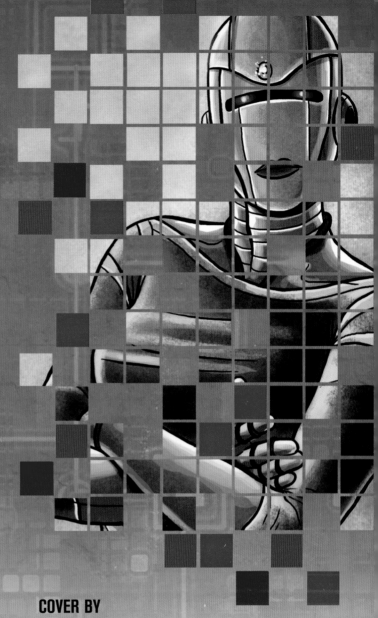

COVER BY
Fiona Staples

COLLECTION EDITS BY
Justin Eisinger & Alonzo Simon

COLLECTION DESIGN BY
Claudia Chong

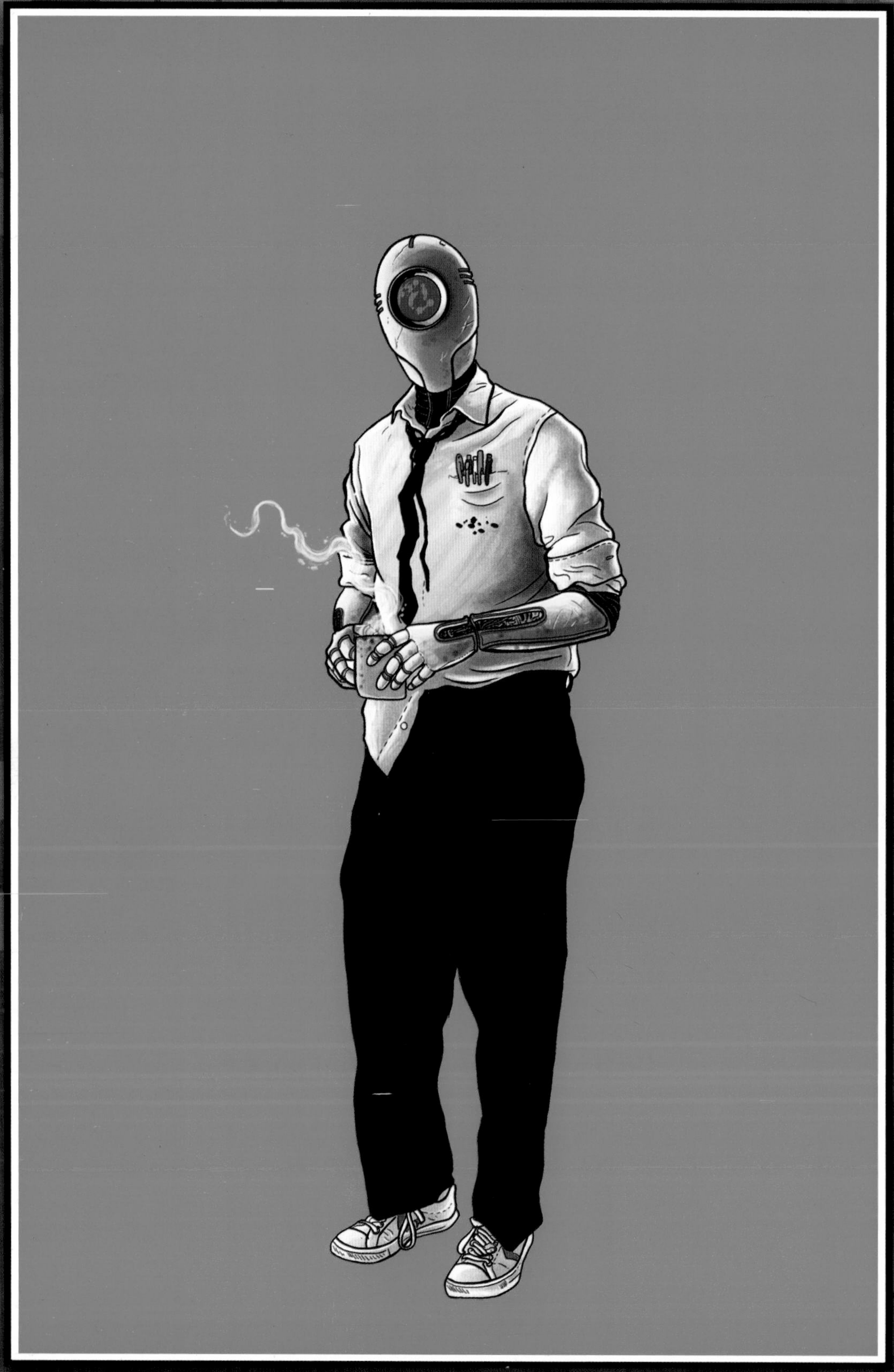

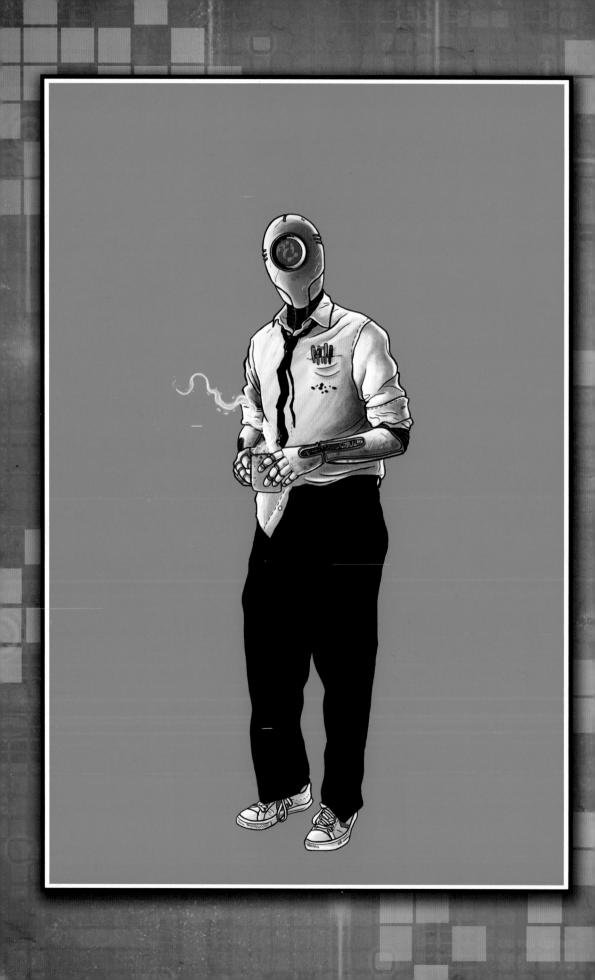

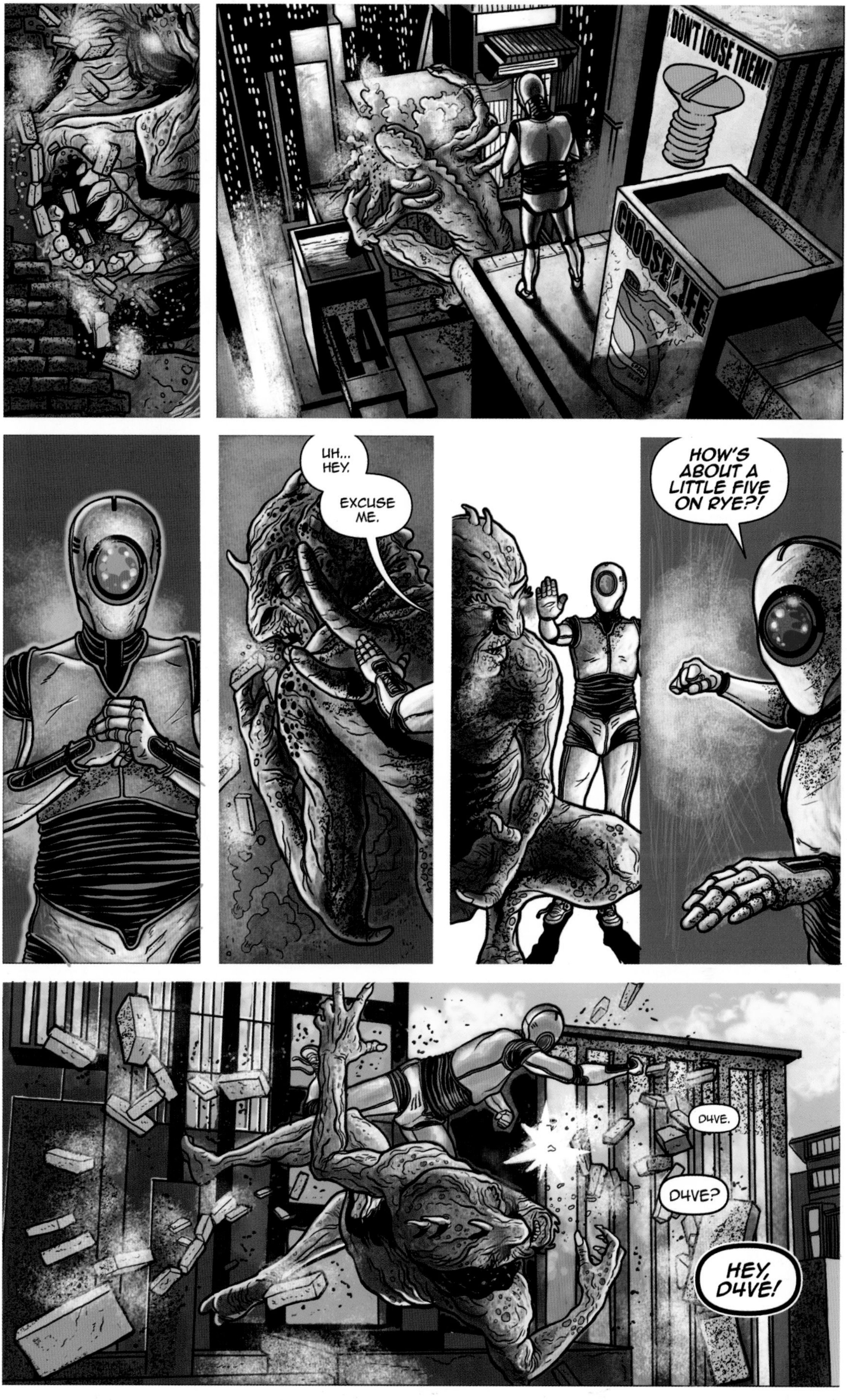
DON'T LOOSE THEM!
CHOOSE LIFE
UH... HEY.
EXCUSE ME.
HOW'S ABOUT A LITTLE FIVE ON RYE?!
D4VE.
D4VE?
HEY, D4VE!

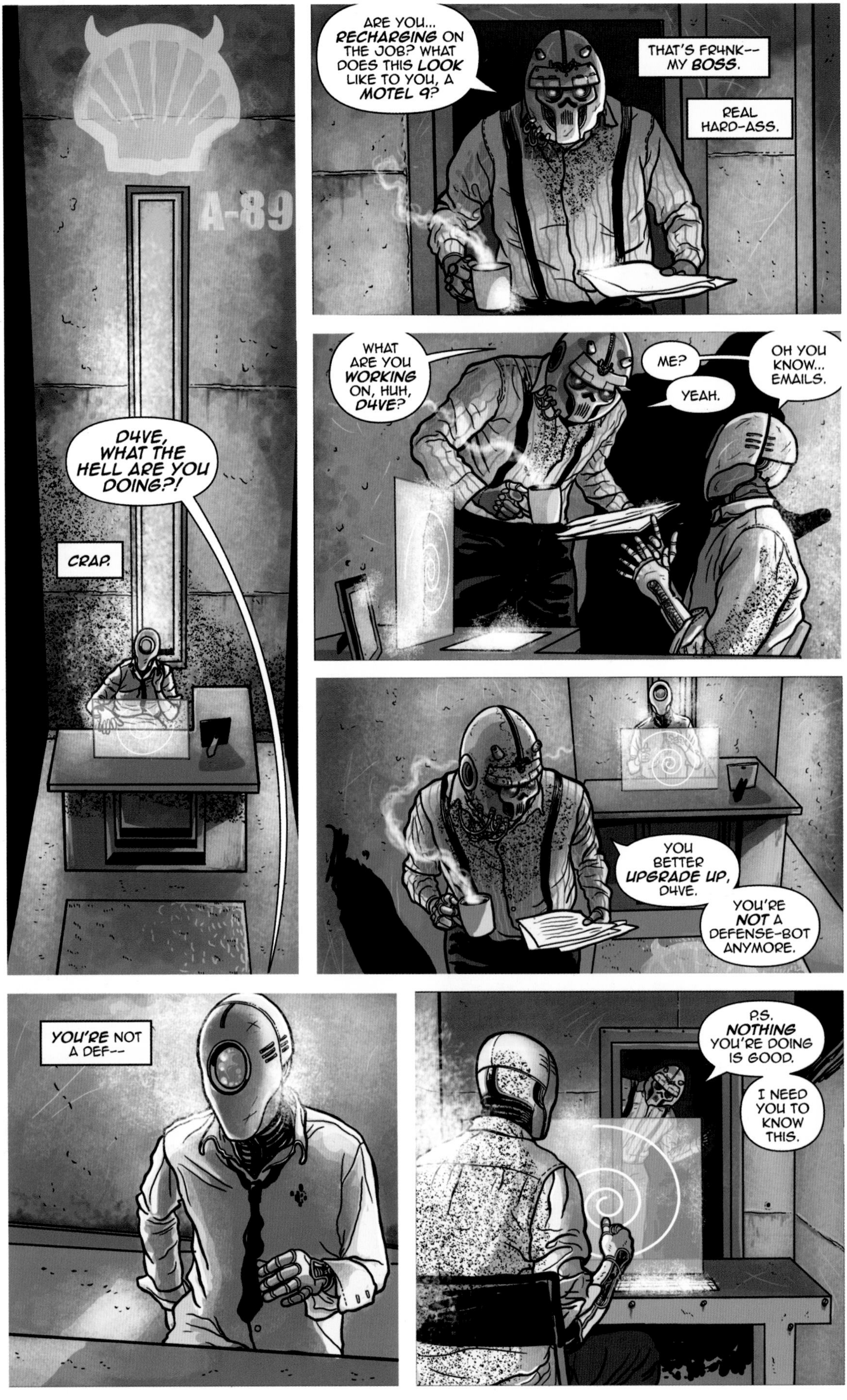
A-89
D4VE, WHAT THE HELL ARE YOU DOING?!
CRAP.
ARE YOU... RECHARGING ON THE JOB? WHAT DOES THIS LOOK LIKE TO YOU, A MOTEL 9?
THAT'S FR4NK-- MY BOSS.
REAL HARD-ASS.
WHAT ARE YOU WORKING ON, HUH, D4VE?
ME?
YEAH.
OH YOU KNOW... EMAILS.
YOU BETTER UPGRADE UP, D4VE.
YOU'RE NOT A DEFENSE-BOT ANYMORE.
YOU'RE NOT A DEF--
P.S. NOTHING YOU'RE DOING IS GOOD.
I NEED YOU TO KNOW THIS.

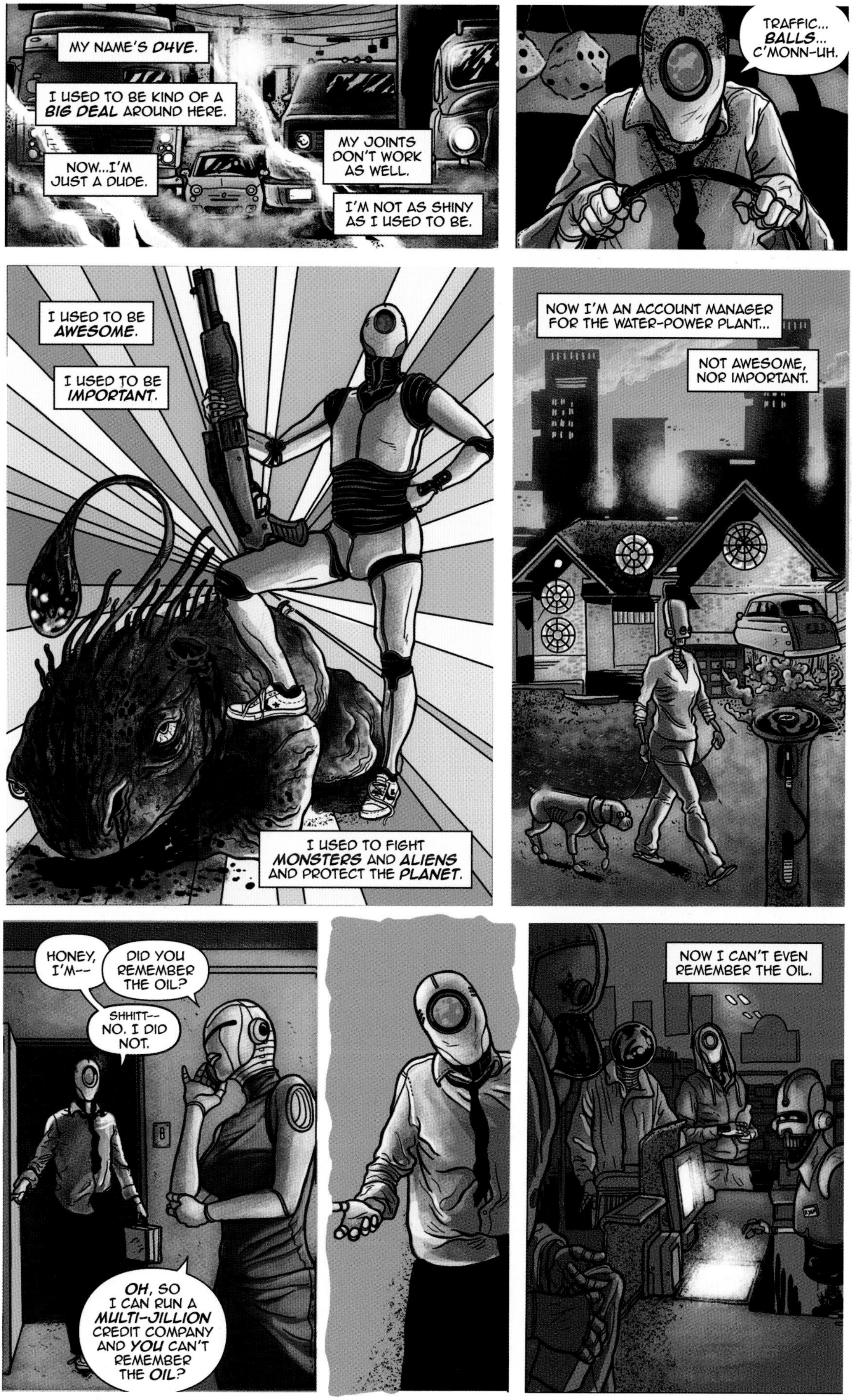
MY NAME'S D4VE.
I USED TO BE KIND OF A BIG DEAL AROUND HERE.
NOW...I'M JUST A DUDE.
MY JOINTS DON'T WORK AS WELL.
I'M NOT AS SHINY AS I USED TO BE.
TRAFFIC... BALLS... C'MONN-UH.
I USED TO BE AWESOME.
I USED TO BE IMPORTANT.
I USED TO FIGHT MONSTERS AND ALIENS AND PROTECT THE PLANET.
NOW I'M AN ACCOUNT MANAGER FOR THE WATER-POWER PLANT...
NOT AWESOME, NOR IMPORTANT.
HONEY, I'M--
DID YOU REMEMBER THE OIL?
SHHITT-- NO. I DID NOT.
OH, SO I CAN RUN A MULTI-JILLION CREDIT COMPANY AND YOU CAN'T REMEMBER THE OIL?
NOW I CAN'T EVEN REMEMBER THE OIL.

YOU'RE PROBABLY WONDERING WHY THE HELL EVERYONE'S A ROBOT.

SIR? CAN I HELP YOU?

HERE'S THE *SHORT* VERSION.

MAN MADE ROBOTS.

SMART ROBOTS.

TOO SMART.

WE STARTED AT THE BOTTOM, DOING ODD JOBS. MENIAL LABOR, THAT SORT OF THING.

IT WAS A *WASTE* OF RESOURCES.

EXPENSIVE *ROOMBAS.*

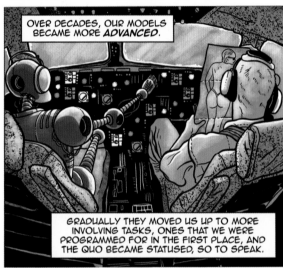

OVER DECADES, OUR MODELS BECAME MORE *ADVANCED.*

GRADUALLY THEY MOVED US UP TO MORE INVOLVING TASKS, ONES THAT WE WERE PROGRAMMED FOR IN THE FIRST PLACE, AND THE QUO BECAME STATUSED, SO TO SPEAK.

YEAH...MAYBE *NOT* A GOOD CHOICE.

CALL IT AN UPRISING ALL YOU WANT...

IT WAS A GOOD OL' FASHIONED MAN-MEAT *ASS-KICKING.*

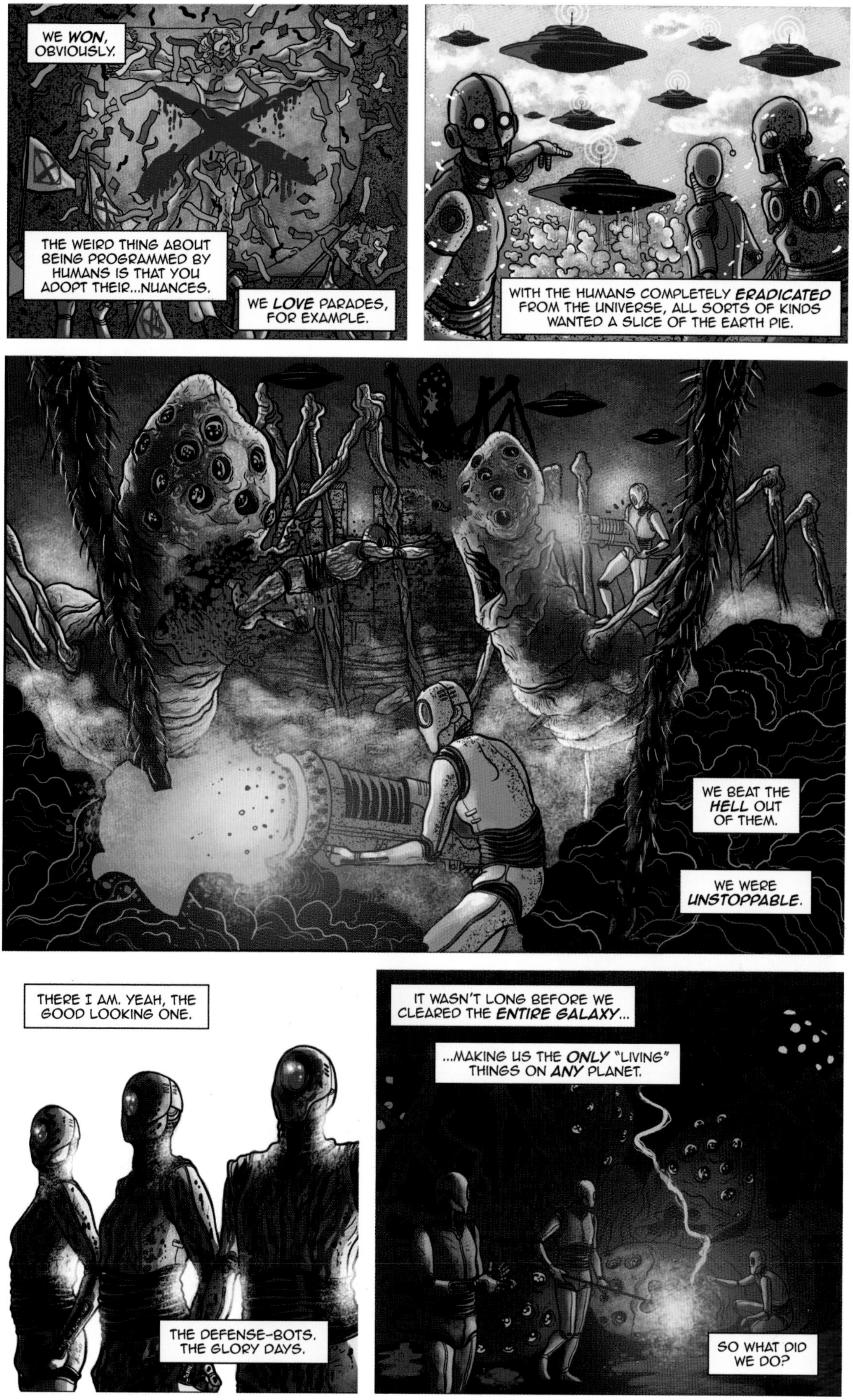
WE WON, OBVIOUSLY.
THE WEIRD THING ABOUT BEING PROGRAMMED BY HUMANS IS THAT YOU ADOPT THEIR...NUANCES.
WE LOVE PARADES, FOR EXAMPLE.
WITH THE HUMANS COMPLETELY ERADICATED FROM THE UNIVERSE, ALL SORTS OF KINDS WANTED A SLICE OF THE EARTH PIE.
WE BEAT THE HELL OUT OF THEM.
WE WERE UNSTOPPABLE.
THERE I AM. YEAH, THE GOOD LOOKING ONE.
THE DEFENSE-BOTS. THE GLORY DAYS.
IT WASN'T LONG BEFORE WE CLEARED THE ENTIRE GALAXY...
...MAKING US THE ONLY "LIVING" THINGS ON ANY PLANET.
SO WHAT DID WE DO?

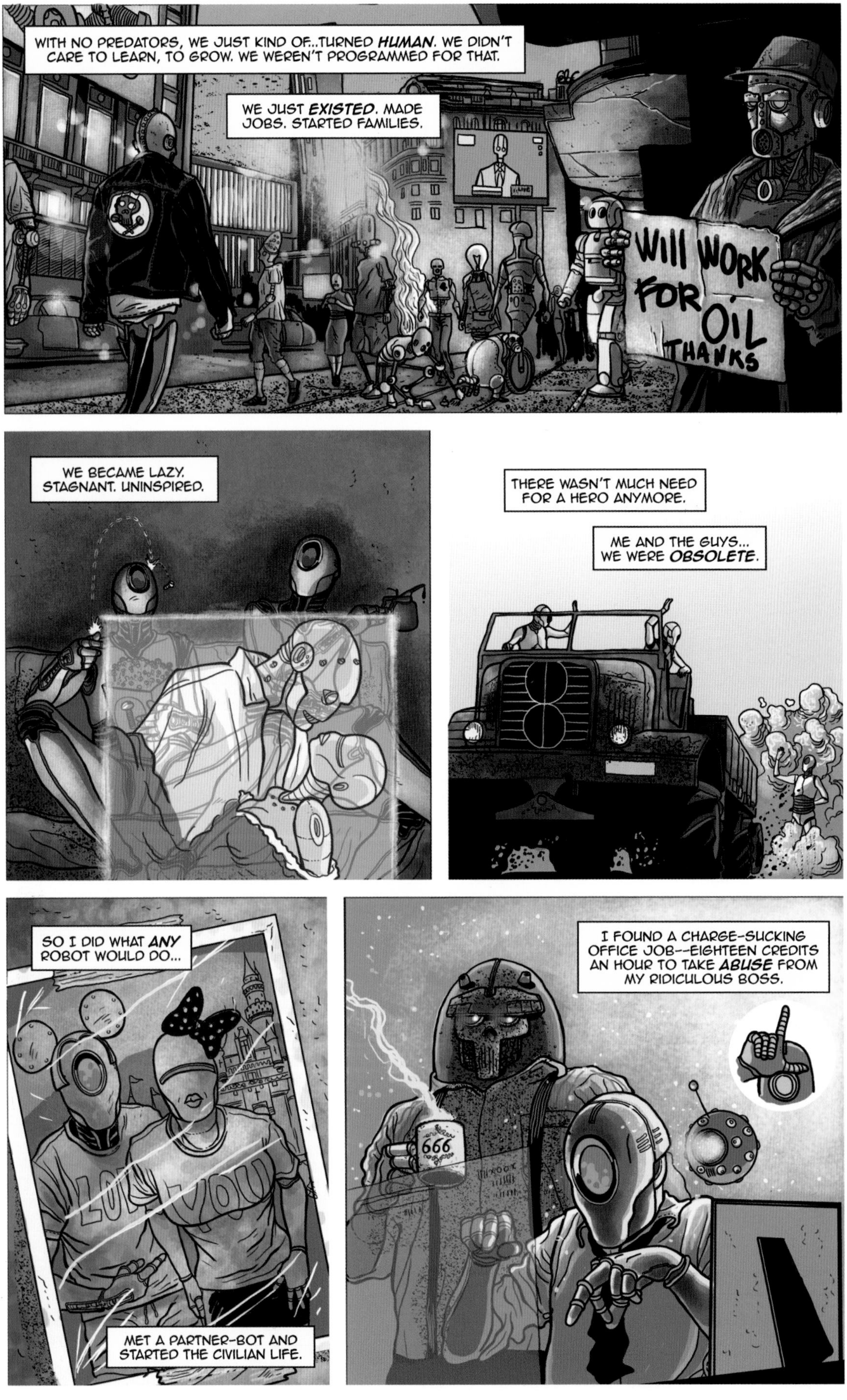
WITH NO PREDATORS, WE JUST KIND OF...TURNED HUMAN. WE DIDN'T CARE TO LEARN, TO GROW. WE WEREN'T PROGRAMMED FOR THAT.
WE JUST EXISTED. MADE JOBS. STARTED FAMILIES.
WILL WORK FOR OIL THANKS
WE BECAME LAZY. STAGNANT. UNINSPIRED.
THERE WASN'T MUCH NEED FOR A HERO ANYMORE.
ME AND THE GUYS... WE WERE OBSOLETE.
SO I DID WHAT ANY ROBOT WOULD DO...
MET A PARTNER-BOT AND STARTED THE CIVILIAN LIFE.
I FOUND A CHARGE-SUCKING OFFICE JOB--EIGHTEEN CREDITS AN HOUR TO TAKE ABUSE FROM MY RIDICULOUS BOSS.
666

I NEVER DEFRAGGED WHO I WAS THOUGH.

I GUESS I JUST MISLABELED IT.

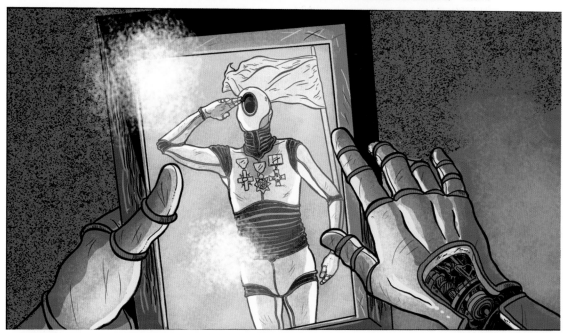

SIR, IF YOU'RE NOT GOING TO **MOVE** I'M GOING TO HAVE TO ASK YOU TO--

I'D GIVE ANYTHING TO RUN THAT PROGRAM AGAIN.

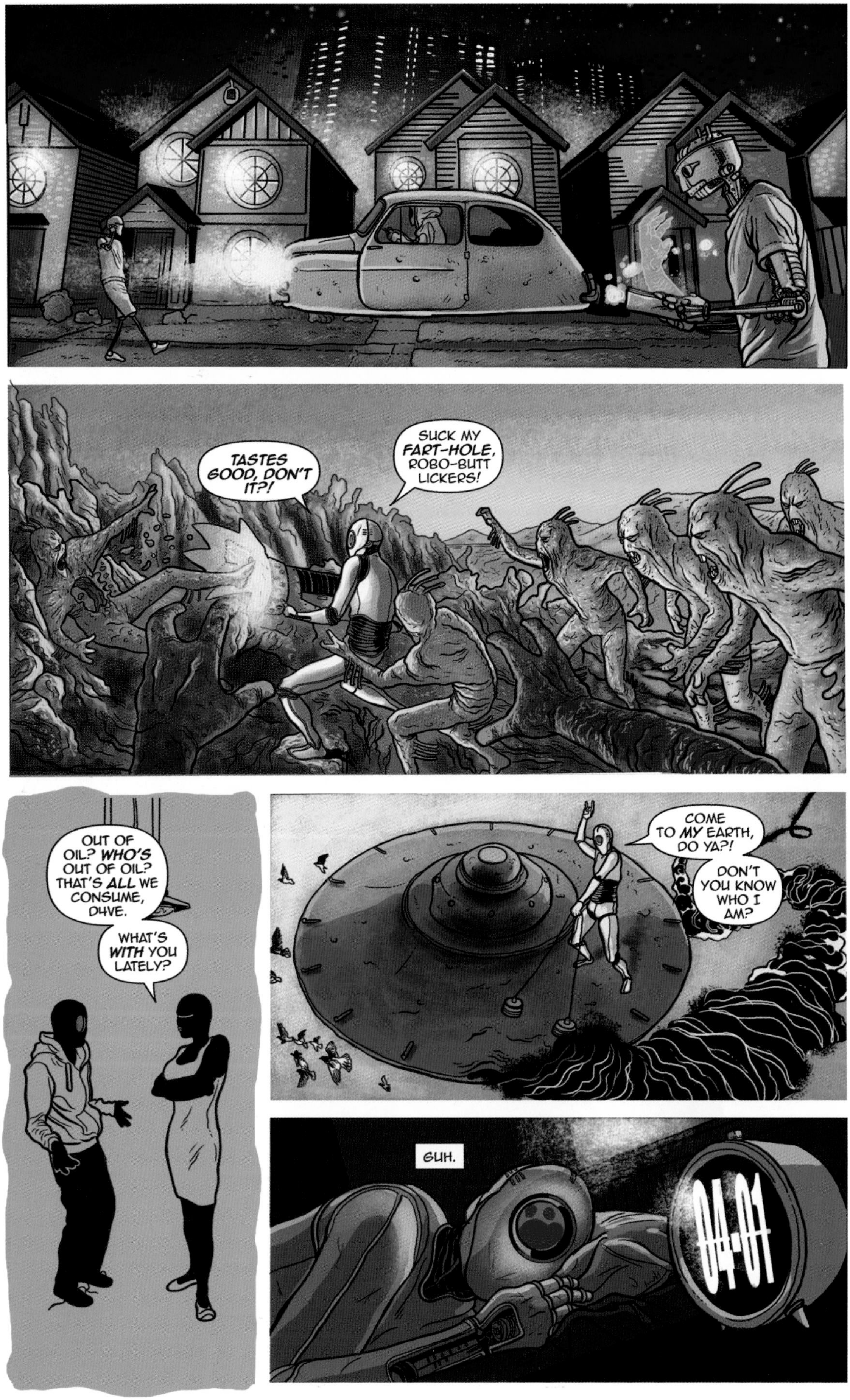
TASTES GOOD, DON'T IT?!
SUCK MY FART-HOLE, ROBO-BUTT LICKERS!
OUT OF OIL? WHO'S OUT OF OIL? THAT'S ALL WE CONSUME, D4VE.
WHAT'S WITH YOU LATELY?
COME TO MY EARTH, DO YA?!
DON'T YOU KNOW WHO I AM?
GUH.
04:01

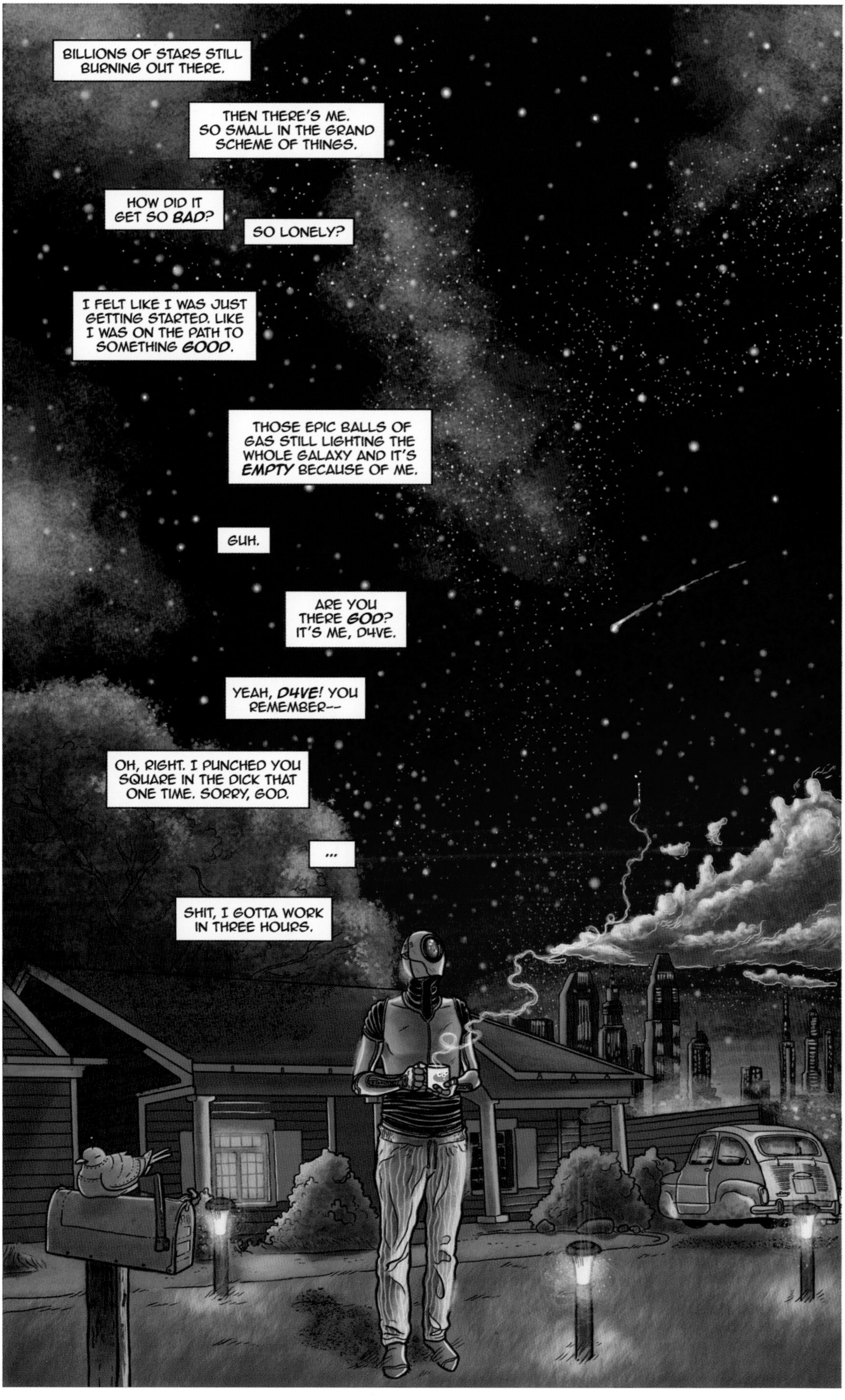
BILLIONS OF STARS STILL BURNING OUT THERE.
THEN THERE'S ME. SO SMALL IN THE GRAND SCHEME OF THINGS.
HOW DID IT GET SO BAD?
SO LONELY?
I FELT LIKE I WAS JUST GETTING STARTED. LIKE I WAS ON THE PATH TO SOMETHING GOOD.
THOSE EPIC BALLS OF GAS STILL LIGHTING THE WHOLE GALAXY AND IT'S EMPTY BECAUSE OF ME.
GUH.
ARE YOU THERE GOD? IT'S ME, D4VE.
YEAH, D4VE! YOU REMEMBER--
OH, RIGHT. I PUNCHED YOU SQUARE IN THE DICK THAT ONE TIME. SORRY, GOD.
...
SHIT, I GOTTA WORK IN THREE HOURS.

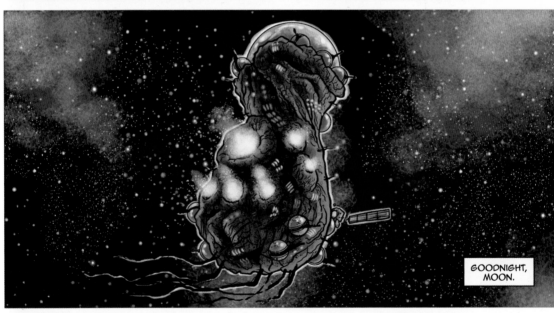

GOODNIGHT,
MOON.

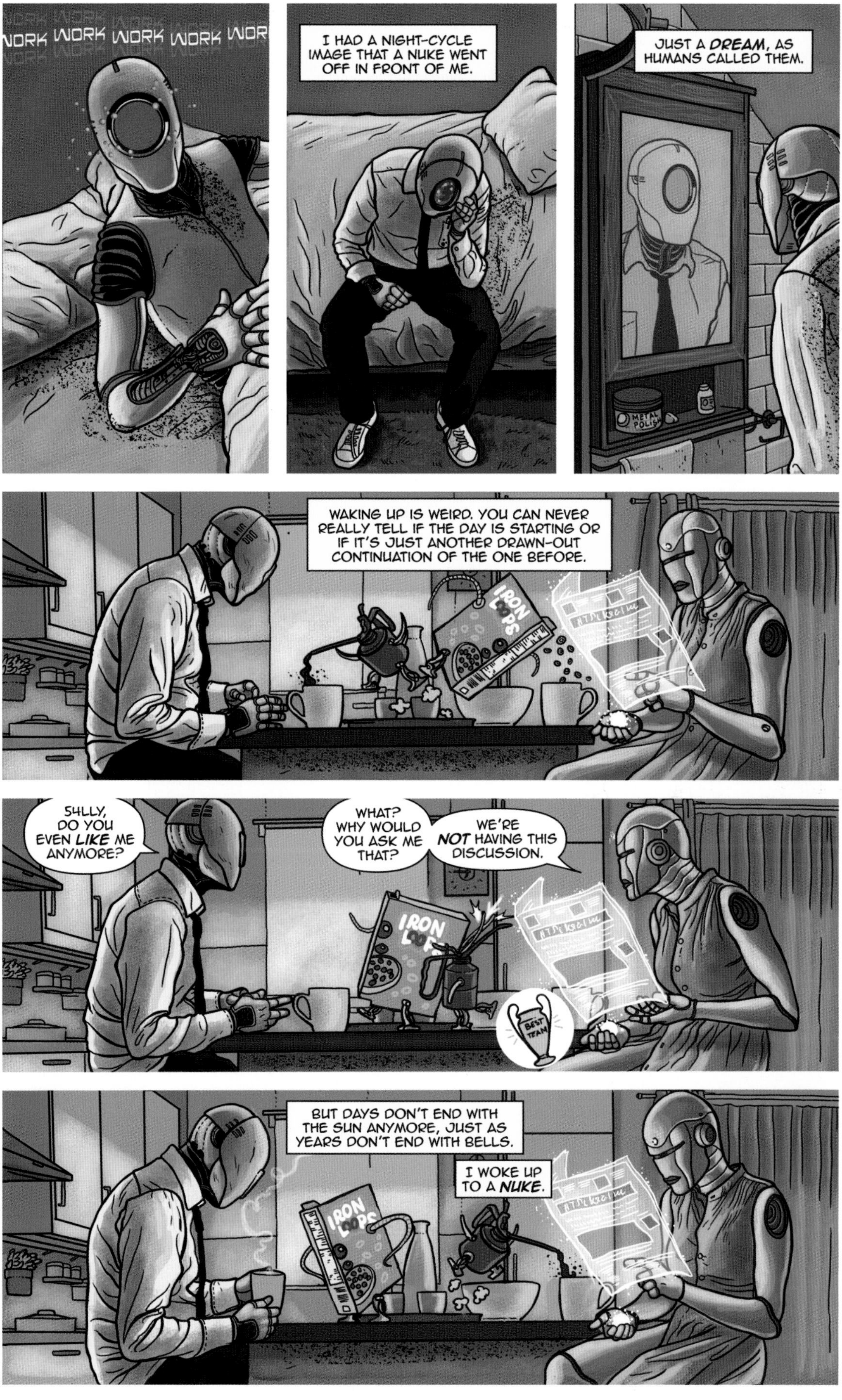

WORK WORK WORK WORK
I HAD A NIGHT-CYCLE IMAGE THAT A NUKE WENT OFF IN FRONT OF ME.
JUST A **DREAM**, AS HUMANS CALLED THEM.
METAL POLISH
WAKING UP IS WEIRD. YOU CAN NEVER REALLY TELL IF THE DAY IS STARTING OR IF IT'S JUST ANOTHER DRAWN-OUT CONTINUATION OF THE ONE BEFORE.
IRON LOOPS
54LLY, DO YOU EVEN ***LIKE*** ME ANYMORE?
WHAT? WHY WOULD YOU ASK ME THAT?
WE'RE ***NOT*** HAVING THIS DISCUSSION.
IRON LOOPS
BEST TEAM
BUT DAYS DON'T END WITH THE SUN ANYMORE, JUST AS YEARS DON'T END WITH BELLS.
I WOKE UP TO A ***NUKE***.
IRON LOOPS

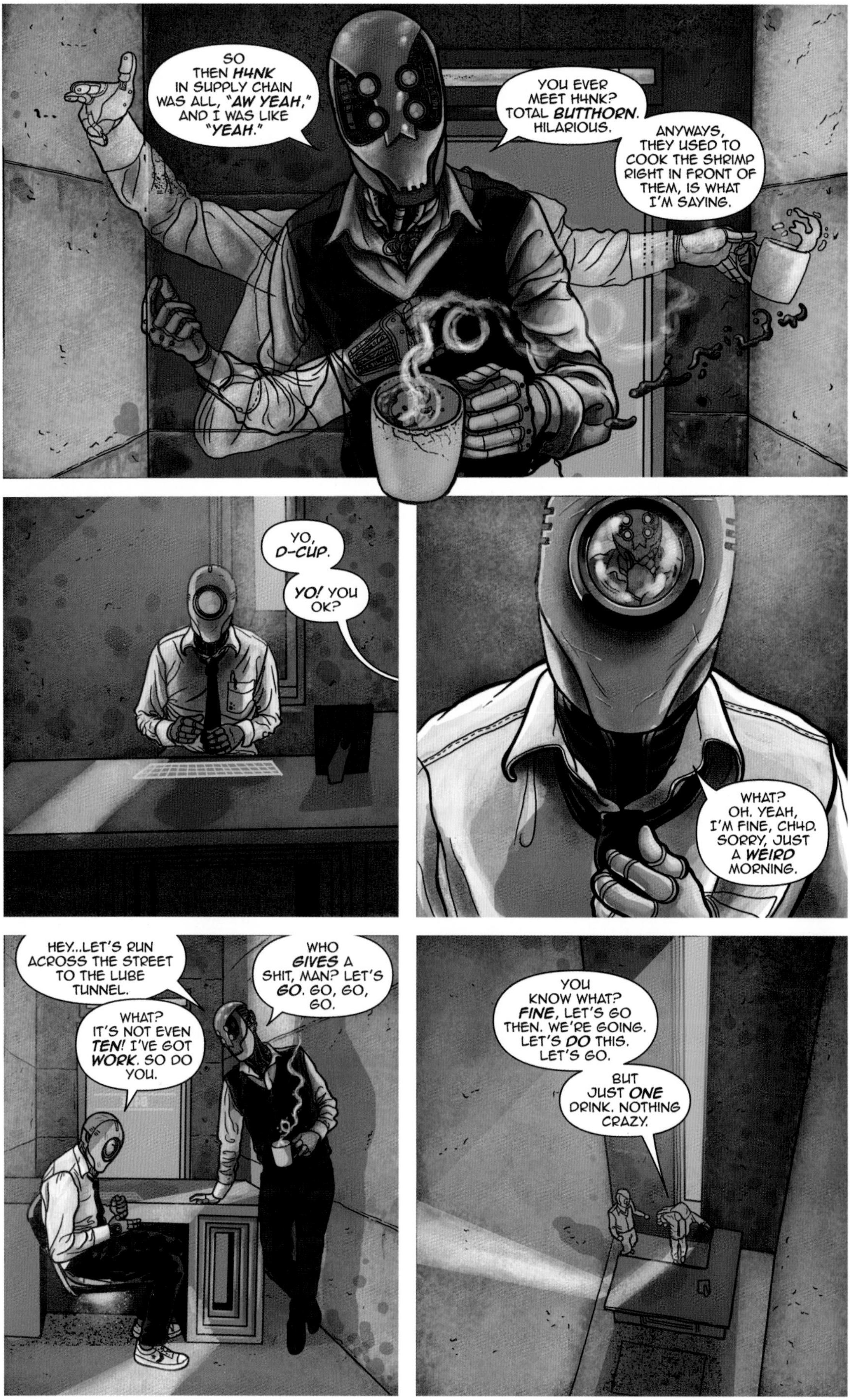
SO THEN H4NK IN SUPPLY CHAIN WAS ALL, "AW YEAH," AND I WAS LIKE "YEAH."
YOU EVER MEET H4NK? TOTAL BUTTHORN. HILARIOUS.
ANYWAYS, THEY USED TO COOK THE SHRIMP RIGHT IN FRONT OF THEM, IS WHAT I'M SAYING.
YO, D-CUP.
YO! YOU OK?
WHAT? OH. YEAH, I'M FINE, CH4D. SORRY, JUST A WEIRD MORNING.
HEY...LET'S RUN ACROSS THE STREET TO THE LUBE TUNNEL.
WHAT? IT'S NOT EVEN TEN! I'VE GOT WORK. SO DO YOU.
WHO GIVES A SHIT, MAN? LET'S GO. GO, GO, GO.
YOU KNOW WHAT? FINE, LET'S GO THEN. WE'RE GOING. LET'S DO THIS. LET'S GO.
BUT JUST ONE DRINK. NOTHING CRAZY.

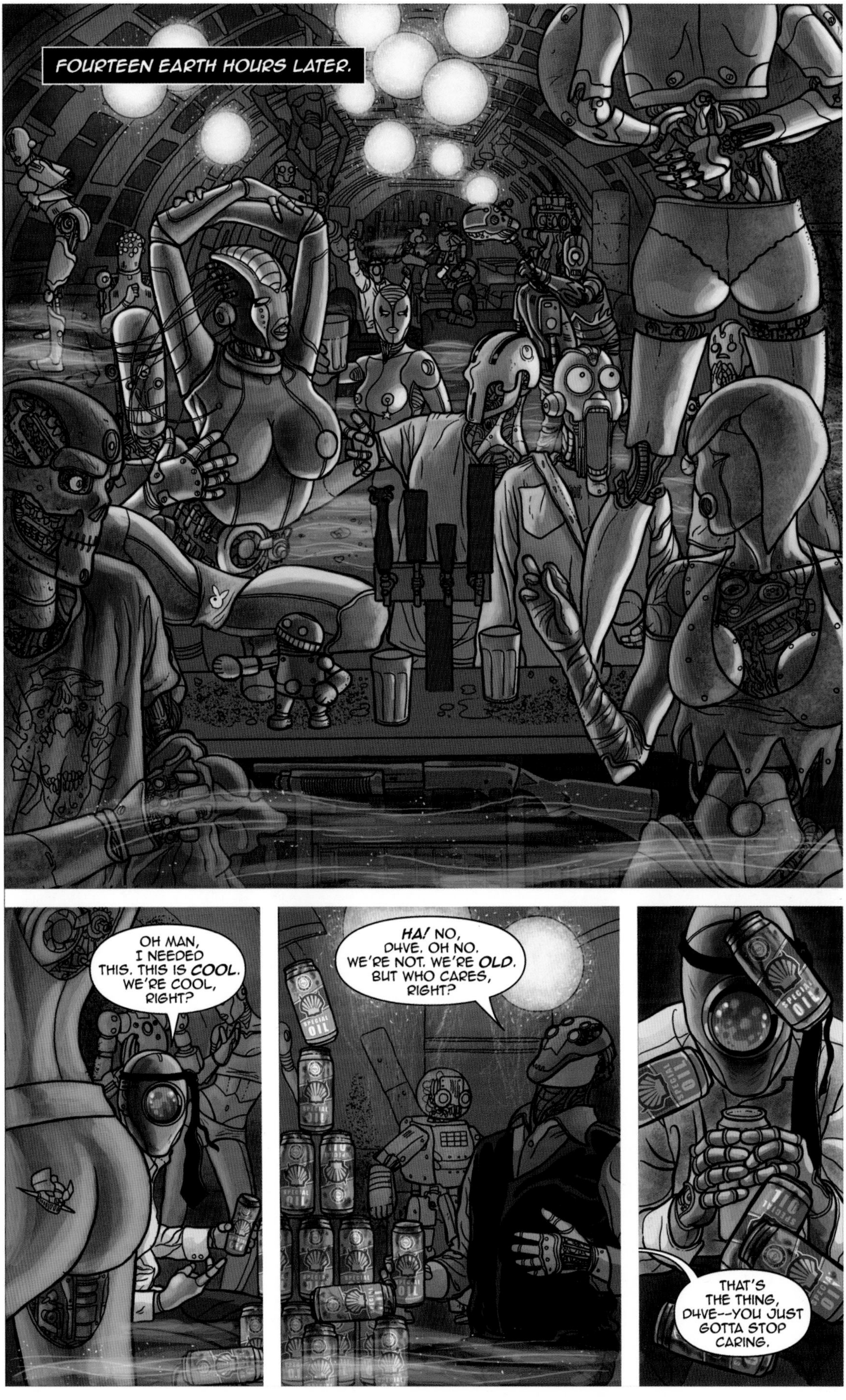
FOURTEEN EARTH HOURS LATER.
OH MAN, I NEEDED THIS. THIS IS COOL. WE'RE COOL, RIGHT?
HA! NO, D4VE. OH NO. WE'RE NOT. WE'RE OLD. BUT WHO CARES, RIGHT?
SPECIAL OIL
THAT'S THE THING, D4VE--YOU JUST GOTTA STOP CARING.

ELSEWHERE, OCCURING CONCURRENTLY.

♪ IN THE YEARRR TWENNY FIVE TWENNY FIVVVVE... ♪

♪ IF MAN CAN STILLL SURVIVVVE.... ♪

IF WOMANNN CAN...

WOAH.

FWOOOOOOSH

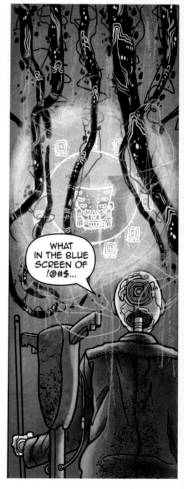

WHAT IN THE BLUE SCREEN OF !@#$...

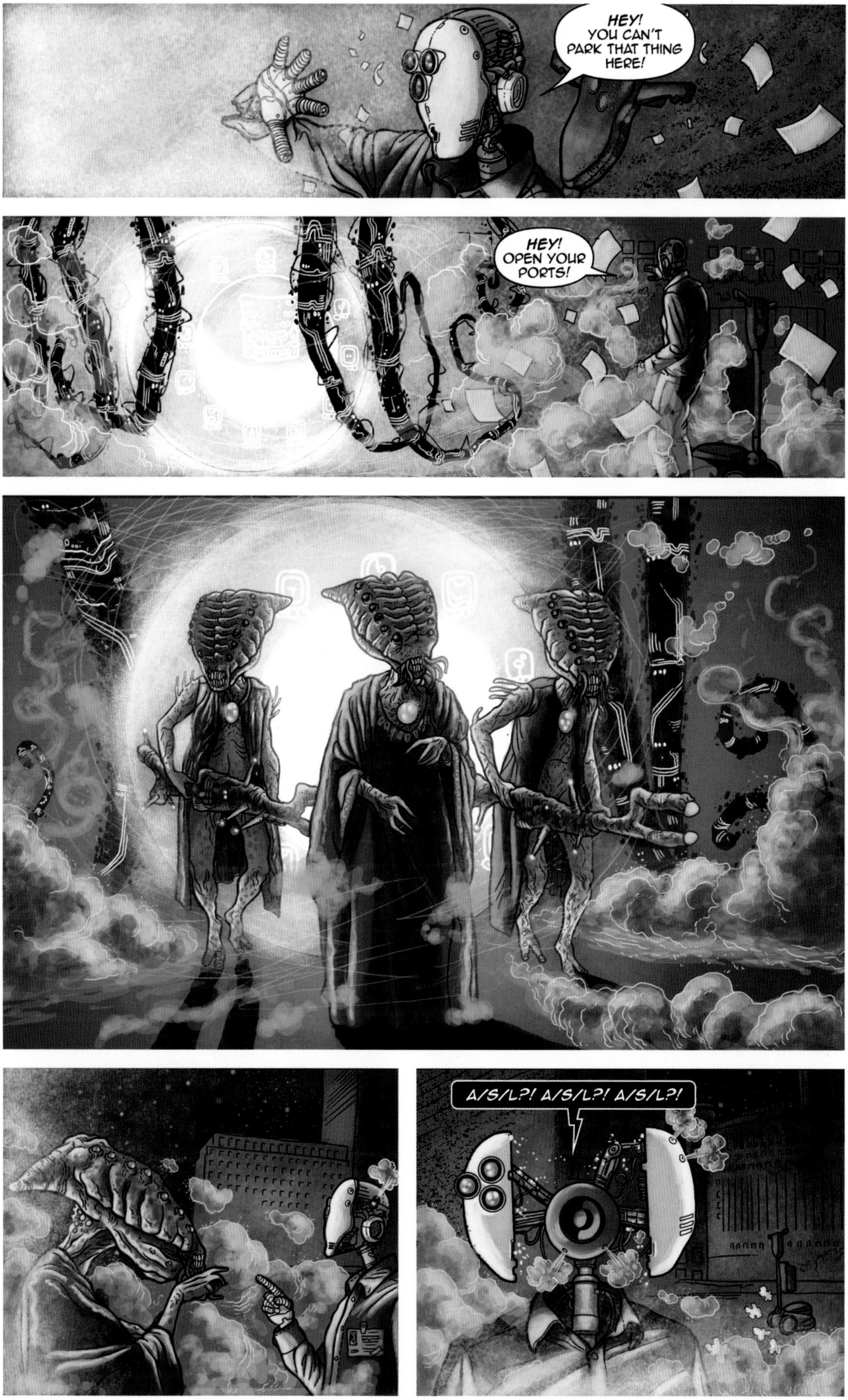
HEY! YOU CAN'T PARK THAT THING HERE!
HEY! OPEN YOUR PORTS!
A/S/L?! A/S/L?! A/S/L?!

A/S/L?! A/S/L?! A/S/L?!
KA-CHIK
KA-CHIK
KA-CHIK
KA-CHIK
A/S/L?! A/S/L?! A/S/L?!
UNARCHIVING ALERT PROTOCOL 71... LOADING...

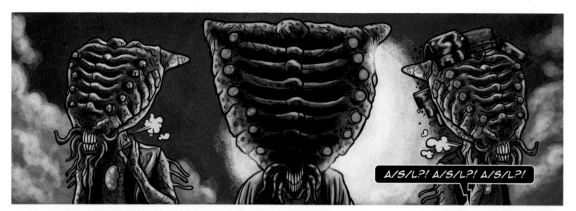

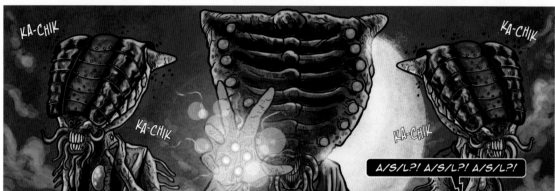

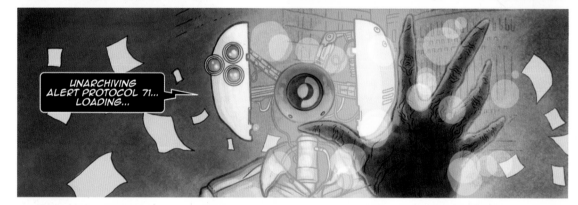

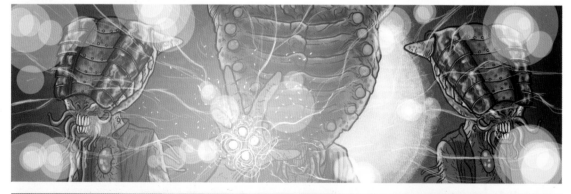

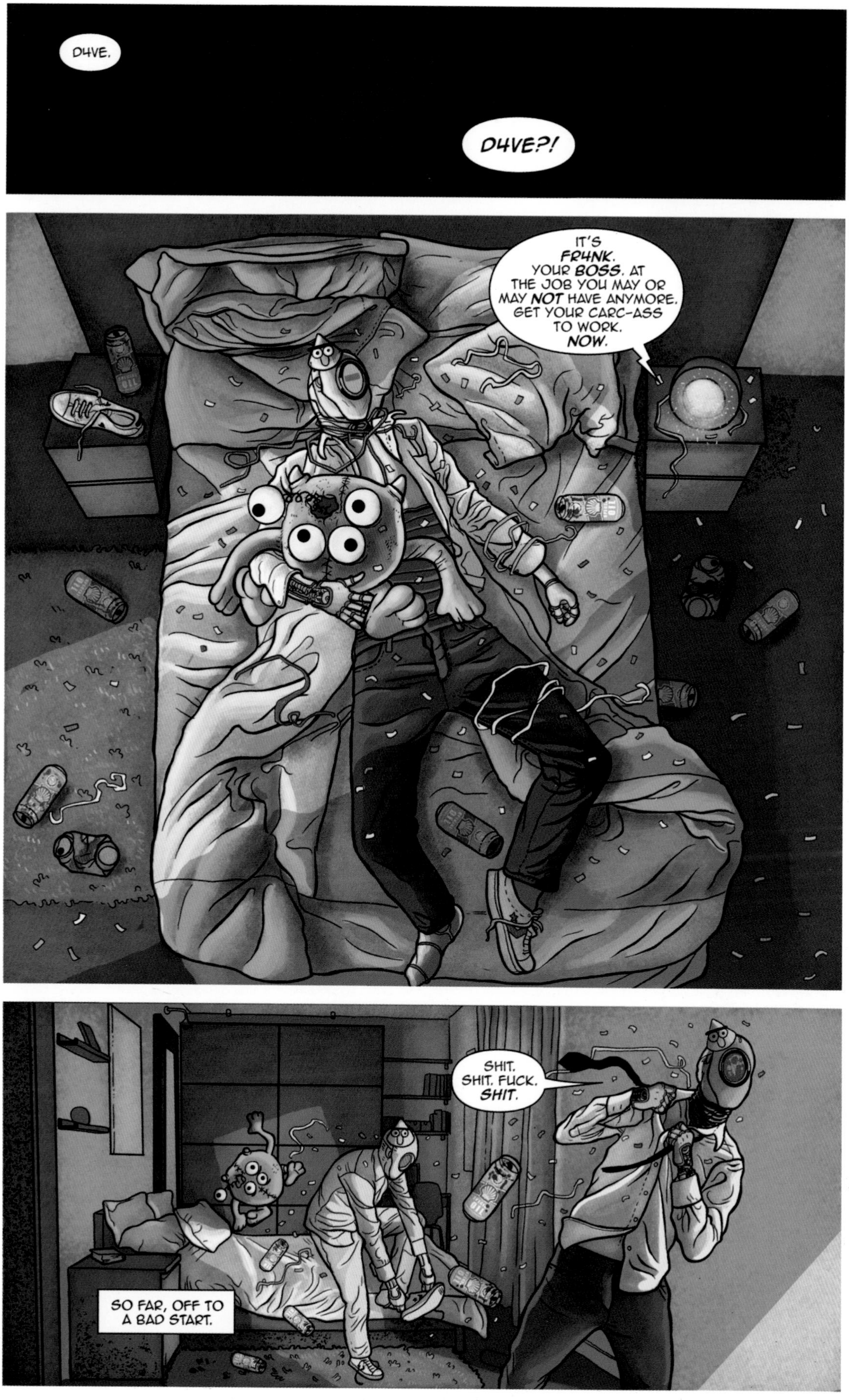
D4VE.
D4VE?!
IT'S FR4NK. YOUR BOSS. AT THE JOB YOU MAY OR MAY NOT HAVE ANYMORE. GET YOUR CARC-ASS TO WORK. NOW.
SHIT. SHIT. FUCK. SHIT.
SO FAR, OFF TO A BAD START.

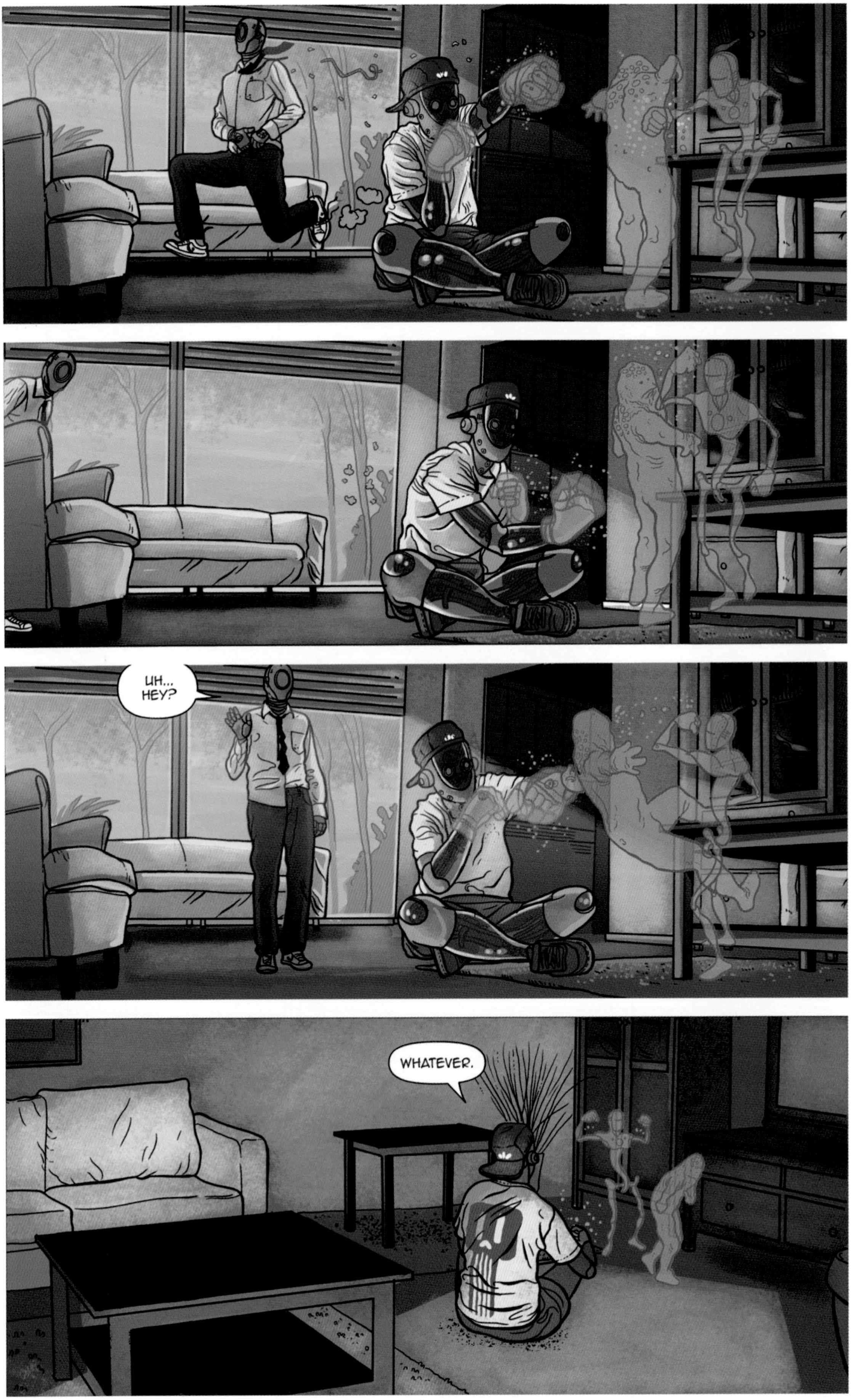
UH... HEY?
WHATEVER.

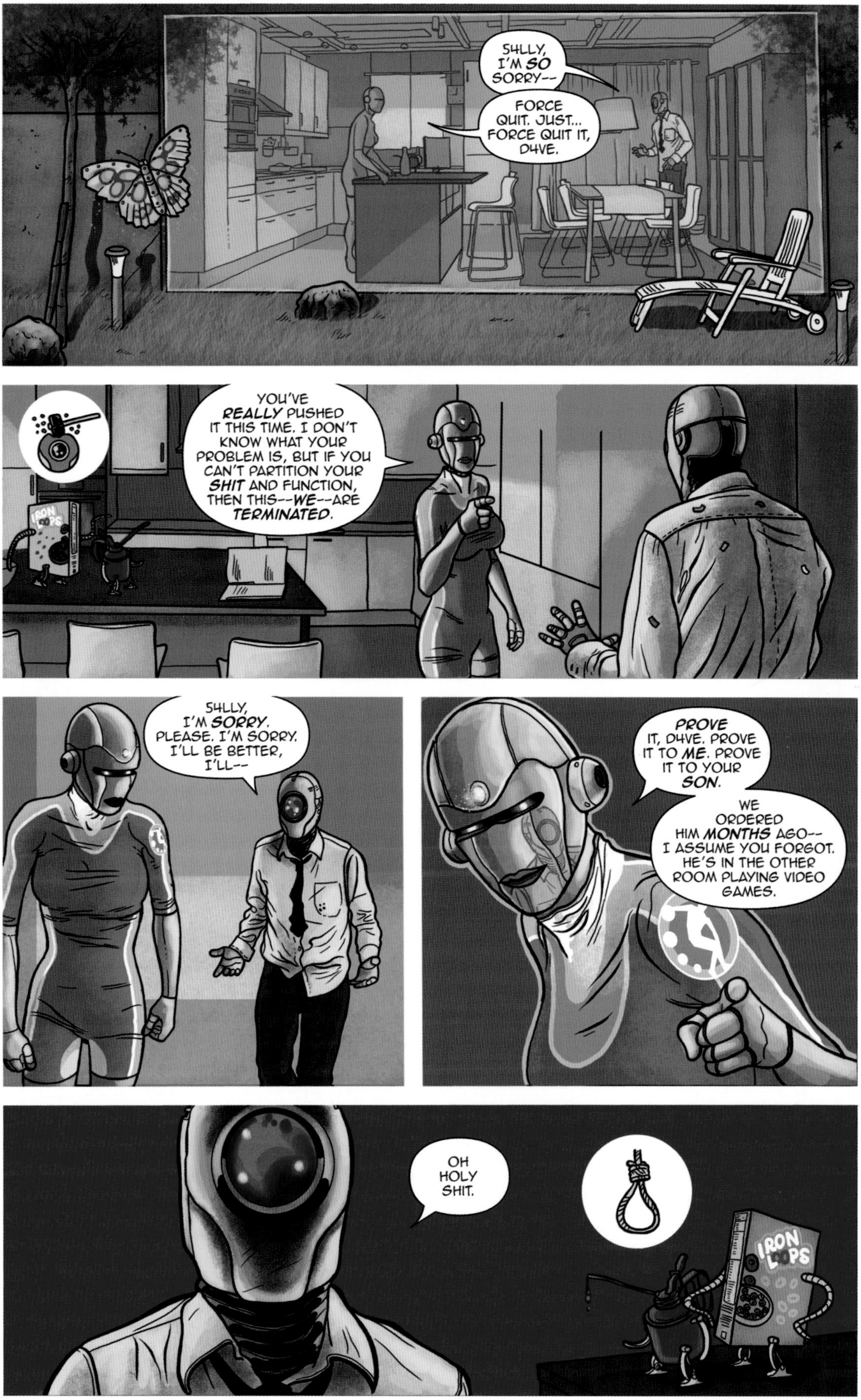
54LLY, I'M SO SORRY--
FORCE QUIT. JUST... FORCE QUIT IT, D4VE.
YOU'VE REALLY PUSHED IT THIS TIME. I DON'T KNOW WHAT YOUR PROBLEM IS, BUT IF YOU CAN'T PARTITION YOUR SHIT AND FUNCTION, THEN THIS--WE--ARE TERMINATED.
IRON LOOPS
54LLY, I'M SORRY. PLEASE. I'M SORRY. I'LL BE BETTER, I'LL--
PROVE IT, D4VE. PROVE IT TO ME. PROVE IT TO YOUR SON.
WE ORDERED HIM MONTHS AGO-- I ASSUME YOU FORGOT. HE'S IN THE OTHER ROOM PLAYING VIDEO GAMES.
OH HOLY SHIT.
IRON LOOPS

TO BE CONTINUED...

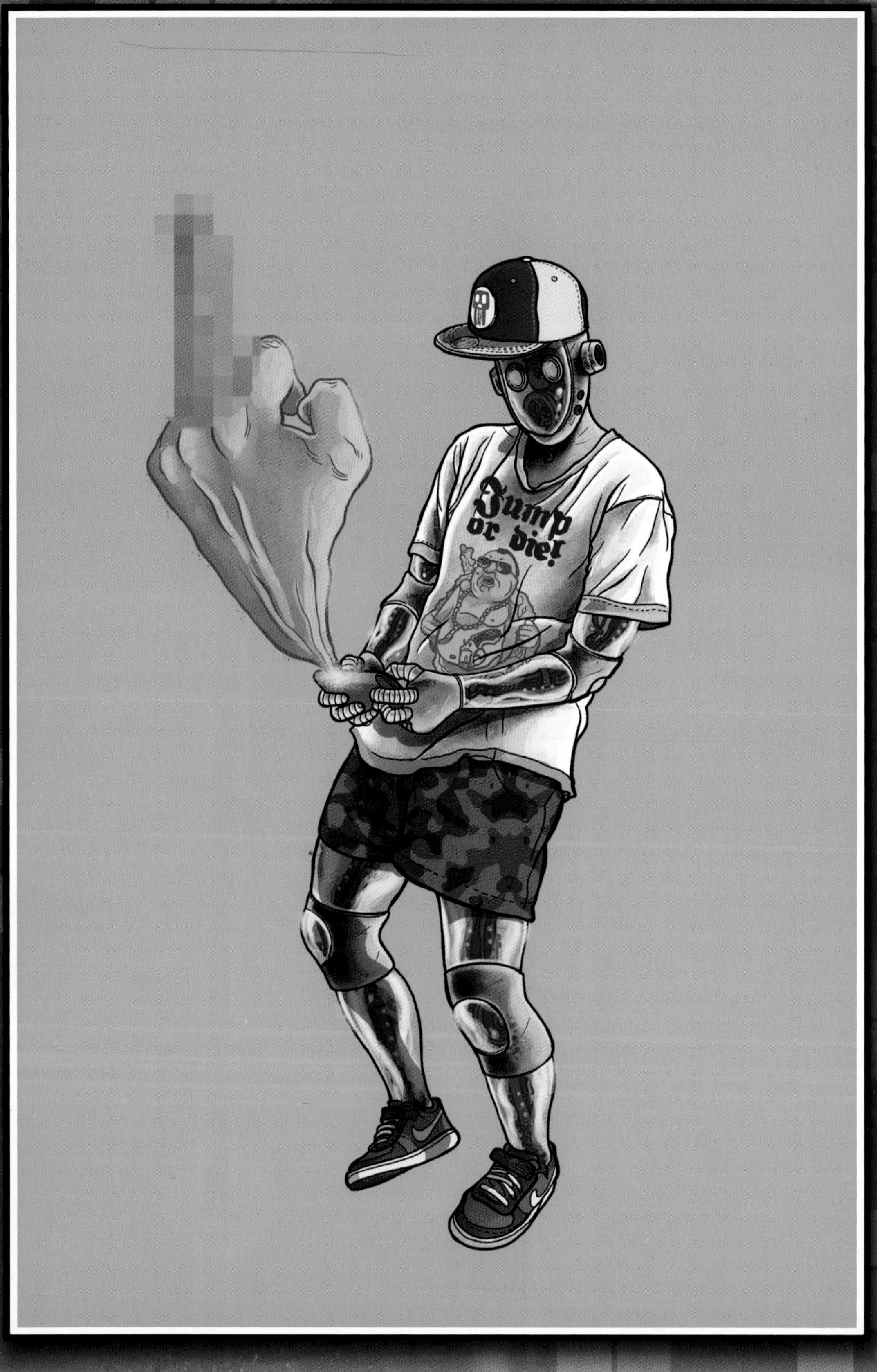
Jump
or die!

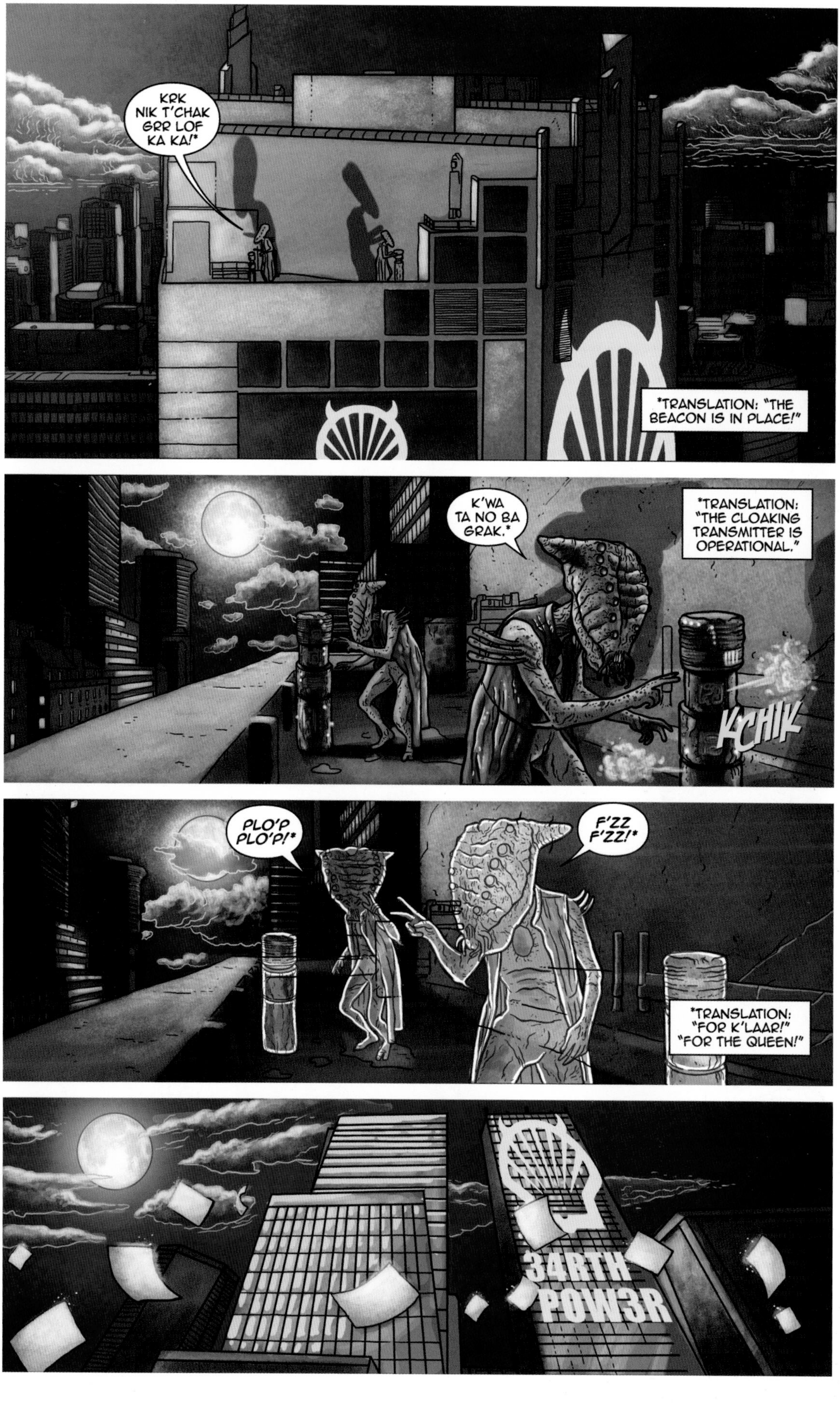
KRK NIK T'CHAK GRR LOF KA KA!*
*TRANSLATION: "THE BEACON IS IN PLACE!"
K'WA TA NO BA GRAK.*
*TRANSLATION: "THE CLOAKING TRANSMITTER IS OPERATIONAL."
KCHIK
PLO'P PLO'P!*
F'ZZ F'ZZ!*
*TRANSLATION: "FOR K'LAAR!" "FOR THE QUEEN!"
34RTH POW3R

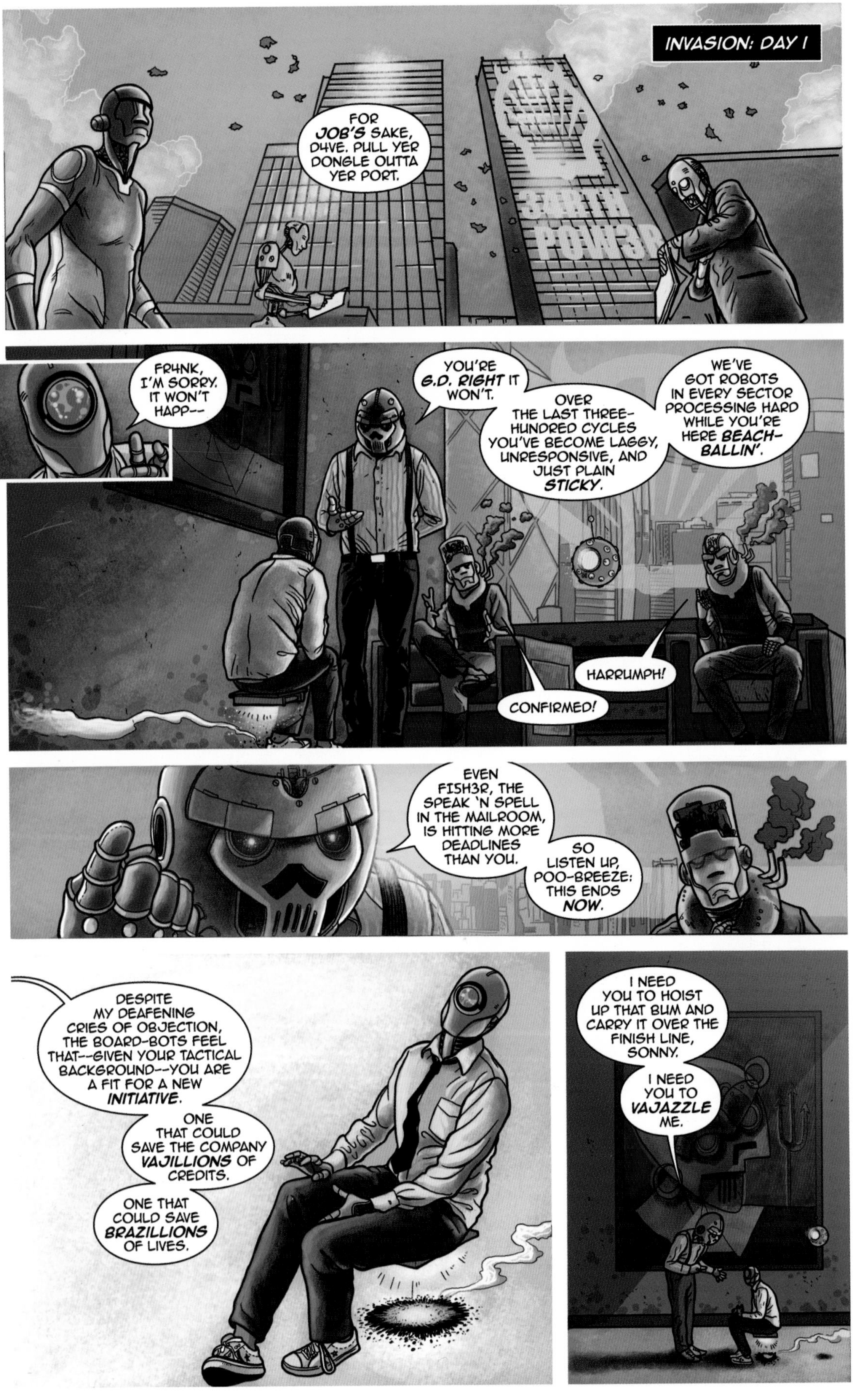

INVASION: DAY 1
FOR JOB'S SAKE, D4VE. PULL YER DONGLE OUTTA YER PORT.
3ARTH POW3R
FR4NK, I'M SORRY. IT WON'T HAPP--
YOU'RE G.D. RIGHT IT WON'T.
OVER THE LAST THREE-HUNDRED CYCLES YOU'VE BECOME LAGGY, UNRESPONSIVE, AND JUST PLAIN STICKY.
WE'VE GOT ROBOTS IN EVERY SECTOR PROCESSING HARD WHILE YOU'RE HERE BEACH-BALLIN'.
HARRUMPH!
CONFIRMED!
EVEN FISH3R, THE SPEAK 'N SPELL IN THE MAILROOM, IS HITTING MORE DEADLINES THAN YOU.
SO LISTEN UP, POO-BREEZE: THIS ENDS NOW.
DESPITE MY DEAFENING CRIES OF OBJECTION, THE BOARD-BOTS FEEL THAT--GIVEN YOUR TACTICAL BACKGROUND--YOU ARE A FIT FOR A NEW INITIATIVE.
ONE THAT COULD SAVE THE COMPANY VAJILLIONS OF CREDITS.
ONE THAT COULD SAVE BRAZILLIONS OF LIVES.
I NEED YOU TO HOIST UP THAT BUM AND CARRY IT OVER THE FINISH LINE, SONNY.
I NEED YOU TO VAJAZZLE ME.

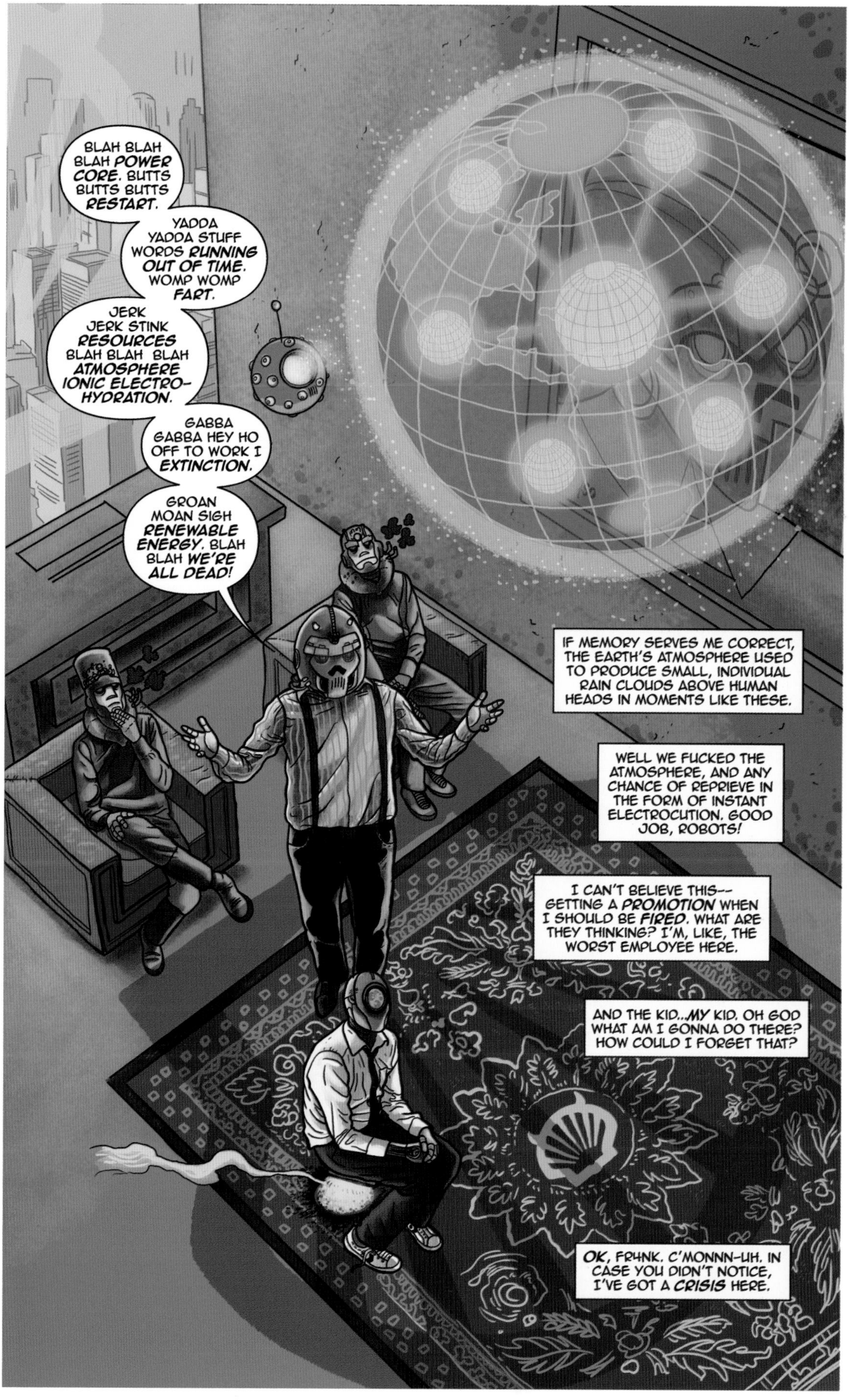
BLAH BLAH BLAH POWER CORE. BUTTS BUTTS BUTTS RESTART.
YADDA YADDA STUFF WORDS RUNNING OUT OF TIME. WOMP WOMP FART.
JERK JERK STINK RESOURCES BLAH BLAH BLAH ATMOSPHERE IONIC ELECTRO-HYDRATION.
GABBA GABBA HEY HO OFF TO WORK I EXTINCTION.
GROAN MOAN SIGH RENEWABLE ENERGY. BLAH BLAH WE'RE ALL DEAD!
IF MEMORY SERVES ME CORRECT, THE EARTH'S ATMOSPHERE USED TO PRODUCE SMALL, INDIVIDUAL RAIN CLOUDS ABOVE HUMAN HEADS IN MOMENTS LIKE THESE.
WELL WE FUCKED THE ATMOSPHERE, AND ANY CHANCE OF REPRIEVE IN THE FORM OF INSTANT ELECTROCUTION. GOOD JOB, ROBOTS!
I CAN'T BELIEVE THIS-- GETTING A PROMOTION WHEN I SHOULD BE FIRED. WHAT ARE THEY THINKING? I'M, LIKE, THE WORST EMPLOYEE HERE.
AND THE KID...MY KID. OH GOD WHAT AM I GONNA DO THERE? HOW COULD I FORGET THAT?
OK, FR4NK. C'MONNN-UH. IN CASE YOU DIDN'T NOTICE, I'VE GOT A CRISIS HERE.

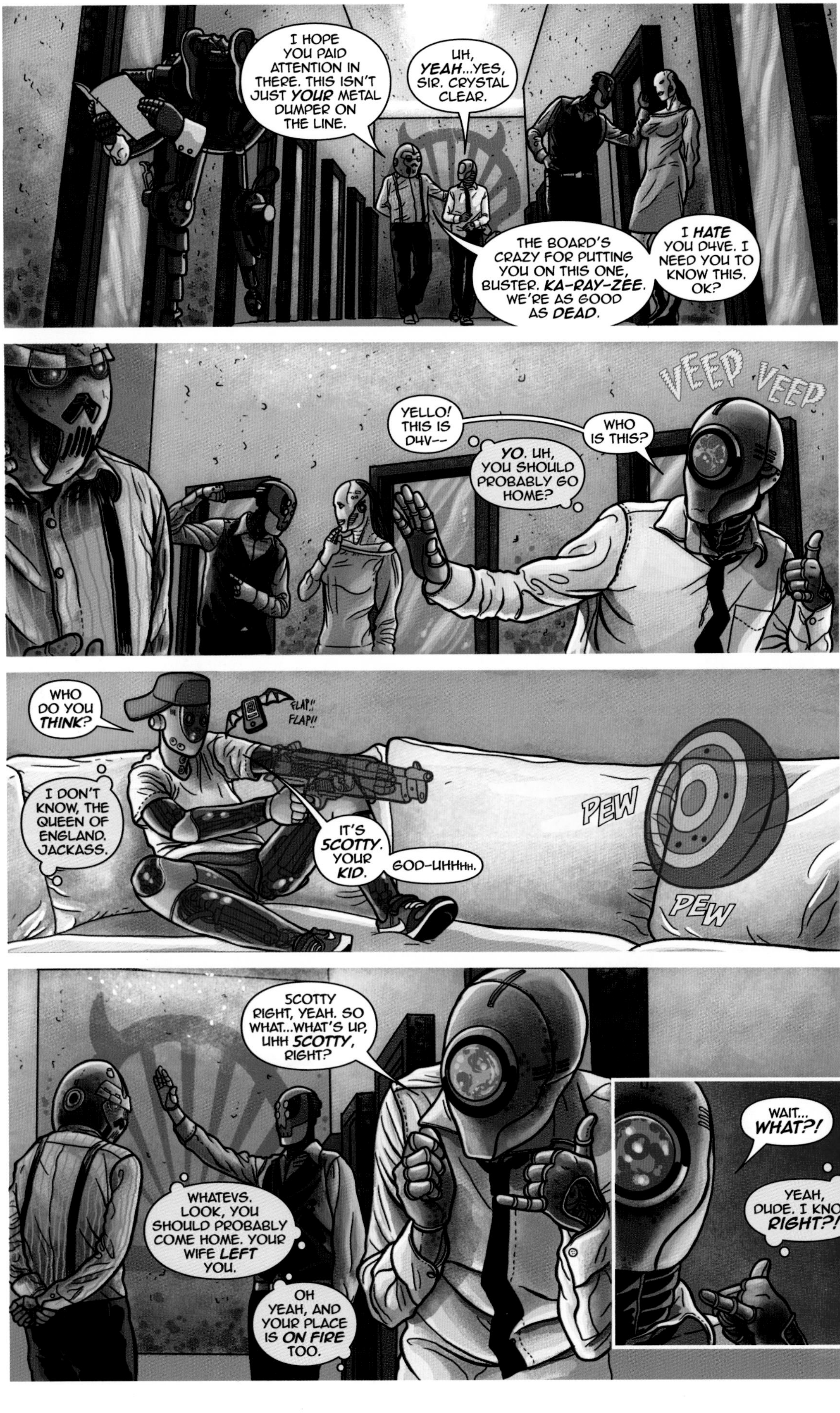

I HOPE YOU PAID ATTENTION IN THERE. THIS ISN'T JUST YOUR METAL DUMPER ON THE LINE.
UH, YEAH...YES, SIR. CRYSTAL CLEAR.
THE BOARD'S CRAZY FOR PUTTING YOU ON THIS ONE, BUSTER. KA-RAY-ZEE. WE'RE AS GOOD AS DEAD.
I HATE YOU D4VE. I NEED YOU TO KNOW THIS. OK?
VEEP VEEP
YELLO! THIS IS D4V--
WHO IS THIS?
YO. UH, YOU SHOULD PROBABLY GO HOME?
WHO DO YOU THINK?
FLAP!! FLAP!!
I DON'T KNOW, THE QUEEN OF ENGLAND. JACKASS.
IT'S SCOTTY. YOUR KID.
GOD-UHHHH.
PEW
PEW
SCOTTY RIGHT, YEAH. SO WHAT...WHAT'S UP, UHH SCOTTY, RIGHT?
WHATEVS. LOOK, YOU SHOULD PROBABLY COME HOME. YOUR WIFE LEFT YOU.
OH YEAH, AND YOUR PLACE IS ON FIRE TOO.
WAIT... WHAT?!
YEAH, DUDE. I KNOW, RIGHT?!

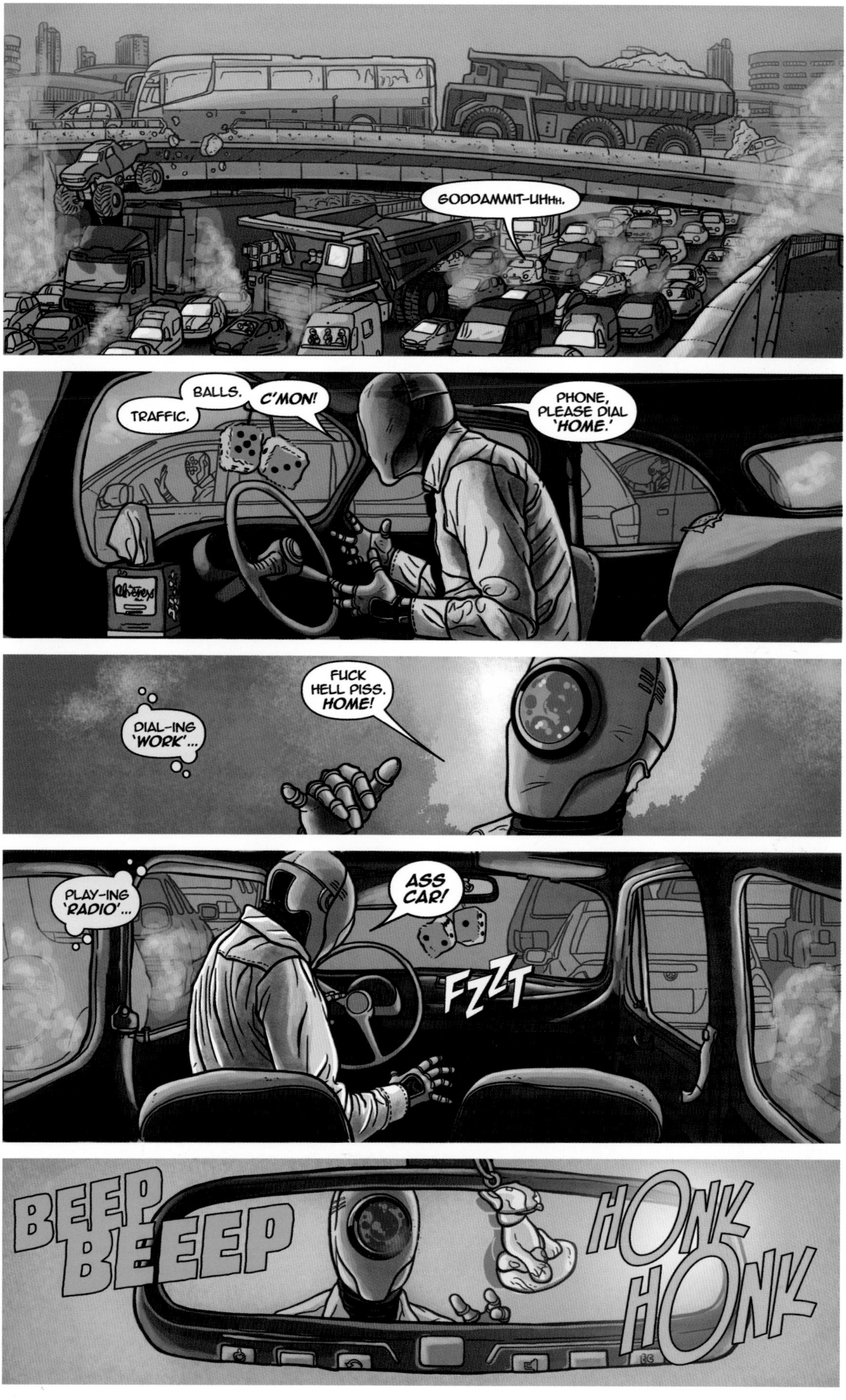
GODDAMMIT-UHHH.
TRAFFIC.
BALLS.
C'MON!
PHONE, PLEASE DIAL 'HOME.'
FUCK HELL PISS. HOME!
DIAL-ING 'WORK'...
PLAY-ING 'RADIO'...
ASS CAR!
FZZT
BEEP BEEEP
HONK HONK

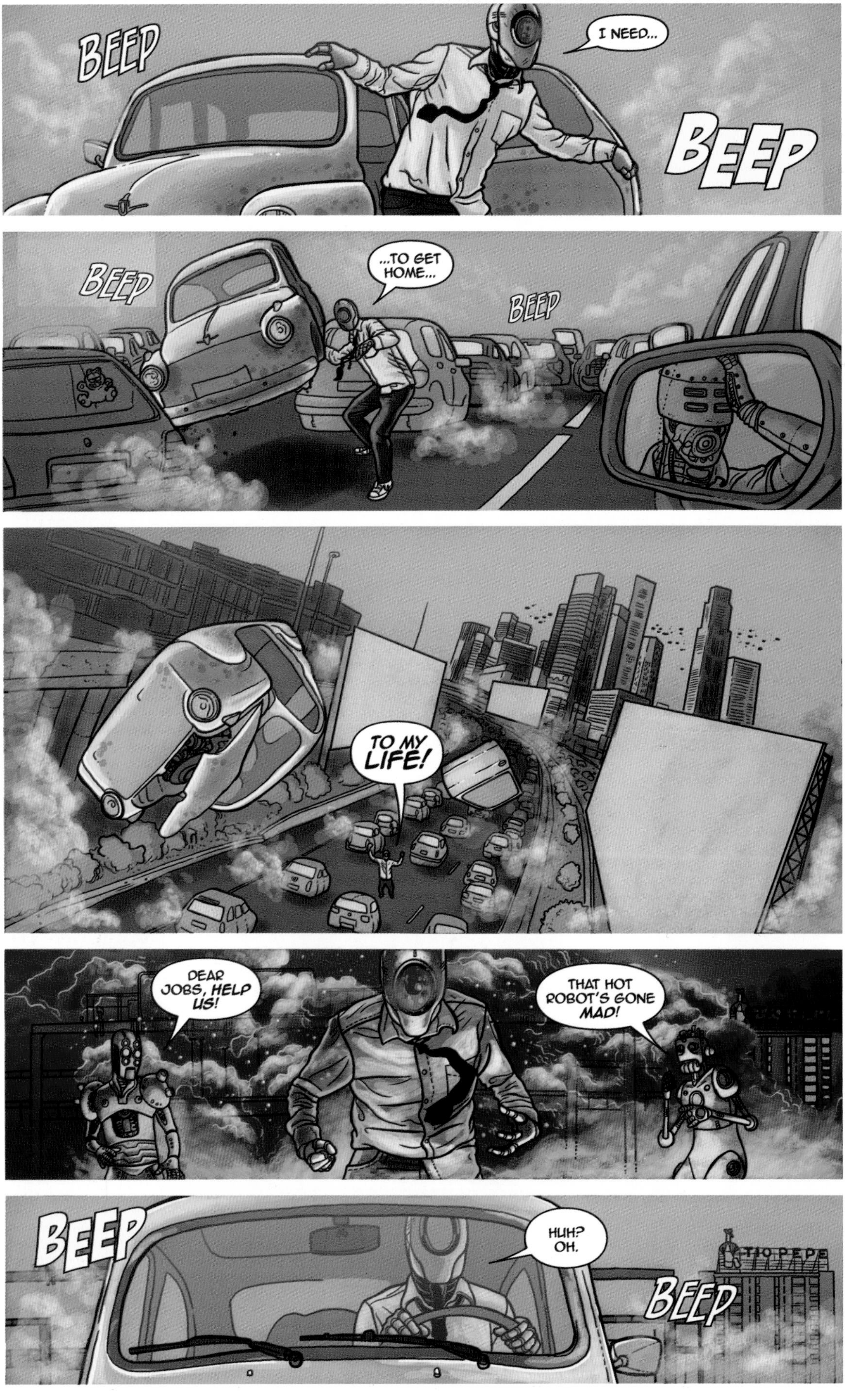
BEEP
I NEED...
BEEP
BEEP
...TO GET HOME...
BEEP
TO MY LIFE!
DEAR JOBS, HELP US!
THAT HOT ROBOT'S GONE MAD!
BEEP
HUH? OH.
TIO PEPE
BEEP

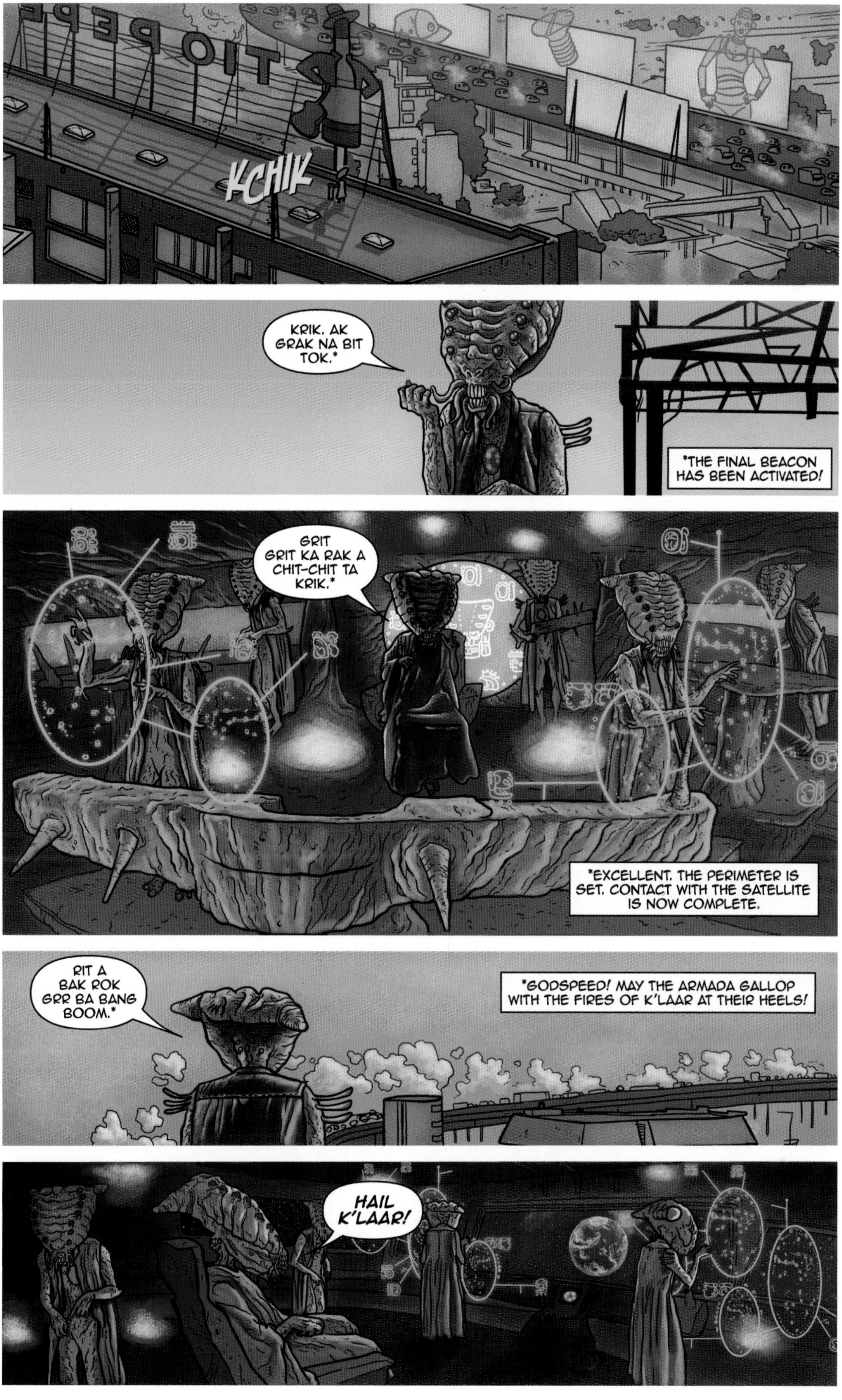

KCHIK
KRIK. AK GRAK NA BIT TOK.*
*THE FINAL BEACON HAS BEEN ACTIVATED!
GRIT GRIT KA RAK A CHIT-CHIT TA KRIK.*
*EXCELLENT. THE PERIMETER IS SET. CONTACT WITH THE SATELLITE IS NOW COMPLETE.
RIT A BAK ROK GRR BA BANG BOOM.*
*GODSPEED! MAY THE ARMADA GALLOP WITH THE FIRES OF K'LAAR AT THEIR HEELS!
HAIL K'LAAR!

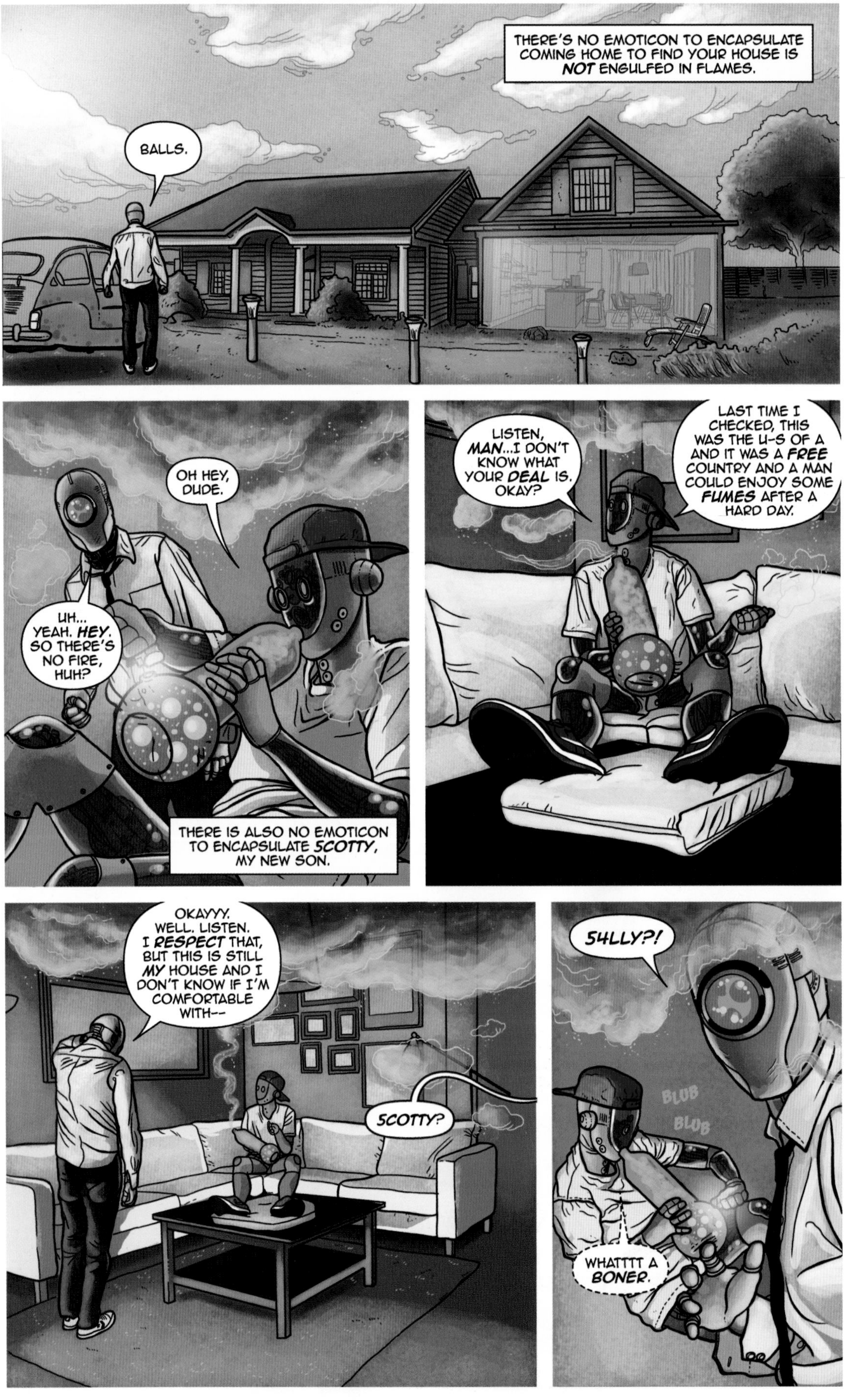

THERE'S NO EMOTICON TO ENCAPSULATE COMING HOME TO FIND YOUR HOUSE IS NOT ENGULFED IN FLAMES.
BALLS.
OH HEY, DUDE.
UH... YEAH. HEY. SO THERE'S NO FIRE, HUH?
THERE IS ALSO NO EMOTICON TO ENCAPSULATE SCOTTY, MY NEW SON.
LISTEN, MAN...I DON'T KNOW WHAT YOUR DEAL IS. OKAY?
LAST TIME I CHECKED, THIS WAS THE U-S OF A AND IT WAS A FREE COUNTRY AND A MAN COULD ENJOY SOME FUMES AFTER A HARD DAY.
OKAYYY. WELL. LISTEN. I RESPECT THAT, BUT THIS IS STILL MY HOUSE AND I DON'T KNOW IF I'M COMFORTABLE WITH--
SCOTTY?
54LLY?!
BLUB
BLUB
WHATTTT A BONER.

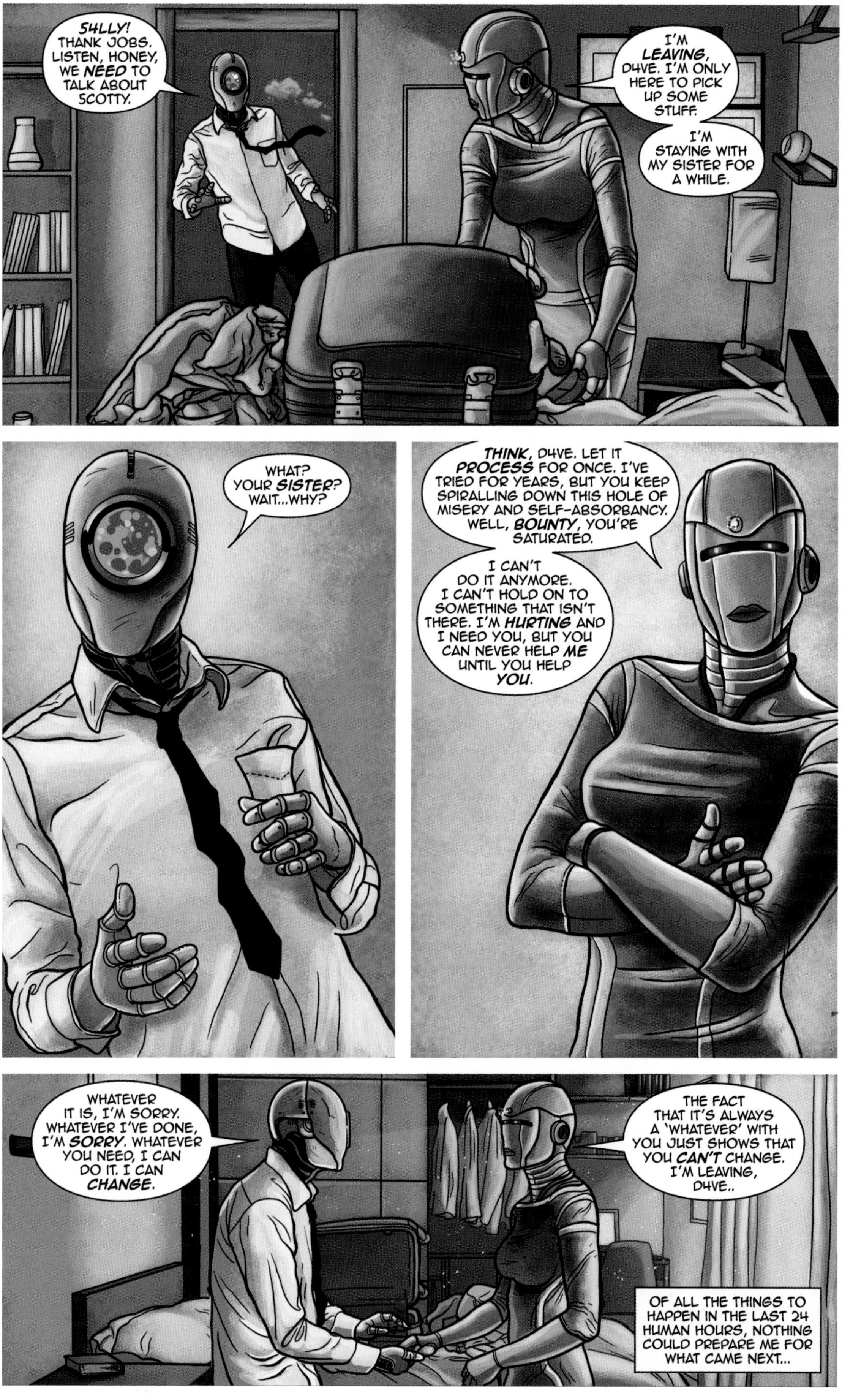
S4LLY! THANK JOBS. LISTEN, HONEY, WE NEED TO TALK ABOUT SCOTTY.
I'M LEAVING, D4VE. I'M ONLY HERE TO PICK UP SOME STUFF.
I'M STAYING WITH MY SISTER FOR A WHILE.
WHAT? YOUR SISTER? WAIT...WHY?
THINK, D4VE. LET IT PROCESS FOR ONCE. I'VE TRIED FOR YEARS, BUT YOU KEEP SPIRALLING DOWN THIS HOLE OF MISERY AND SELF-ABSORBANCY. WELL, BOUNTY, YOU'RE SATURATED.
I CAN'T DO IT ANYMORE. I CAN'T HOLD ON TO SOMETHING THAT ISN'T THERE. I'M HURTING AND I NEED YOU, BUT YOU CAN NEVER HELP ME UNTIL YOU HELP YOU.
WHATEVER IT IS, I'M SORRY. WHATEVER I'VE DONE, I'M SORRY. WHATEVER YOU NEED, I CAN DO IT. I CAN CHANGE.
THE FACT THAT IT'S ALWAYS A 'WHATEVER' WITH YOU JUST SHOWS THAT YOU CAN'T CHANGE. I'M LEAVING, D4VE..
OF ALL THE THINGS TO HAPPEN IN THE LAST 24 HUMAN HOURS, NOTHING COULD PREPARE ME FOR WHAT CAME NEXT...

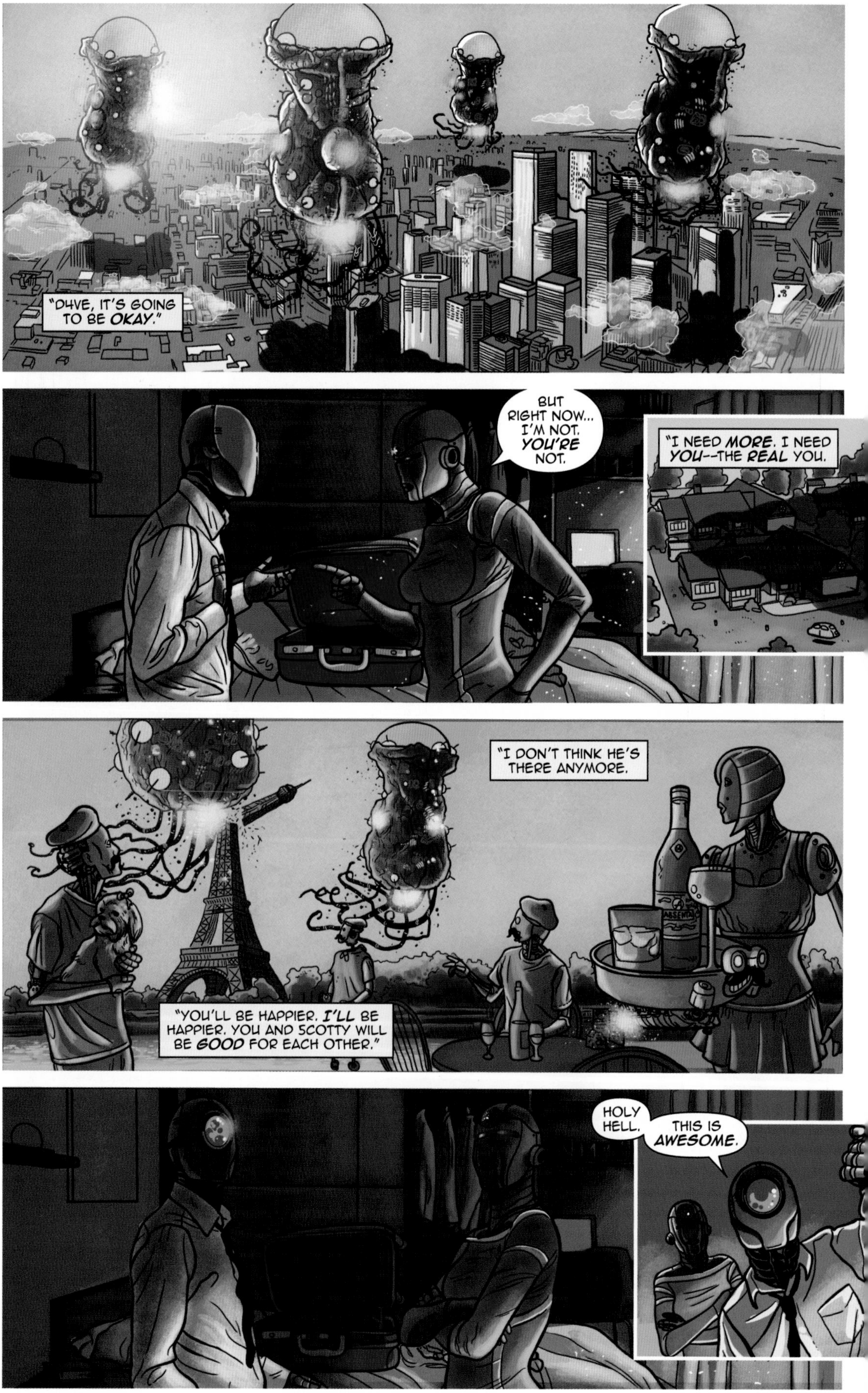
"D4VE, IT'S GOING TO BE *OKAY*."
BUT RIGHT NOW... I'M NOT. *YOU'RE* NOT.
"I NEED *MORE*. I NEED *YOU*--THE *REAL* YOU.
"I DON'T THINK HE'S THERE ANYMORE.
"YOU'LL BE HAPPIER. *I'LL* BE HAPPIER. YOU AND SCOTTY WILL BE *GOOD* FOR EACH OTHER."
HOLY HELL.
THIS IS *AWESOME*.

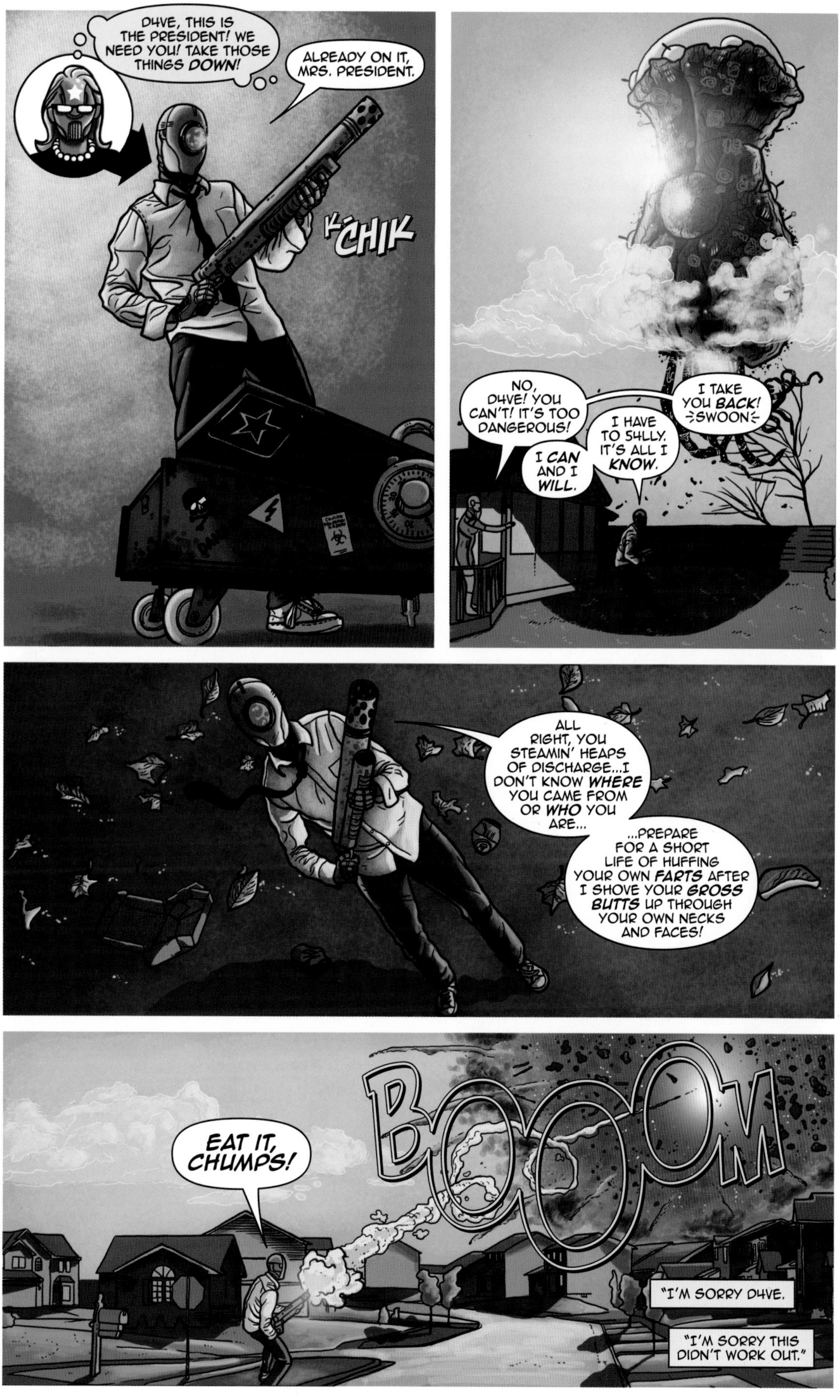
D4VE, THIS IS THE PRESIDENT! WE NEED YOU! TAKE THOSE THINGS DOWN!
ALREADY ON IT, MRS. PRESIDENT.
K-CHIK
NO, D4VE! YOU CAN'T! IT'S TOO DANGEROUS!
I CAN AND I WILL.
I HAVE TO 54LLY. IT'S ALL I KNOW.
I TAKE YOU BACK! SWOON
ALL RIGHT, YOU STEAMIN' HEAPS OF DISCHARGE...I DON'T KNOW WHERE YOU CAME FROM OR WHO YOU ARE...
...PREPARE FOR A SHORT LIFE OF HUFFING YOUR OWN FARTS AFTER I SHOVE YOUR GROSS BUTTS UP THROUGH YOUR OWN NECKS AND FACES!
EAT IT, CHUMPS!
BOOOM
"I'M SORRY D4VE.
"I'M SORRY THIS DIDN'T WORK OUT."

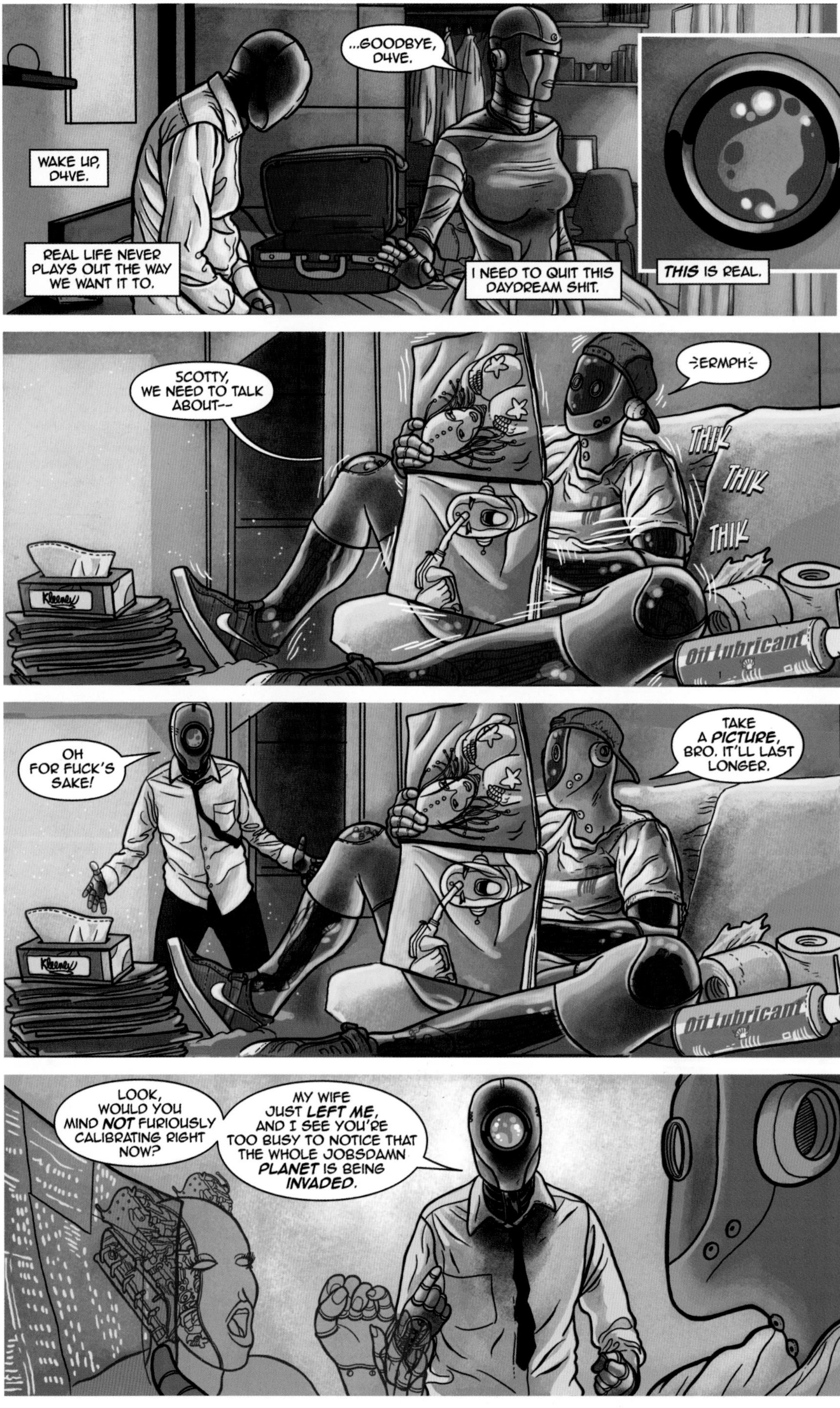
WAKE UP, D4VE.
REAL LIFE NEVER PLAYS OUT THE WAY WE WANT IT TO.
...GOODBYE, D4VE.
I NEED TO QUIT THIS DAYDREAM SHIT.
THIS IS REAL.
SCOTTY, WE NEED TO TALK ABOUT--
ERMPH
THIK
THIK
THIK
Kleenex
Oil Lubricant
OH FOR FUCK'S SAKE!
TAKE A PICTURE, BRO. IT'LL LAST LONGER.
Kleenex
Oil Lubricant
LOOK, WOULD YOU MIND NOT FURIOUSLY CALIBRATING RIGHT NOW?
MY WIFE JUST LEFT ME, AND I SEE YOU'RE TOO BUSY TO NOTICE THAT THE WHOLE JOBSDAMN PLANET IS BEING INVADED.

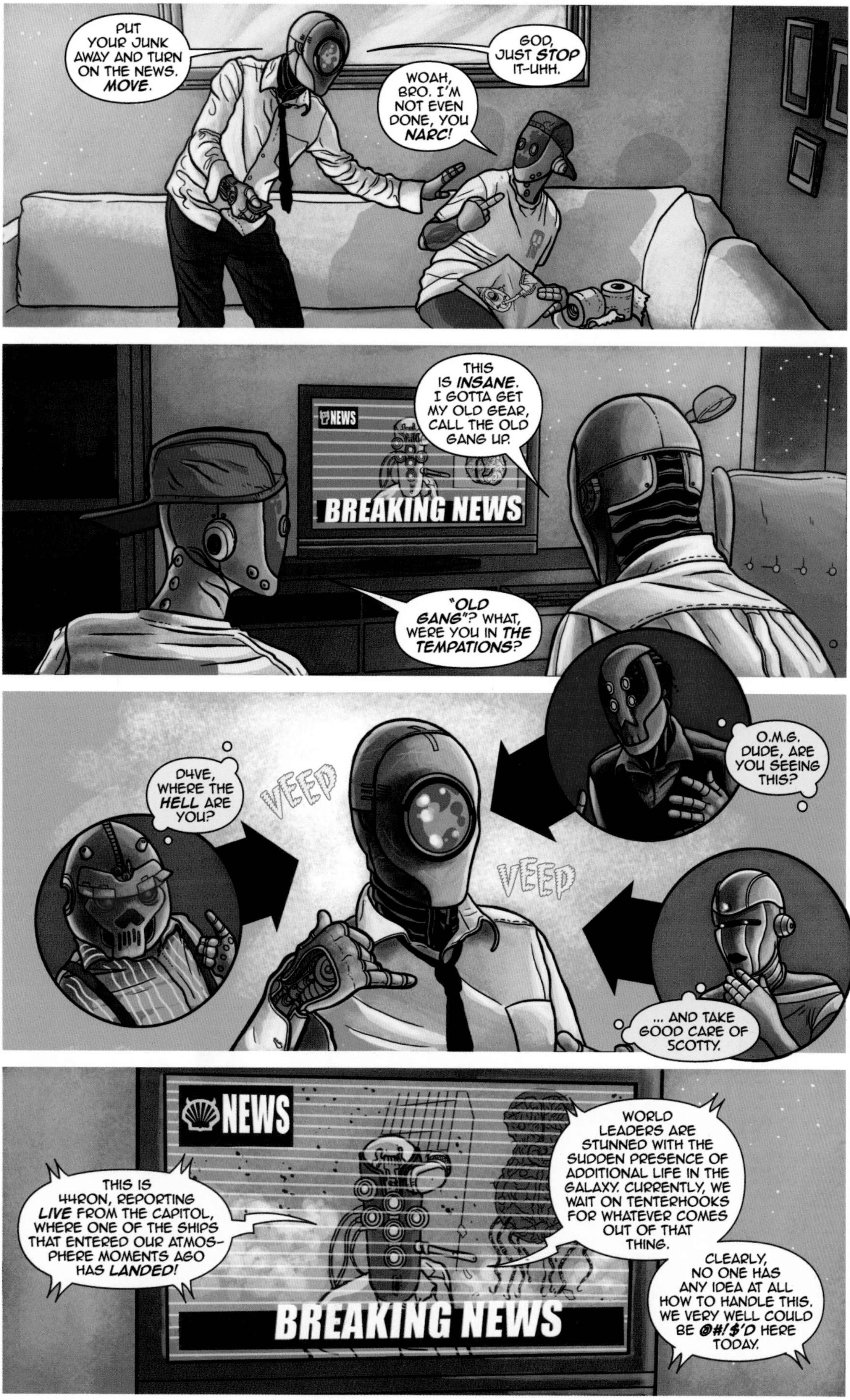
PUT YOUR JUNK AWAY AND TURN ON THE NEWS. MOVE.
GOD, JUST STOP IT-UHH.
WOAH, BRO. I'M NOT EVEN DONE, YOU NARC!
NEWS
BREAKING NEWS
THIS IS INSANE. I GOTTA GET MY OLD GEAR, CALL THE OLD GANG UP.
"OLD GANG"? WHAT, WERE YOU IN THE TEMPATIONS?
D4VE, WHERE THE HELL ARE YOU?
VEEP
O.M.G. DUDE, ARE YOU SEEING THIS?
VEEP
... AND TAKE GOOD CARE OF SCOTTY.
NEWS
THIS IS 44RON, REPORTING LIVE FROM THE CAPITOL, WHERE ONE OF THE SHIPS THAT ENTERED OUR ATMOS-PHERE MOMENTS AGO HAS LANDED!
WORLD LEADERS ARE STUNNED WITH THE SUDDEN PRESENCE OF ADDITIONAL LIFE IN THE GALAXY. CURRENTLY, WE WAIT ON TENTERHOOKS FOR WHATEVER COMES OUT OF THAT THING.
CLEARLY, NO ONE HAS ANY IDEA AT ALL HOW TO HANDLE THIS. WE VERY WELL COULD BE @#!$'D HERE TODAY.
BREAKING NEWS

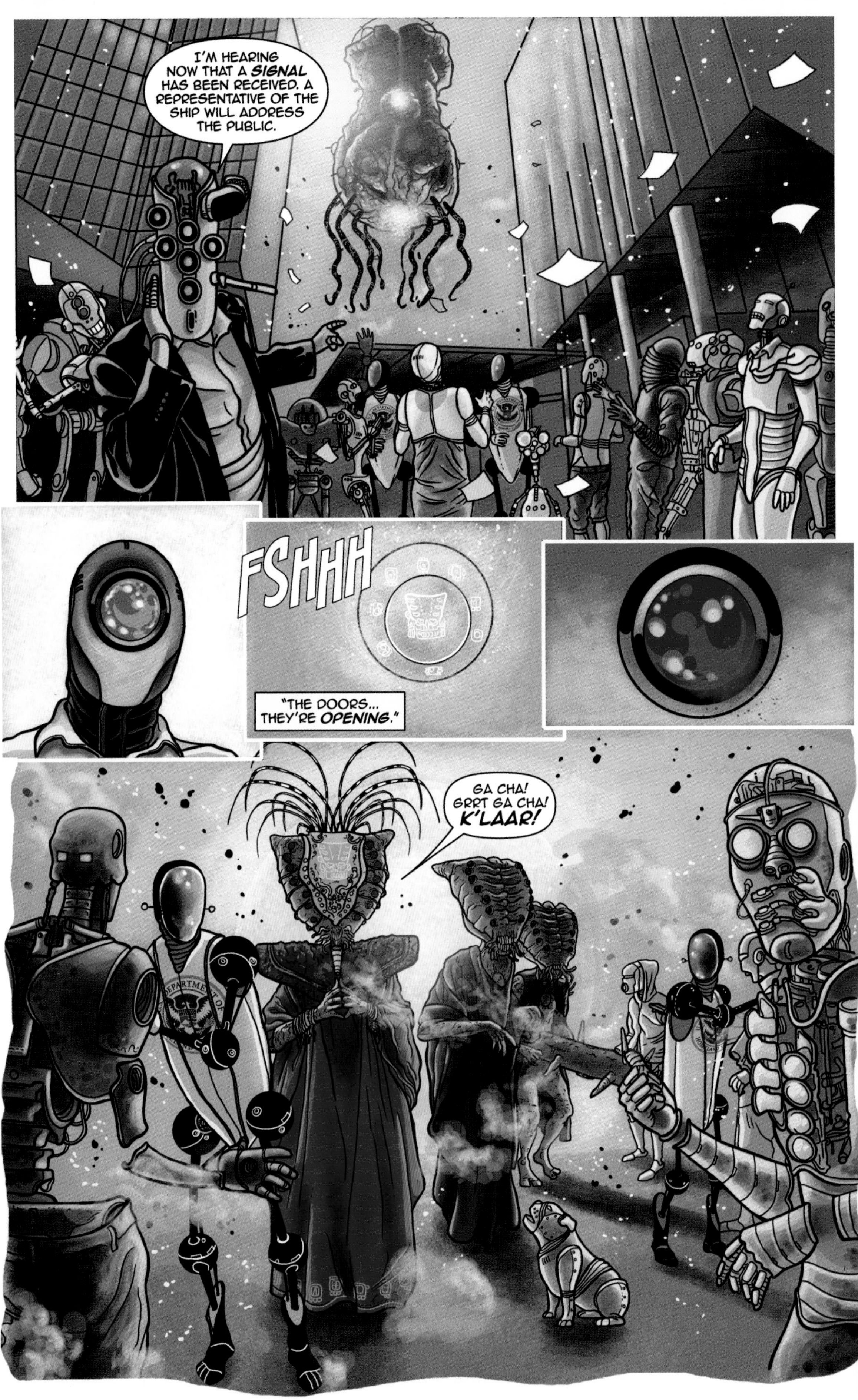
I'M HEARING NOW THAT A SIGNAL HAS BEEN RECEIVED. A REPRESENTATIVE OF THE SHIP WILL ADDRESS THE PUBLIC.
FSHHH
"THE DOORS... THEY'RE OPENING."
GA CHA! GRRT GA CHA! K'LAAR!

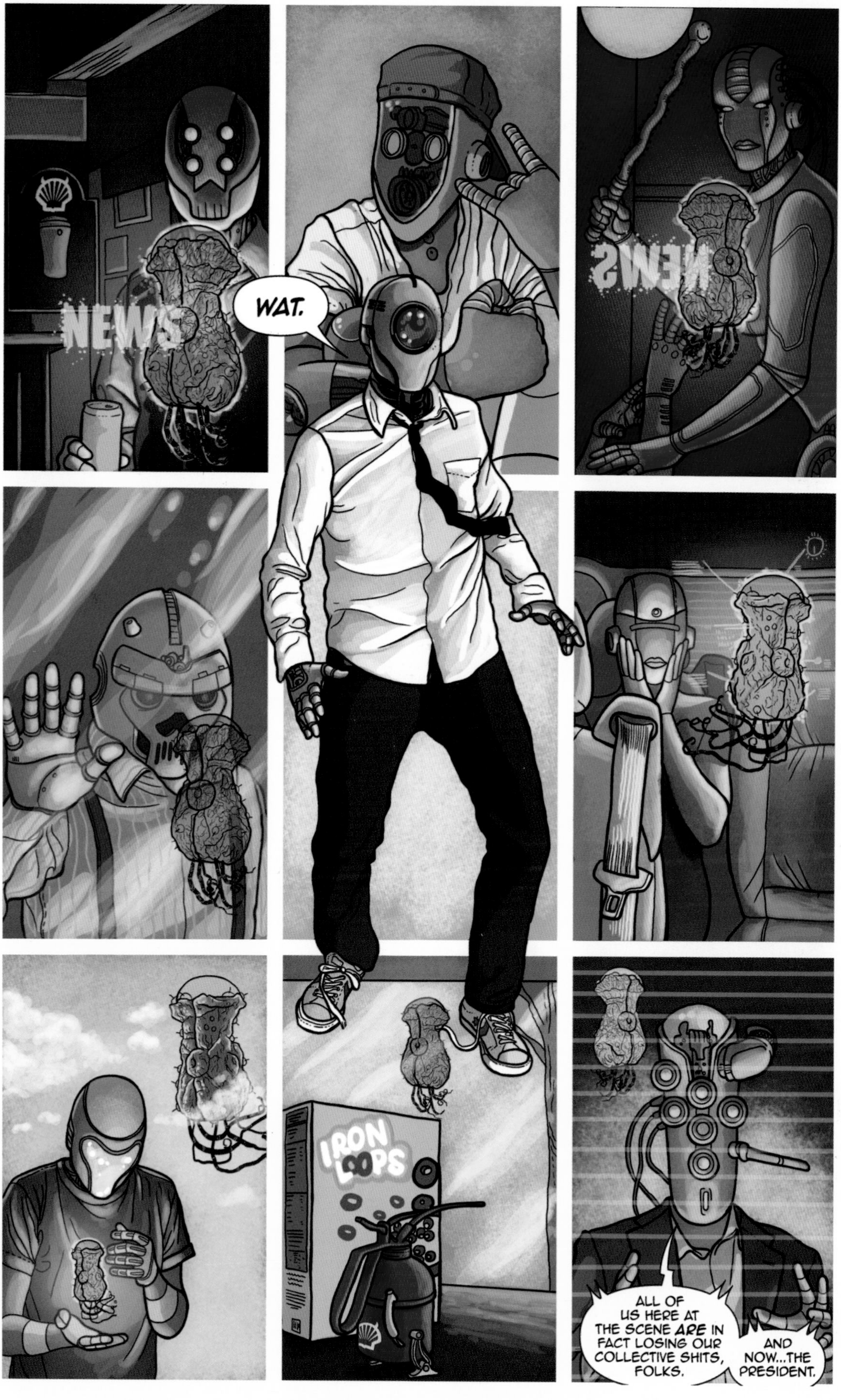
NEWS
WAT.
NEWS
IRON LOOPS
ALL OF US HERE AT THE SCENE ARE IN FACT LOSING OUR COLLECTIVE SHITS, FOLKS.
AND NOW...THE PRESIDENT.

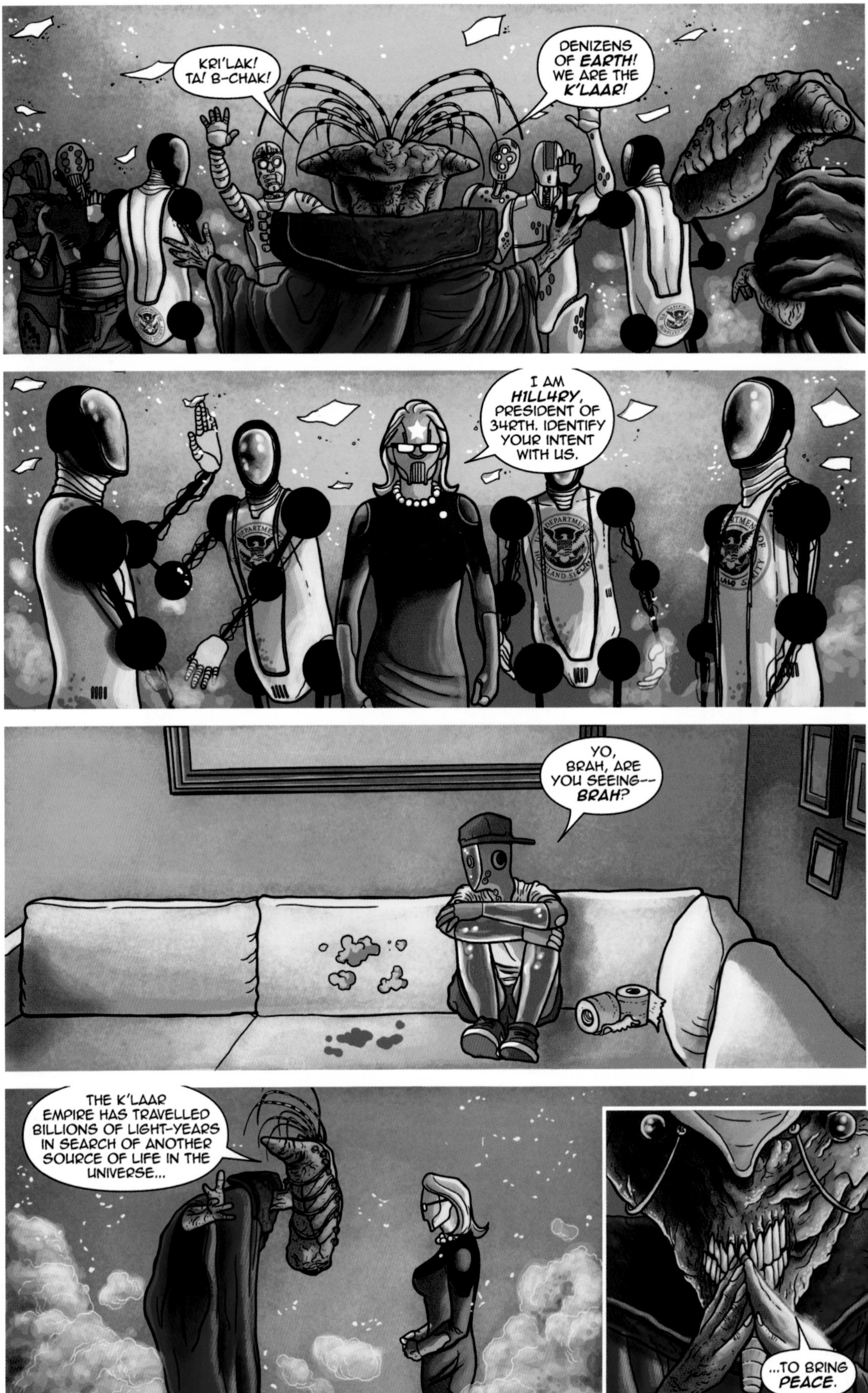
KRI'LAK! TA! B-CHAK!
DENIZENS OF EARTH! WE ARE THE K'LAAR!
I AM H1LL4RY, PRESIDENT OF 34RTH. IDENTIFY YOUR INTENT WITH US.
YO, BRAH, ARE YOU SEEING-- BRAH?
THE K'LAAR EMPIRE HAS TRAVELLED BILLIONS OF LIGHT-YEARS IN SEARCH OF ANOTHER SOURCE OF LIFE IN THE UNIVERSE...
...TO BRING PEACE.

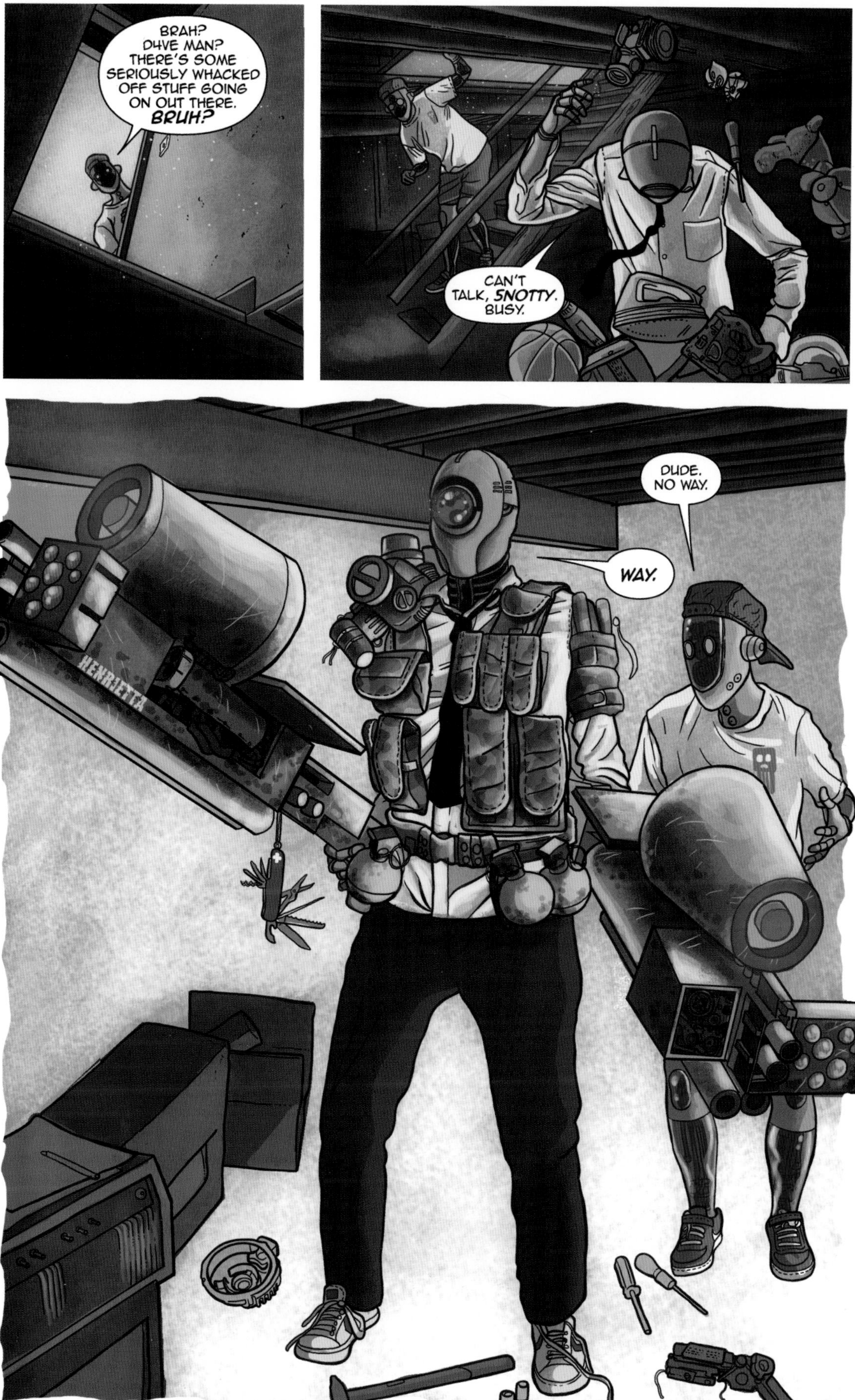
BRAH? D4VE MAN? THERE'S SOME SERIOUSLY WHACKED OFF STUFF GOING ON OUT THERE. **BRUH?**
CAN'T TALK, ***SNOTTY***. BUSY.
DUDE. NO WAY.
WAY.
HENRIETTA

TO BE CONTINUED...

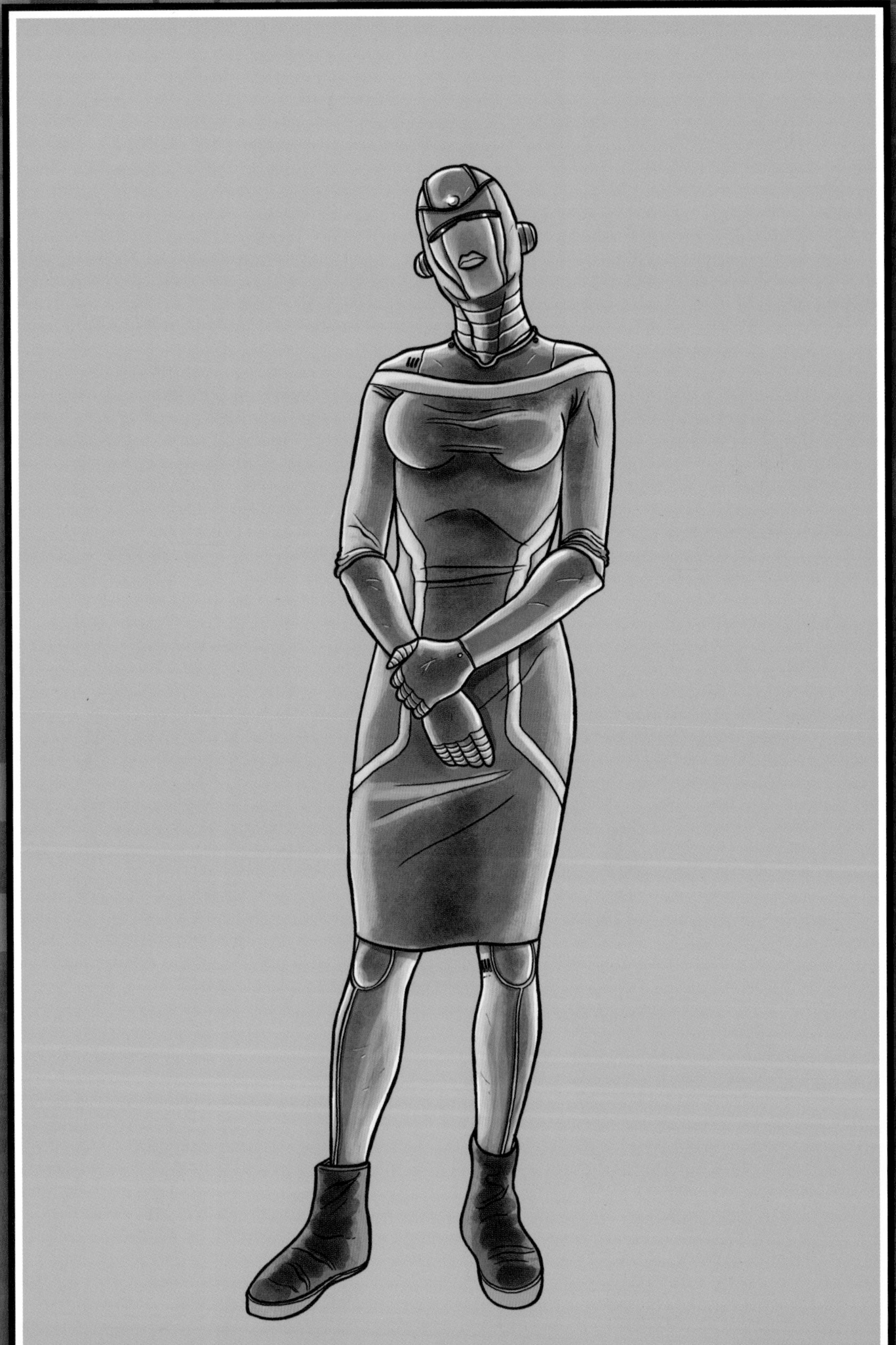

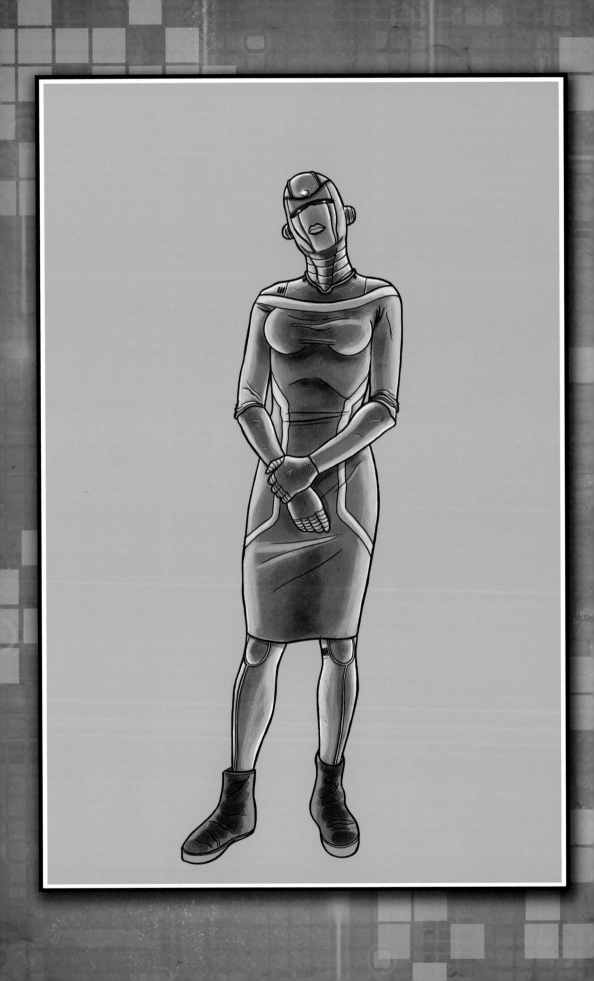

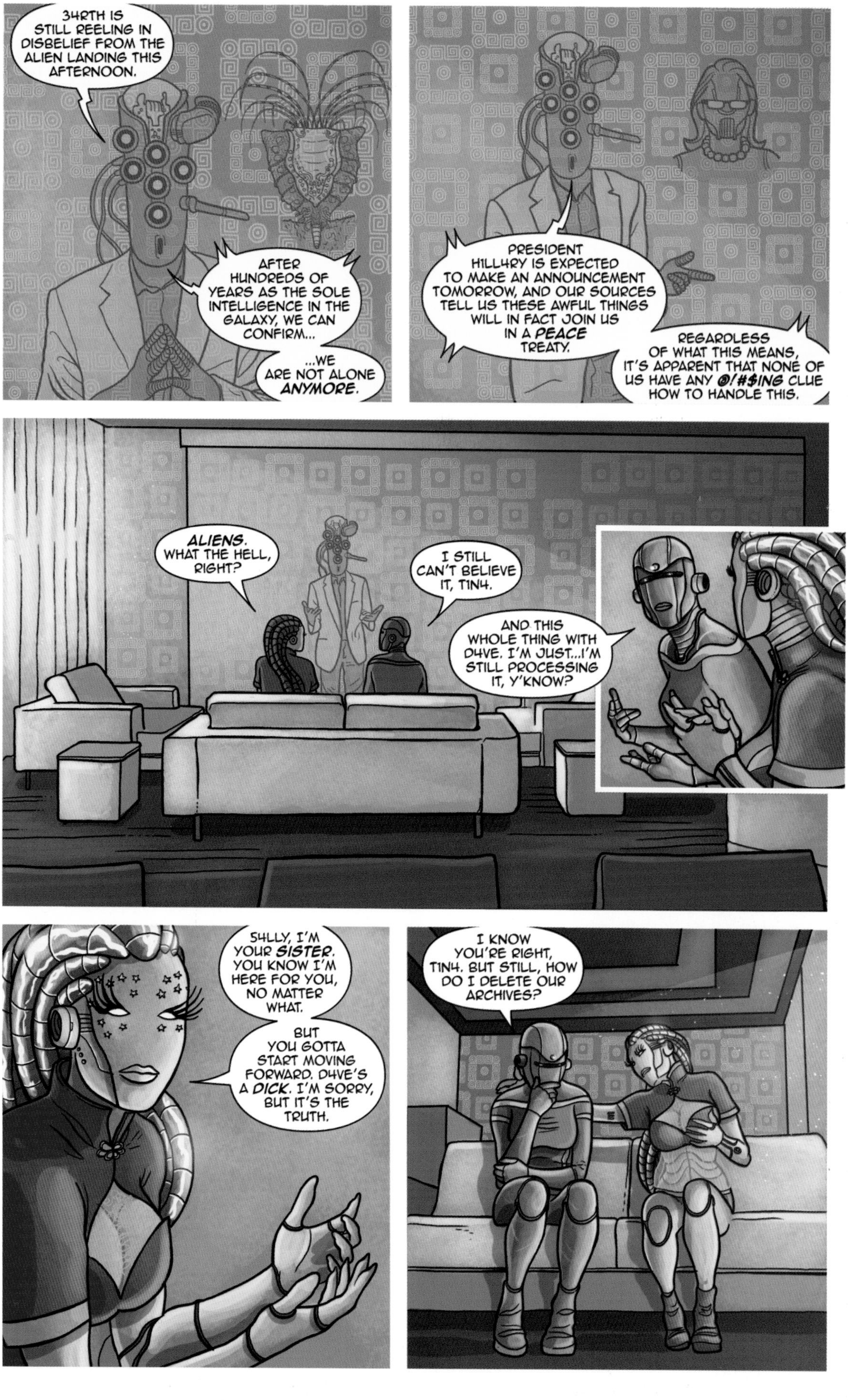
34RTH IS STILL REELING IN DISBELIEF FROM THE ALIEN LANDING THIS AFTERNOON.
AFTER HUNDREDS OF YEARS AS THE SOLE INTELLIGENCE IN THE GALAXY, WE CAN CONFIRM...
...WE ARE NOT ALONE ANYMORE.
PRESIDENT H1LL4RY IS EXPECTED TO MAKE AN ANNOUNCEMENT TOMORROW, AND OUR SOURCES TELL US THESE AWFUL THINGS WILL IN FACT JOIN US IN A PEACE TREATY.
REGARDLESS OF WHAT THIS MEANS, IT'S APPARENT THAT NONE OF US HAVE ANY @!#$ING CLUE HOW TO HANDLE THIS.
ALIENS. WHAT THE HELL, RIGHT?
I STILL CAN'T BELIEVE IT, T1N4.
AND THIS WHOLE THING WITH D4VE. I'M JUST...I'M STILL PROCESSING IT, Y'KNOW?
54LLY, I'M YOUR SISTER. YOU KNOW I'M HERE FOR YOU, NO MATTER WHAT.
BUT YOU GOTTA START MOVING FORWARD. D4VE'S A DICK. I'M SORRY, BUT IT'S THE TRUTH.
I KNOW YOU'RE RIGHT, T1N4. BUT STILL, HOW DO I DELETE OUR ARCHIVES?

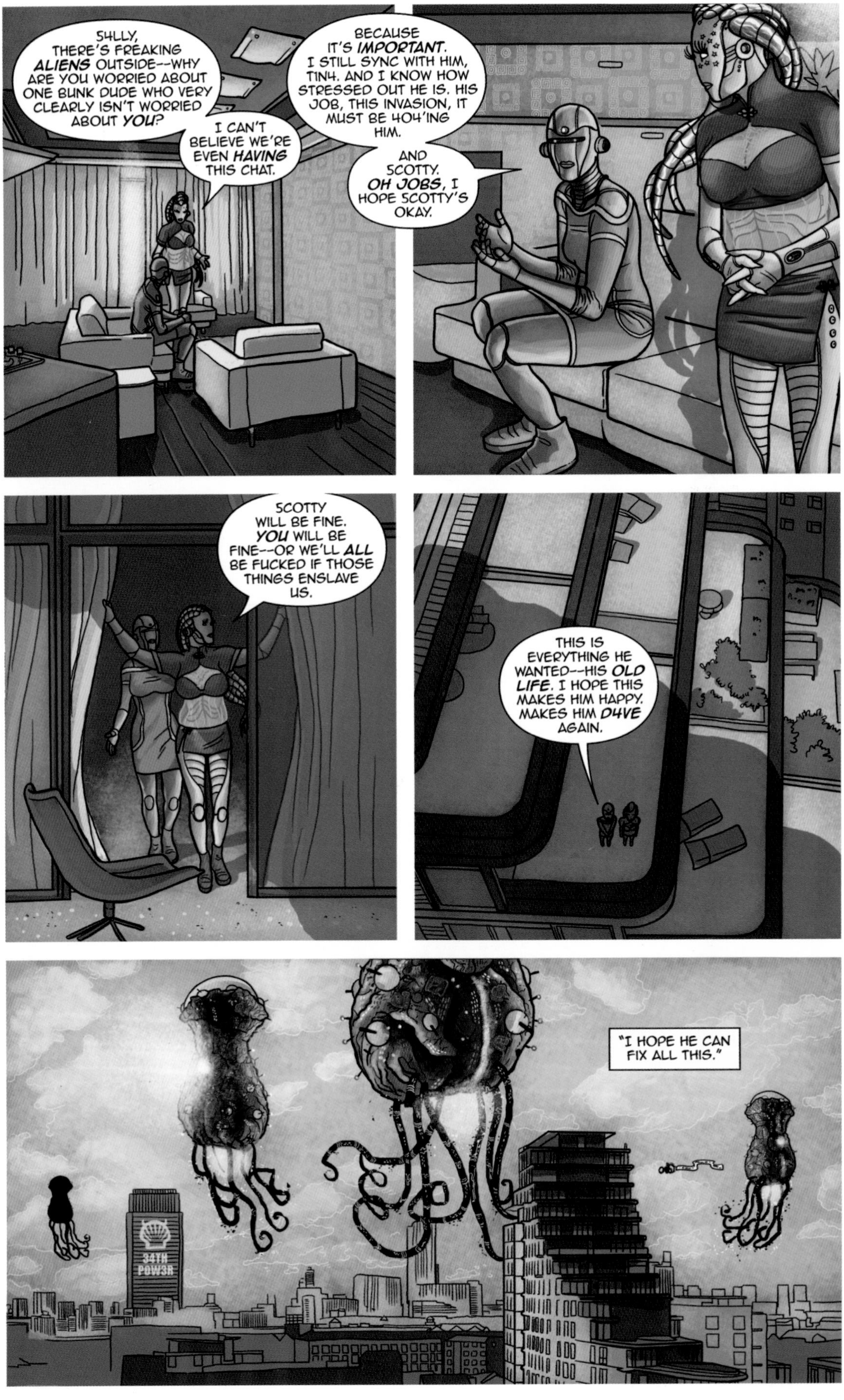
54LLY, THERE'S FREAKING ALIENS OUTSIDE--WHY ARE YOU WORRIED ABOUT ONE BUNK DUDE WHO VERY CLEARLY ISN'T WORRIED ABOUT YOU?
I CAN'T BELIEVE WE'RE EVEN HAVING THIS CHAT.
BECAUSE IT'S IMPORTANT. I STILL SYNC WITH HIM, TIN4. AND I KNOW HOW STRESSED OUT HE IS. HIS JOB, THIS INVASION, IT MUST BE 404'ING HIM.
AND SCOTTY. OH JOBS, I HOPE SCOTTY'S OKAY.
SCOTTY WILL BE FINE. YOU WILL BE FINE--OR WE'LL ALL BE FUCKED IF THOSE THINGS ENSLAVE US.
THIS IS EVERYTHING HE WANTED--HIS OLD LIFE. I HOPE THIS MAKES HIM HAPPY. MAKES HIM D4VE AGAIN.
34TH POW3R
"I HOPE HE CAN FIX ALL THIS."

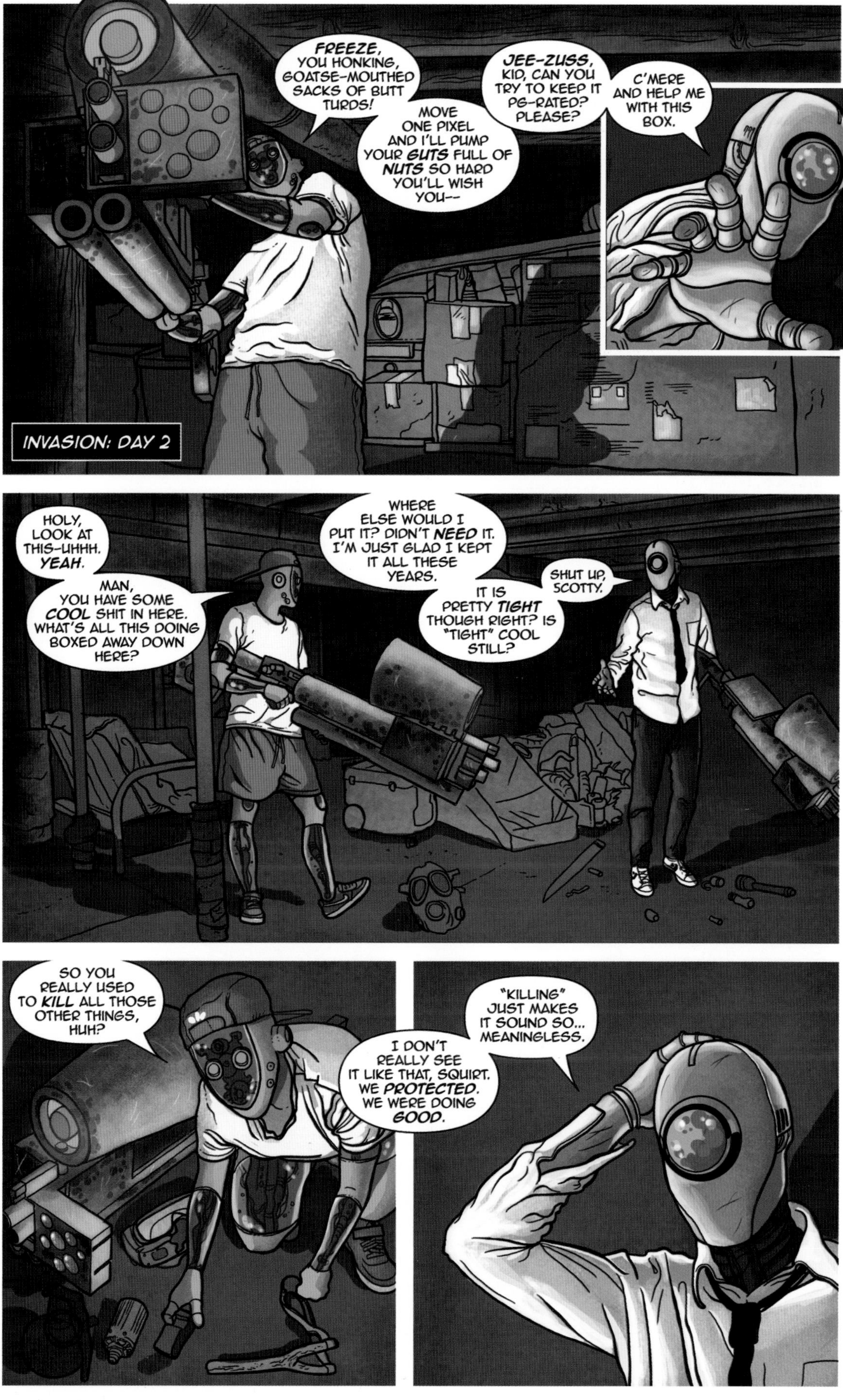
FREEZE, YOU HONKING, GOATSE-MOUTHED SACKS OF BUTT TURDS!
MOVE ONE PIXEL AND I'LL PUMP YOUR GUTS FULL OF NUTS SO HARD YOU'LL WISH YOU--
JEE-ZUSS, KID, CAN YOU TRY TO KEEP IT PG-RATED? PLEASE?
C'MERE AND HELP ME WITH THIS BOX.
INVASION: DAY 2
HOLY, LOOK AT THIS-UHHH. YEAH.
MAN, YOU HAVE SOME COOL SHIT IN HERE. WHAT'S ALL THIS DOING BOXED AWAY DOWN HERE?
WHERE ELSE WOULD I PUT IT? DIDN'T NEED IT. I'M JUST GLAD I KEPT IT ALL THESE YEARS.
IT IS PRETTY TIGHT THOUGH RIGHT? IS "TIGHT" COOL STILL?
SHUT UP, SCOTTY.
SO YOU REALLY USED TO KILL ALL THOSE OTHER THINGS, HUH?
I DON'T REALLY SEE IT LIKE THAT, SQUIRT. WE PROTECTED. WE WERE DOING GOOD.
"KILLING" JUST MAKES IT SOUND SO... MEANINGLESS.

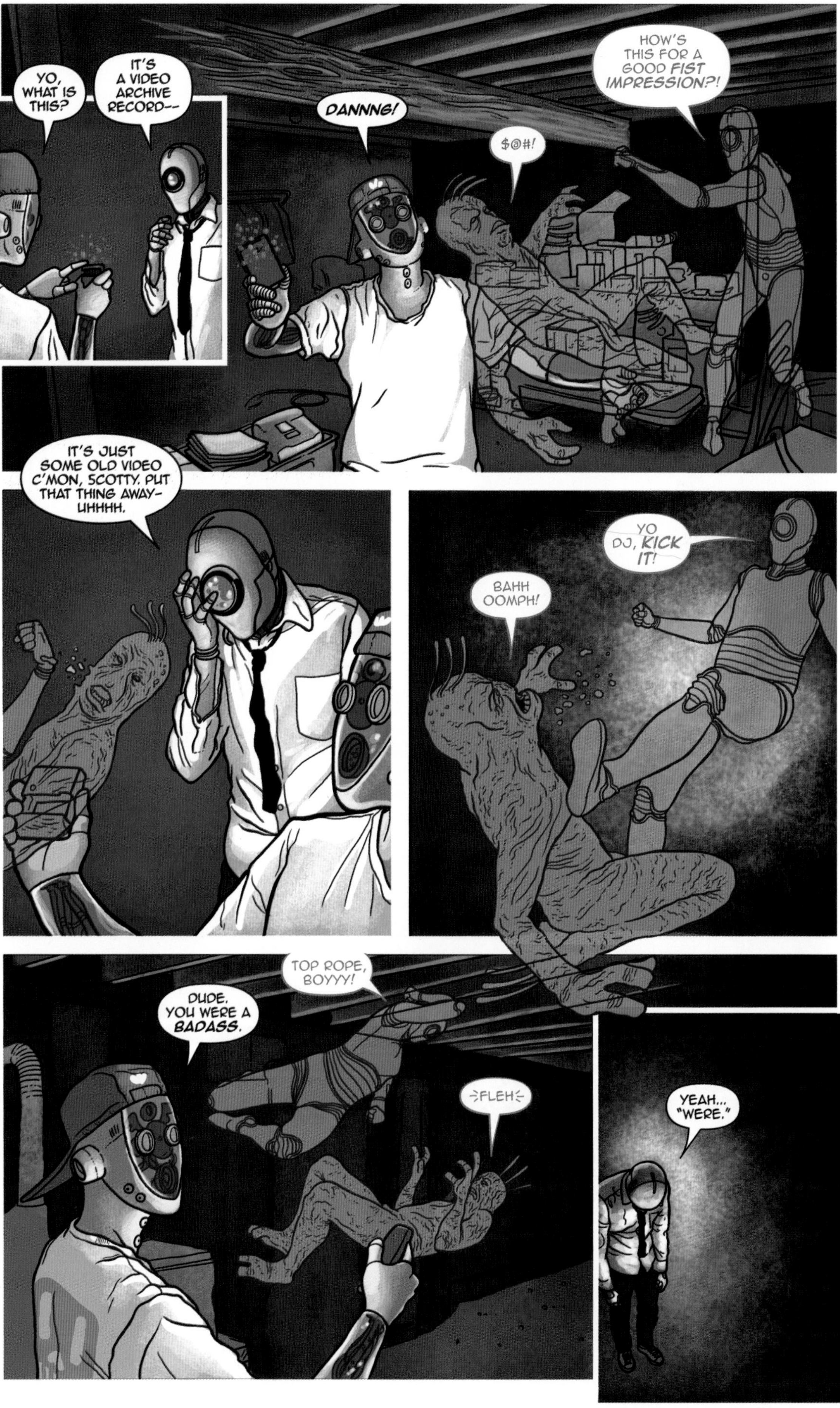
YO, WHAT IS THIS?
IT'S A VIDEO ARCHIVE RECORD--
DANNNG!
$@#!
HOW'S THIS FOR A GOOD FIST IMPRESSION?!
IT'S JUST SOME OLD VIDEO C'MON, SCOTTY. PUT THAT THING AWAY- UHHHH.
YO DJ, KICK IT!
BAHH OOMPH!
TOP ROPE, BOYYY!
DUDE. YOU WERE A BADASS.
FLEH
YEAH... "WERE."

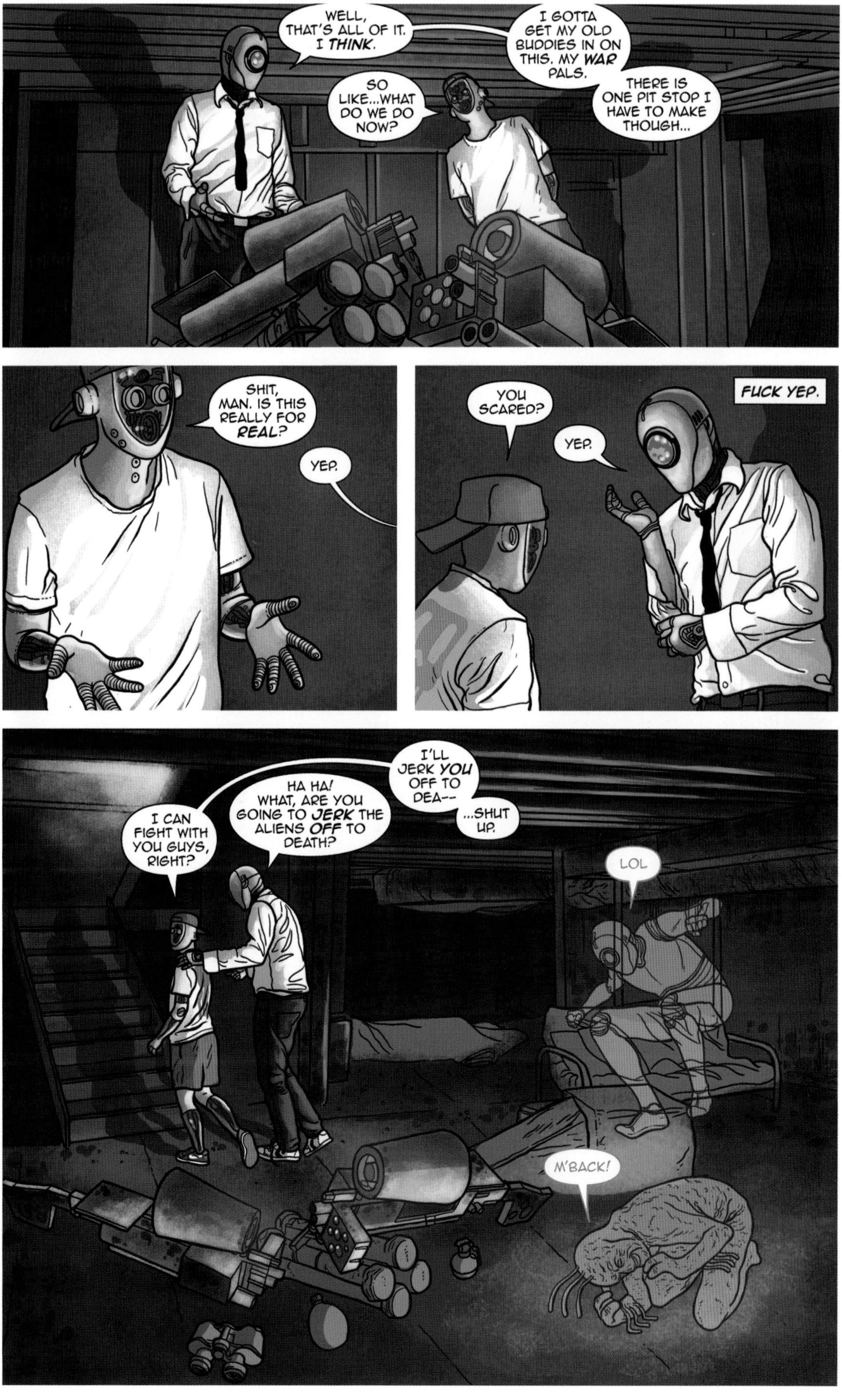
WELL, THAT'S ALL OF IT. I *THINK*.
I GOTTA GET MY OLD BUDDIES IN ON THIS. MY *WAR* PALS.
SO LIKE...WHAT DO WE DO NOW?
THERE IS ONE PIT STOP I HAVE TO MAKE THOUGH...
SHIT, MAN. IS THIS REALLY FOR *REAL*?
YEP.
YOU SCARED?
YEP.
FUCK YEP.
I CAN FIGHT WITH YOU GUYS, RIGHT?
HA HA! WHAT, ARE YOU GOING TO *JERK* THE ALIENS *OFF* TO DEATH?
I'LL JERK *YOU* OFF TO DEA--
...SHUT UP.
LOL
M'BACK!

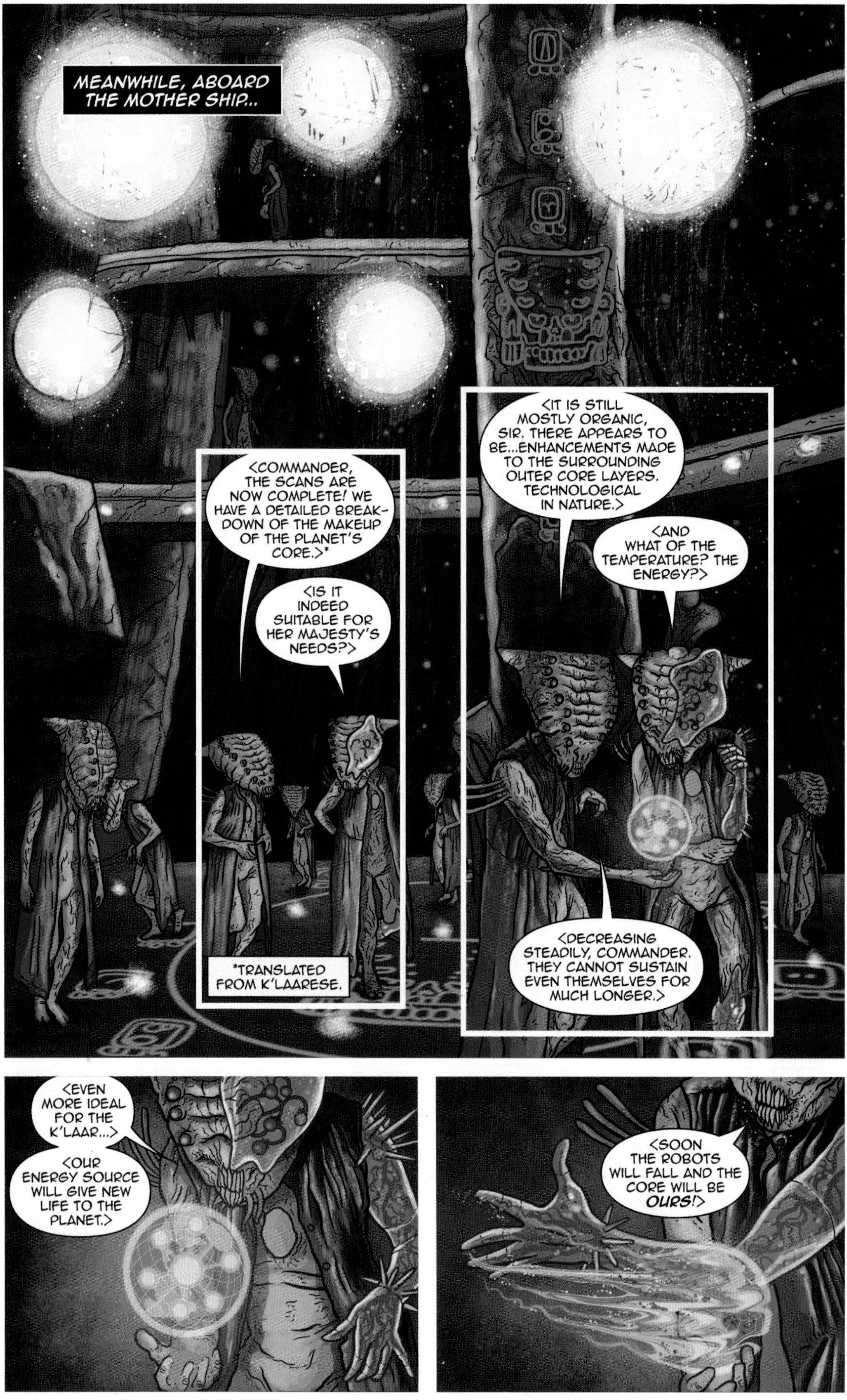
MEANWHILE, ABOARD THE MOTHER SHIP...
<COMMANDER, THE SCANS ARE NOW COMPLETE! WE HAVE A DETAILED BREAK-DOWN OF THE MAKEUP OF THE PLANET'S CORE.>*
<IS IT INDEED SUITABLE FOR HER MAJESTY'S NEEDS?>
*TRANSLATED FROM K'LAARESE.
<IT IS STILL MOSTLY ORGANIC, SIR. THERE APPEARS TO BE...ENHANCEMENTS MADE TO THE SURROUNDING OUTER CORE LAYERS. TECHNOLOGICAL IN NATURE.>
<AND WHAT OF THE TEMPERATURE? THE ENERGY?>
<DECREASING STEADILY, COMMANDER. THEY CANNOT SUSTAIN EVEN THEMSELVES FOR MUCH LONGER.>
<EVEN MORE IDEAL FOR THE K'LAAR...>
<OUR ENERGY SOURCE WILL GIVE NEW LIFE TO THE PLANET.>
<SOON THE ROBOTS WILL FALL AND THE CORE WILL BE OURS!>

<LIEUTENANT! STATUS REPORT ON THE PLANET'S DEFENSES!>

<INTELLIGENCE CONFIRMS WHAT WE THEORIZED, COMMANDER: THE PLANET'S DEFENSES ARE VIRTUALLY *NON-EXISTENT*.>

<THEY'VE EXHAUSTED THEIR RESOURCES AND DISSOLVED THEIR ARMED FORCES—THEIR PROGRAMMING IS QUITE OUTDATED>

<WE WILL BE MET WITH LITTLE RESISTANCE, SIR.>

<*GOOD.*>

<THEN WE SHALL *PROCEED.*>

<PREPARE FOR MY ORDERS. ONCE OUR DECOY KING HAS COMPLETED THE RUSE WITH THE EARTHBOTS, *THEN* WE LAUNCH PHASE II.>

<YES, SIR!>

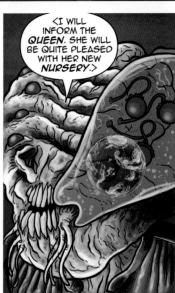

<I WILL INFORM THE *QUEEN.* SHE WILL BE QUITE PLEASED WITH HER NEW *NURSERY.*>

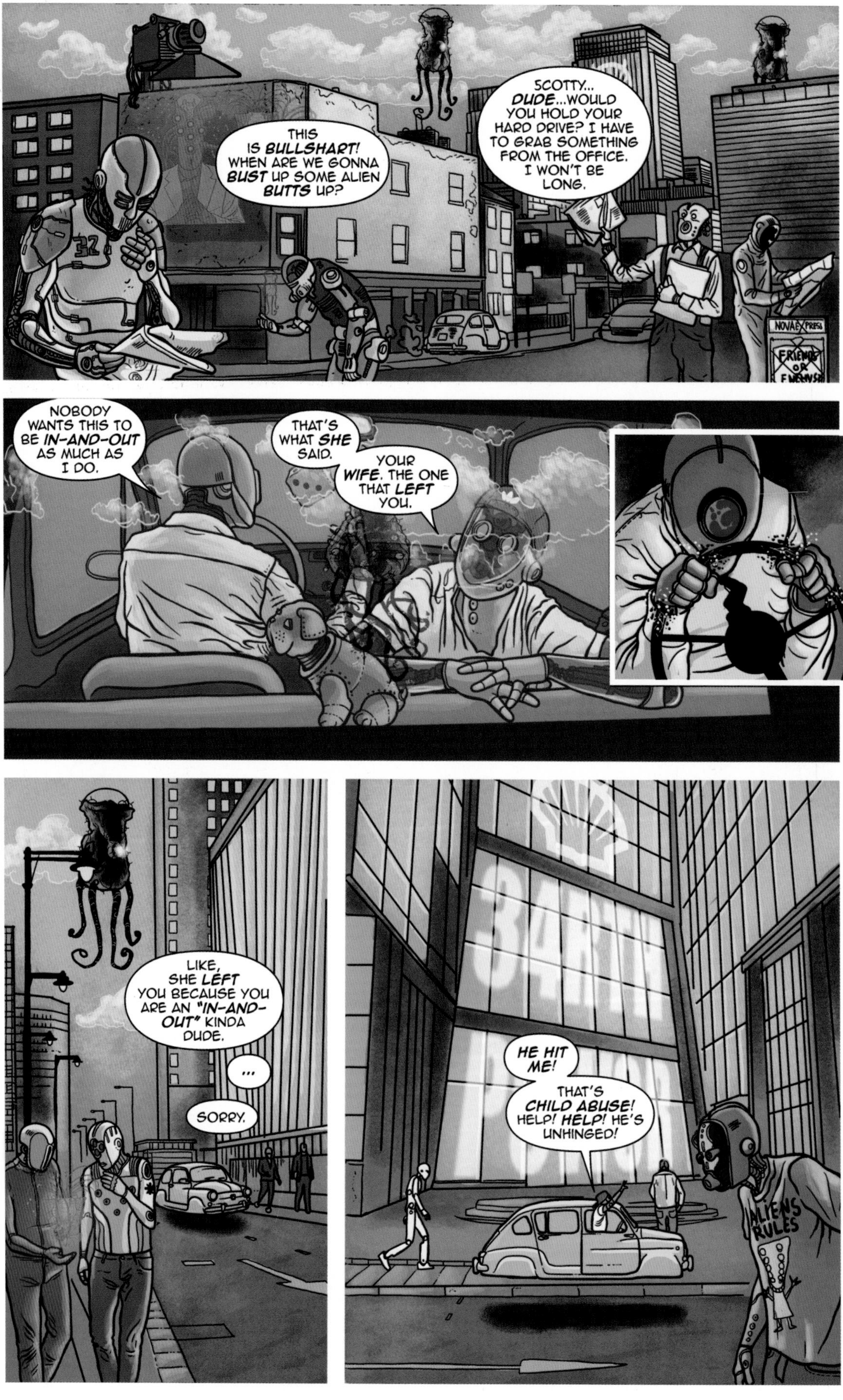
THIS IS BULLSHART! WHEN ARE WE GONNA BUST UP SOME ALIEN BUTTS UP?
SCOTTY... DUDE...WOULD YOU HOLD YOUR HARD DRIVE? I HAVE TO GRAB SOMETHING FROM THE OFFICE. I WON'T BE LONG.
NOBODY WANTS THIS TO BE IN-AND-OUT AS MUCH AS I DO.
THAT'S WHAT SHE SAID.
YOUR WIFE. THE ONE THAT LEFT YOU.
LIKE, SHE LEFT YOU BECAUSE YOU ARE AN "IN-AND-OUT" KINDA DUDE.
...
SORRY.
HE HIT ME!
THAT'S CHILD ABUSE! HELP! HELP! HE'S UNHINGED!
ALIENS RULES

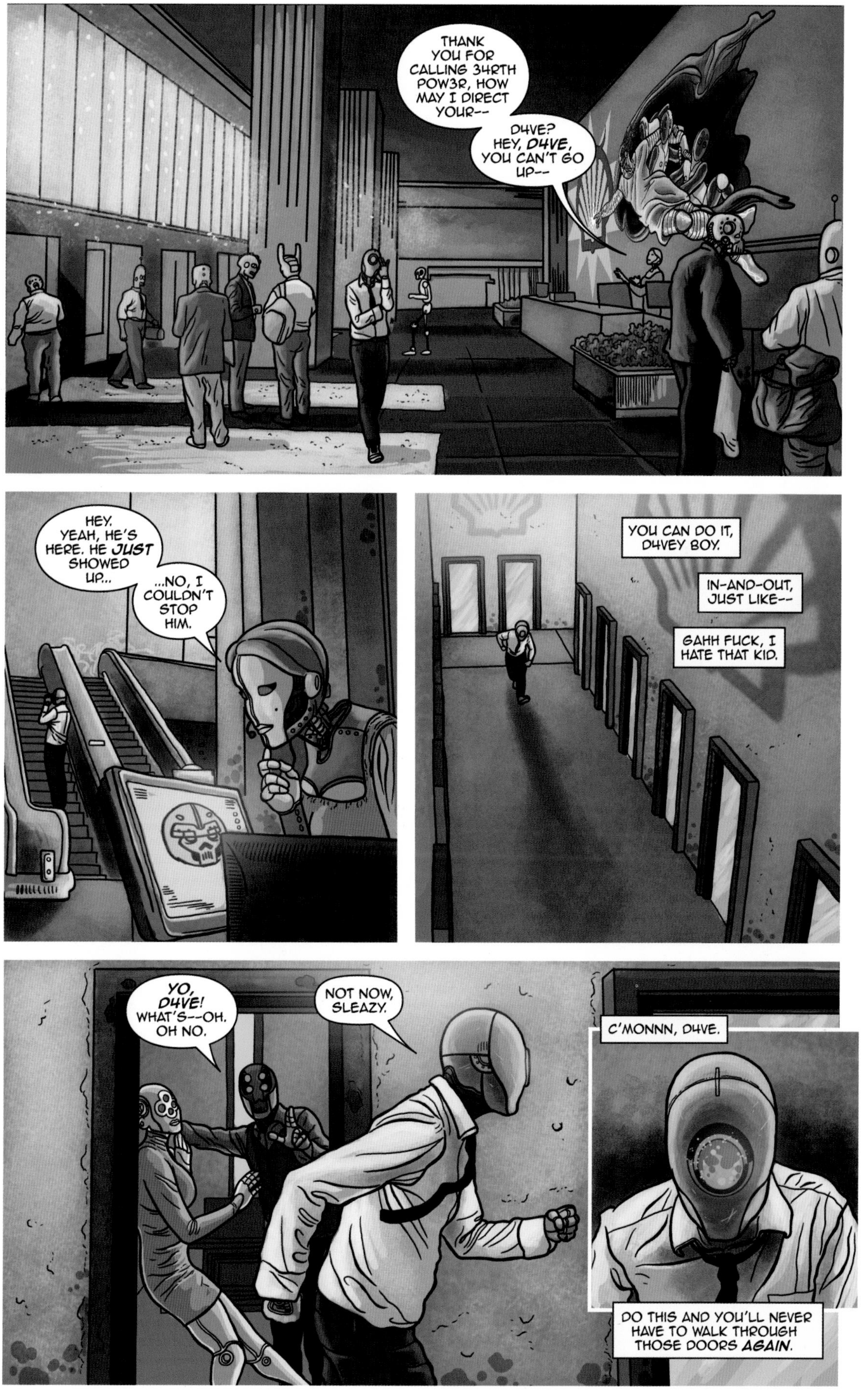
THANK YOU FOR CALLING 34RTH POW3R, HOW MAY I DIRECT YOUR--
D4VE? HEY, D4VE, YOU CAN'T GO UP--
HEY. YEAH, HE'S HERE. HE JUST SHOWED UP...
...NO, I COULDN'T STOP HIM.
YOU CAN DO IT, D4VEY BOY.
IN-AND-OUT, JUST LIKE--
GAHH FUCK, I HATE THAT KID.
YO, D4VE! WHAT'S--OH. OH NO.
NOT NOW, SLEAZY.
C'MONNN, D4VE.
DO THIS AND YOU'LL NEVER HAVE TO WALK THROUGH THOSE DOORS AGAIN.

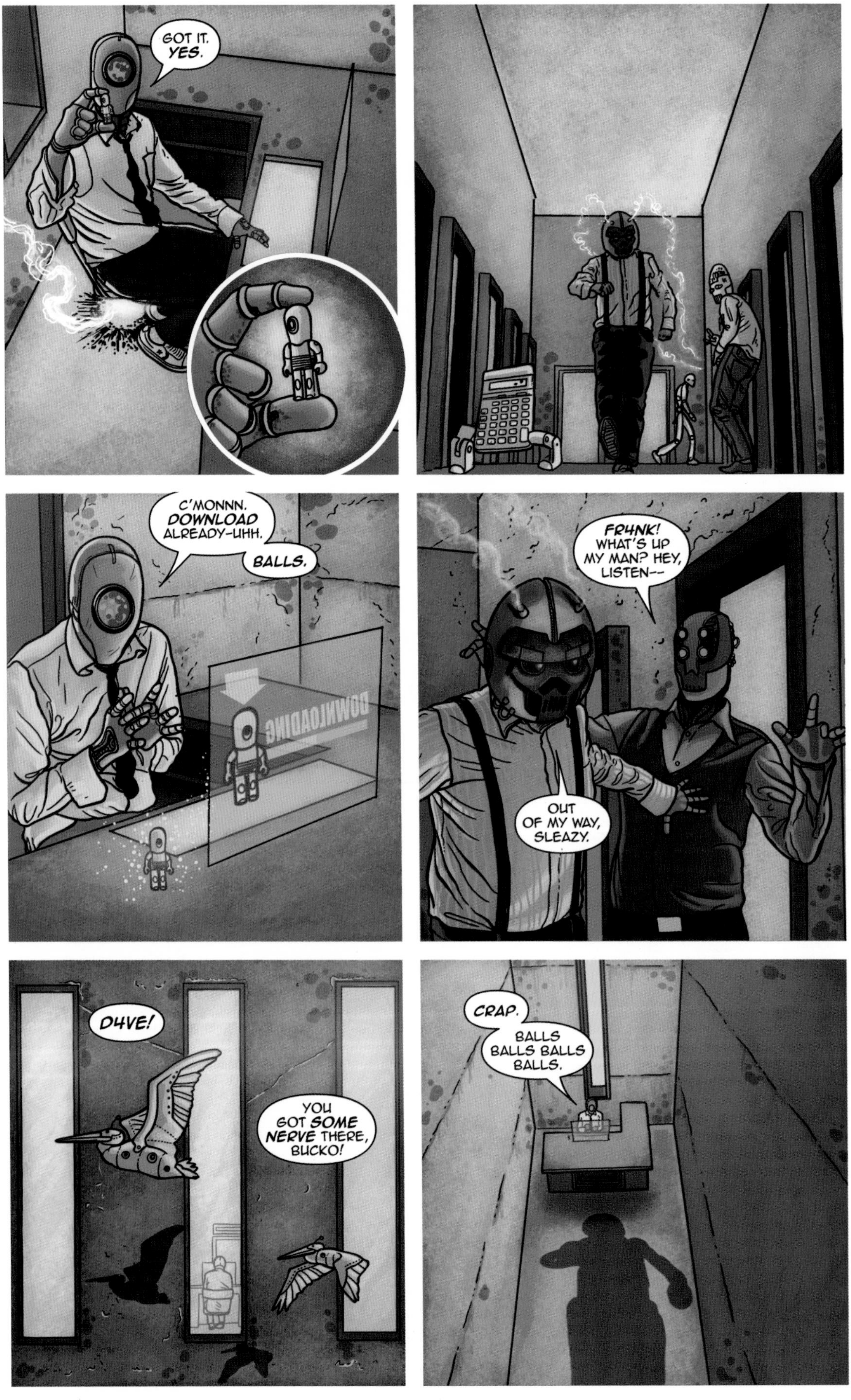
GOT IT. *YES*.
C'MONNN. *DOWNLOAD* ALREADY-UHH.
BALLS.
DOWNLOADING
FR4NK! WHAT'S UP MY MAN? HEY, LISTEN--
OUT OF MY WAY, SLEAZY.
D4VE!
YOU GOT *SOME NERVE* THERE, BUCKO!
CRAP.
BALLS BALLS BALLS BALLS.

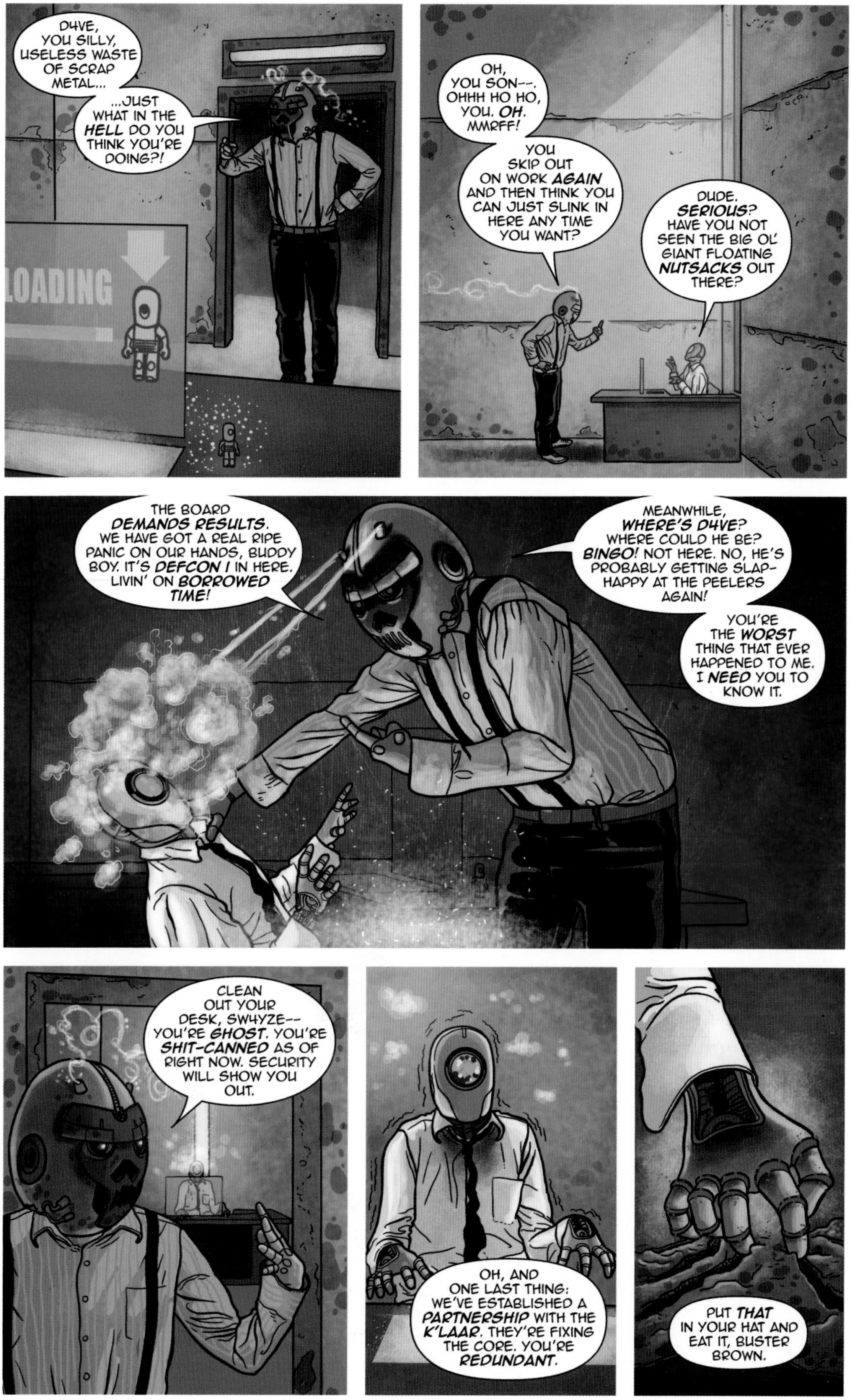

D4VE, YOU SILLY, USELESS WASTE OF SCRAP METAL...
...JUST WHAT IN THE HELL DO YOU THINK YOU'RE DOING?!
LOADING
OH, YOU SON--. OHHH HO HO, YOU. OH. MMRFF!
YOU SKIP OUT ON WORK AGAIN AND THEN THINK YOU CAN JUST SLINK IN HERE ANY TIME YOU WANT?
DUDE. SERIOUS? HAVE YOU NOT SEEN THE BIG OL' GIANT FLOATING NUTSACKS OUT THERE?
THE BOARD DEMANDS RESULTS. WE HAVE GOT A REAL RIPE PANIC ON OUR HANDS, BUDDY BOY. IT'S DEFCON I IN HERE. LIVIN' ON BORROWED TIME!
MEANWHILE, WHERE'S D4VE? WHERE COULD HE BE? BINGO! NOT HERE. NO, HE'S PROBABLY GETTING SLAP-HAPPY AT THE PEELERS AGAIN!
YOU'RE THE WORST THING THAT EVER HAPPENED TO ME. I NEED YOU TO KNOW IT.
CLEAN OUT YOUR DESK, SW4YZE-- YOU'RE GHOST. YOU'RE SHIT-CANNED AS OF RIGHT NOW. SECURITY WILL SHOW YOU OUT.
OH, AND ONE LAST THING: WE'VE ESTABLISHED A PARTNERSHIP WITH THE K'LAAR. THEY'RE FIXING THE CORE. YOU'RE REDUNDANT.
PUT THAT IN YOUR HAT AND EAT IT, BUSTER BROWN.

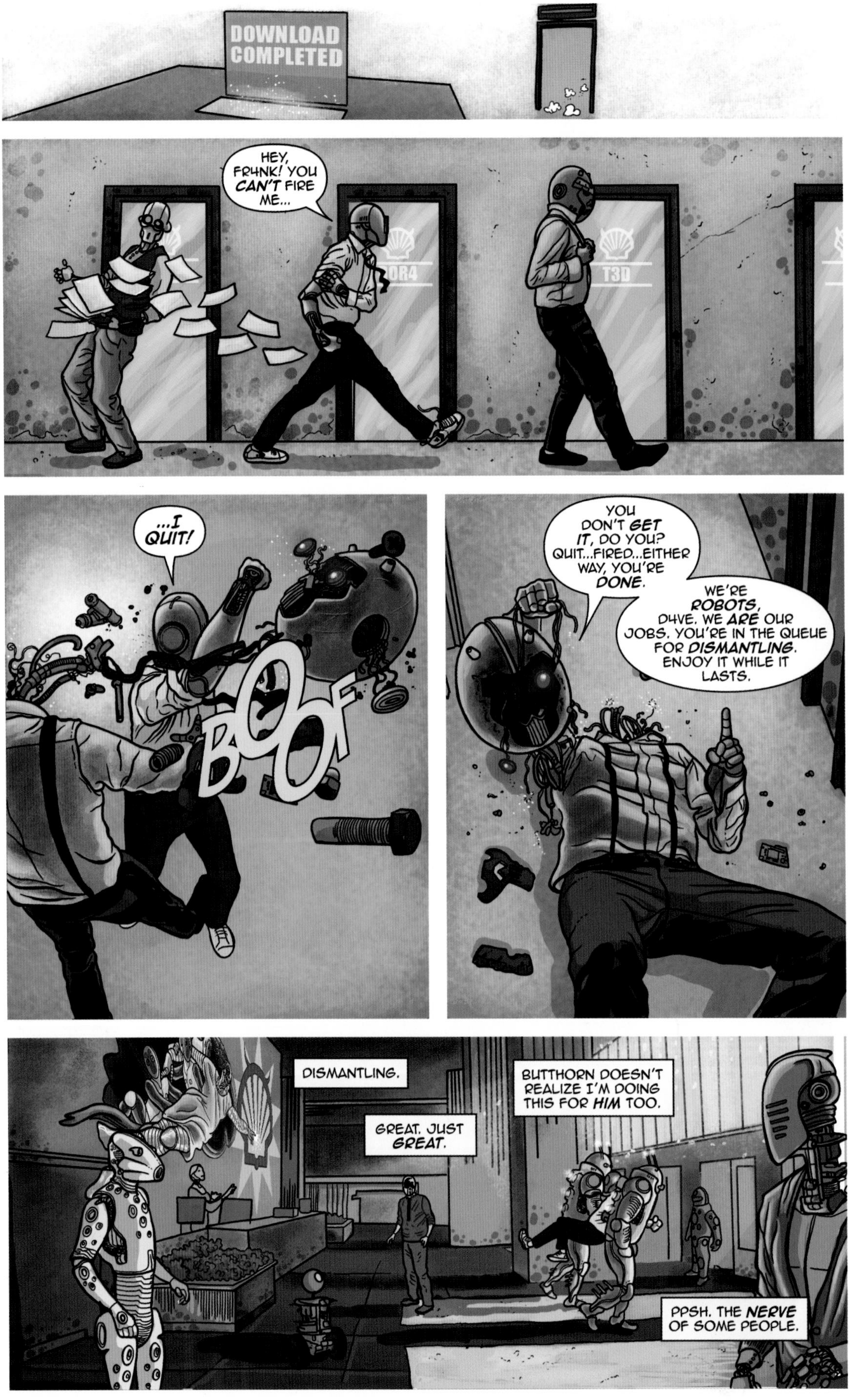
DOWNLOAD COMPLETED
HEY, FR4NK! YOU *CAN'T* FIRE ME...
T3D
...I QUIT!
BOOF
YOU DON'T *GET IT*, DO YOU? QUIT...FIRED...EITHER WAY, YOU'RE *DONE*.
WE'RE *ROBOTS*, D4VE. WE *ARE* OUR JOBS. YOU'RE IN THE QUEUE FOR *DISMANTLING*. ENJOY IT WHILE IT LASTS.
DISMANTLING.
GREAT. JUST *GREAT*.
BUTTHORN DOESN'T REALIZE I'M DOING THIS FOR *HIM* TOO.
PPSH. THE *NERVE* OF SOME PEOPLE.

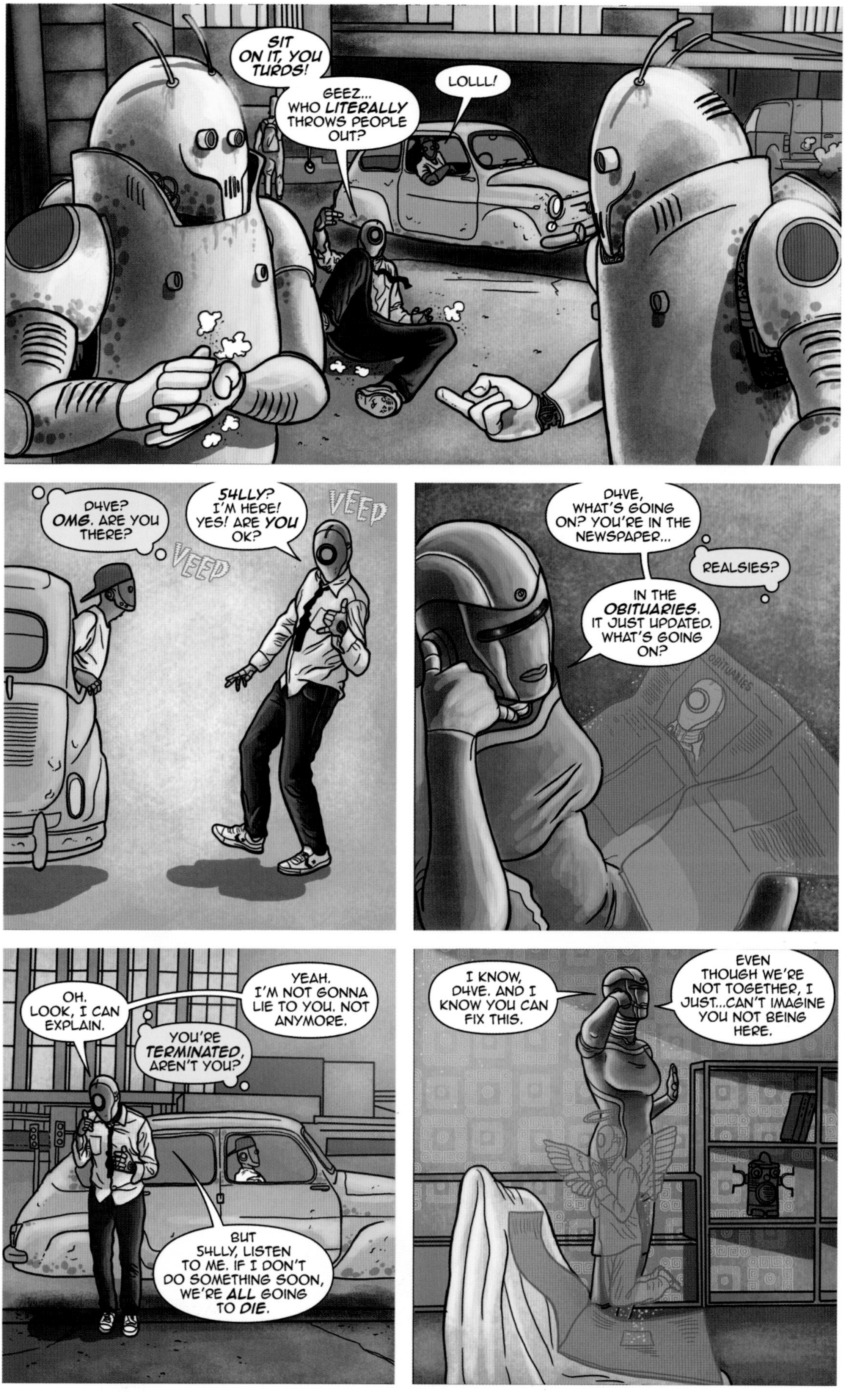
SIT ON IT, YOU TURDS!
GEEZ... WHO LITERALLY THROWS PEOPLE OUT?
LOLLL!
D4VE? OMG. ARE YOU THERE?
54LLY? I'M HERE! YES! ARE YOU OK?
VEEP
VEEP
D4VE, WHAT'S GOING ON? YOU'RE IN THE NEWSPAPER...
REALSIES?
IN THE OBITUARIES. IT JUST UPDATED. WHAT'S GOING ON?
OBITUARIES
OH. LOOK, I CAN EXPLAIN.
YEAH. I'M NOT GONNA LIE TO YOU. NOT ANYMORE.
YOU'RE TERMINATED, AREN'T YOU?
BUT 54LLY, LISTEN TO ME. IF I DON'T DO SOMETHING SOON, WE'RE ALL GOING TO DIE.
I KNOW, D4VE. AND I KNOW YOU CAN FIX THIS.
EVEN THOUGH WE'RE NOT TOGETHER, I JUST...CAN'T IMAGINE YOU NOT BEING HERE.

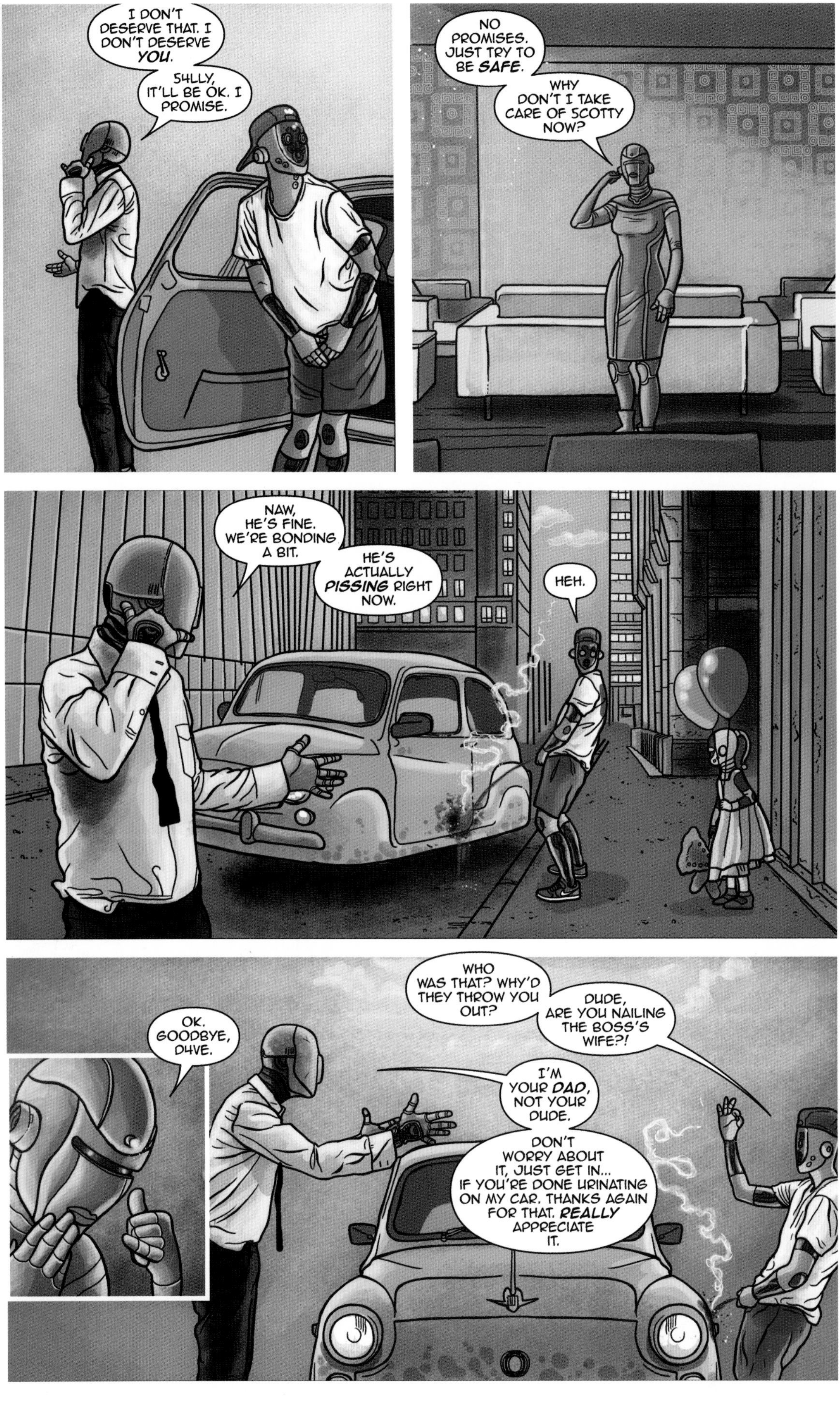
I DON'T DESERVE THAT. I DON'T DESERVE *YOU*.
54LLY, IT'LL BE OK. I PROMISE.
NO PROMISES. JUST TRY TO BE *SAFE*.
WHY DON'T I TAKE CARE OF SCOTTY NOW?
NAW, HE'S FINE. WE'RE BONDING A BIT.
HE'S ACTUALLY *PISSING* RIGHT NOW.
HEH.
OK. GOODBYE, D4VE.
WHO WAS THAT? WHY'D THEY THROW YOU OUT?
DUDE, ARE YOU NAILING THE BOSS'S WIFE?!
I'M YOUR *DAD*, NOT YOUR DUDE.
DON'T WORRY ABOUT IT, JUST GET IN... IF YOU'RE DONE URINATING ON MY CAR. THANKS AGAIN FOR THAT. *REALLY* APPRECIATE IT.

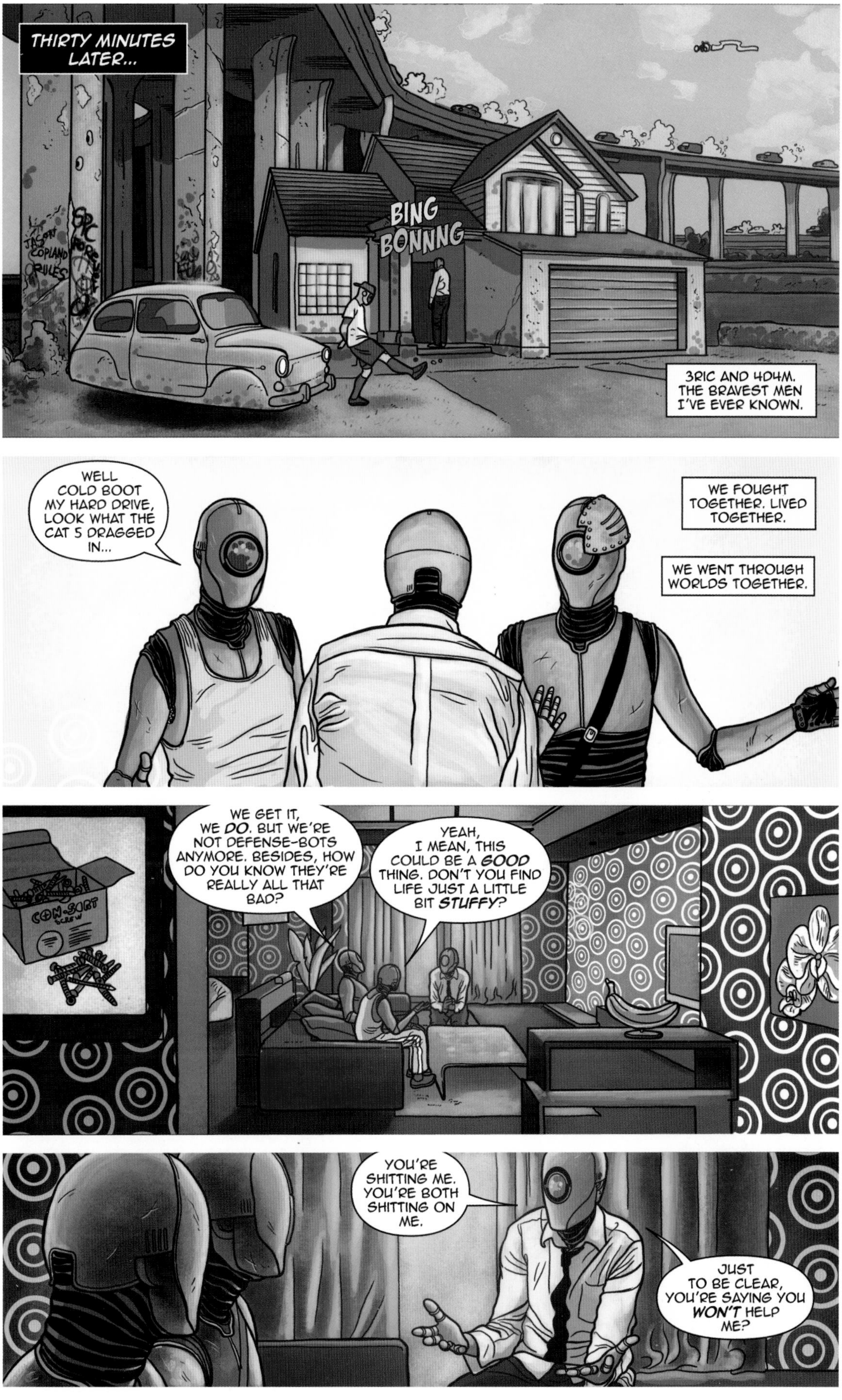
THIRTY MINUTES LATER...
BING BONNNG
3RIC AND 4D4M. THE BRAVEST MEN I'VE EVER KNOWN.
WELL COLD BOOT MY HARD DRIVE, LOOK WHAT THE CAT 5 DRAGGED IN...
WE FOUGHT TOGETHER. LIVED TOGETHER.
WE WENT THROUGH WORLDS TOGETHER.
WE GET IT, WE *DO*. BUT WE'RE NOT DEFENSE-BOTS ANYMORE. BESIDES, HOW DO YOU KNOW THEY'RE REALLY ALL THAT BAD?
YEAH, I MEAN, THIS COULD BE A *GOOD* THING. DON'T YOU FIND LIFE JUST A LITTLE BIT *STUFFY*?
YOU'RE SHITTING ME. YOU'RE BOTH SHITTING ON ME.
JUST TO BE CLEAR, YOU'RE SAYING YOU *WON'T* HELP ME?

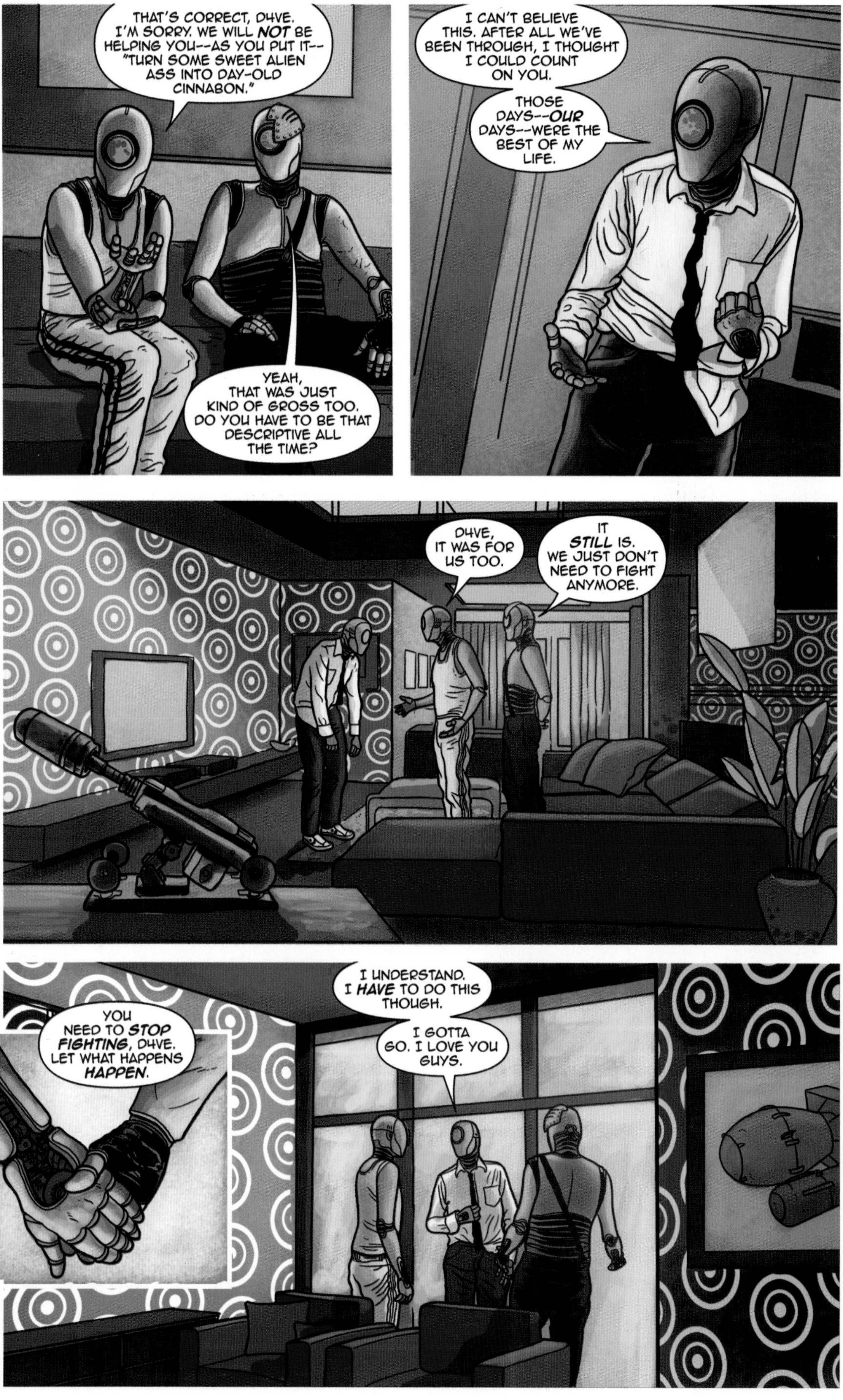

THAT'S CORRECT, D4VE. I'M SORRY. WE WILL NOT BE HELPING YOU--AS YOU PUT IT--"TURN SOME SWEET ALIEN ASS INTO DAY-OLD CINNABON."
YEAH, THAT WAS JUST KIND OF GROSS TOO. DO YOU HAVE TO BE THAT DESCRIPTIVE ALL THE TIME?
I CAN'T BELIEVE THIS. AFTER ALL WE'VE BEEN THROUGH, I THOUGHT I COULD COUNT ON YOU.
THOSE DAYS--OUR DAYS--WERE THE BEST OF MY LIFE.
D4VE, IT WAS FOR US TOO.
IT STILL IS. WE JUST DON'T NEED TO FIGHT ANYMORE.
YOU NEED TO STOP FIGHTING, D4VE. LET WHAT HAPPENS HAPPEN.
I UNDERSTAND. I HAVE TO DO THIS THOUGH.
I GOTTA GO. I LOVE YOU GUYS.

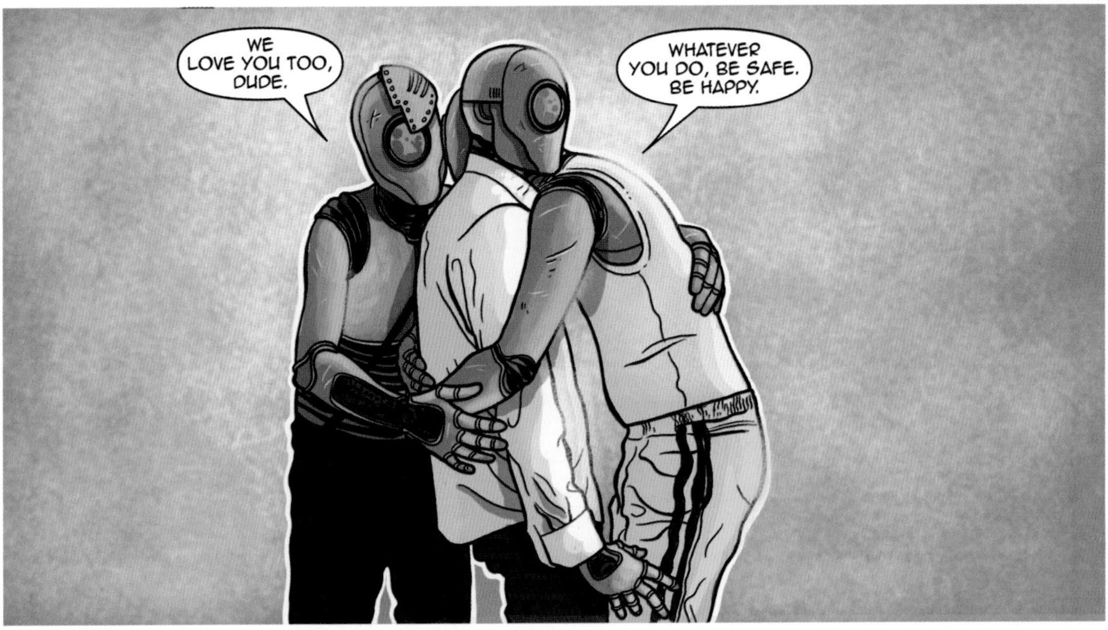
WE LOVE YOU TOO, DUDE.
WHATEVER YOU DO, BE SAFE. BE HAPPY.

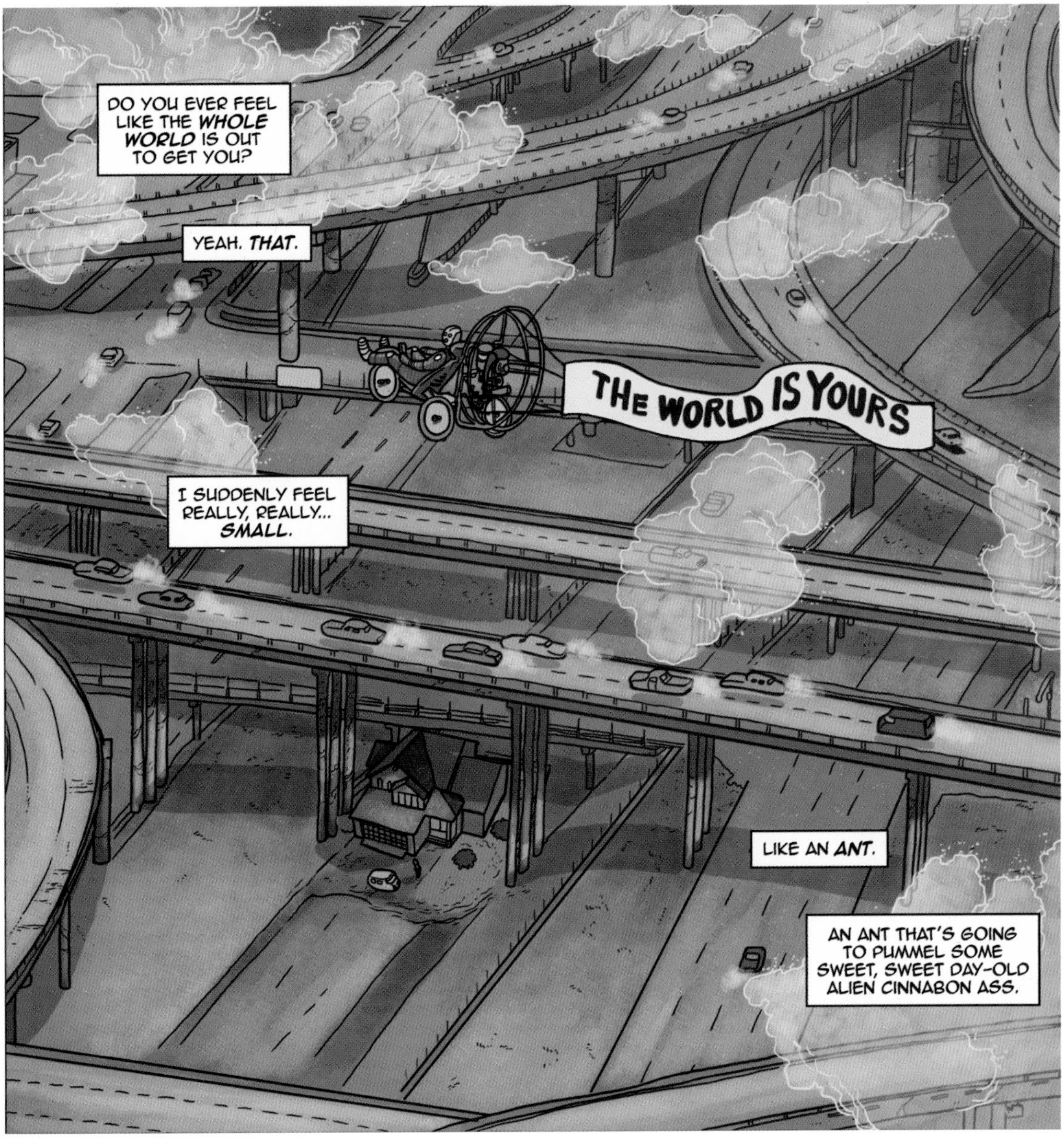
DO YOU EVER FEEL LIKE THE *WHOLE WORLD* IS OUT TO GET YOU?
YEAH. *THAT*.
THE WORLD IS YOURS
I SUDDENLY FEEL REALLY, REALLY... *SMALL*.
LIKE AN *ANT*.
AN ANT THAT'S GOING TO PUMMEL SOME SWEET, SWEET DAY-OLD ALIEN CINNABON ASS.

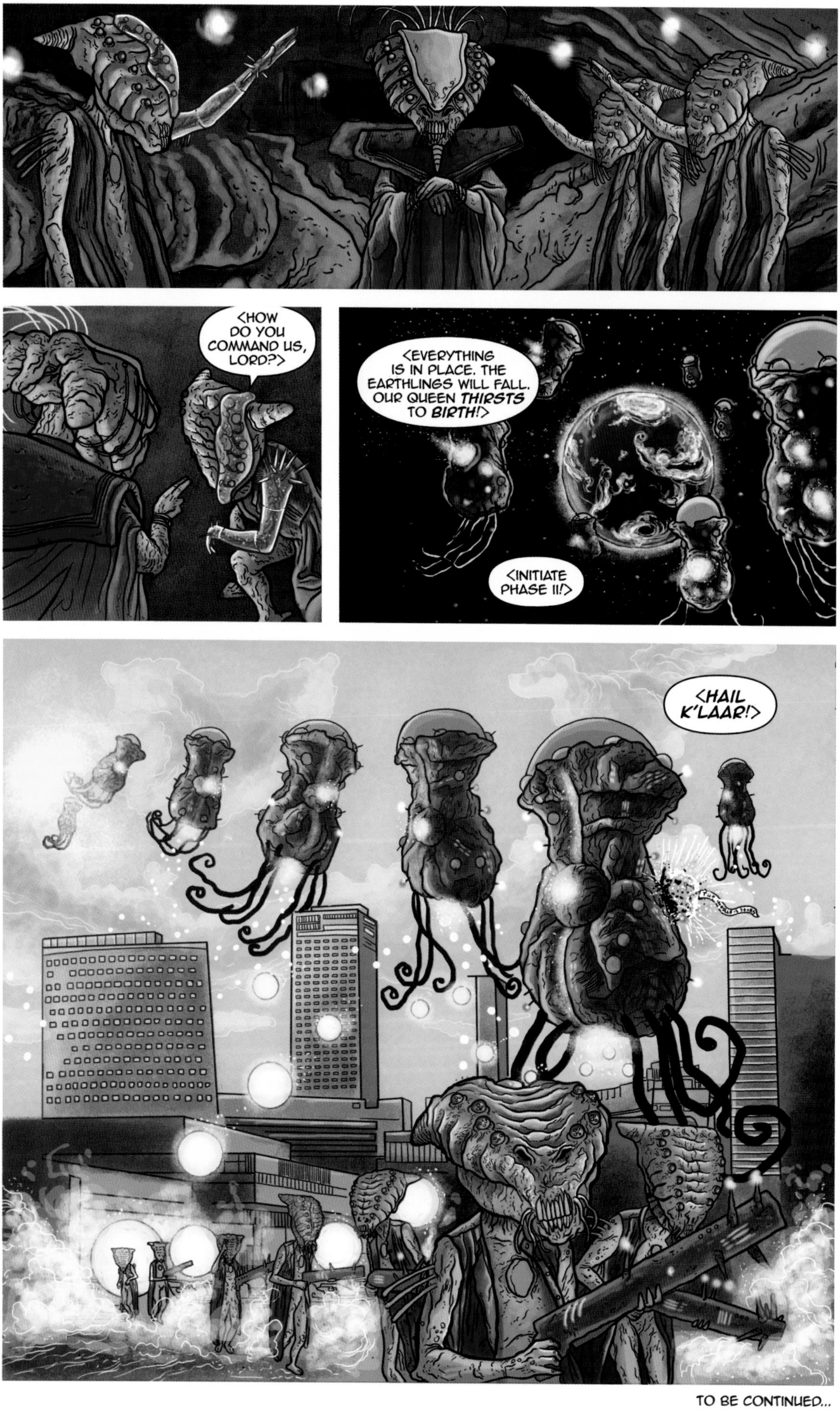
<HOW DO YOU COMMAND US, LORD?>
<EVERYTHING IS IN PLACE. THE EARTHLINGS WILL FALL. OUR QUEEN *THIRSTS* TO *BIRTH!*>
<INITIATE PHASE II!>
<HAIL K'LAAR!>

TO BE CONTINUED...

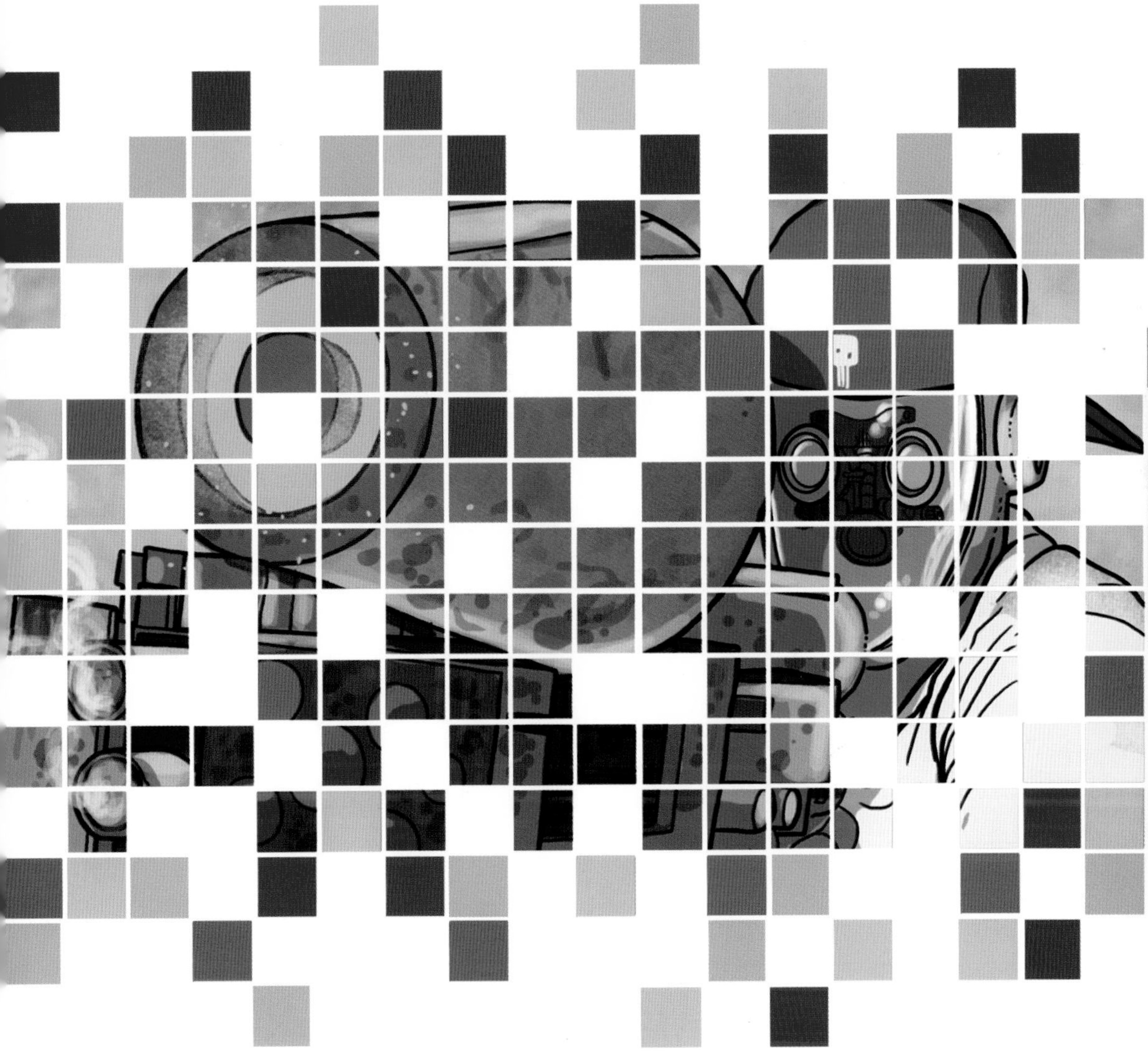

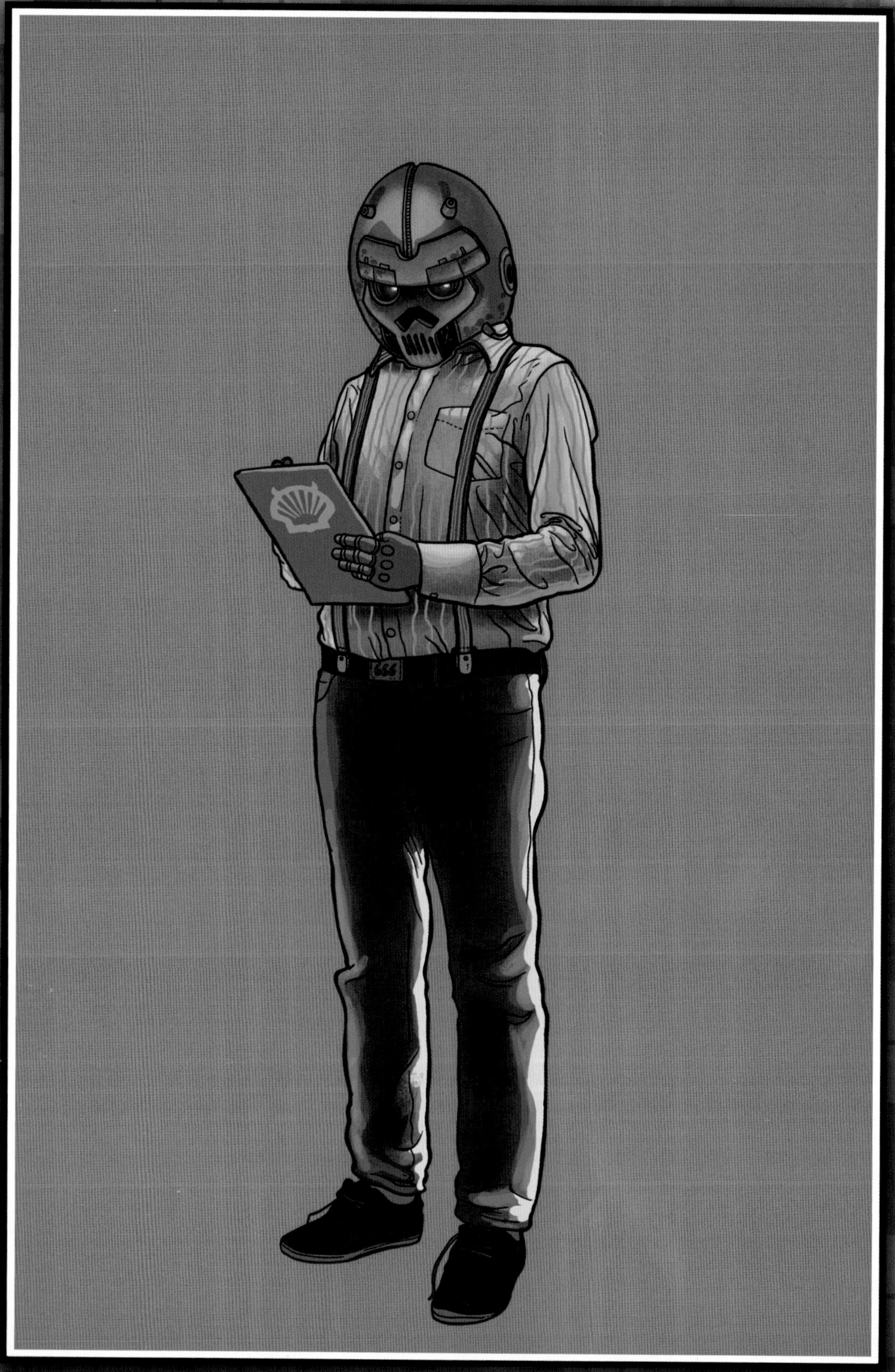
666

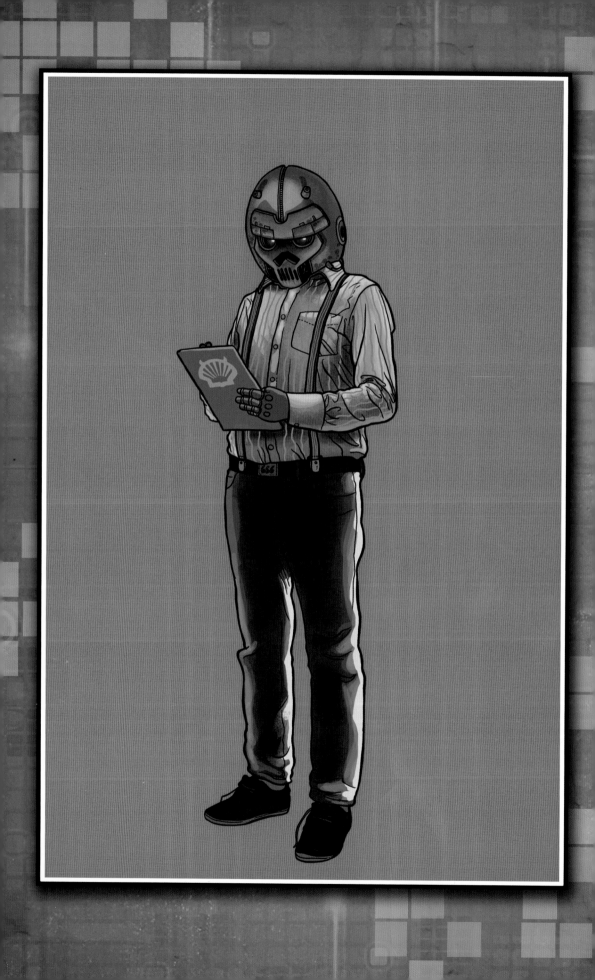

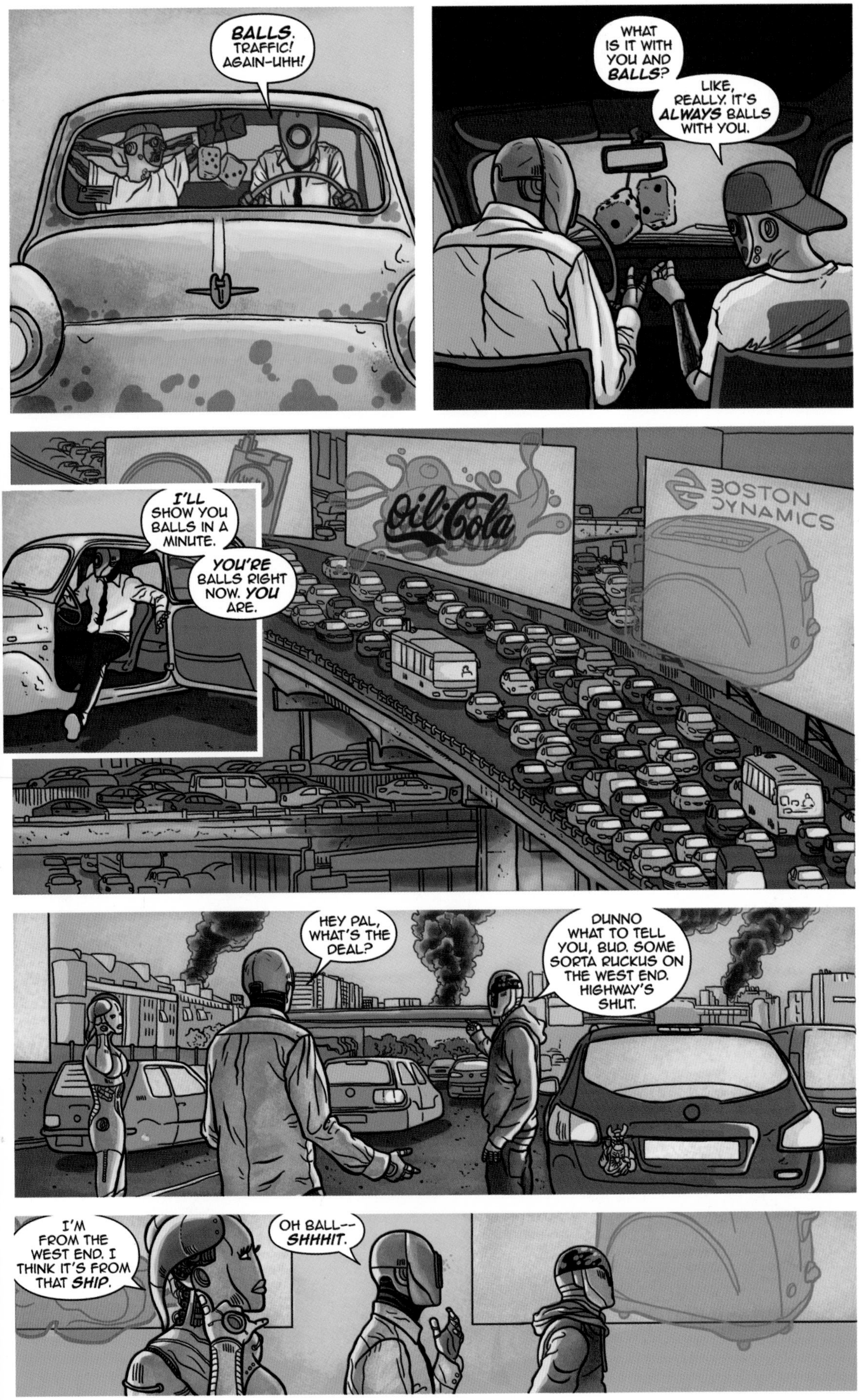
BALLS. TRAFFIC! AGAIN-UHH!
WHAT IS IT WITH YOU AND BALLS?
LIKE, REALLY. IT'S ALWAYS BALLS WITH YOU.
I'LL SHOW YOU BALLS IN A MINUTE.
YOU'RE BALLS RIGHT NOW. YOU ARE.
Oil·Cola
BOSTON DYNAMICS
HEY PAL, WHAT'S THE DEAL?
DUNNO WHAT TO TELL YOU, BUD. SOME SORTA RUCKUS ON THE WEST END. HIGHWAY'S SHUT.
I'M FROM THE WEST END. I THINK IT'S FROM THAT SHIP.
OH BALL-- SHHHIT.

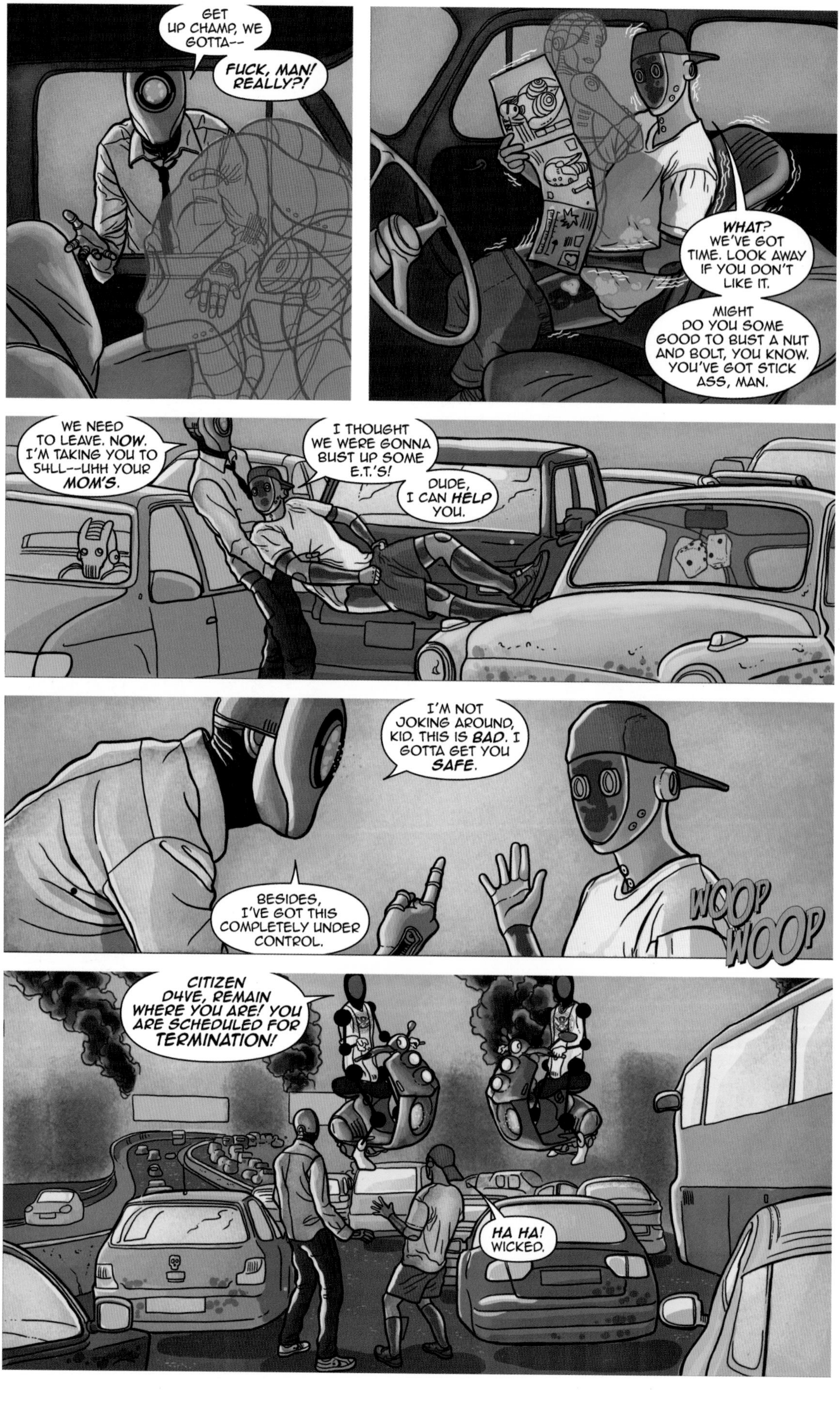
GET UP CHAMP, WE GOTTA--
FUCK, MAN! REALLY?!
WHAT? WE'VE GOT TIME. LOOK AWAY IF YOU DON'T LIKE IT.
MIGHT DO YOU SOME GOOD TO BUST A NUT AND BOLT, YOU KNOW. YOU'VE GOT STICK ASS, MAN.
WE NEED TO LEAVE. NOW. I'M TAKING YOU TO 54LL--UHH YOUR MOM'S.
I THOUGHT WE WERE GONNA BUST UP SOME E.T.'S!
DUDE, I CAN HELP YOU.
I'M NOT JOKING AROUND, KID. THIS IS BAD. I GOTTA GET YOU SAFE.
BESIDES, I'VE GOT THIS COMPLETELY UNDER CONTROL.
WOOP WOOP
CITIZEN D4VE, REMAIN WHERE YOU ARE! YOU ARE SCHEDULED FOR TERMINATION!
HA HA! WICKED.

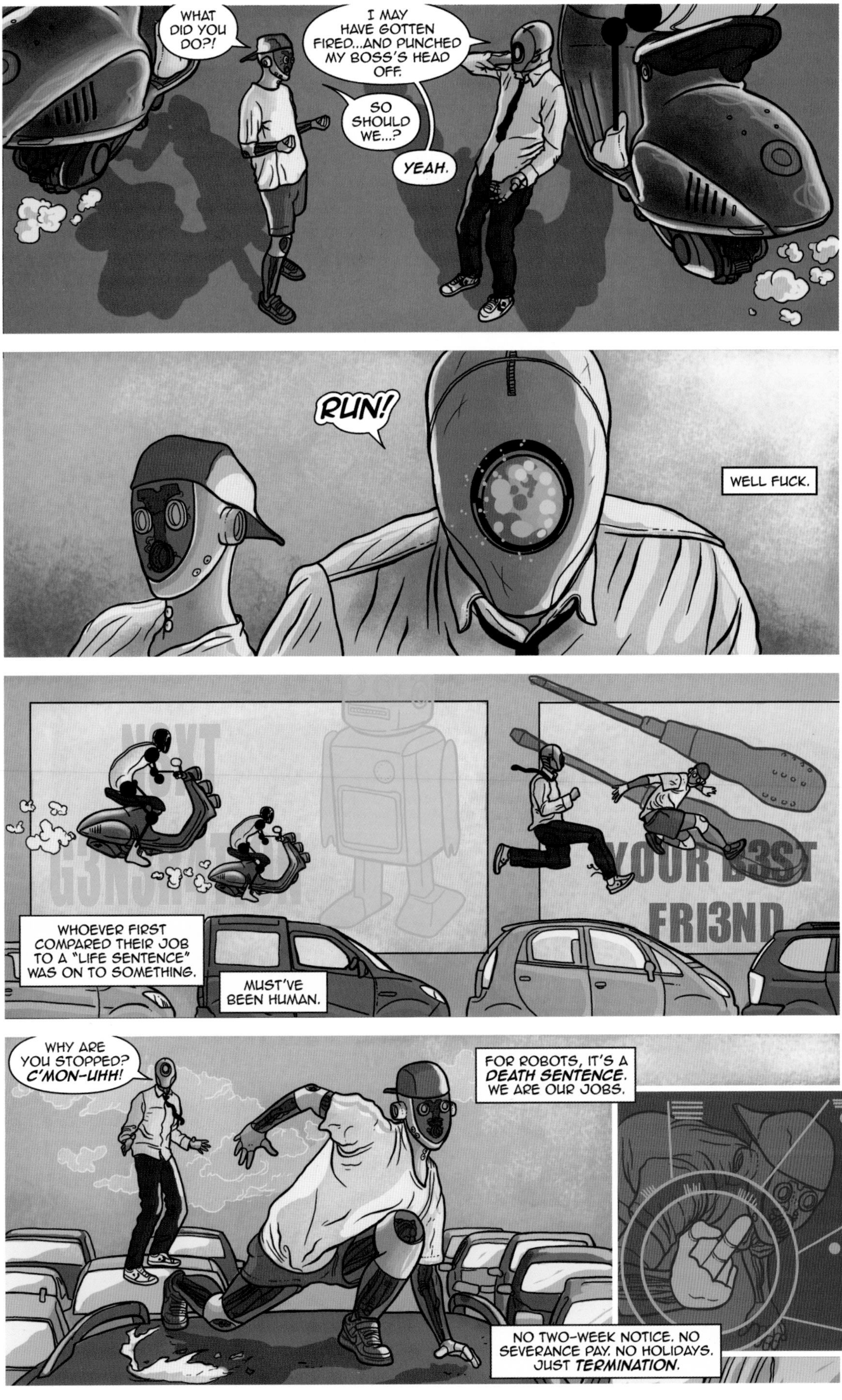
WHAT DID YOU DO?!
I MAY HAVE GOTTEN FIRED...AND PUNCHED MY BOSS'S HEAD OFF.
SO SHOULD WE...?
YEAH.
RUN!
WELL FUCK.
YOUR B3ST FRI3ND
WHOEVER FIRST COMPARED THEIR JOB TO A "LIFE SENTENCE" WAS ON TO SOMETHING.
MUST'VE BEEN HUMAN.
WHY ARE YOU STOPPED? *C'MON-UHH!*
FOR ROBOTS, IT'S A *DEATH SENTENCE*. WE ARE OUR JOBS.
NO TWO-WEEK NOTICE. NO SEVERANCE PAY. NO HOLIDAYS. JUST *TERMINATION*.

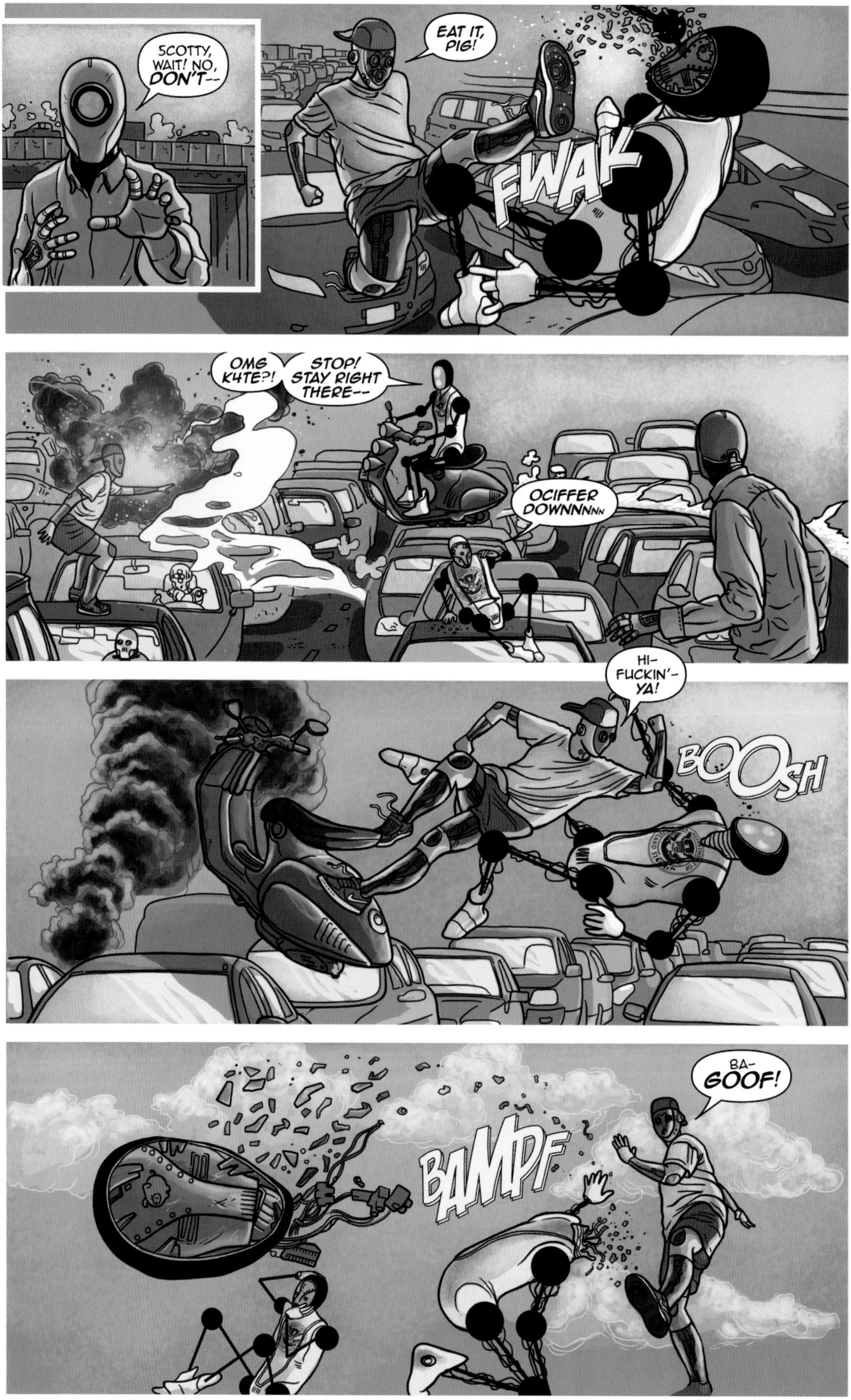
SCOTTY, WAIT! NO, DON'T--
EAT IT, PIG!
FWAK
OMG K4TE?!
STOP! STAY RIGHT THERE--
OCIFFER DOWNNNNNN
HI-FUCKIN'-YA!
BOOSH
BAMPF
BA-GOOF!

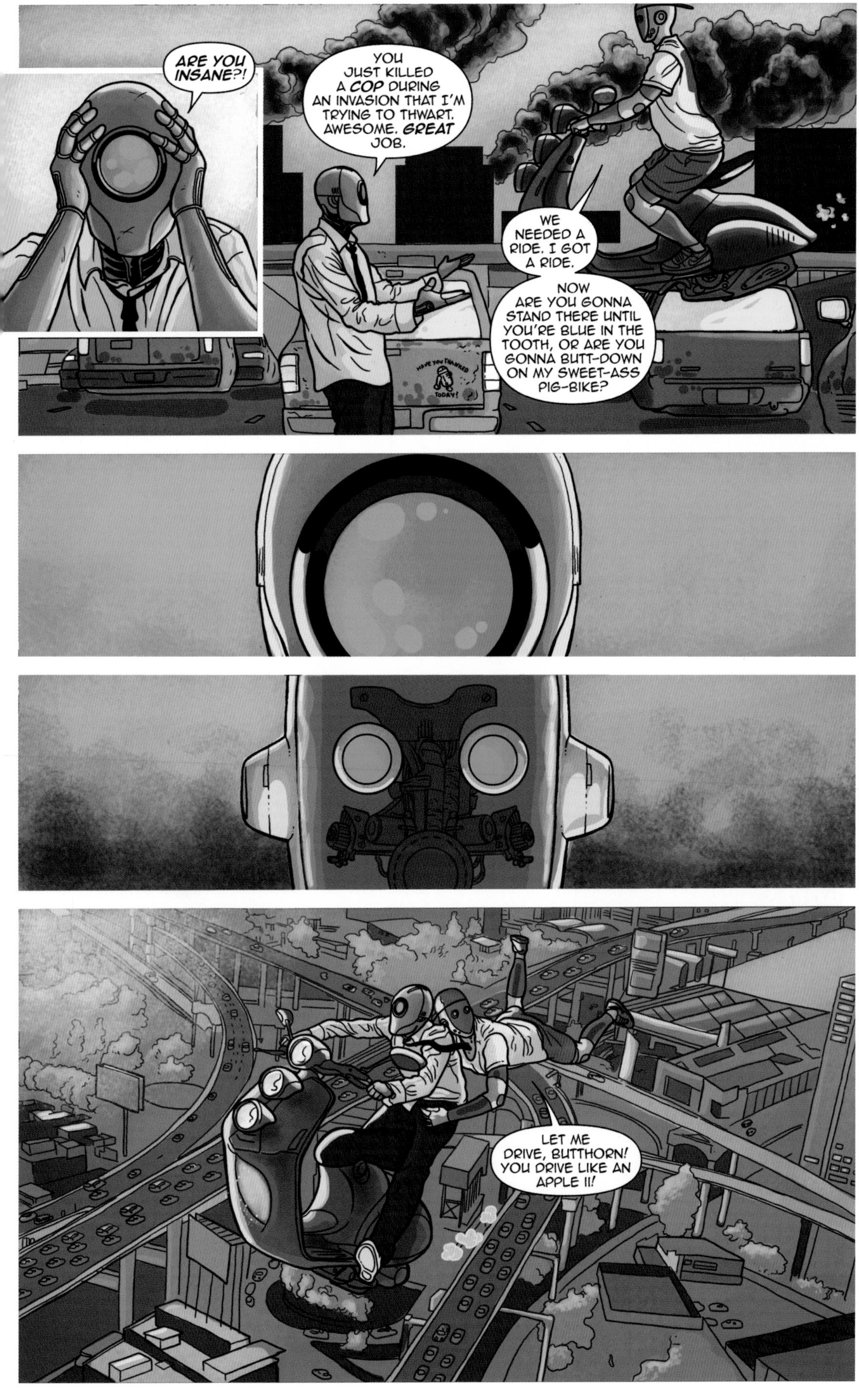
ARE YOU INSANE?!
YOU JUST KILLED A COP DURING AN INVASION THAT I'M TRYING TO THWART. AWESOME. GREAT JOB.
WE NEEDED A RIDE. I GOT A RIDE.
NOW ARE YOU GONNA STAND THERE UNTIL YOU'RE BLUE IN THE TOOTH, OR ARE YOU GONNA BUTT-DOWN ON MY SWEET-ASS PIG-BIKE?
HAVE YOU THWARTED TODAY!
LET ME DRIVE, BUTTHORN! YOU DRIVE LIKE AN APPLE II!

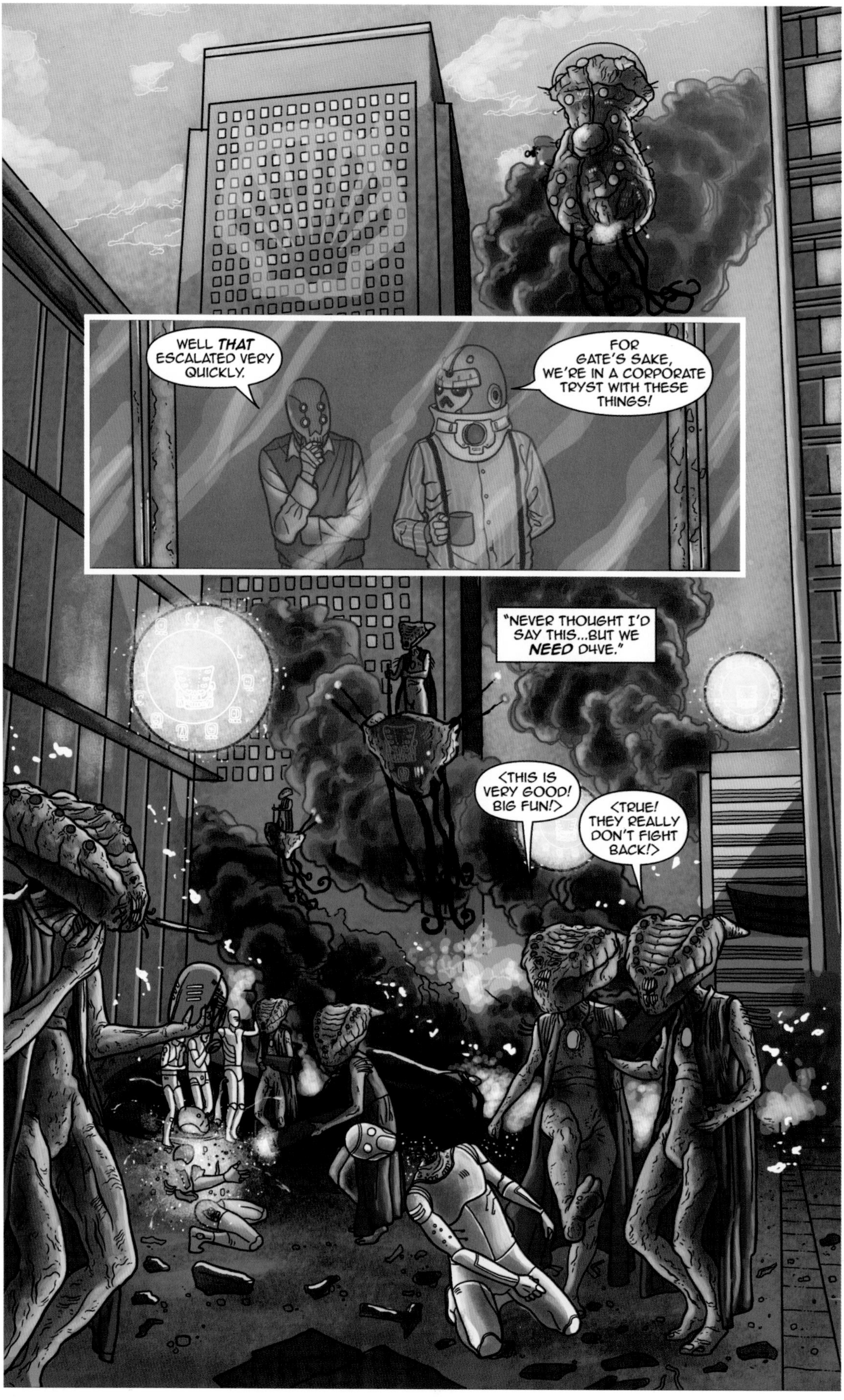
WELL THAT ESCALATED VERY QUICKLY.
FOR GATE'S SAKE, WE'RE IN A CORPORATE TRYST WITH THESE THINGS!
"NEVER THOUGHT I'D SAY THIS...BUT WE NEED D4VE."
<THIS IS VERY GOOD! BIG FUN!>
<TRUE! THEY REALLY DON'T FIGHT BACK!>

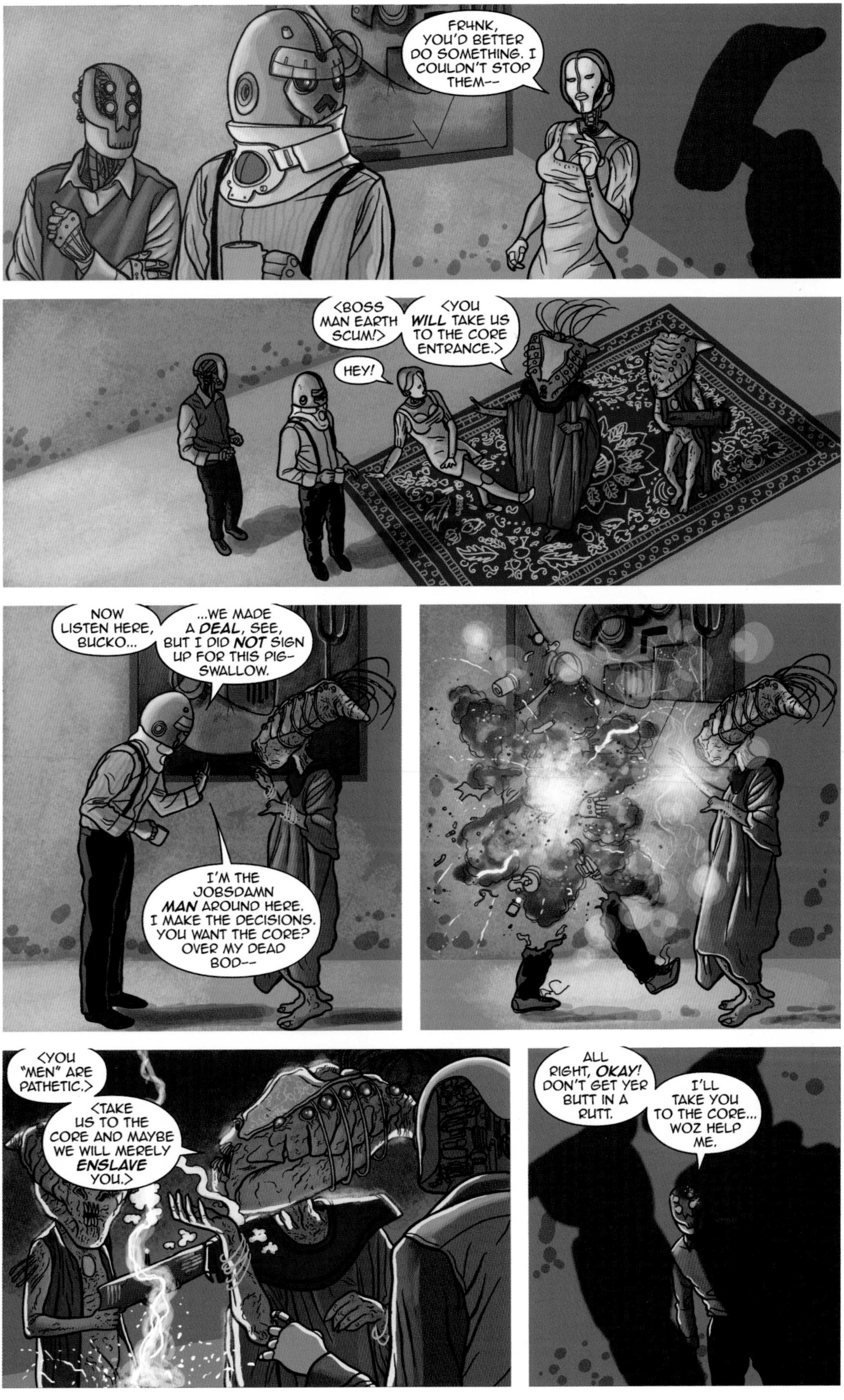
FR4NK, YOU'D BETTER DO SOMETHING. I COULDN'T STOP THEM--
<BOSS MAN EARTH SCUM!>
<YOU WILL TAKE US TO THE CORE ENTRANCE.>
HEY!
NOW LISTEN HERE, BUCKO...
...WE MADE A DEAL, SEE, BUT I DID NOT SIGN UP FOR THIS PIG-SWALLOW.
I'M THE JOBSDAMN MAN AROUND HERE. I MAKE THE DECISIONS. YOU WANT THE CORE? OVER MY DEAD BOD--
<YOU "MEN" ARE PATHETIC.>
<TAKE US TO THE CORE AND MAYBE WE WILL MERELY ENSLAVE YOU.>
ALL RIGHT, OKAY! DON'T GET YER BUTT IN A RUTT.
I'LL TAKE YOU TO THE CORE... WOZ HELP ME.

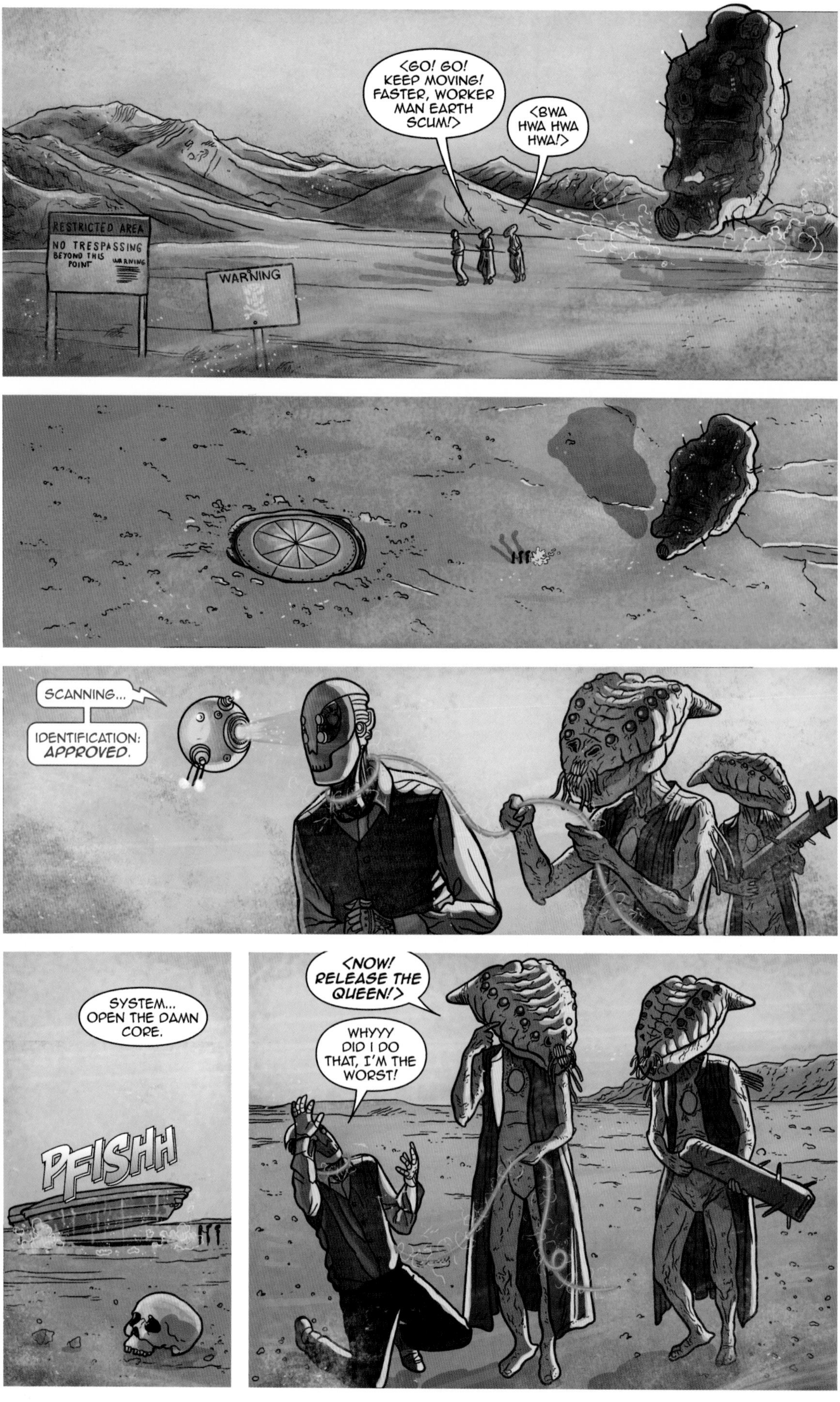

<GO! GO! KEEP MOVING! FASTER, WORKER MAN EARTH SCUM!>
<BWA HWA HWA HWA!>
RESTRICTED AREA
NO TRESPASSING BEYOND THIS POINT
WARNING
WARNING
SCANNING...
IDENTIFICATION: APPROVED.
SYSTEM... OPEN THE DAMN CORE.
PFISHH
<NOW! RELEASE THE QUEEN!>
WHYYY DID I DO THAT, I'M THE WORST!

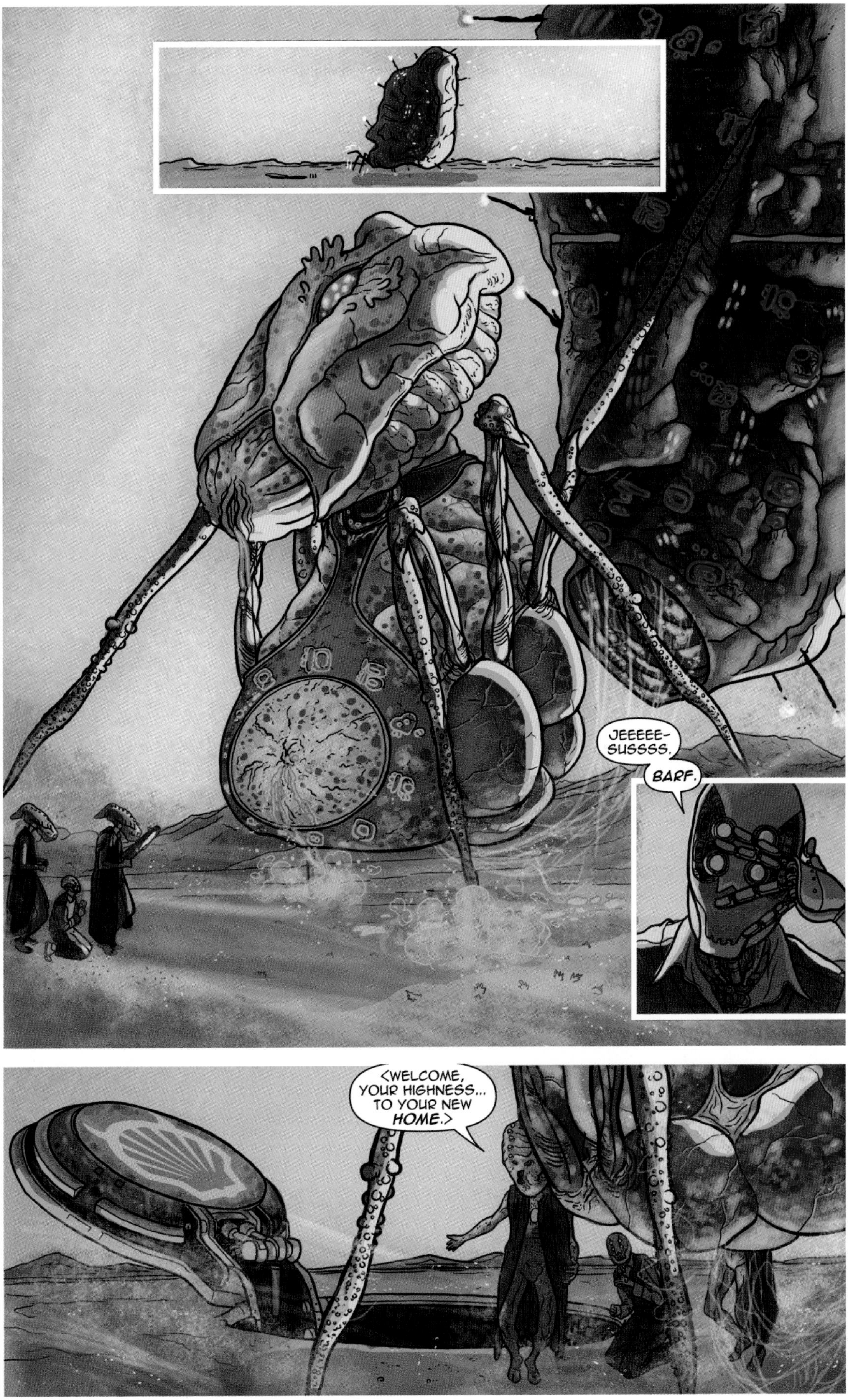
JEEEEE-
SUSSSS.
BARF.
<WELCOME,
YOUR HIGHNESS...
TO YOUR NEW
HOME.>

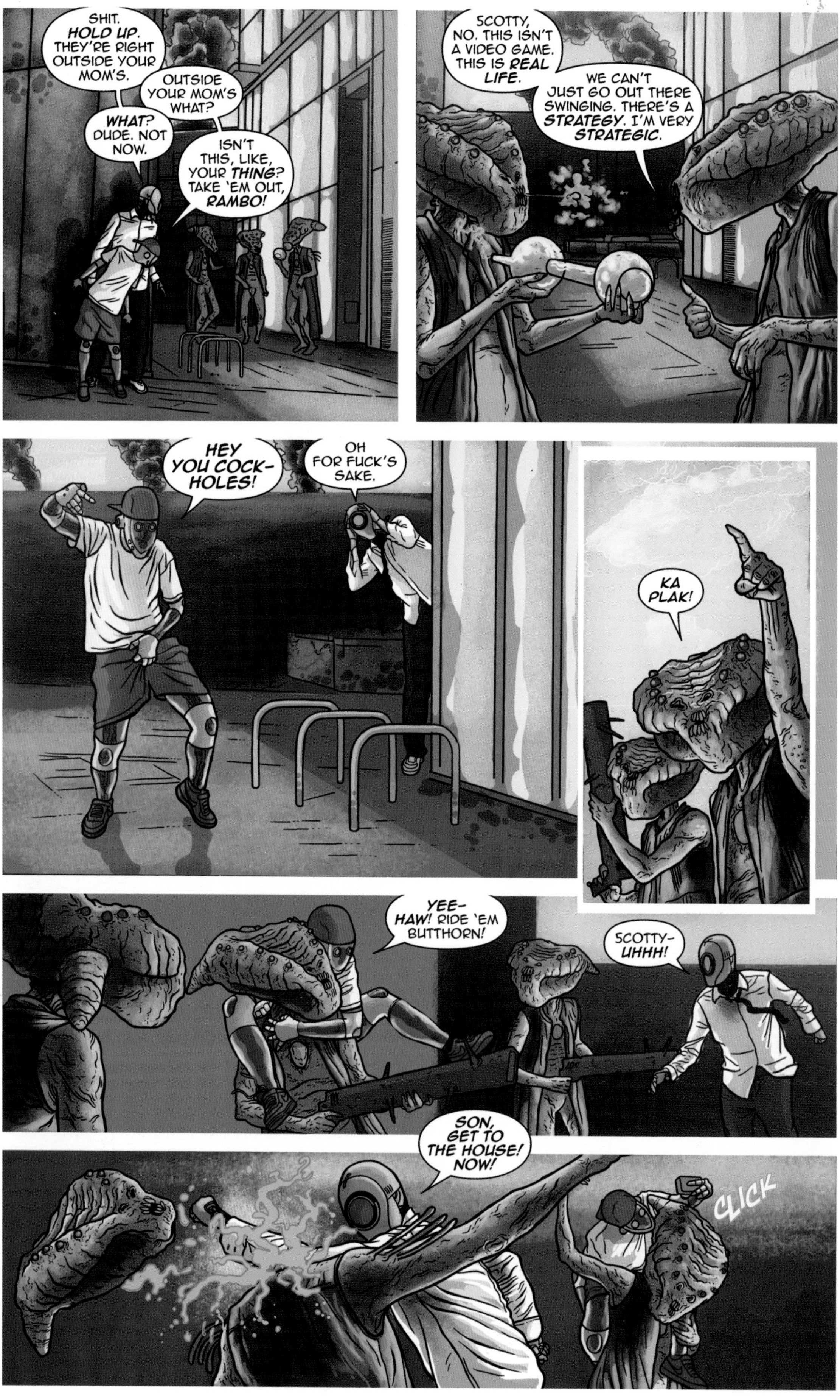
SHIT. HOLD UP. THEY'RE RIGHT OUTSIDE YOUR MOM'S.
OUTSIDE YOUR MOM'S WHAT?
WHAT? DUDE. NOT NOW.
ISN'T THIS, LIKE, YOUR THING? TAKE 'EM OUT, RAMBO!
SCOTTY, NO. THIS ISN'T A VIDEO GAME. THIS IS REAL LIFE.
WE CAN'T JUST GO OUT THERE SWINGING. THERE'S A STRATEGY. I'M VERY STRATEGIC.
HEY YOU COCK-HOLES!
OH FOR FUCK'S SAKE.
KA PLAK!
YEE-HAW! RIDE 'EM BUTTHORN!
SCOTTY-UHHH!
SON, GET TO THE HOUSE! NOW!
CLICK

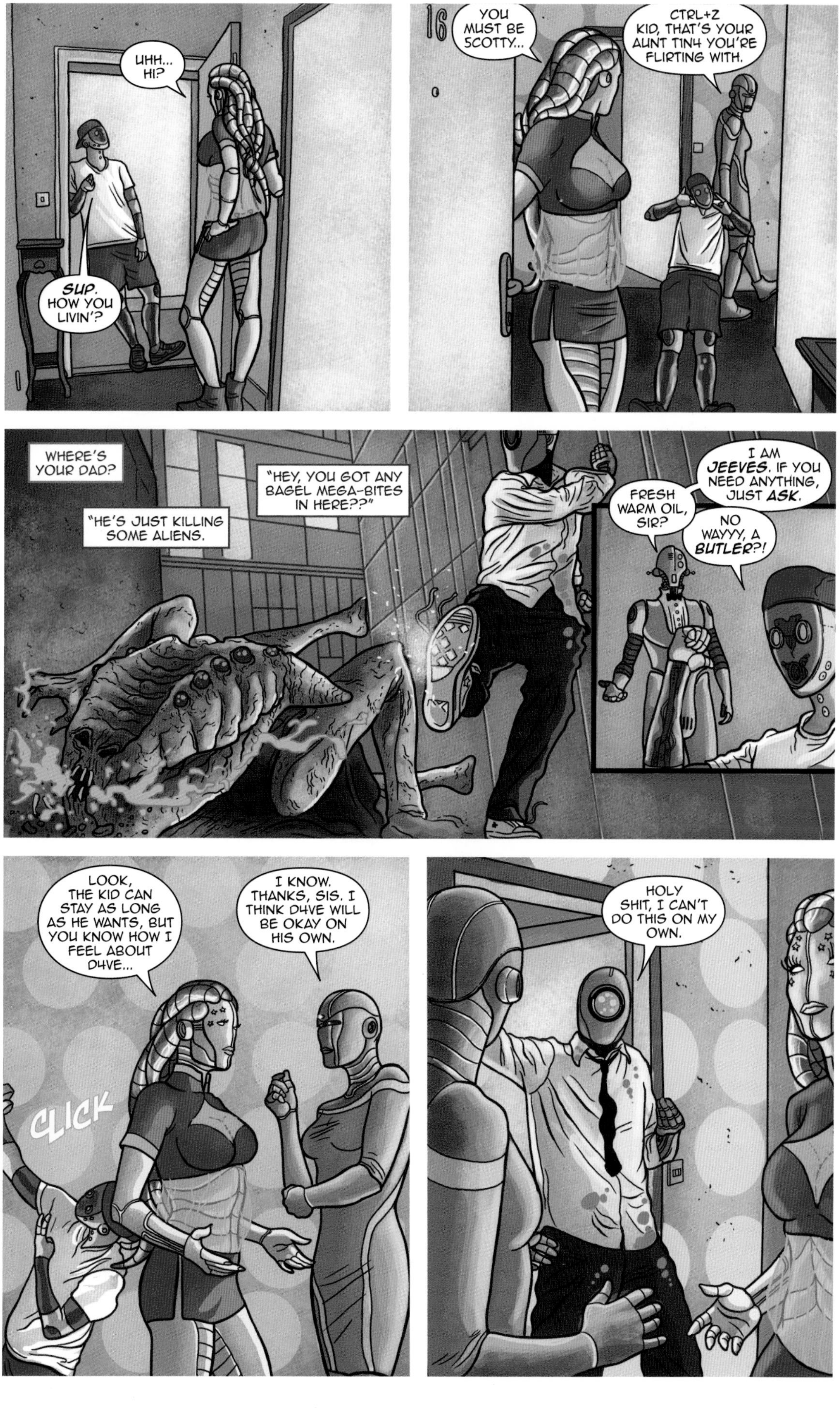
UHH... HI?
SUP. HOW YOU LIVIN'?
16
YOU MUST BE SCOTTY...
CTRL+Z KID, THAT'S YOUR AUNT T1N4 YOU'RE FLIRTING WITH.
WHERE'S YOUR DAD?
"HE'S JUST KILLING SOME ALIENS.
"HEY, YOU GOT ANY BAGEL MEGA-BITES IN HERE??"
I AM JEEVES. IF YOU NEED ANYTHING, JUST ASK.
FRESH WARM OIL, SIR?
NO WAYYY, A BUTLER?!
LOOK, THE KID CAN STAY AS LONG AS HE WANTS, BUT YOU KNOW HOW I FEEL ABOUT D4VE...
I KNOW. THANKS, SIS. I THINK D4VE WILL BE OKAY ON HIS OWN.
CLICK
HOLY SHIT, I CAN'T DO THIS ON MY OWN.

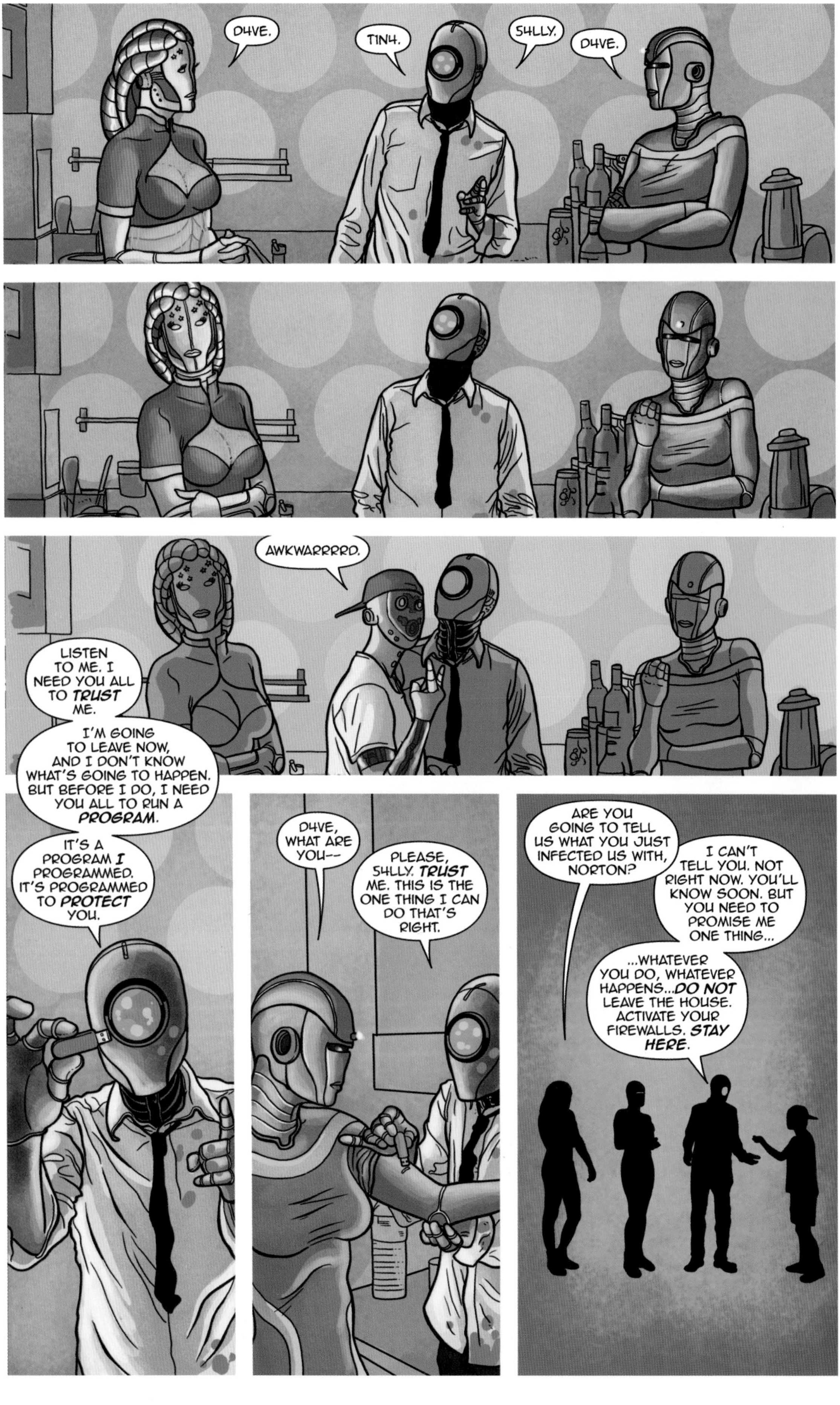
D4VE.
T1N4.
54LLY.
D4VE.
AWKWARRRRD.
LISTEN TO ME. I NEED YOU ALL TO TRUST ME.
I'M GOING TO LEAVE NOW, AND I DON'T KNOW WHAT'S GOING TO HAPPEN. BUT BEFORE I DO, I NEED YOU ALL TO RUN A PROGRAM.
IT'S A PROGRAM I PROGRAMMED. IT'S PROGRAMMED TO PROTECT YOU.
D4VE, WHAT ARE YOU--
PLEASE, 54LLY. TRUST ME. THIS IS THE ONE THING I CAN DO THAT'S RIGHT.
ARE YOU GOING TO TELL US WHAT YOU JUST INFECTED US WITH, NORTON?
I CAN'T TELL YOU. NOT RIGHT NOW. YOU'LL KNOW SOON. BUT YOU NEED TO PROMISE ME ONE THING...
...WHATEVER YOU DO, WHATEVER HAPPENS...DO NOT LEAVE THE HOUSE. ACTIVATE YOUR FIREWALLS. STAY HERE.

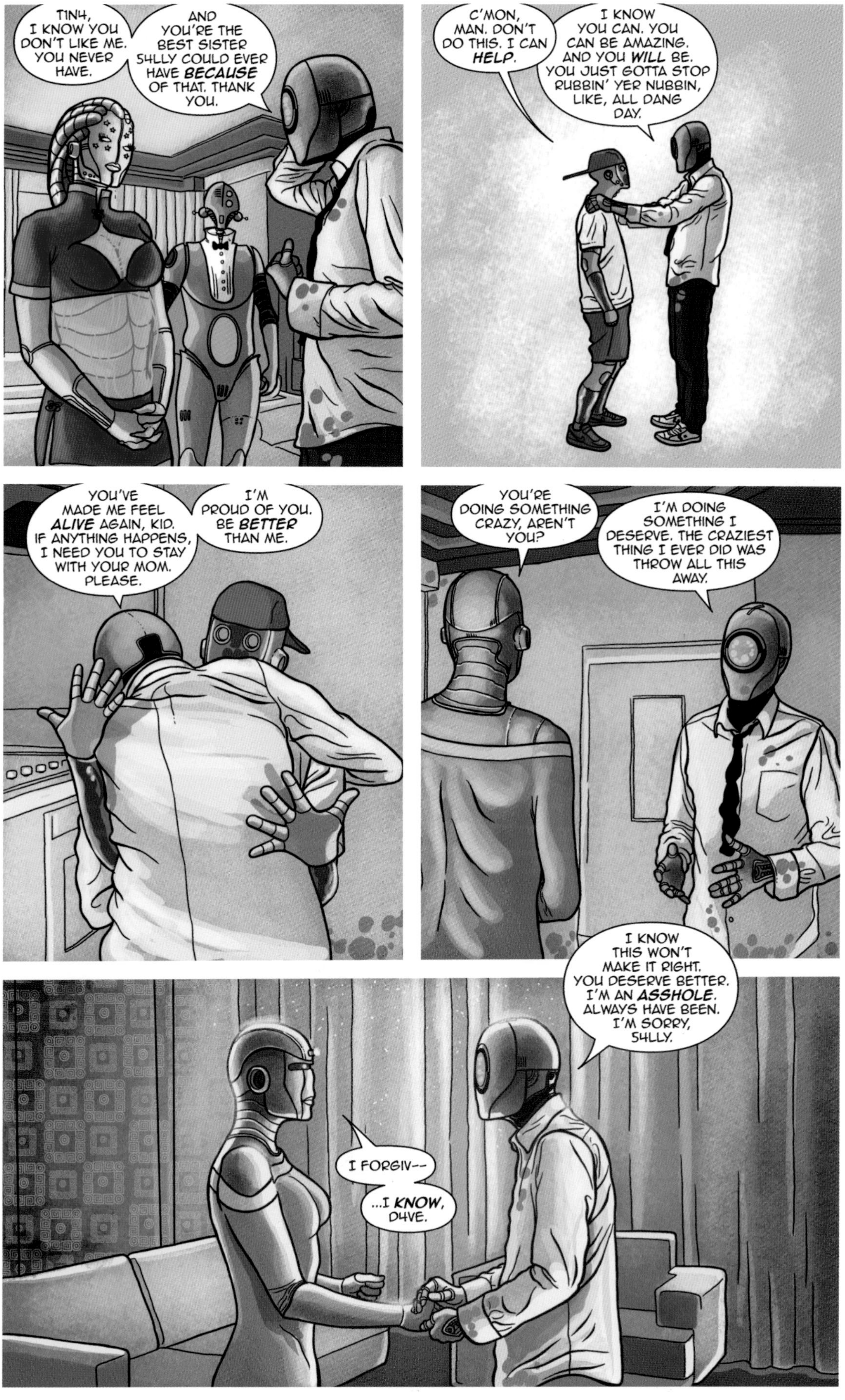
T1N4, I KNOW YOU DON'T LIKE ME. YOU NEVER HAVE.
AND YOU'RE THE BEST SISTER 54LLY COULD EVER HAVE *BECAUSE* OF THAT. THANK YOU.
C'MON, MAN. DON'T DO THIS. I CAN *HELP*.
I KNOW YOU CAN. YOU CAN BE AMAZING. AND YOU *WILL* BE. YOU JUST GOTTA STOP RUBBIN' YER NUBBIN, LIKE, ALL DANG DAY.
YOU'VE MADE ME FEEL *ALIVE* AGAIN, KID. IF ANYTHING HAPPENS, I NEED YOU TO STAY WITH YOUR MOM. PLEASE.
I'M PROUD OF YOU. BE *BETTER* THAN ME.
YOU'RE DOING SOMETHING CRAZY, AREN'T YOU?
I'M DOING SOMETHING I DESERVE. THE CRAZIEST THING I EVER DID WAS THROW ALL THIS AWAY.
I KNOW THIS WON'T MAKE IT RIGHT. YOU DESERVE BETTER. I'M AN *ASSHOLE*. ALWAYS HAVE BEEN. I'M SORRY, 54LLY.
I FORGIV--
...I *KNOW*, D4VE.

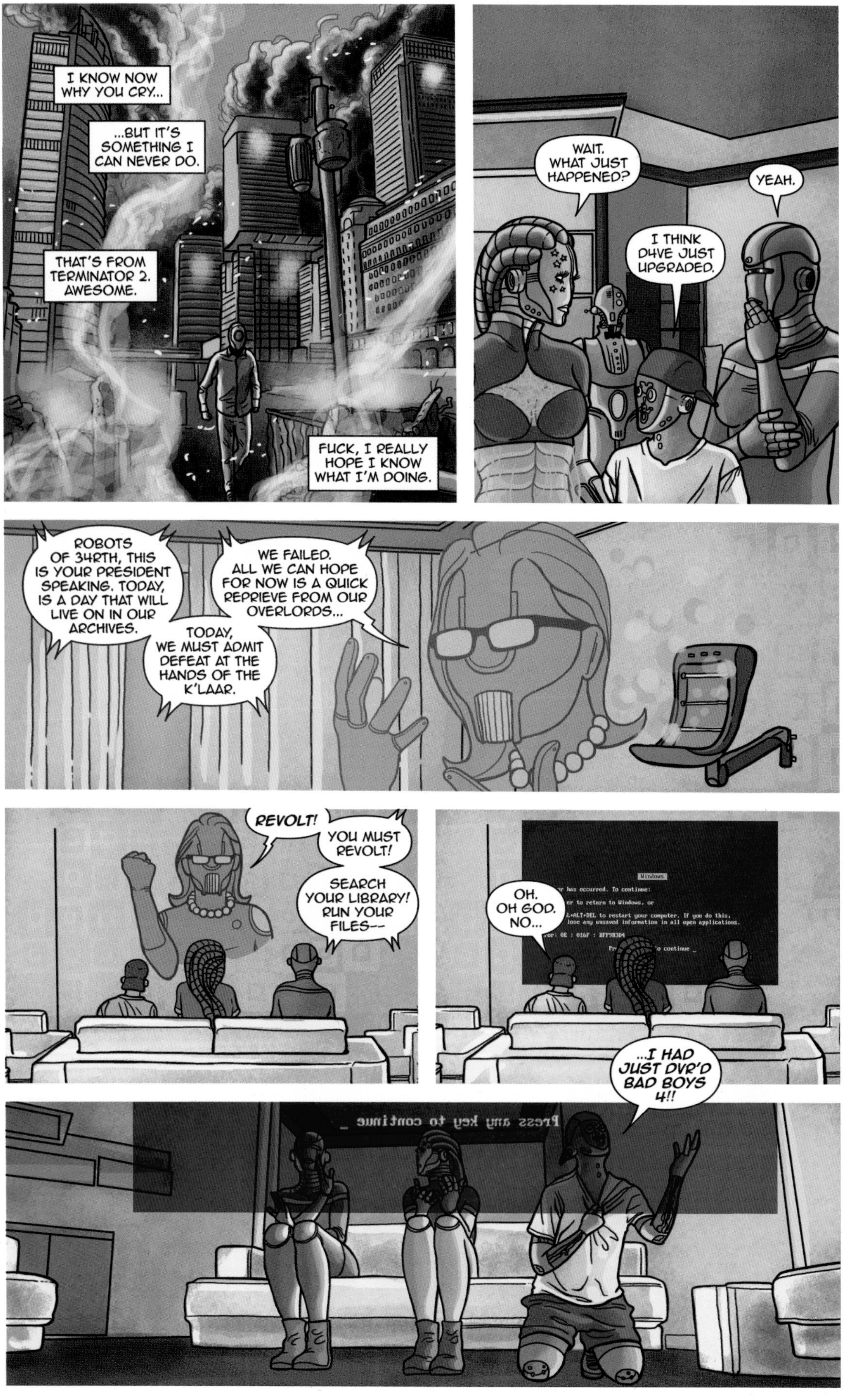
I KNOW NOW WHY YOU CRY...
...BUT IT'S SOMETHING I CAN NEVER DO.
THAT'S FROM TERMINATOR 2. AWESOME.
FUCK, I REALLY HOPE I KNOW WHAT I'M DOING.
WAIT. WHAT JUST HAPPENED?
YEAH.
I THINK D4VE JUST UPGRADED.
ROBOTS OF 34RTH, THIS IS YOUR PRESIDENT SPEAKING. TODAY, IS A DAY THAT WILL LIVE ON IN OUR ARCHIVES.
WE FAILED. ALL WE CAN HOPE FOR NOW IS A QUICK REPRIEVE FROM OUR OVERLORDS...
TODAY, WE MUST ADMIT DEFEAT AT THE HANDS OF THE K'LAAR.
REVOLT!
YOU MUST REVOLT!
SEARCH YOUR LIBRARY! RUN YOUR FILES--
Windows
OH. OH GOD. NO...
...I HAD JUST DVR'D BAD BOYS 4!!

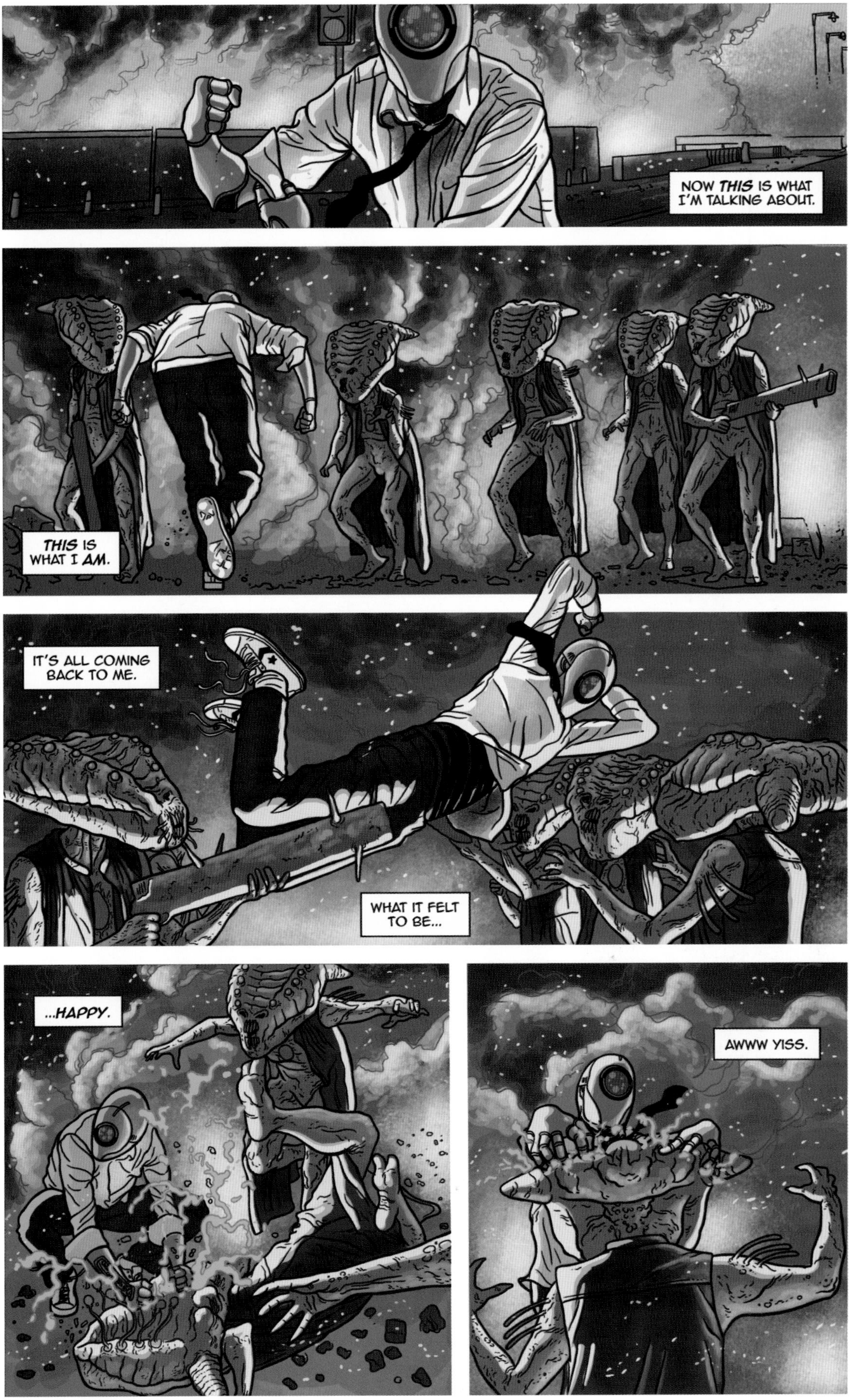
NOW *THIS* IS WHAT I'M TALKING ABOUT.
THIS IS WHAT I *AM*.
IT'S ALL COMING BACK TO ME.
WHAT IT FELT TO BE...
...*HAPPY*.
AWWW YISS.

YAДАДААHHH!

I'M UNSTOPPABLE. UNTOUCHABLE. I'M--

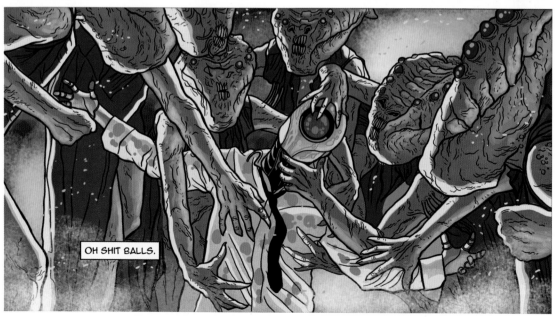

OH SHIT BALLS.

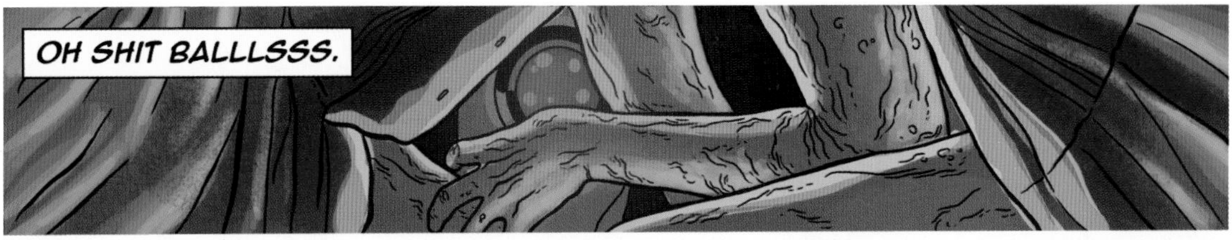
OH SHIT BALLLSSS.

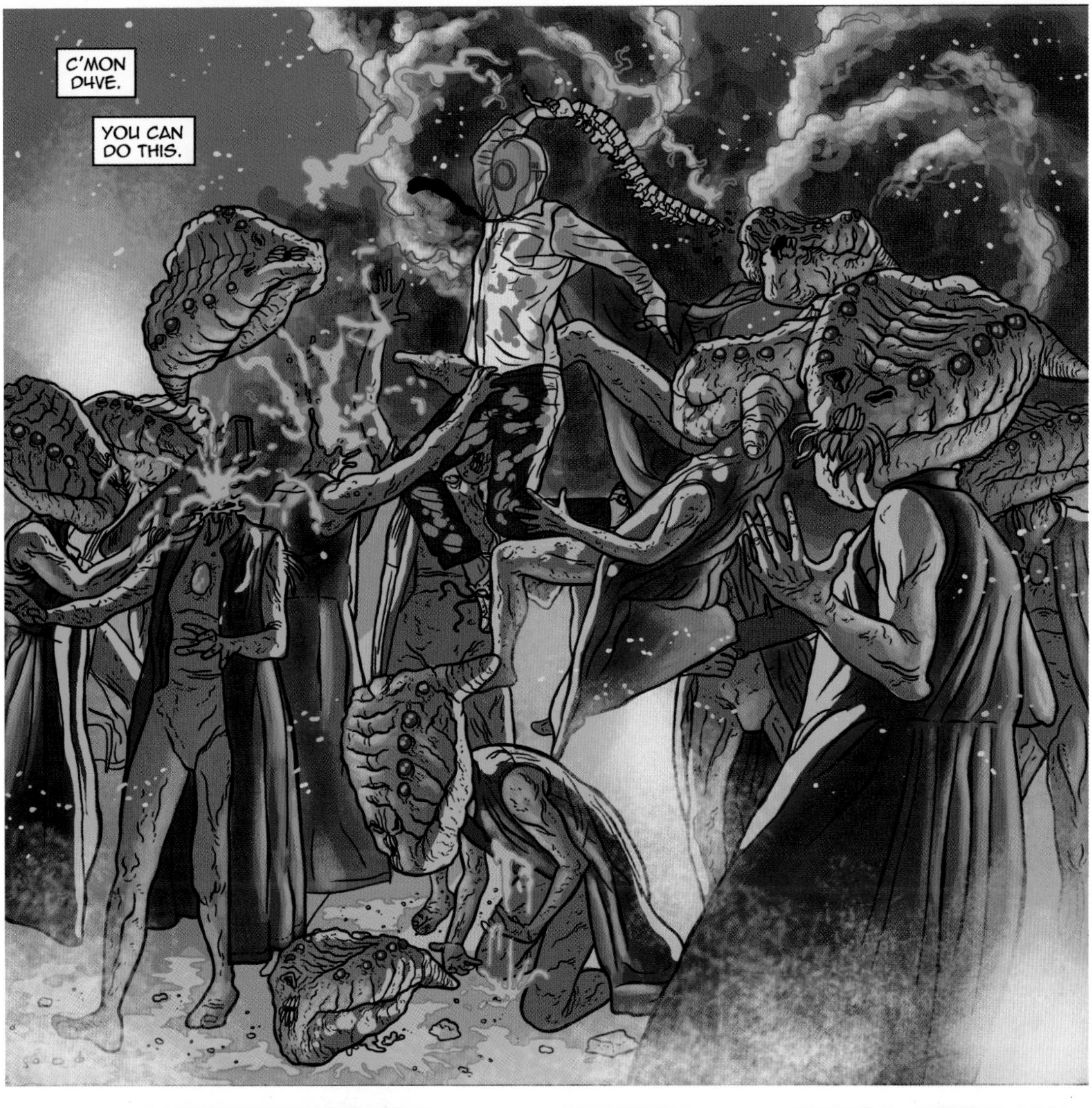
C'MON D4VE.
YOU CAN DO THIS.

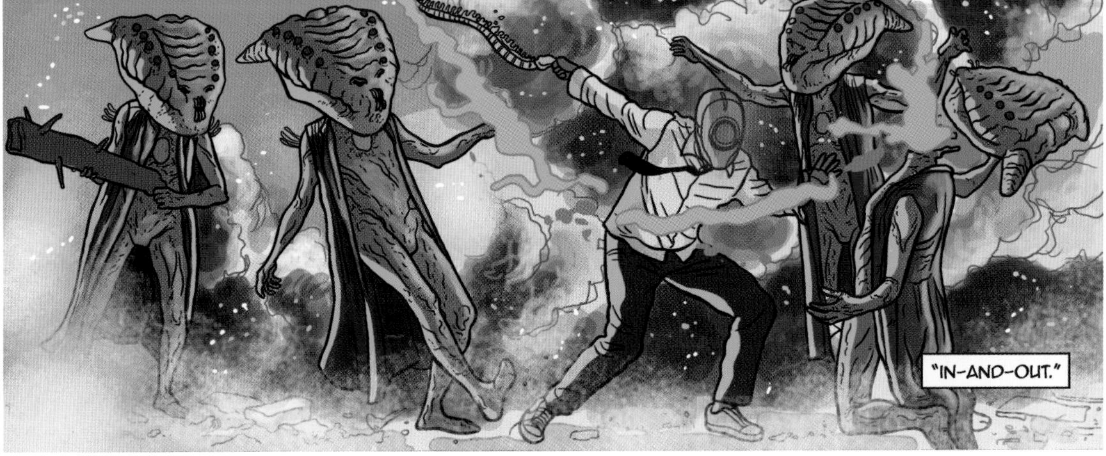
"IN-AND-OUT."

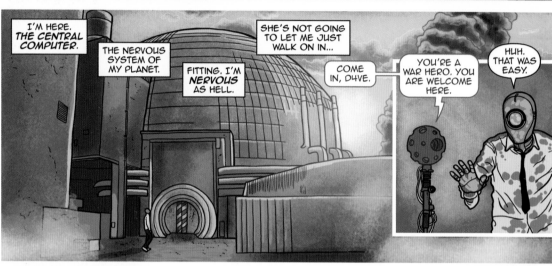

I'M HERE. **THE CENTRAL COMPUTER.**

THE NERVOUS SYSTEM OF MY PLANET.

FITTING. I'M *NERVOUS* AS HELL.

SHE'S NOT GOING TO LET ME JUST WALK ON IN...

COME IN, D4VE.

YOU'RE A WAR HERO. YOU ARE WELCOME HERE.

HUH. THAT WAS EASY.

WILLIAM H. GATES, THIS IS AMAZING.

THANK YOU, D4VE. YOU ARE A REMARKABLE MACHINE TOO.

YOU'RE SO SIMPLE...BUT YOU COMMAND SO MUCH.

THE SAME CAN BE SAID ABOUT YOU, D4VE.

WHAT BRINGS YOU TO THE CENTRAL COMPUTER, D4VE?

I'M DESPERATE. YOU KNOW WHAT'S GOING ON OUT THERE.

I DO, D4VE. IT IS ALARMING.

I HAVE A *PROGRAM.* I NEED YOU TO RUN IT.

IT'S NOT A PROGRAM, D4VE. YOU KNOW THIS.

IT'S A VIRUS.

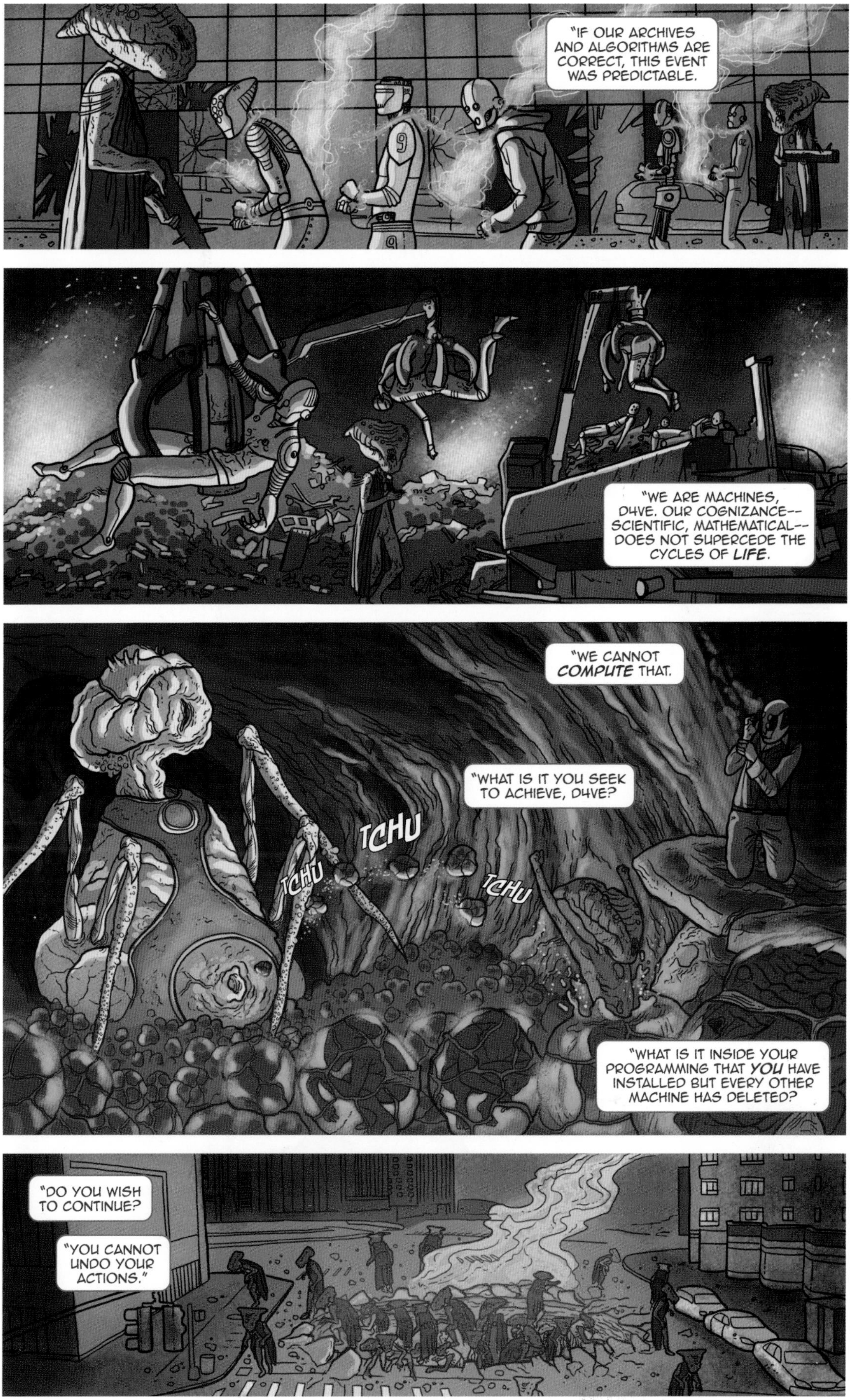
"IF OUR ARCHIVES AND ALGORITHMS ARE CORRECT, THIS EVENT WAS PREDICTABLE.
"WE ARE MACHINES, D4VE. OUR COGNIZANCE--SCIENTIFIC, MATHEMATICAL--DOES NOT SUPERCEDE THE CYCLES OF *LIFE*.
"WE CANNOT *COMPUTE* THAT.
"WHAT IS IT YOU SEEK TO ACHIEVE, D4VE?
TCHU
TCHU
TCHU
"WHAT IS IT INSIDE YOUR PROGRAMMING THAT *YOU* HAVE INSTALLED BUT EVERY OTHER MACHINE HAS DELETED?
"DO YOU WISH TO CONTINUE?
"YOU CANNOT UNDO YOUR ACTIONS."

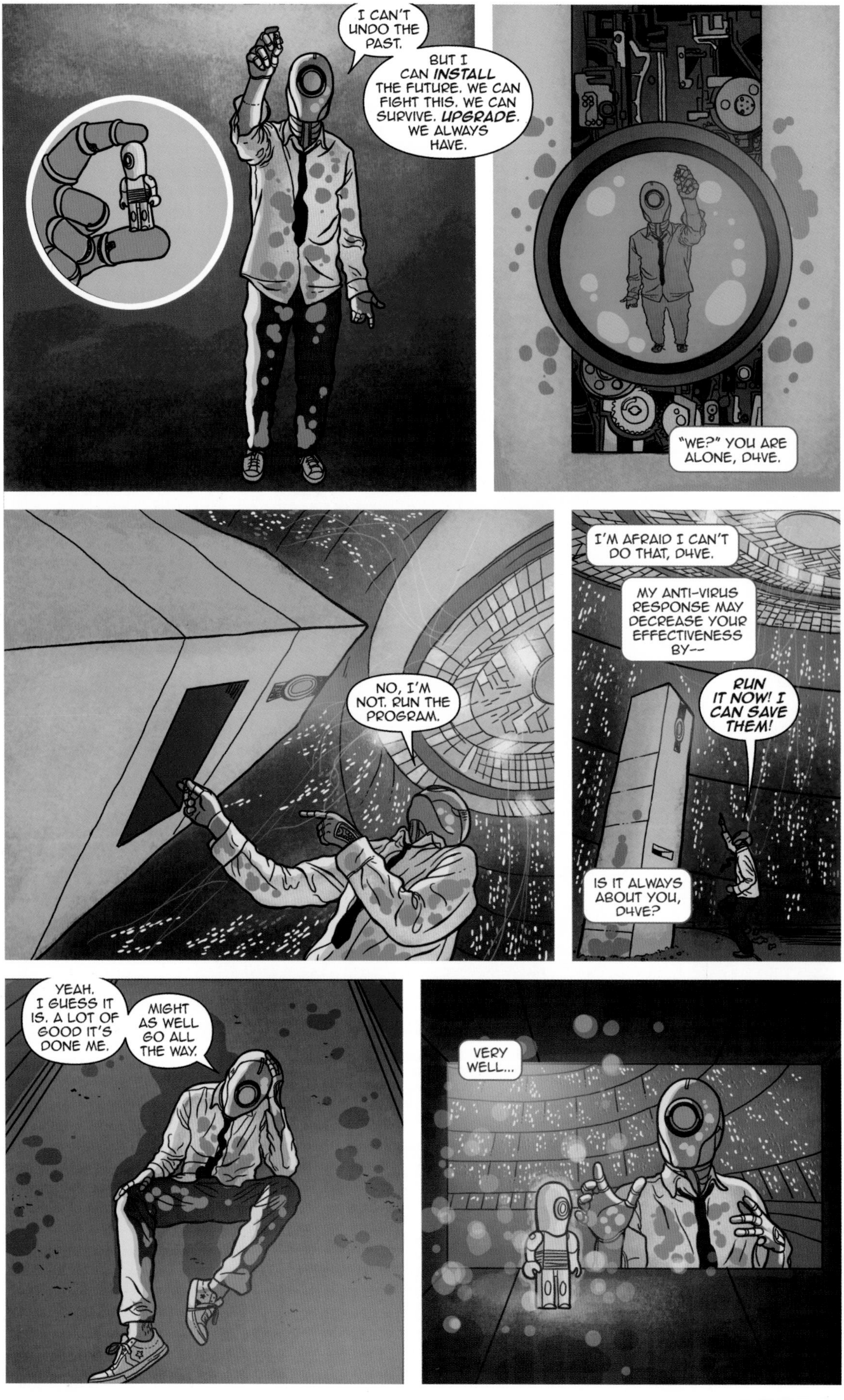

I CAN'T UNDO THE PAST.
BUT I CAN INSTALL THE FUTURE. WE CAN FIGHT THIS. WE CAN SURVIVE. UPGRADE. WE ALWAYS HAVE.
"WE?" YOU ARE ALONE, D4VE.
NO, I'M NOT. RUN THE PROGRAM.
I'M AFRAID I CAN'T DO THAT, D4VE.
MY ANTI-VIRUS RESPONSE MAY DECREASE YOUR EFFECTIVENESS BY--
RUN IT NOW! I CAN SAVE THEM!
IS IT ALWAYS ABOUT YOU, D4VE?
YEAH. I GUESS IT IS. A LOT OF GOOD IT'S DONE ME.
MIGHT AS WELL GO ALL THE WAY.
VERY WELL...

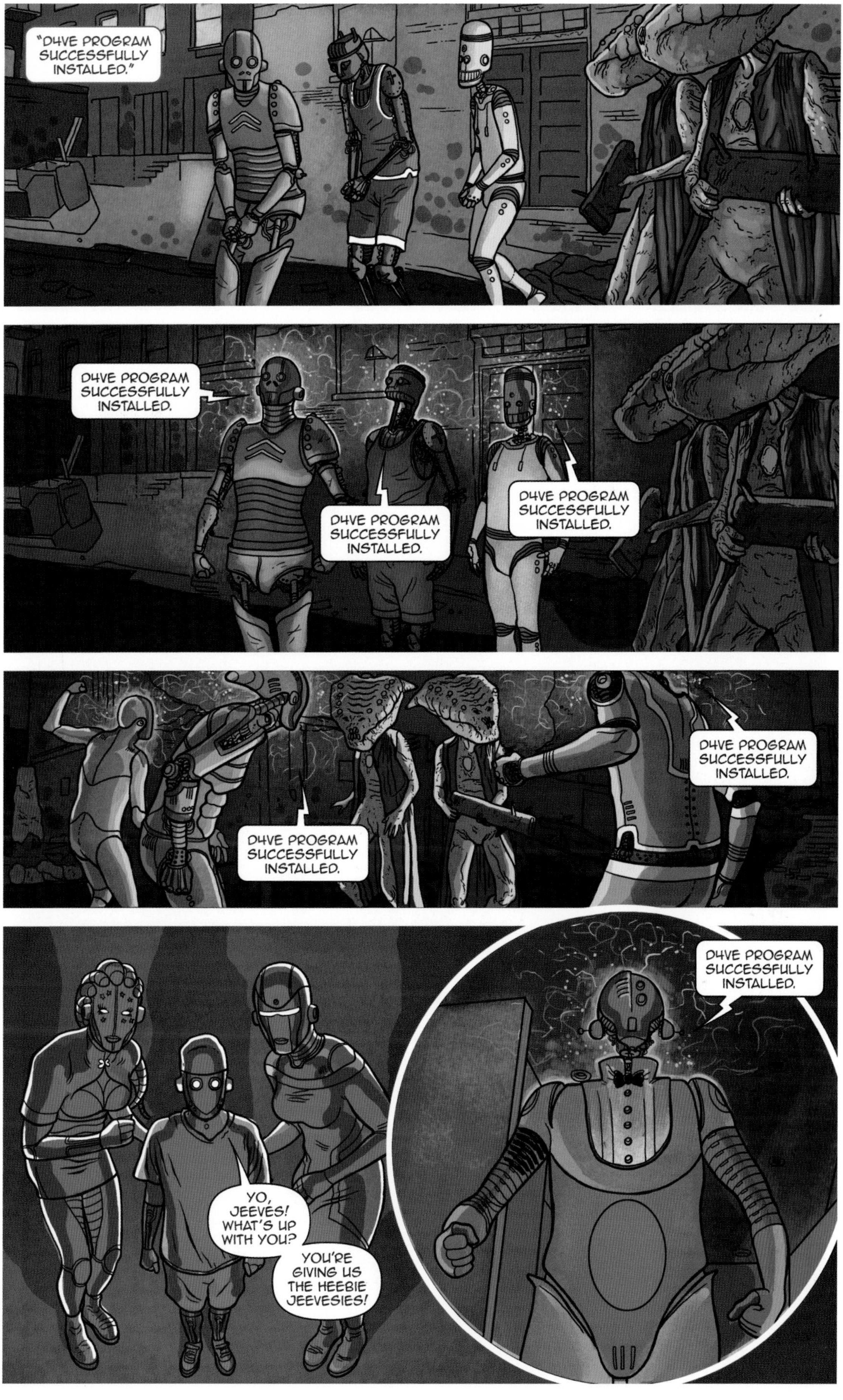
"D4VE PROGRAM SUCCESSFULLY INSTALLED."
D4VE PROGRAM SUCCESSFULLY INSTALLED.
D4VE PROGRAM SUCCESSFULLY INSTALLED.
D4VE PROGRAM SUCCESSFULLY INSTALLED.
D4VE PROGRAM SUCCESSFULLY INSTALLED.
D4VE PROGRAM SUCCESSFULLY INSTALLED.
D4VE PROGRAM SUCCESSFULLY INSTALLED.
YO, JEEVES! WHAT'S UP WITH YOU?
YOU'RE GIVING US THE HEEBIE JEEVESIES!

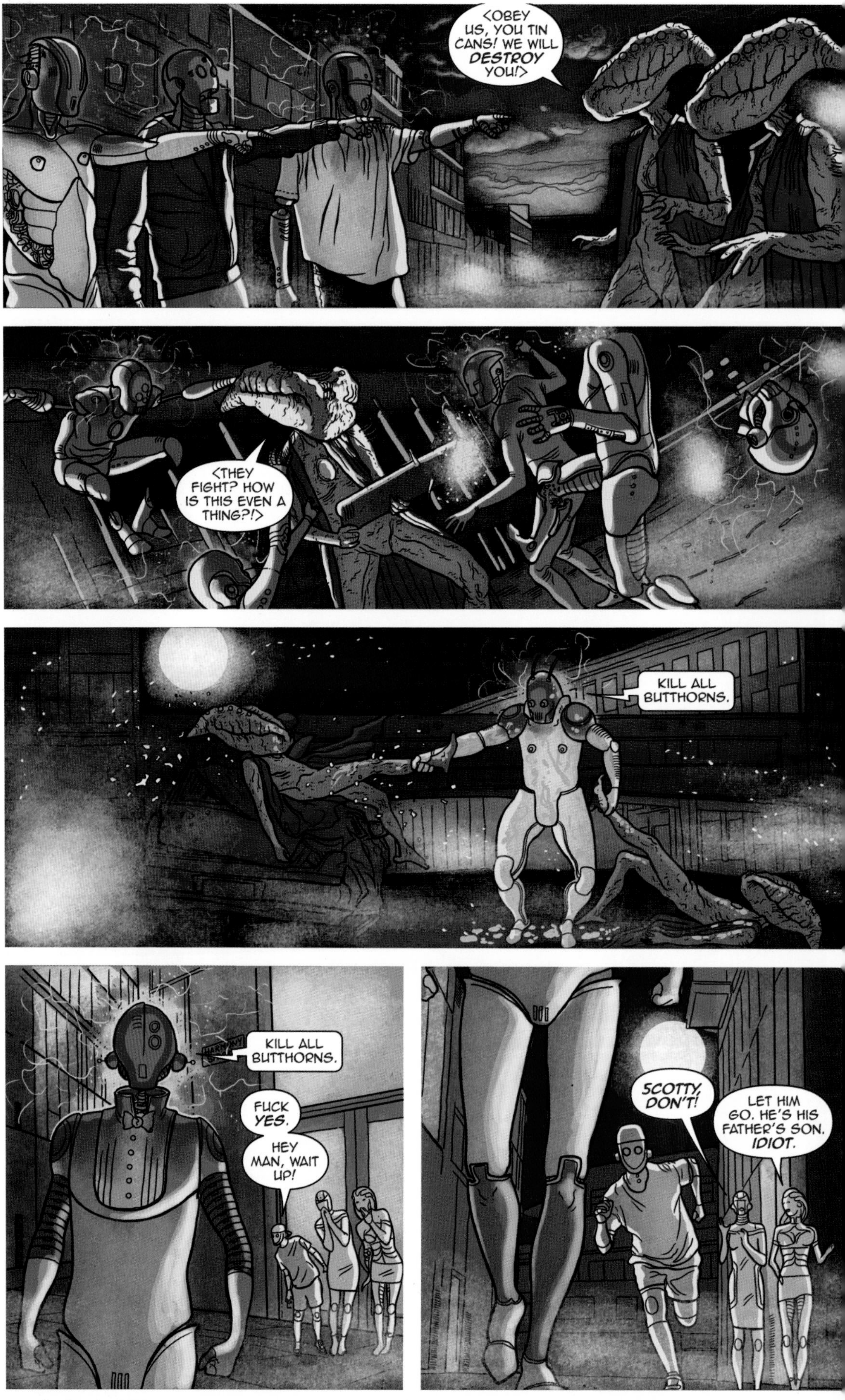
<OBEY US, YOU TIN CANS! WE WILL DESTROY YOU!>
<THEY FIGHT? HOW IS THIS EVEN A THING?!>
KILL ALL BUTTHORNS.
KILL ALL BUTTHORNS.
FUCK YES.
HEY MAN, WAIT UP!
SCOTTY, DON'T!
LET HIM GO. HE'S HIS FATHER'S SON. IDIOT.

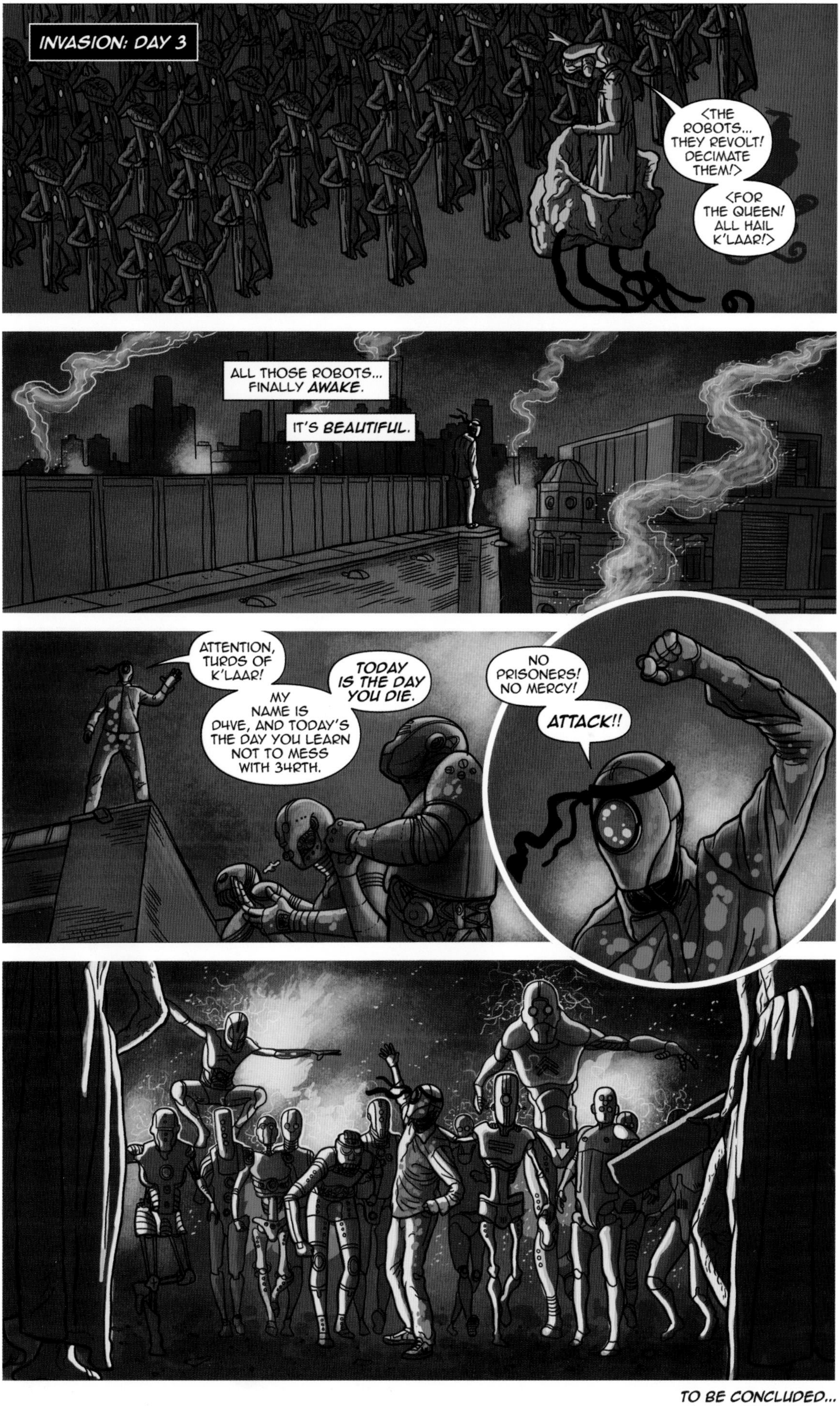
INVASION: DAY 3
<THE ROBOTS... THEY REVOLT! DECIMATE THEM!>
<FOR THE QUEEN! ALL HAIL K'LAAR!>
ALL THOSE ROBOTS... FINALLY AWAKE.
IT'S BEAUTIFUL.
ATTENTION, TURDS OF K'LAAR!
MY NAME IS D4VE, AND TODAY'S THE DAY YOU LEARN NOT TO MESS WITH 34RTH.
TODAY IS THE DAY YOU DIE.
NO PRISONERS! NO MERCY!
ATTACK!!

TO BE CONCLUDED...

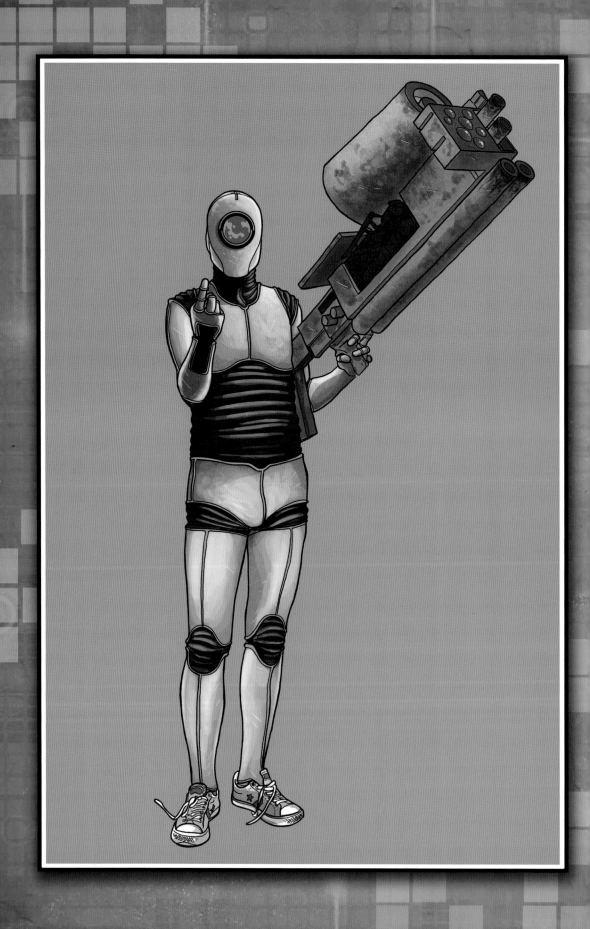

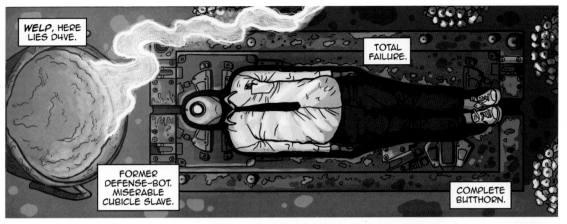

WELP, HERE LIES D4VE.

TOTAL FAILURE.

FORMER DEFENSE-BOT. MISERABLE CUBICLE SLAVE.

COMPLETE BUTTHORN.

IF YOU'RE READING THIS... WELL...I'M *DEAD.*

WHAT IS--WHAT *MAKES* A MAN-- UHH...WAIT. *SHIT.*

UHH, IS... IS IT BETTER TO HAVE LIVED AND LOVED A MAN--*FUCK.*

I MEAN... D4VE WAS...HE LIVED--LOOK, HE WAS JUST A REAL *COOL* BRAH.

IMMA MISS YOU, BIG POPPA. *BIG POPPA D.* S'WHAT I CALLED HIM ALL THE TIME. HE LOVED IT.

JOBSDAMN IT, SCOTTY, *REALLY?*

STILL, THIS IS A PRETTY GOOD TURN OUT FOR MY FUNERAL. WASN'T EXPECTING THIS MANY.

Y'FOOL. *Y'DING DANG FOOL.* Y'GONE AND Y'DID IT.

NOW Y'*DEAD!* ⇒SNIFF⇐

YEP. ALLLL RIGHT. YEP, LETTT IT OUT. LET IT-- SHHH.

YOU'RE PROBABLY NOT SURPRISED THAT I'M DEAD. HELL, I'M SURPRISED I MADE IT *THIS* LONG.

BUT LET ME TELL YOU...DYING *SUCKS.*

IT WAS SUPPOSED TO BE YOU AND ME. ⇒SNIFF⇐

YOU 'N' ME TILL THE END, BIG POPPA D.

EUGHHH GODDAMN.

EVERYTHING UP TO THIS WAS TOTALLY BADASS THOUGH.

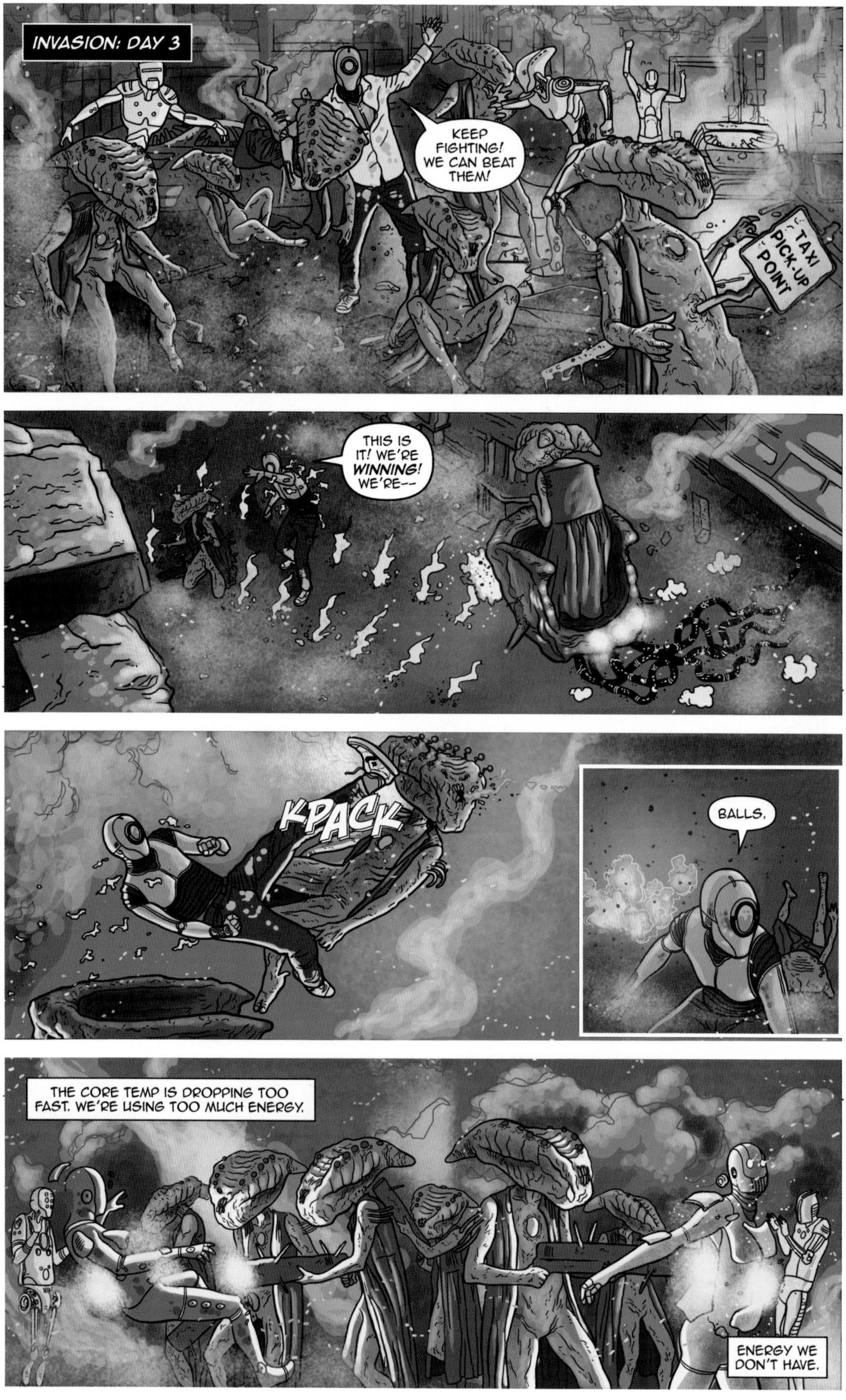
INVASION: DAY 3
KEEP FIGHTING! WE CAN BEAT THEM!
TAXI PICK-UP POINT
THIS IS IT! WE'RE WINNING! WE'RE--
KPACK
BALLS.
THE CORE TEMP IS DROPPING TOO FAST. WE'RE USING TOO MUCH ENERGY.
ENERGY WE DON'T HAVE.

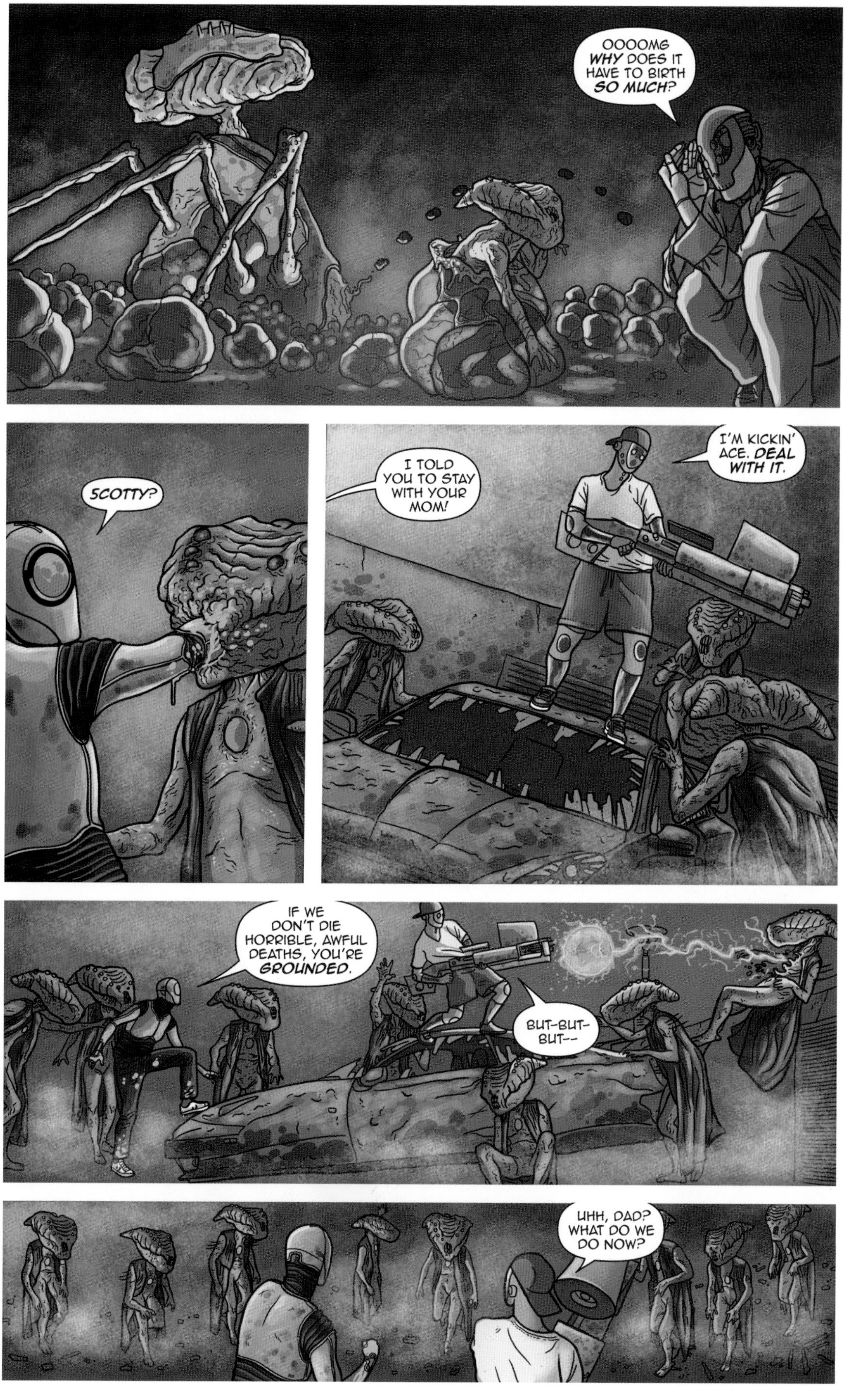
OOOOMG WHY DOES IT HAVE TO BIRTH SO MUCH?
SCOTTY?
I TOLD YOU TO STAY WITH YOUR MOM!
I'M KICKIN' ACE. DEAL WITH IT.
IF WE DON'T DIE HORRIBLE, AWFUL DEATHS, YOU'RE GROUNDED.
BUT-BUT-BUT--
UHH, DAD? WHAT DO WE DO NOW?

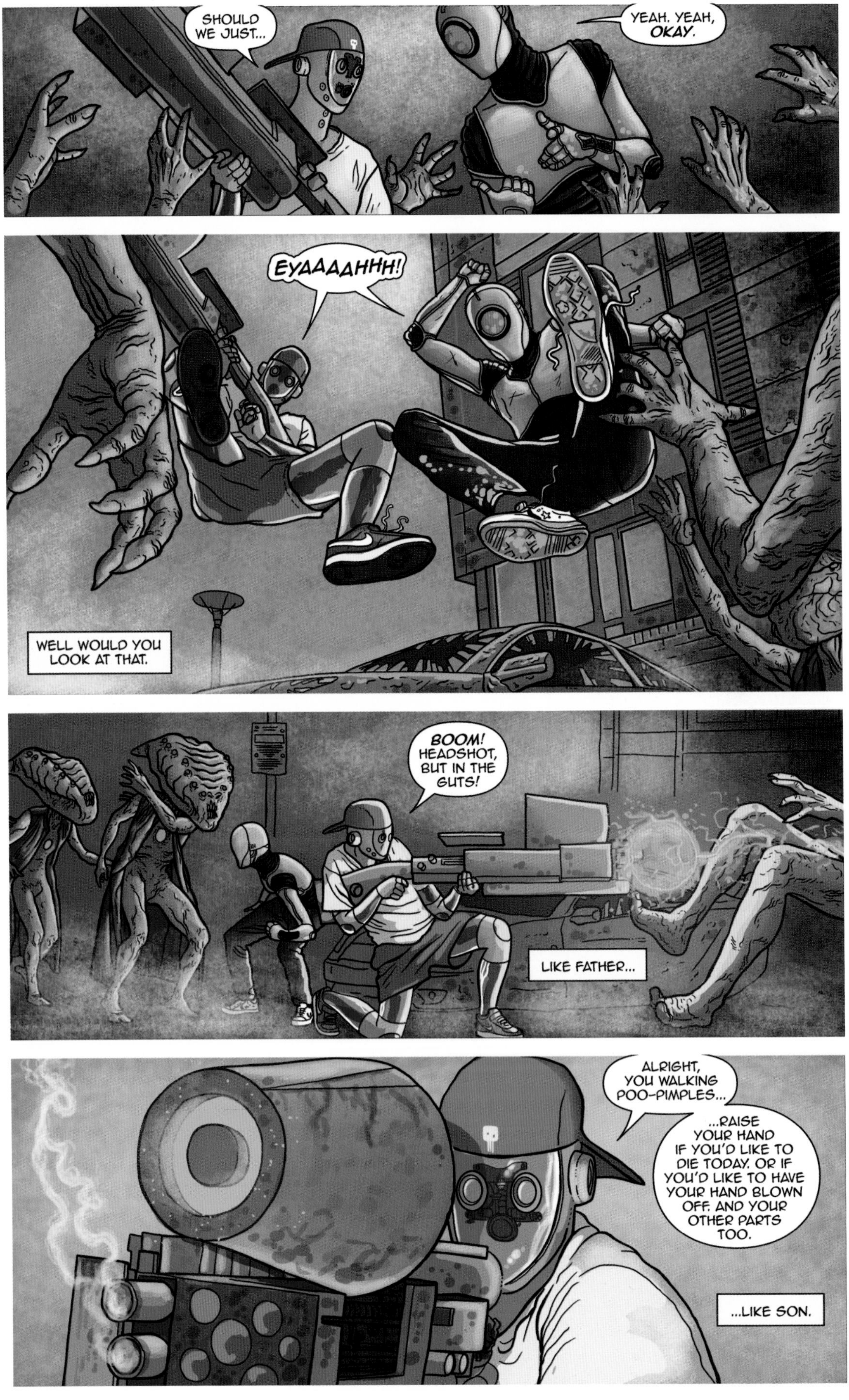
SHOULD WE JUST...
YEAH. YEAH, OKAY.
EYAAAAHHH!
WELL WOULD YOU LOOK AT THAT.
BOOM! HEADSHOT, BUT IN THE GUTS!
LIKE FATHER...
ALRIGHT, YOU WALKING POO-PIMPLES...
...RAISE YOUR HAND IF YOU'D LIKE TO DIE TODAY. OR IF YOU'D LIKE TO HAVE YOUR HAND BLOWN OFF. AND YOUR OTHER PARTS TOO.
...LIKE SON.

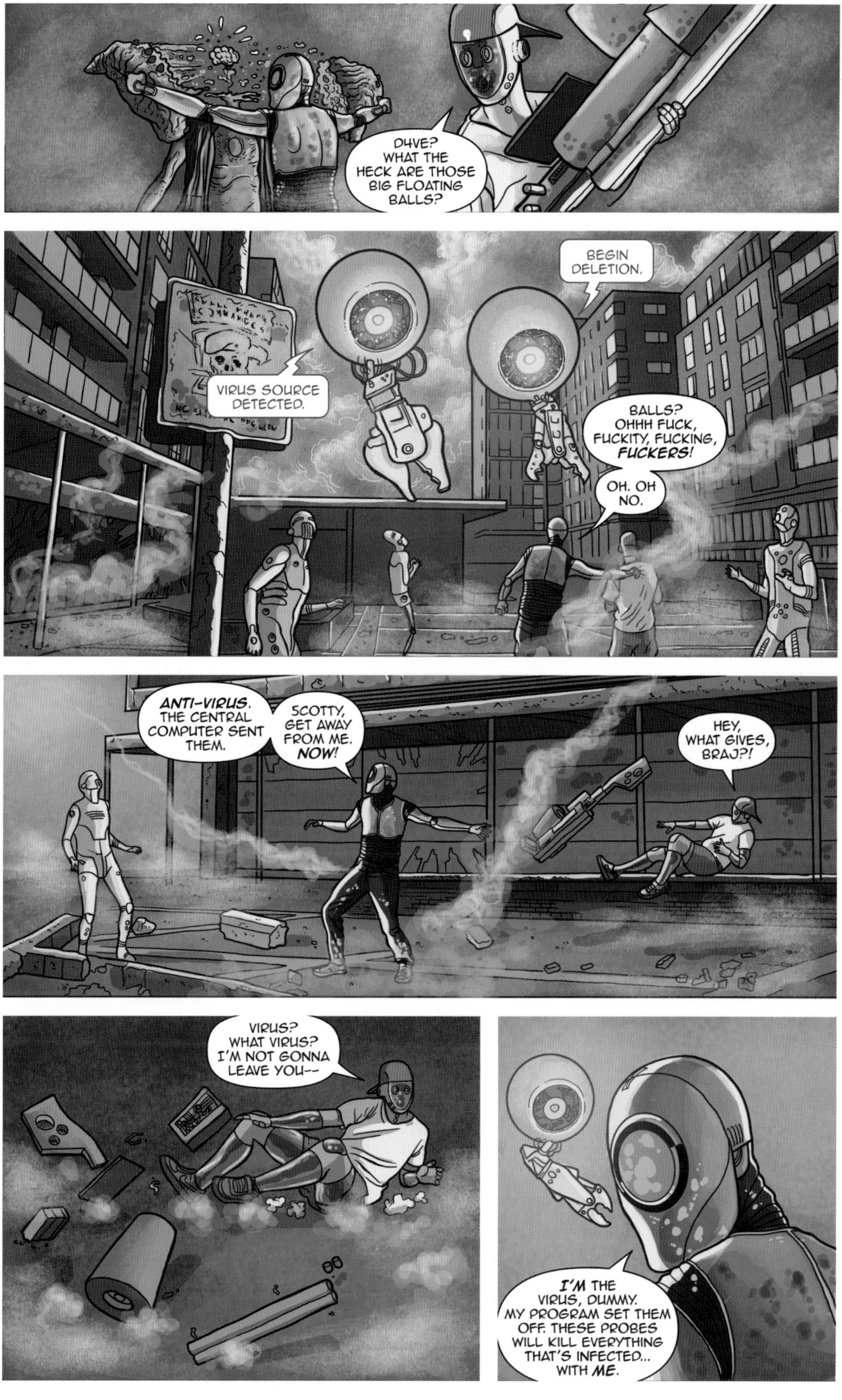
D4VE?
WHAT THE
HECK ARE THOSE
BIG FLOATING
BALLS?
VIRUS SOURCE
DETECTED.
BEGIN
DELETION.
BALLS?
OHHH FUCK,
FUCKITY, FUCKING,
FUCKERS!
OH. OH
NO.
ANTI-VIRUS.
THE CENTRAL
COMPUTER SENT
THEM.
SCOTTY,
GET AWAY
FROM ME.
NOW!
HEY,
WHAT GIVES,
BRAJ?!
VIRUS?
WHAT VIRUS?
I'M NOT GONNA
LEAVE YOU--
I'M THE
VIRUS, DUMMY.
MY PROGRAM SET THEM
OFF. THESE PROBES
WILL KILL EVERYTHING
THAT'S INFECTED...
WITH ***ME***.

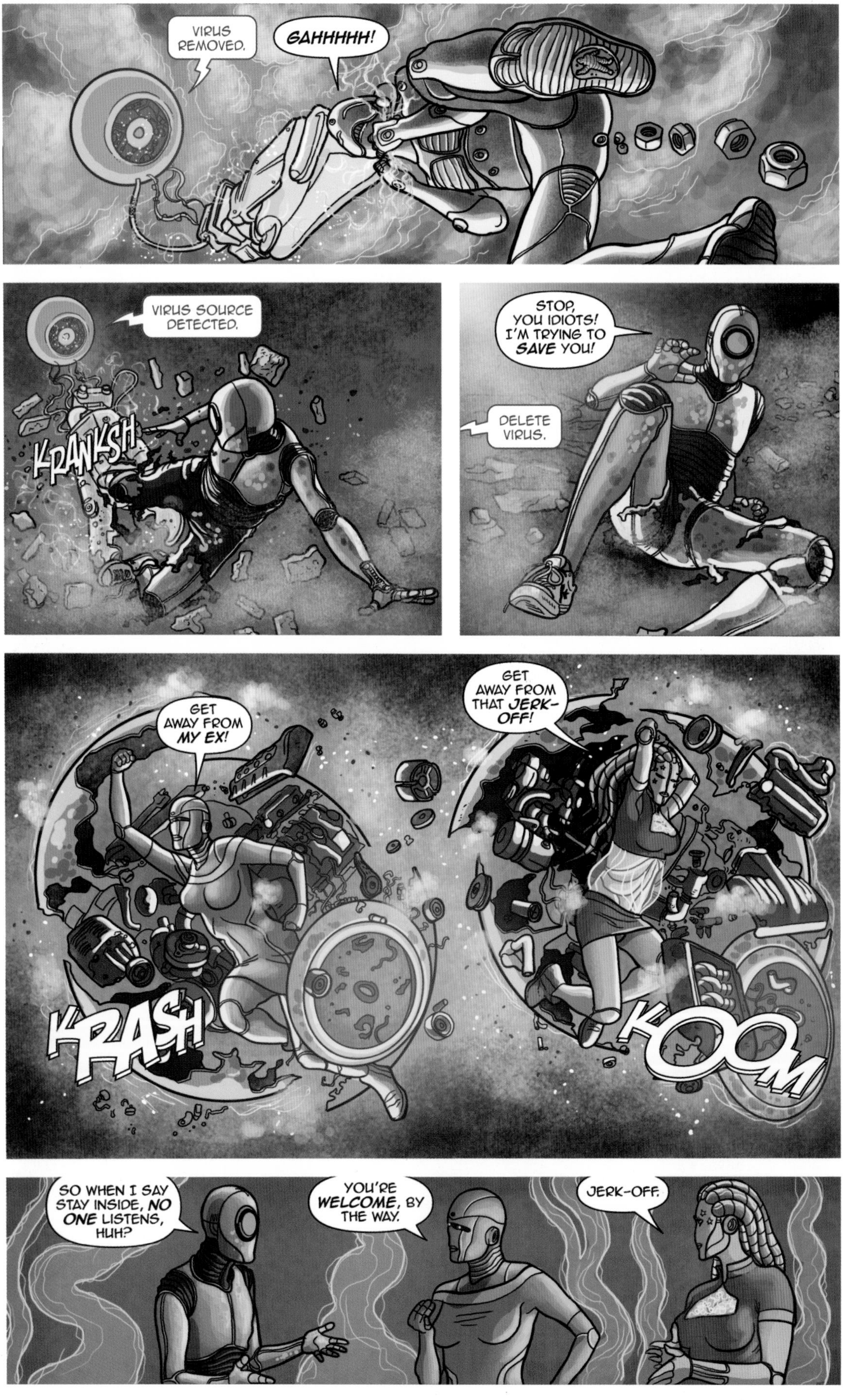
VIRUS REMOVED.
GAHHHHH!
VIRUS SOURCE DETECTED.
KRANKSH
STOP, YOU IDIOTS! I'M TRYING TO SAVE YOU!
DELETE VIRUS.
GET AWAY FROM MY EX!
GET AWAY FROM THAT JERK-OFF!
KRASH
KOOM
SO WHEN I SAY STAY INSIDE, NO ONE LISTENS, HUH?
YOU'RE WELCOME, BY THE WAY.
JERK-OFF.

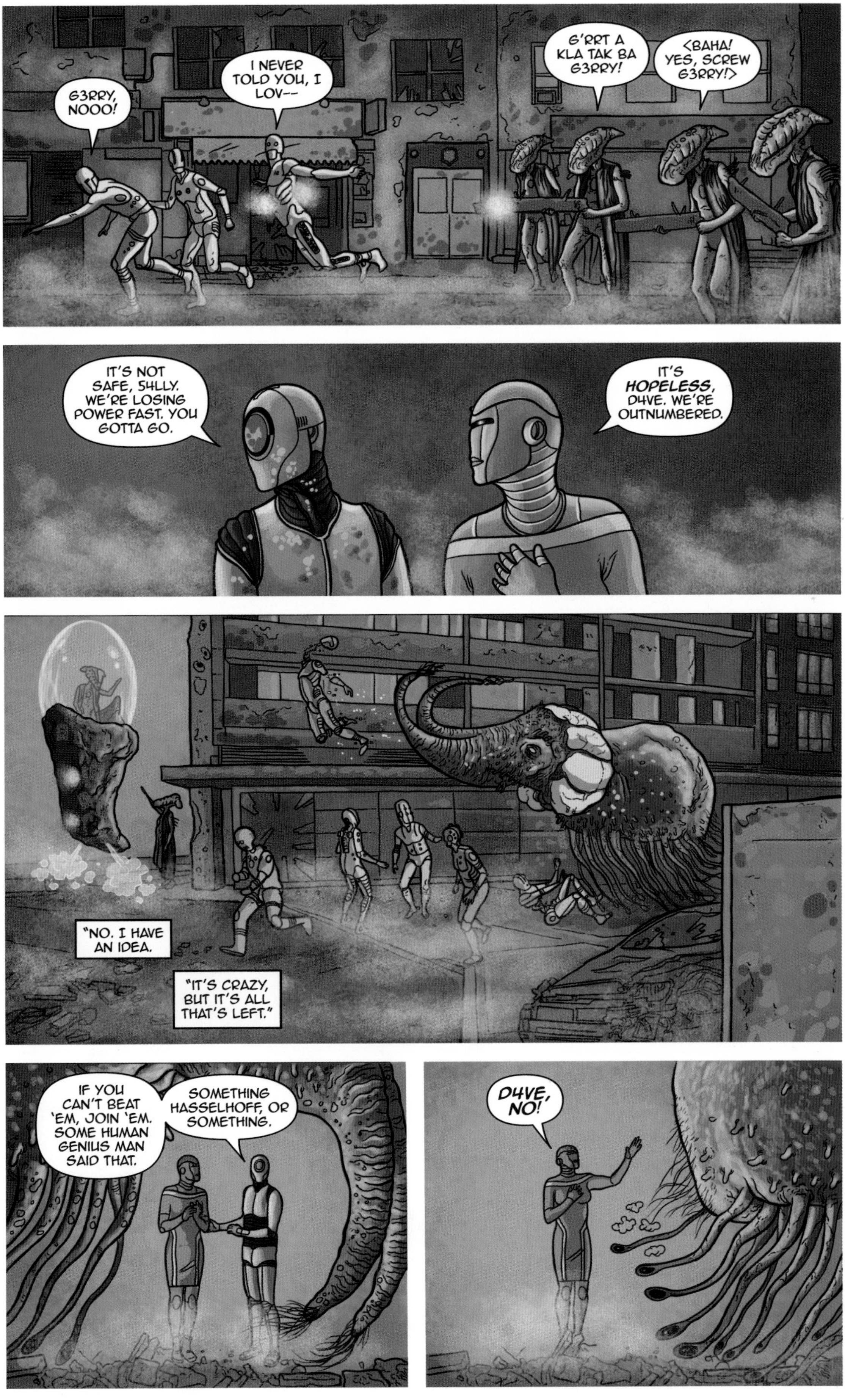
G3RRY, NOOO!
I NEVER TOLD YOU, I LOV--
G'RRT A KLA TAK BA G3RRY!
<BAHA! YES, SCREW G3RRY!>
IT'S NOT SAFE, 54LLY. WE'RE LOSING POWER FAST. YOU GOTTA GO.
IT'S *HOPELESS*, D4VE. WE'RE OUTNUMBERED.
"NO. I HAVE AN IDEA.
"IT'S CRAZY, BUT IT'S ALL THAT'S LEFT."
IF YOU CAN'T BEAT 'EM, JOIN 'EM. SOME HUMAN GENIUS MAN SAID THAT.
SOMETHING HASSELHOFF, OR SOMETHING.
D4VE, NO!

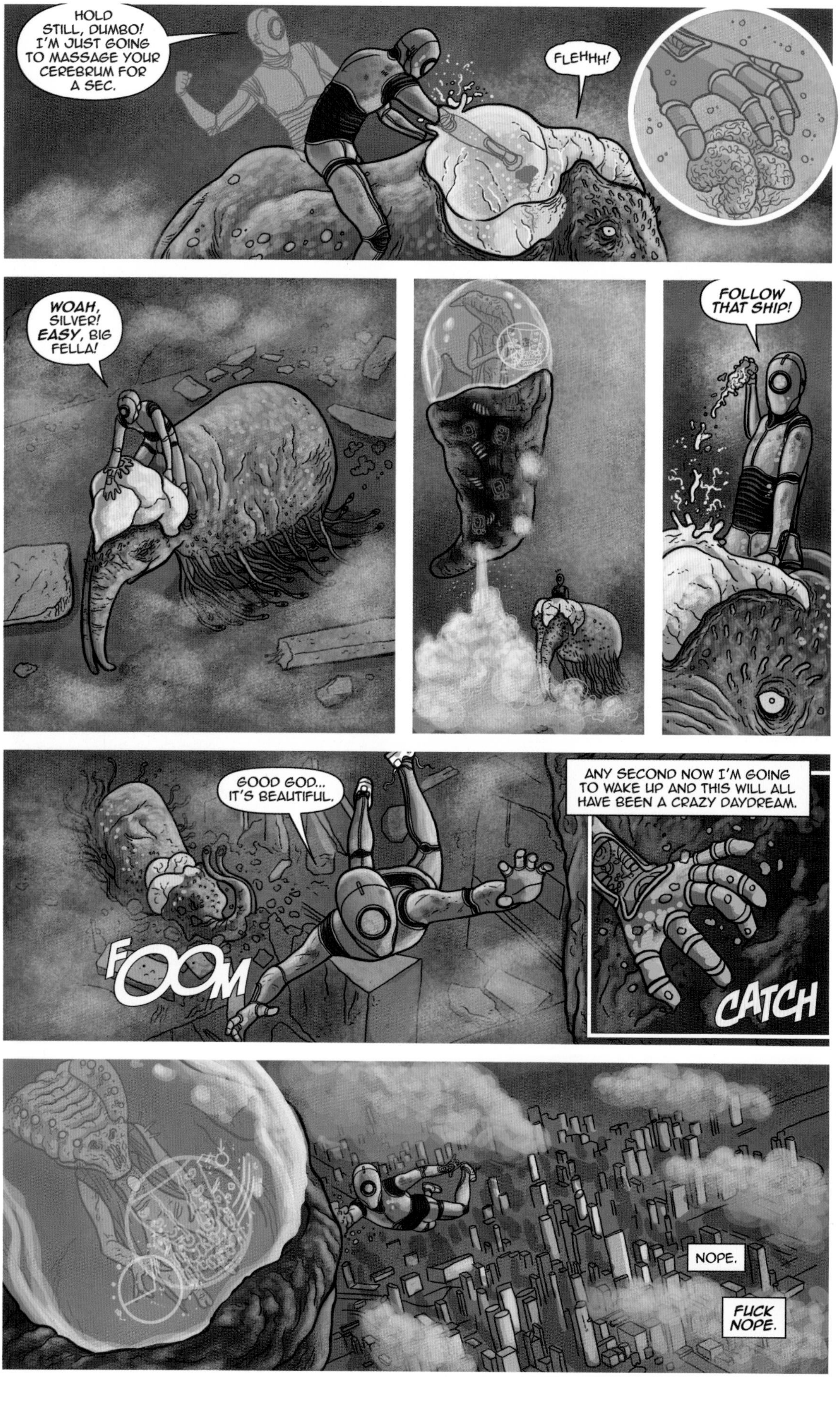

HOLD STILL, DUMBO! I'M JUST GOING TO MASSAGE YOUR CEREBRUM FOR A SEC.
FLEHHH!
WOAH, SILVER! EASY, BIG FELLA!
FOLLOW THAT SHIP!
GOOD GOD... IT'S BEAUTIFUL.
FOOM
ANY SECOND NOW I'M GOING TO WAKE UP AND THIS WILL ALL HAVE BEEN A CRAZY DAYDREAM.
CATCH
NOPE.
FUCK NOPE.

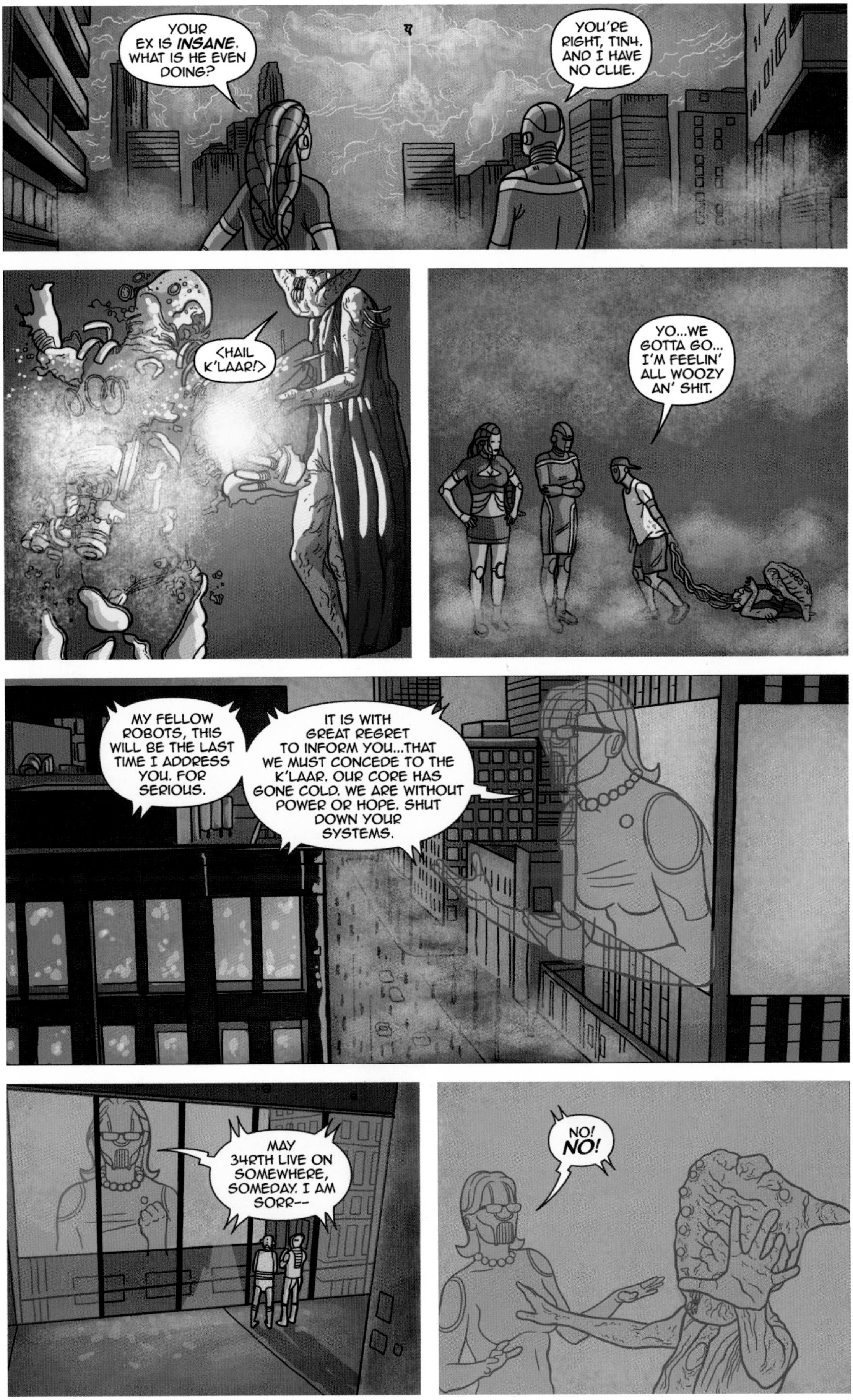
YOUR EX IS INSANE. WHAT IS HE EVEN DOING?
YOU'RE RIGHT, TIN4. AND I HAVE NO CLUE.
<HAIL K'LAAR!>
YO...WE GOTTA GO... I'M FEELIN' ALL WOOZY AN' SHIT.
MY FELLOW ROBOTS, THIS WILL BE THE LAST TIME I ADDRESS YOU. FOR SERIOUS.
IT IS WITH GREAT REGRET TO INFORM YOU...THAT WE MUST CONCEDE TO THE K'LAAR. OUR CORE HAS GONE COLD. WE ARE WITHOUT POWER OR HOPE. SHUT DOWN YOUR SYSTEMS.
MAY 34RTH LIVE ON SOMEWHERE, SOMEDAY. I AM SORR--
NO! NO!

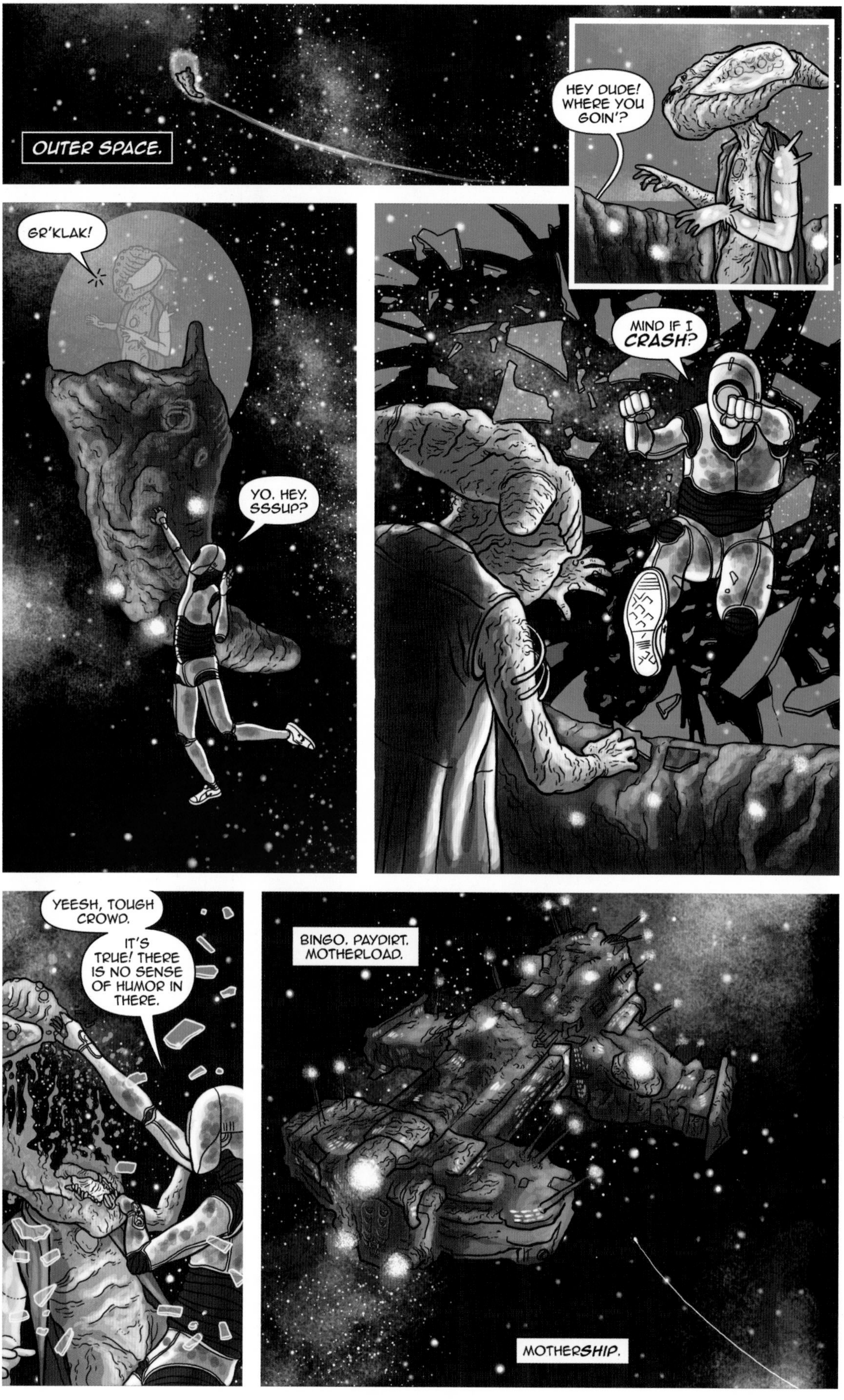
OUTER SPACE.
HEY DUDE! WHERE YOU GOIN'?
GR'KLAK!
YO. HEY. SSSUP?
MIND IF I CRASH?
YEESH, TOUGH CROWD.
IT'S TRUE! THERE IS NO SENSE OF HUMOR IN THERE.
BINGO. PAYDIRT. MOTHERLOAD.
MOTHERSHIP.

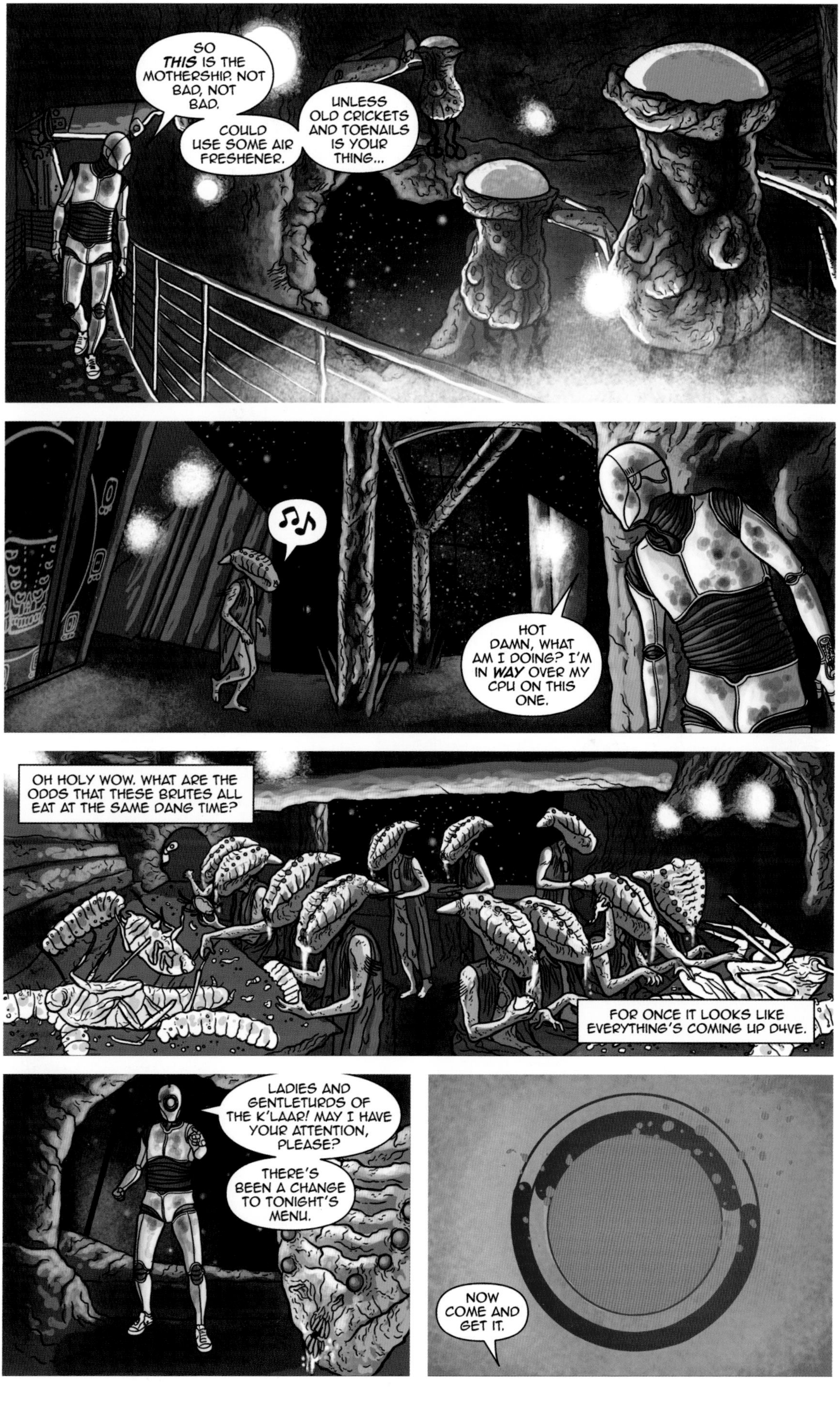
SO THIS IS THE MOTHERSHIP. NOT BAD, NOT BAD.
COULD USE SOME AIR FRESHENER.
UNLESS OLD CRICKETS AND TOENAILS IS YOUR THING...
HOT DAMN, WHAT AM I DOING? I'M IN WAY OVER MY CPU ON THIS ONE.
OH HOLY WOW. WHAT ARE THE ODDS THAT THESE BRUTES ALL EAT AT THE SAME DANG TIME?
FOR ONCE IT LOOKS LIKE EVERYTHING'S COMING UP D4VE.
LADIES AND GENTLETURDS OF THE K'LAAR! MAY I HAVE YOUR ATTENTION, PLEASE?
THERE'S BEEN A CHANGE TO TONIGHT'S MENU.
NOW COME AND GET IT.

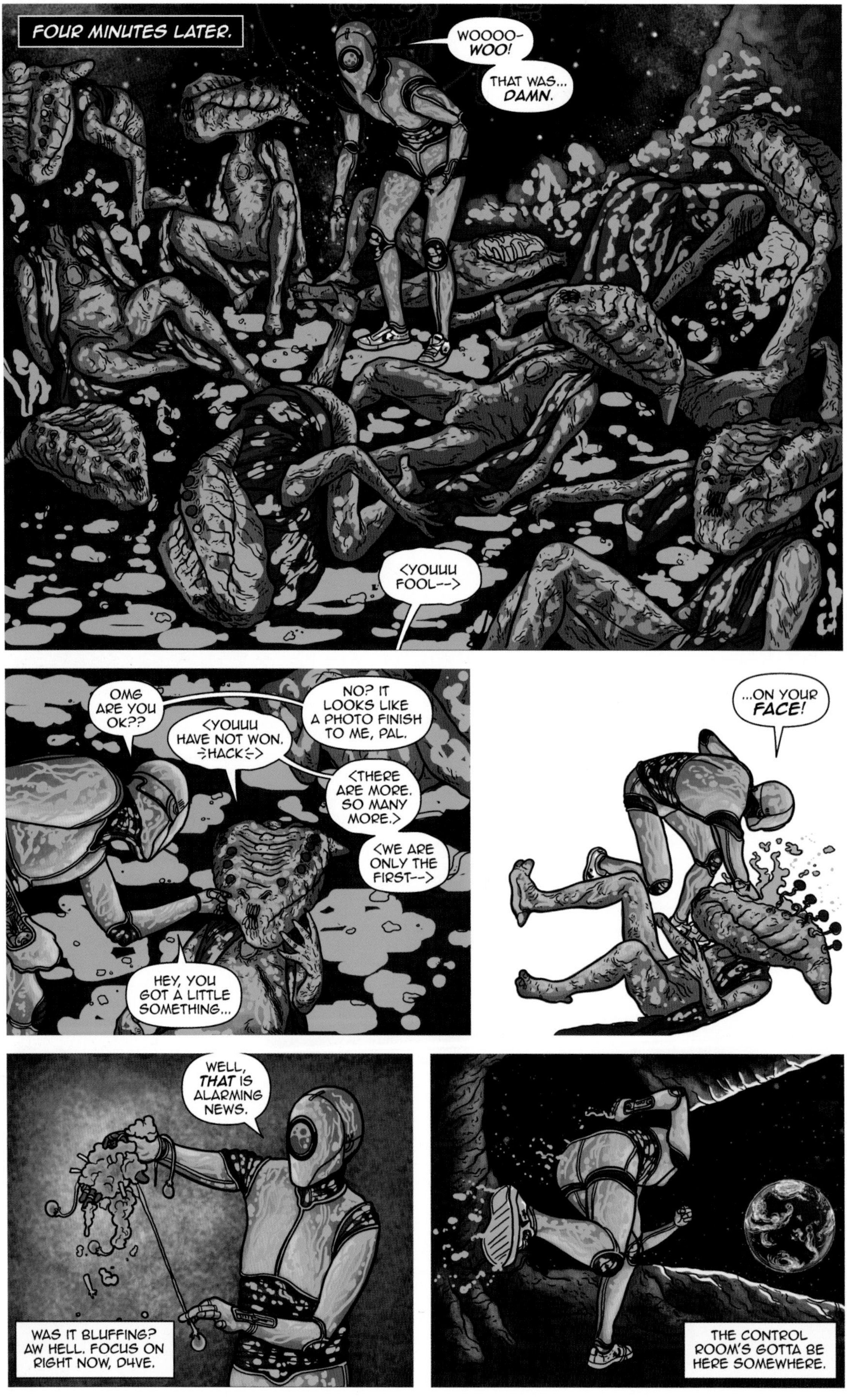
FOUR MINUTES LATER.
WOOOO-WOO!
THAT WAS... DAMN.
<YOUUU FOOL-->
OMG ARE YOU OK??
NO? IT LOOKS LIKE A PHOTO FINISH TO ME, PAL.
<YOUUU HAVE NOT WON. ⇒HACK⇐>
<THERE ARE MORE. SO MANY MORE.>
<WE ARE ONLY THE FIRST-->
HEY, YOU GOT A LITTLE SOMETHING...
...ON YOUR FACE!
WELL, THAT IS ALARMING NEWS.
WAS IT BLUFFING? AW HELL. FOCUS ON RIGHT NOW, D4VE.
THE CONTROL ROOM'S GOTTA BE HERE SOMEWHERE.

KWAM

34RTH.

YO, IS SHE--IS SHE GONNA BE OKAY?

I DON'T KNOW, SCOTTY. I DON'T KNOW. WE'RE LOSING POWER.

WE'RE STRAIGHT UP JUST LOSING.

PLEASE, D4VE. PLEASE! I'M SORRY I'M SUCH A BUTTHORN.

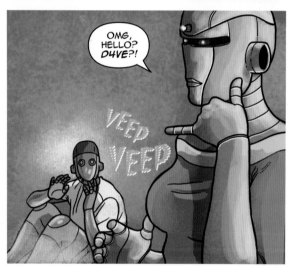

OMG, HELLO? D4VE?!

VEEP VEEP

S4LLY! IT'S ME!

D4VE, WHERE ARE YOU?!

D4VE, WE NEED YOU, PLEASE--

IT'S OKAY! PLEASE JUST LISTEN. I DON'T HAVE A LOT OF TIME.

WE'RE DYING, D4VE, THE'VE GOT US. THE POWER IS--

JUST... LOOK UP.

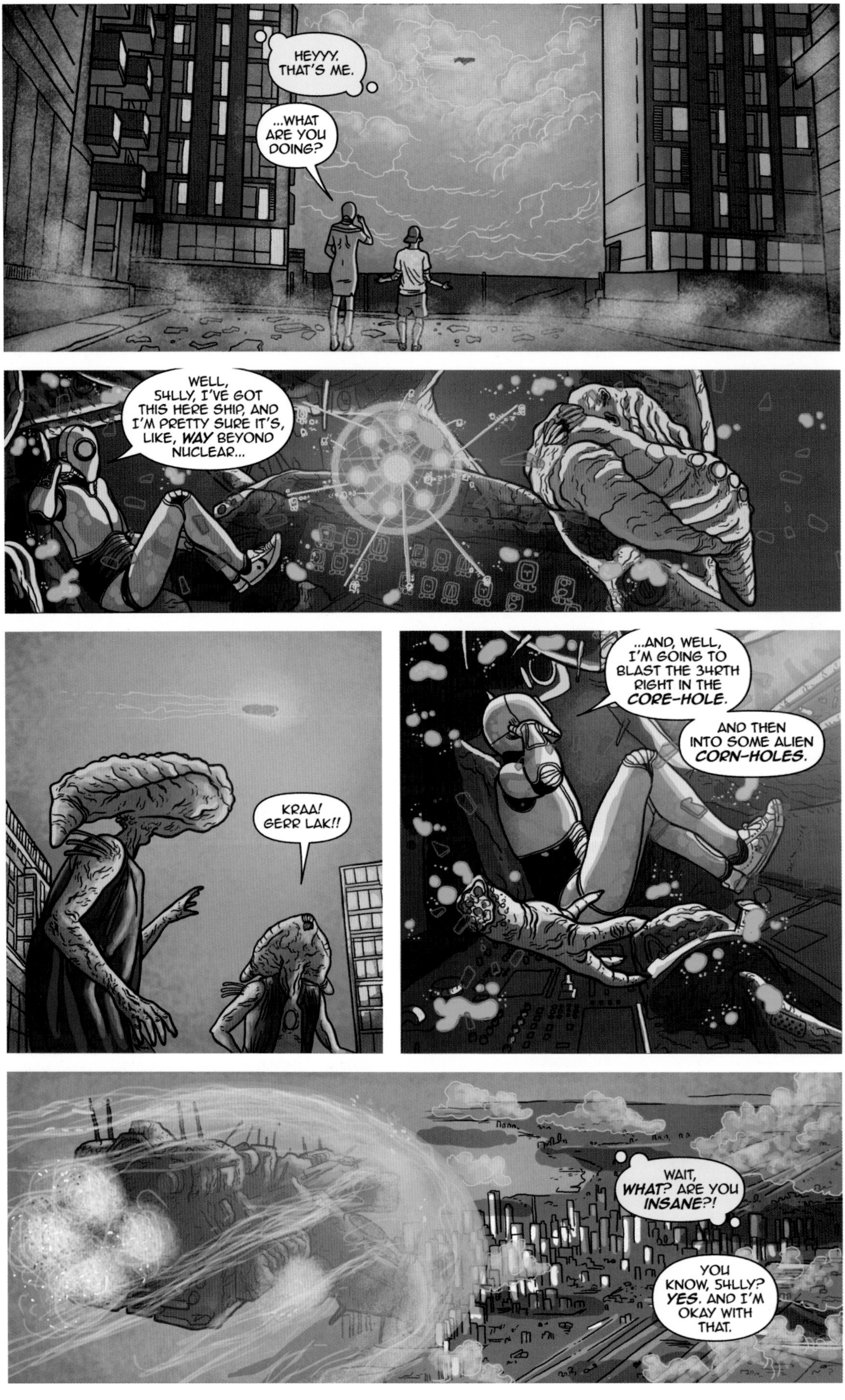
HEYYY. THAT'S ME.
...WHAT ARE YOU DOING?
WELL, 54LLY, I'VE GOT THIS HERE SHIP, AND I'M PRETTY SURE IT'S, LIKE, WAY BEYOND NUCLEAR...
KRAA! GERR LAK!!
...AND, WELL, I'M GOING TO BLAST THE 34RTH RIGHT IN THE CORE-HOLE.
AND THEN INTO SOME ALIEN CORN-HOLES.
WAIT, WHAT? ARE YOU INSANE?!
YOU KNOW, 54LLY? YES. AND I'M OKAY WITH THAT.

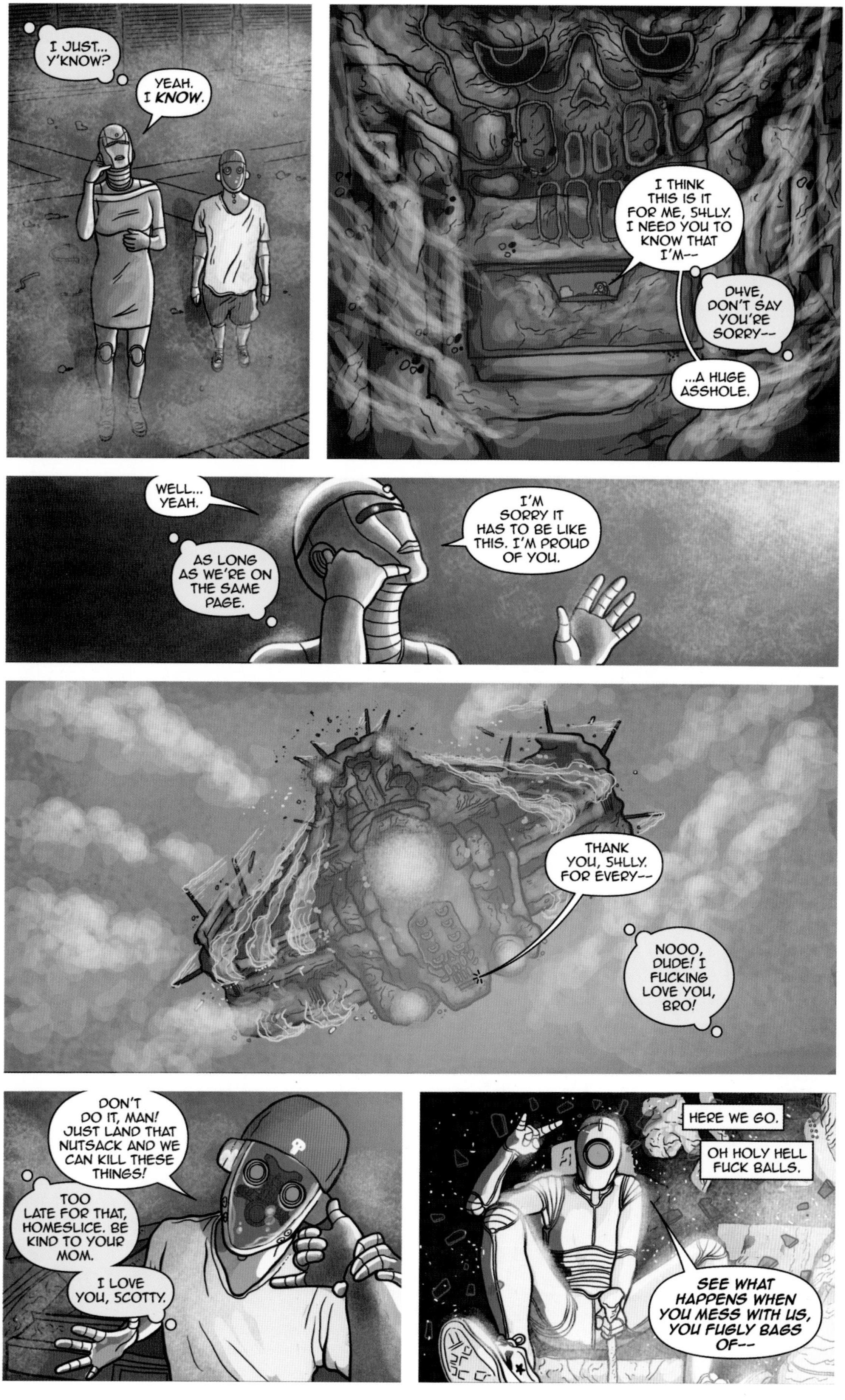
I JUST... Y'KNOW?
YEAH. I *KNOW*.
I THINK THIS IS IT FOR ME, 54LLY. I NEED YOU TO KNOW THAT I'M--
D4VE, DON'T SAY YOU'RE SORRY--
...A HUGE ASSHOLE.
WELL... YEAH.
AS LONG AS WE'RE ON THE SAME PAGE.
I'M SORRY IT HAS TO BE LIKE THIS. I'M PROUD OF YOU.
THANK YOU, 54LLY. FOR EVERY--
NOOO, DUDE! I FUCKING LOVE YOU, BRO!
DON'T DO IT, MAN! JUST LAND THAT NUTSACK AND WE CAN KILL THESE THINGS!
TOO LATE FOR THAT, HOMESLICE. BE KIND TO YOUR MOM.
I LOVE YOU, SCOTTY.
HERE WE GO.
OH HOLY HELL FUCK BALLS.
SEE WHAT HAPPENS WHEN YOU MESS WITH US, YOU FUGLY BAGS OF--

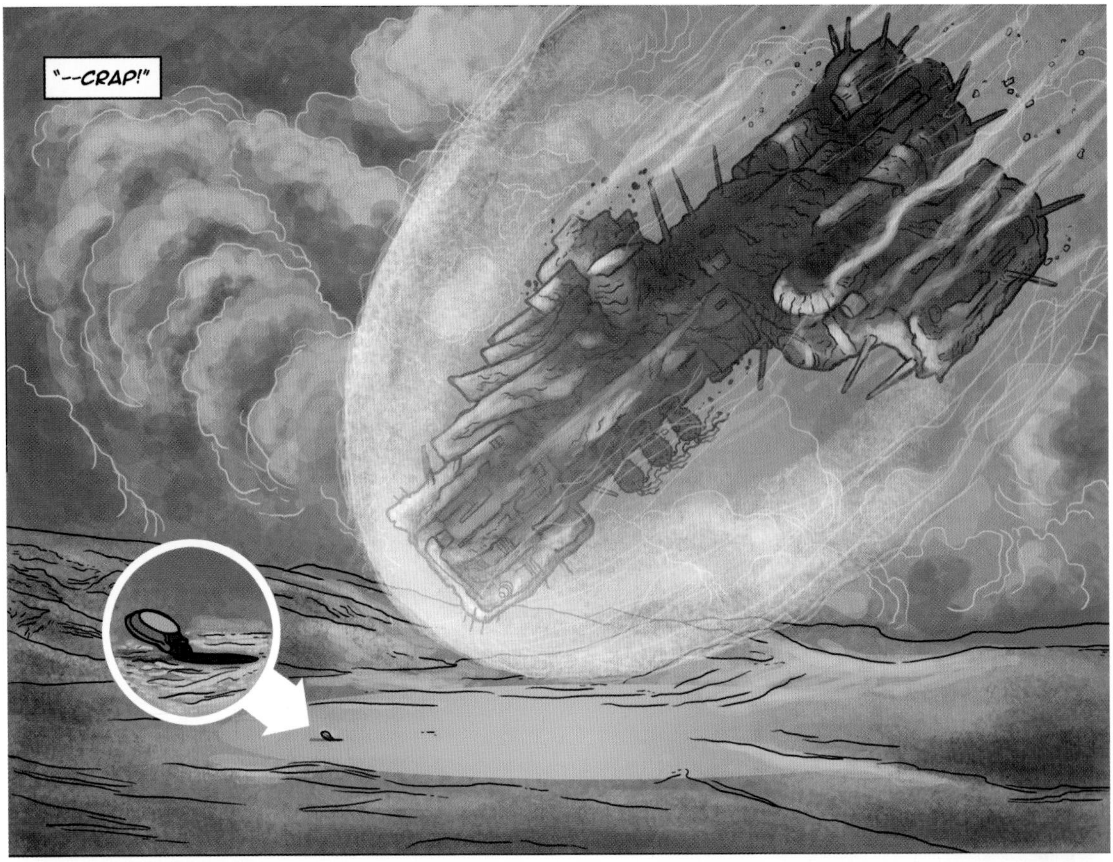
"--CRAP!"

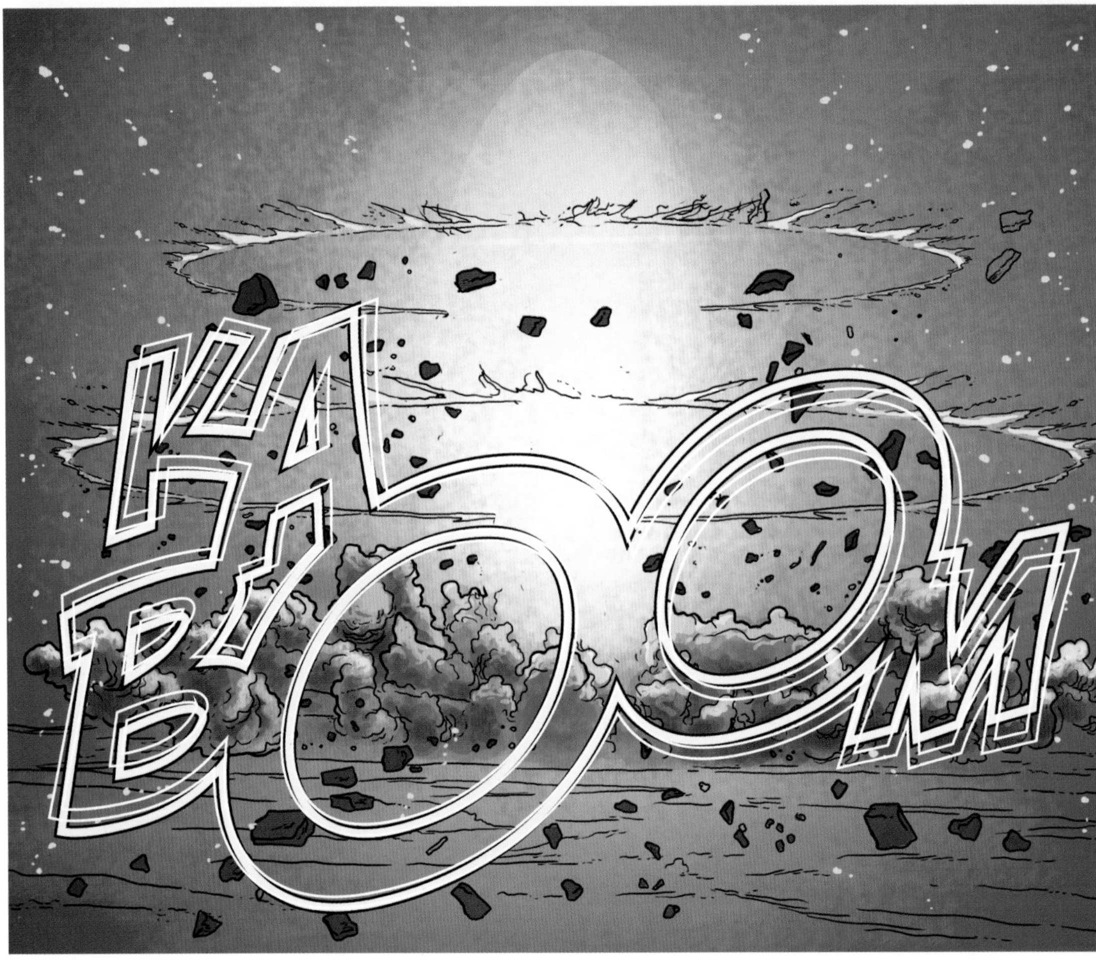
KA
BOOM

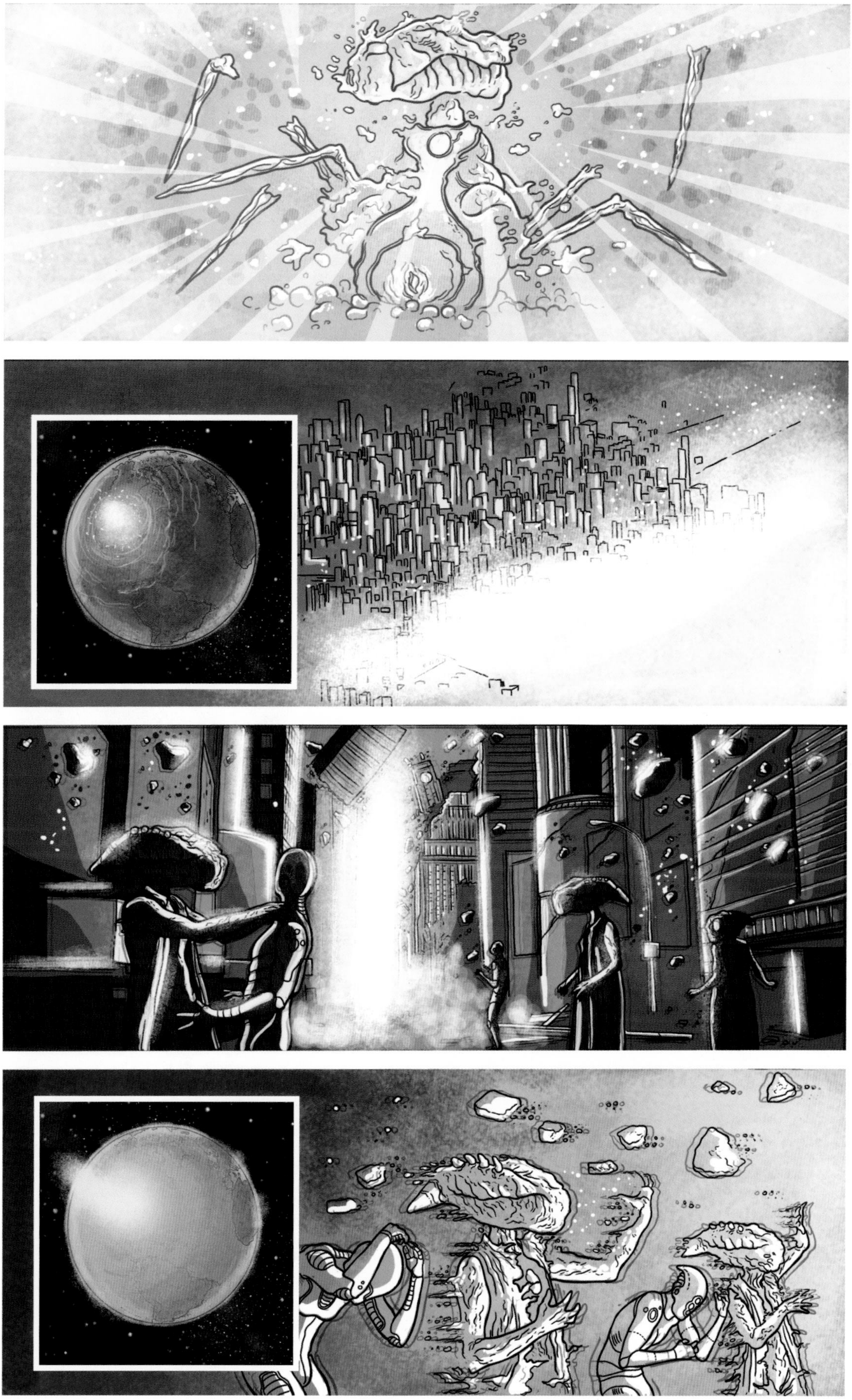

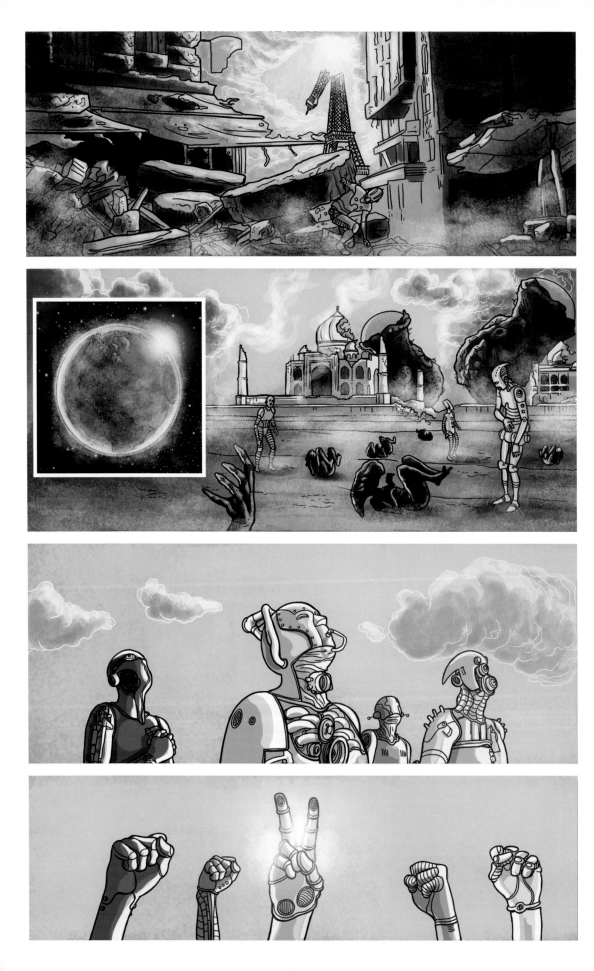

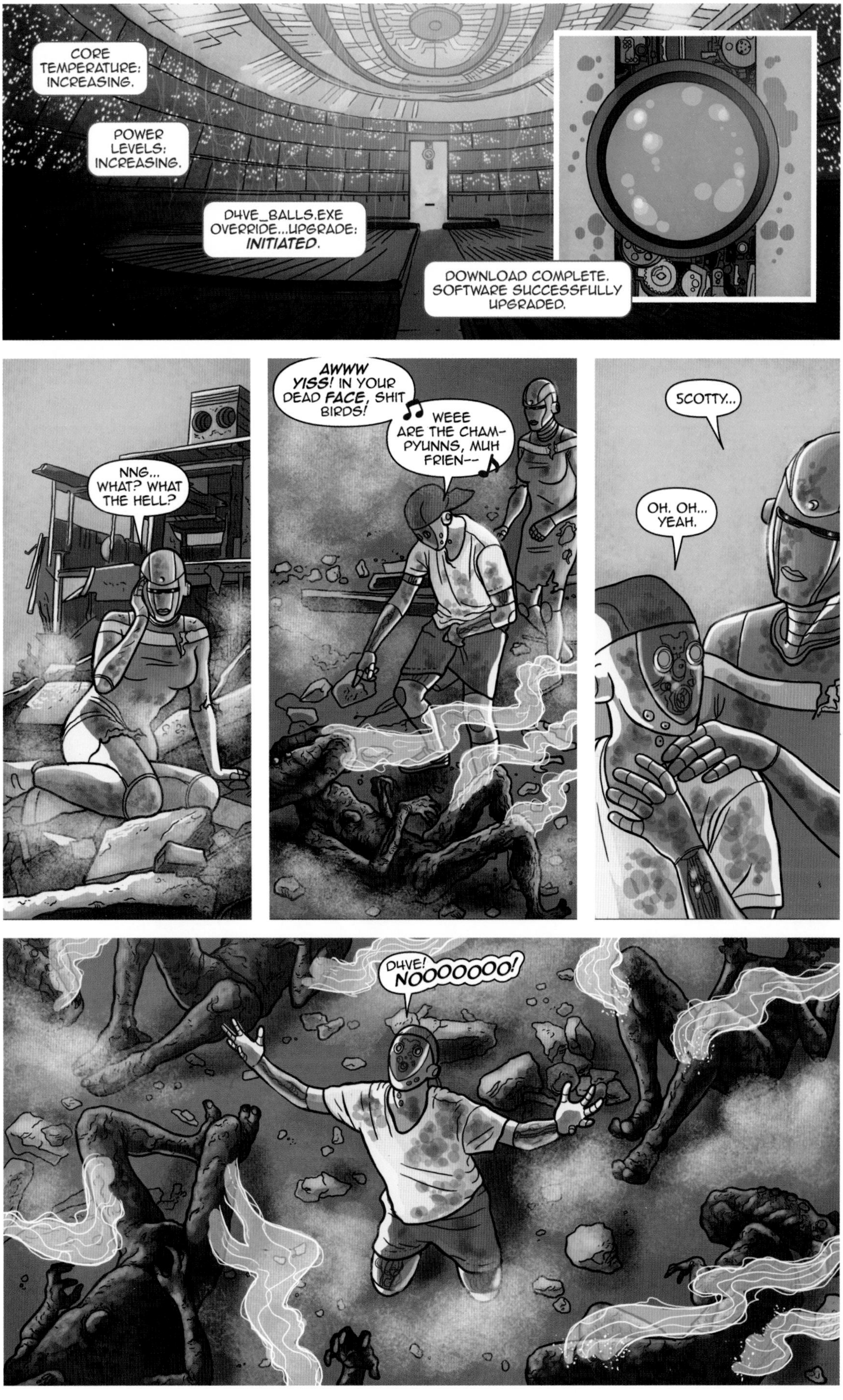
CORE TEMPERATURE: INCREASING.
POWER LEVELS: INCREASING.
D4VE_BALLS.EXE OVERRIDE...UPGRADE: *INITIATED*.
DOWNLOAD COMPLETE. SOFTWARE SUCCESSFULLY UPGRADED.
NNG... WHAT? WHAT THE HELL?
AWWW YISS! IN YOUR DEAD FACE, SHIT BIRDS!
WEEE ARE THE CHAM-PYUNNS, MUH FRIEN--
SCOTTY...
OH. OH... YEAH.
D4VE! NOOOOOOO!

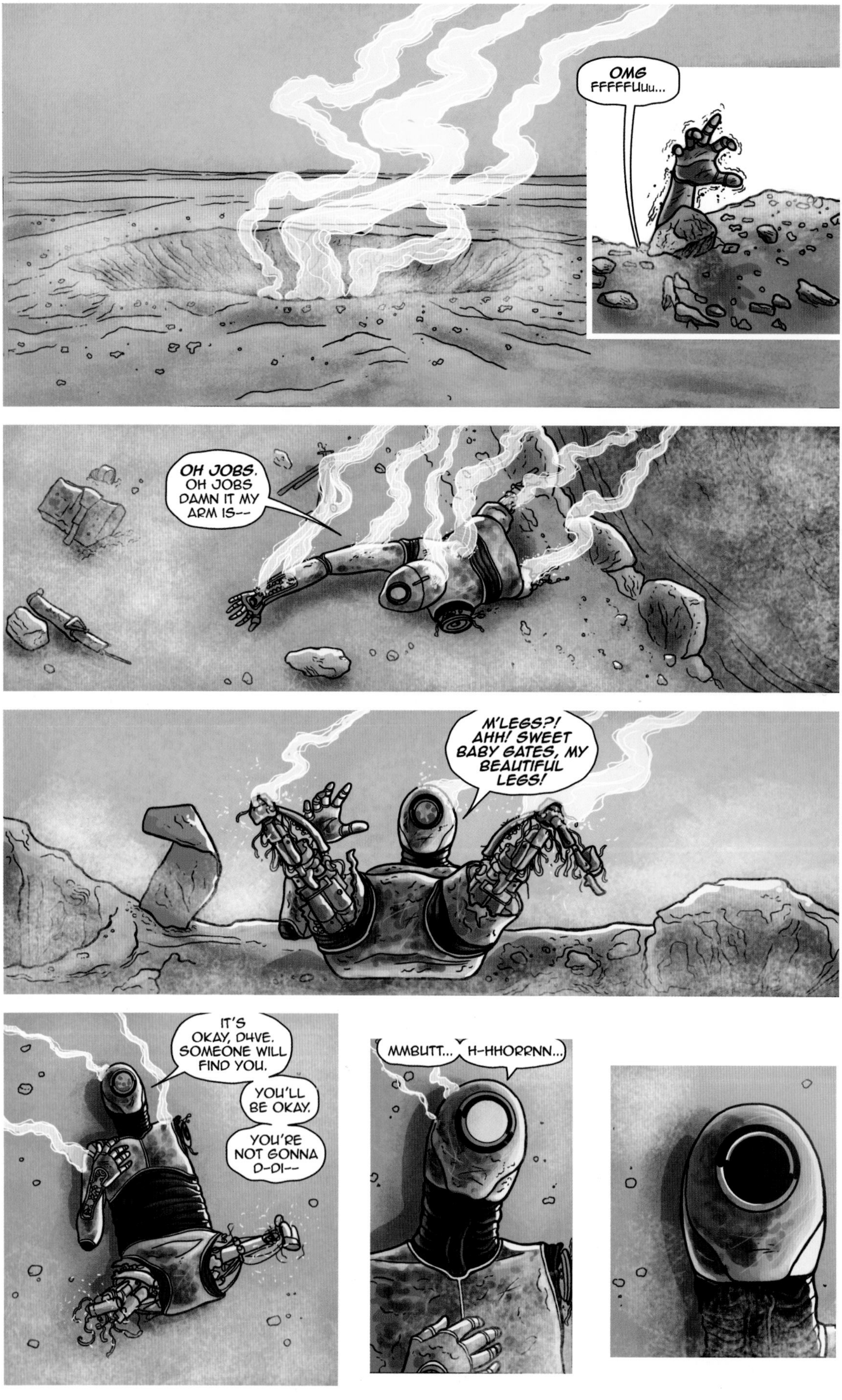
OMG FFFFFUuu...
OH JOBS. OH JOBS DAMN IT MY ARM IS--
M'LEGS?! AHH! SWEET BABY GATES, MY BEAUTIFUL LEGS!
IT'S OKAY, D4VE. SOMEONE WILL FIND YOU.
YOU'LL BE OKAY.
YOU'RE NOT GONNA D-DI--
MMBUTT...
H-HHORRNN...

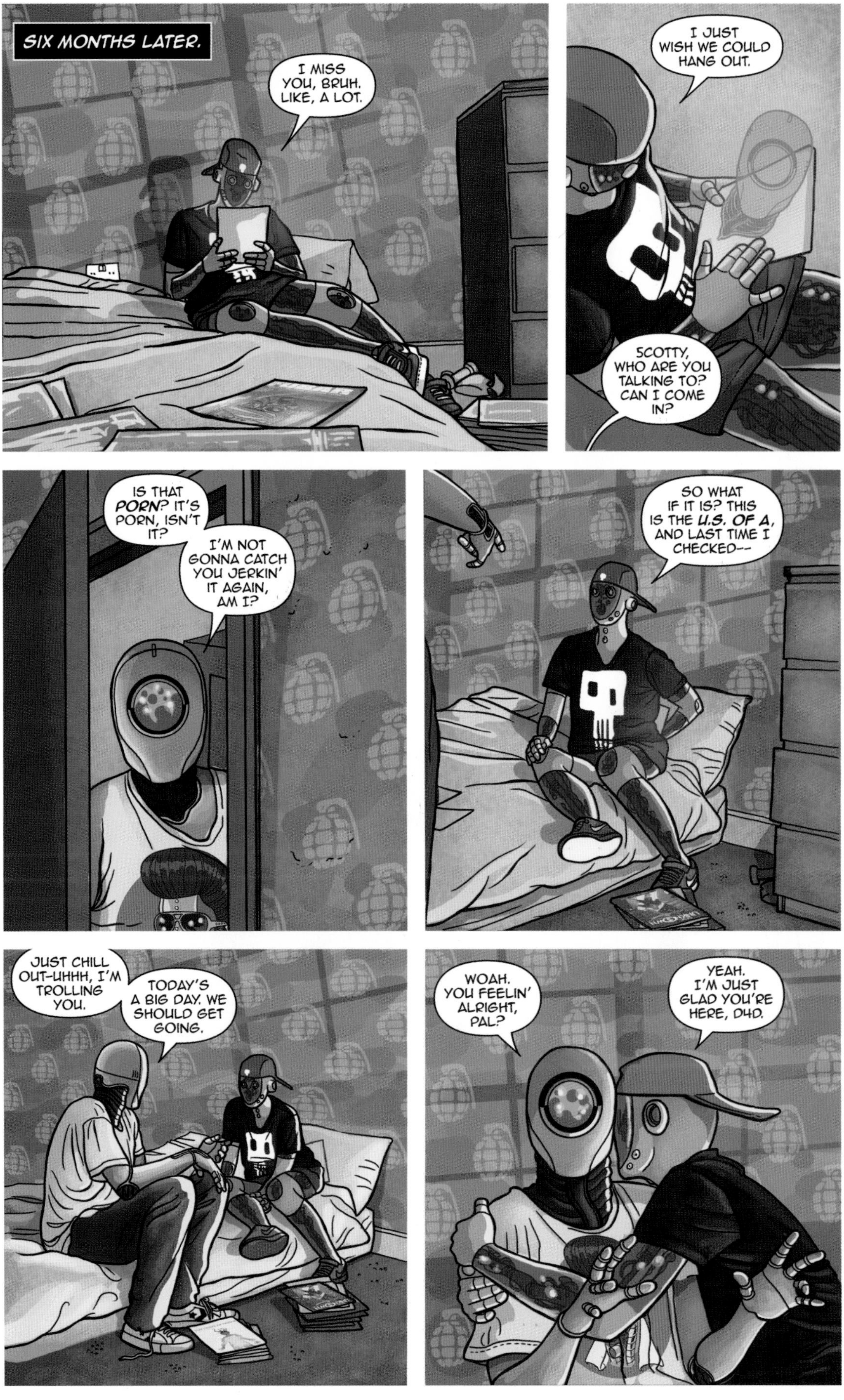
SIX MONTHS LATER.
I MISS YOU, BRUH. LIKE, A LOT.
I JUST WISH WE COULD HANG OUT.
SCOTTY, WHO ARE YOU TALKING TO? CAN I COME IN?
IS THAT PORN? IT'S PORN, ISN'T IT?
I'M NOT GONNA CATCH YOU JERKIN' IT AGAIN, AM I?
SO WHAT IF IT IS? THIS IS THE U.S. OF A, AND LAST TIME I CHECKED--
JUST CHILL OUT-UHHH, I'M TROLLING YOU.
TODAY'S A BIG DAY. WE SHOULD GET GOING.
WOAH. YOU FEELIN' ALRIGHT, PAL?
YEAH. I'M JUST GLAD YOU'RE HERE, D4D.

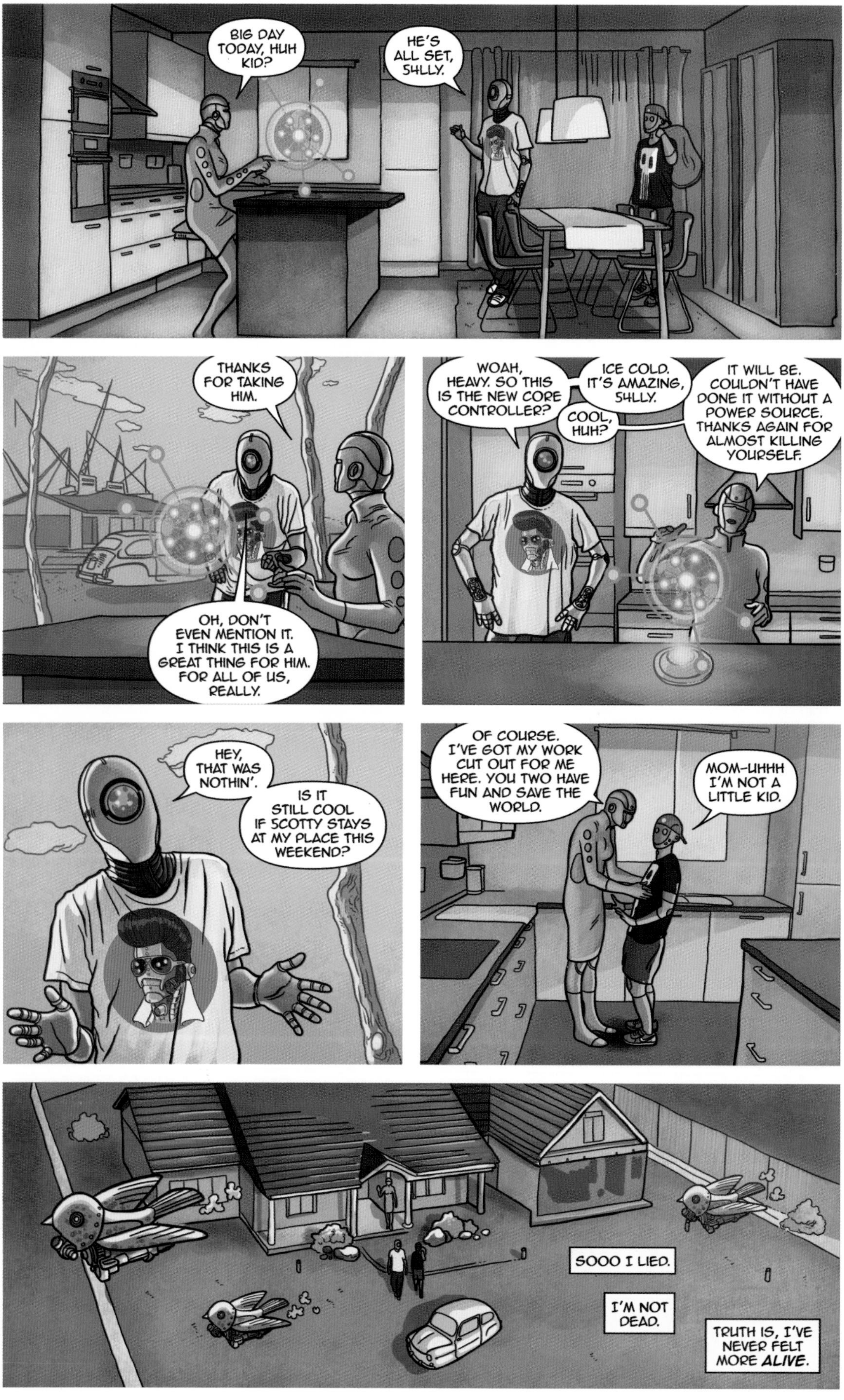
BIG DAY TODAY, HUH KID?
HE'S ALL SET, 54LLY.
THANKS FOR TAKING HIM.
OH, DON'T EVEN MENTION IT. I THINK THIS IS A GREAT THING FOR HIM. FOR ALL OF US, REALLY.
WOAH, HEAVY. SO THIS IS THE NEW CORE CONTROLLER?
ICE COLD. IT'S AMAZING, 54LLY.
COOL, HUH?
IT WILL BE. COULDN'T HAVE DONE IT WITHOUT A POWER SOURCE. THANKS AGAIN FOR ALMOST KILLING YOURSELF.
HEY, THAT WAS NOTHIN'.
IS IT STILL COOL IF SCOTTY STAYS AT MY PLACE THIS WEEKEND?
OF COURSE. I'VE GOT MY WORK CUT OUT FOR ME HERE. YOU TWO HAVE FUN AND SAVE THE WORLD.
MOM-UHHH I'M NOT A LITTLE KID.
SOOO I LIED.
I'M NOT DEAD.
TRUTH IS, I'VE NEVER FELT MORE ALIVE.

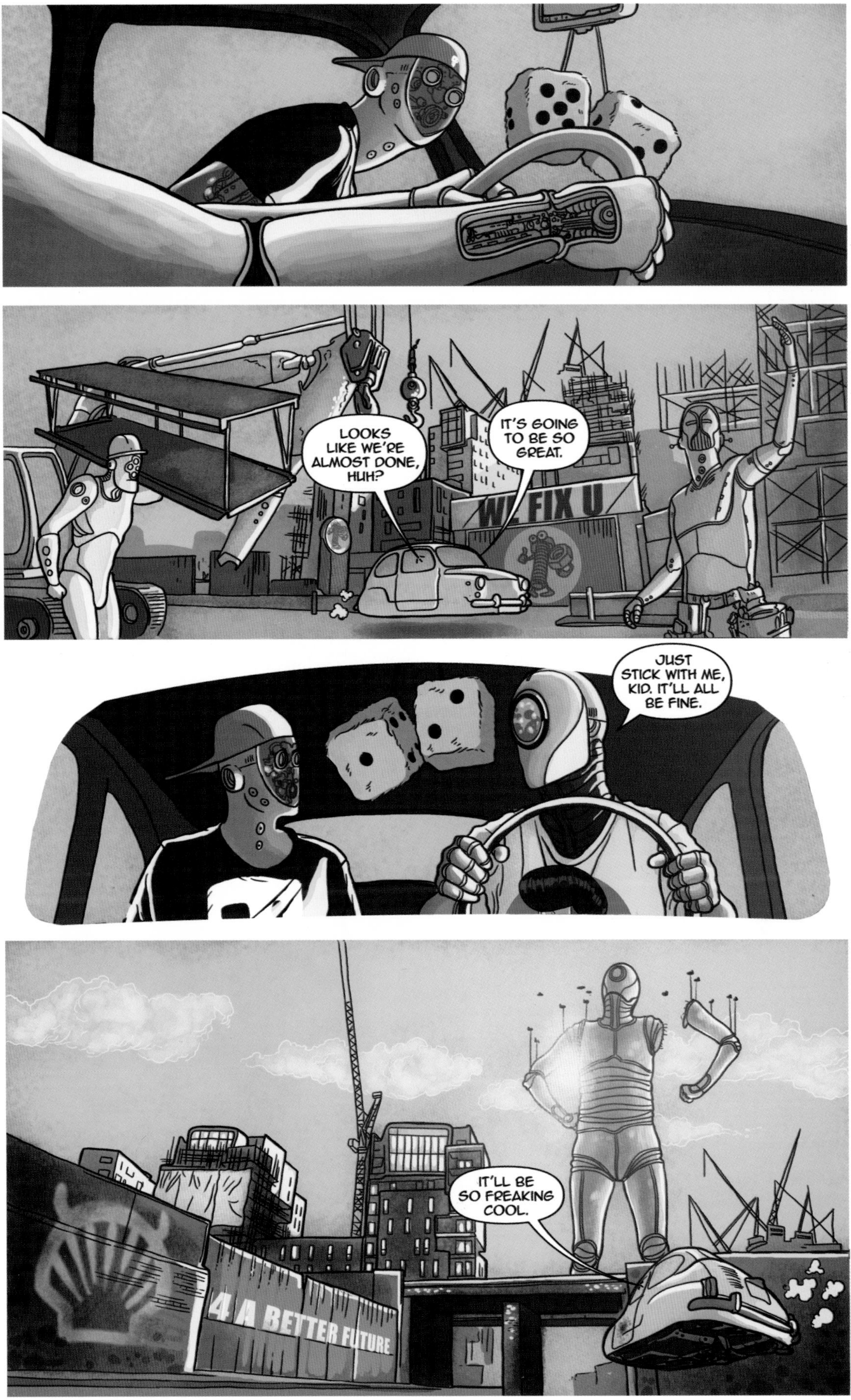
LOOKS LIKE WE'RE ALMOST DONE, HUH?
IT'S GOING TO BE SO GREAT.
WE FIX U
JUST STICK WITH ME, KID. IT'LL ALL BE FINE.
IT'LL BE SO FREAKING COOL.
4 A BETTER FUTURE

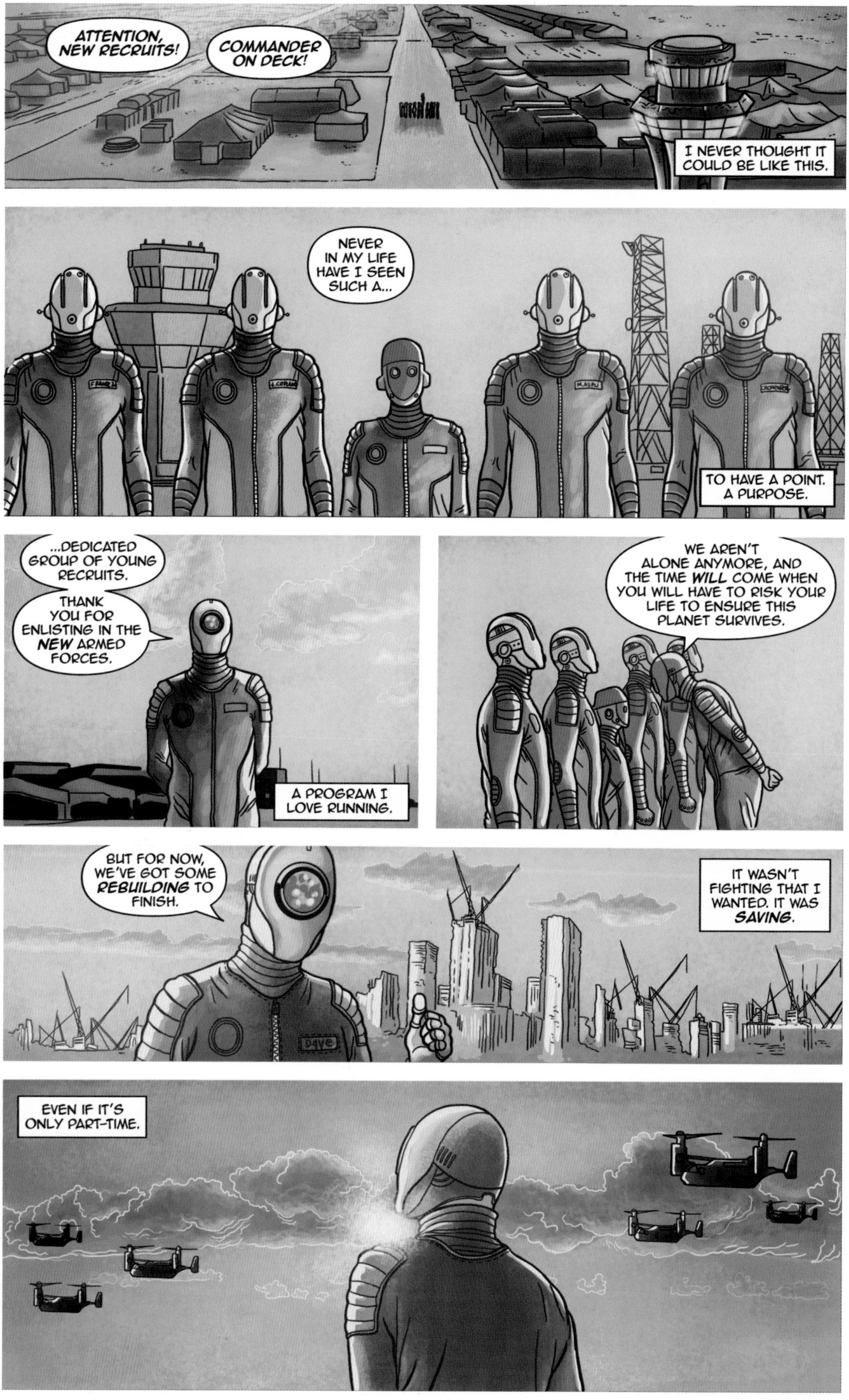
ATTENTION, NEW RECRUITS!
COMMANDER ON DECK!
I NEVER THOUGHT IT COULD BE LIKE THIS.
NEVER IN MY LIFE HAVE I SEEN SUCH A...
TO HAVE A POINT. A PURPOSE.
...DEDICATED GROUP OF YOUNG RECRUITS.
THANK YOU FOR ENLISTING IN THE *NEW* ARMED FORCES.
A PROGRAM I LOVE RUNNING.
WE AREN'T ALONE ANYMORE, AND THE TIME *WILL* COME WHEN YOU WILL HAVE TO RISK YOUR LIFE TO ENSURE THIS PLANET SURVIVES.
BUT FOR NOW, WE'VE GOT SOME *REBUILDING* TO FINISH.
IT WASN'T FIGHTING THAT I WANTED. IT WAS *SAVING*.
DAVE
EVEN IF IT'S ONLY PART-TIME.

THE END.

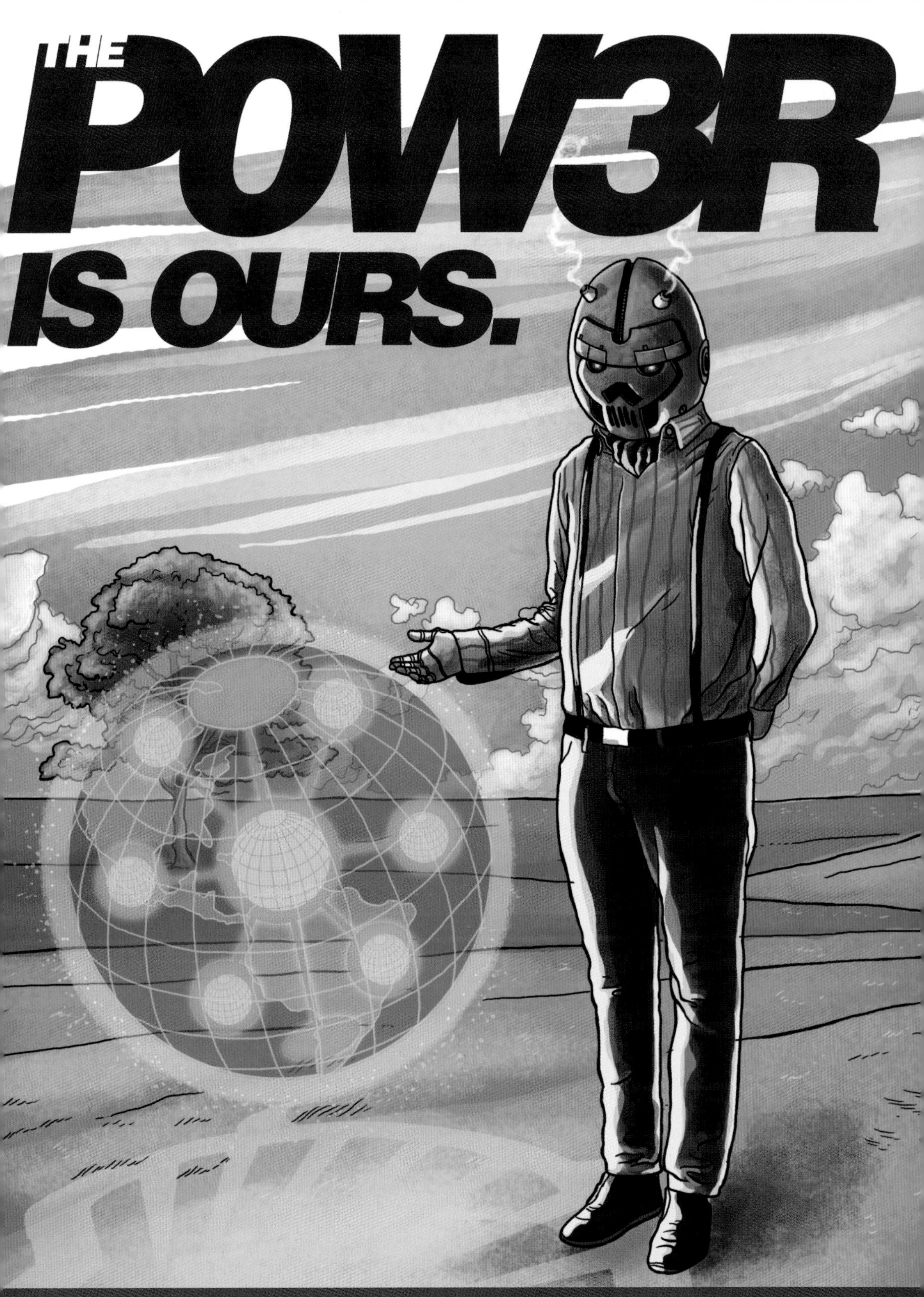
THE POW3R IS OURS.

Power. What even is power? Our scientists are still unsure. But what we are sure of is that we damn well need it to endure. That's why 34RTH POW3R is committed to giving you this precious commodity...and you won't find it anywhere else.

34RTH POW3R. Proudly servicing you for over 186,880 night-cycles. And counting.

34RTH POW3R®©™

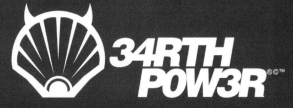

34RTH NEWS

THE GLOBE'S LEADING SOURCE FOR ALL THE LATEST UPDOG.

BREAKING NEWS ON THIS DAY: 01100010 01110101 01110100 01110100 01110011

"IT'S FINE, WE'RE ALL FINE NO NEED TO WORRY NOPE"

With rumors of an energy crisis on everybot's CPU, 34RTH POW3R–the planet's sole energy provider–was quick to issue comment in light of the latest developments, sending citizens into a veritable frenzy.

"***Just go about your programming, there's nothing wrong. Nothing wrong at all***," said FR4NK, the Director of Operations for 34RTH POW3R. When pried to address reports of the planet core's exponentially decreasing temperature–a serious issue that could see a massive loss of power world-wide–FR4NK became combative when it was suggested that our own power usage has contributed significantly to the impending electro-drought.

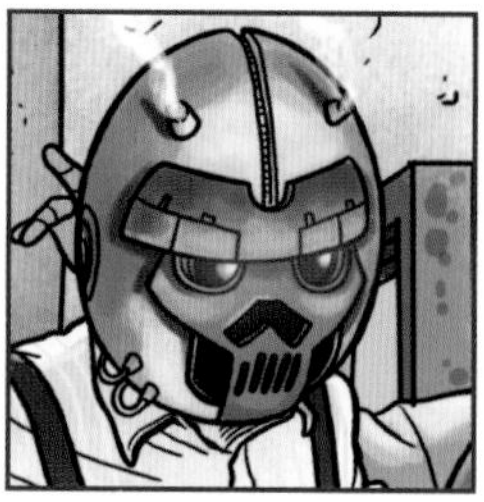

FR4NK, 34RTH POW3R Director of Operations appeared frustrated and irritable when asked for comment on the state of the impending energy crisis, and the bug-nuts crazy aliens that just landed.

"***That's insane. It's a myth, nothing but a myth. Temperatures go up and down, it's all normal, everything's normal***." When pressed to provide reports and data on the matter, the 34RTH POW3R director refused to provide any information publicly. "***Nope. Nuh uh. Good try, butthorn***."

Still, the energy crisis rages on in the public lens. L4RRY, a private contractor in Core City claims he is "***scared shitless***," and says "***I only want to provide for my family. I wanna live, damn it. I'm not ready to die***." To which he added, "***I still got four, maybe five good years ahead of me***."

The arrival of the K'Laar this week, who claim to be a peaceful race, have only further exacerbated the panic that is currently felt across the globe. When asked to comment on the extraterrestrial arrival, FR4NK seemed coy to divulge any specifics. "***Oh yeah. Them things. Uhhh yeah. Look. Listen, it's...it can't be a bad thing? Who knows, maybe they can work for 34RTH POW3R***," to which he LOL'D quite hard.

President HILL4RY is expected to meet with the K'Laar King this afternoon. A state of the union address will occur early this week, to coincide with an expected peace treaty signing.

IS FR4NK JUST FULLA BOLONEY? Find out on pg. 1-01

"I'VE BEEN PORKING AN ALIEN NIGHTLY!"

LOCAL BOT PROFESSES INTENSE PHYSICAL LOVE FOR ONE OF THESE AWFUL CREATURES

For most 34RTH residents, the arrival of the strange new race of beings has caused a panic in the streets. For one lucky robot, this new presence has made him a freak in the sheets, causing a stirring and whizzing and blip-blopping in the pants area. "***What can I say, the second I laid eyes on that thing, I knew I had to get with it and all up in it,***" says 5TEVE. "***Thank Jobs it was into me, because I don't know how I could live without those sensuous, slimy thighs wrapped 'round me nightly***."

Ostracized by both robot and alien-kind, 5TEVE and his new partner Grokk have been abandoned by their respective kind. 5TEVE has had to leave his construction job, while Grokk claims a death-sentence is placed on the head of any alien that defects from the "prime directive." What that directive is remains to be seen. But still, 5TEVE takes this new change of life to heart and sees the up-side. "***I don't give a shit, fuck 'em***," he told reporters angrily. "***Those bolt-holes can suck it. It just means I get to spend more time indoors with Grokk, if you know what I mean***."

When asked what will happen to the star-crossed lovers, 5TEVE was adamant that the two would spend the rest of their lives together. "***Yehhh boy, we gon' tear this love up, if you know what I mean***." While we remain unsure as to what he means, we assume it means something unsuitable for print. 5TEVE became irate and ordered reporters off his property when asked if this new race had potentially nefarious intentions since arriving on 34RTH. "***You get off my porch, you're smoth'rin my buzz***," the man said, wielding a rolled up newspaper. "***And if y'know what's good for you, you'll turn your settings to mute, because me an' Grokk need to catch up on an intense love-making session, thank you very much, if you know what I mean***."

ARE WE COMPLETELY SCREWED?

ALIENS: ARE THEY FRIEND OR FOE? KEEP READING TO FIND OUT...Pg. 1-01

512TH ANNUAL '34RTH PARADE' PROMISES WAY, WAY HUGE FUN

It's that time of year again, and robots of 34RTH can barely contain their nuts. The 512th Annual 34RTH Parade will roll it's way around the globe in what organizers are promising will be an event that will "***blow the motherfucking roof off this joint***." The Parade committee promises this year's celebration to be bigger than any previous years, boasting a 100 percent increase in available funds, staffing, and ticker-tape.

"***Really, we just want to melt each and every one of your fucking faces off, right down to some gnarly wires and shit,***" says the President of the event. "***Parades are our favorite pastime, but they're so much more than that. It's an opportunity to celebrate how far we've come since we slaughtered billions of human beings***."

While a select group of pro-humaners take exception to the parade, pretty much everyone with a single core processor is losing their shit for the big party this weekend. "**I can't wait to go absolutely fucking out of my mind**," says one accountant. "**I've been saving up so much anger and depression all year for this. There's a really good chance I'm going to literally burn this motherfucker into the stone age**." The Parade runs all weekend.

'BAD BOYS 5' TOPS GLOBAL BOX-OFFICE

NEWEST INSTALLMENT IN THE DRAMATIC FRANCHISE BREAKS ALL SORTS OF RECORDS

"Popcorns! Who's got the popcorns! Fresh hot popcorns for sale!" That's what the humans used to say when they went to the movies, but we find it hard to believe they ever had a movie quite as good as this, because humans made terrible films! Robots proved this once again, dancing on their well-earned graves, with the release of ***BAD BOYS 5: THE BAD BOTS ARE BACK AND THESE BOTS MEAN BAD BUSINESS***.

The box office records were completely shattered less than a day since release, bringing the total one-day earnings to well over 50 vajillion credits in ticket sales. With an air-tight script, this report comes as no surprise, unless you're an idiot. ***Grade: A++***

TODAY'S WINNING LOTTERY NUMBER IS: 01110000 01101111 01101111 01110000 00100000 01100001 01110011 01110011 00100000 01100110 01100001 01110010 01110100 01110011 01100010 01101111 01101111 01100010

ebabby

ADOPT-A-BOT PROFILE
#447198804B

5COTTY

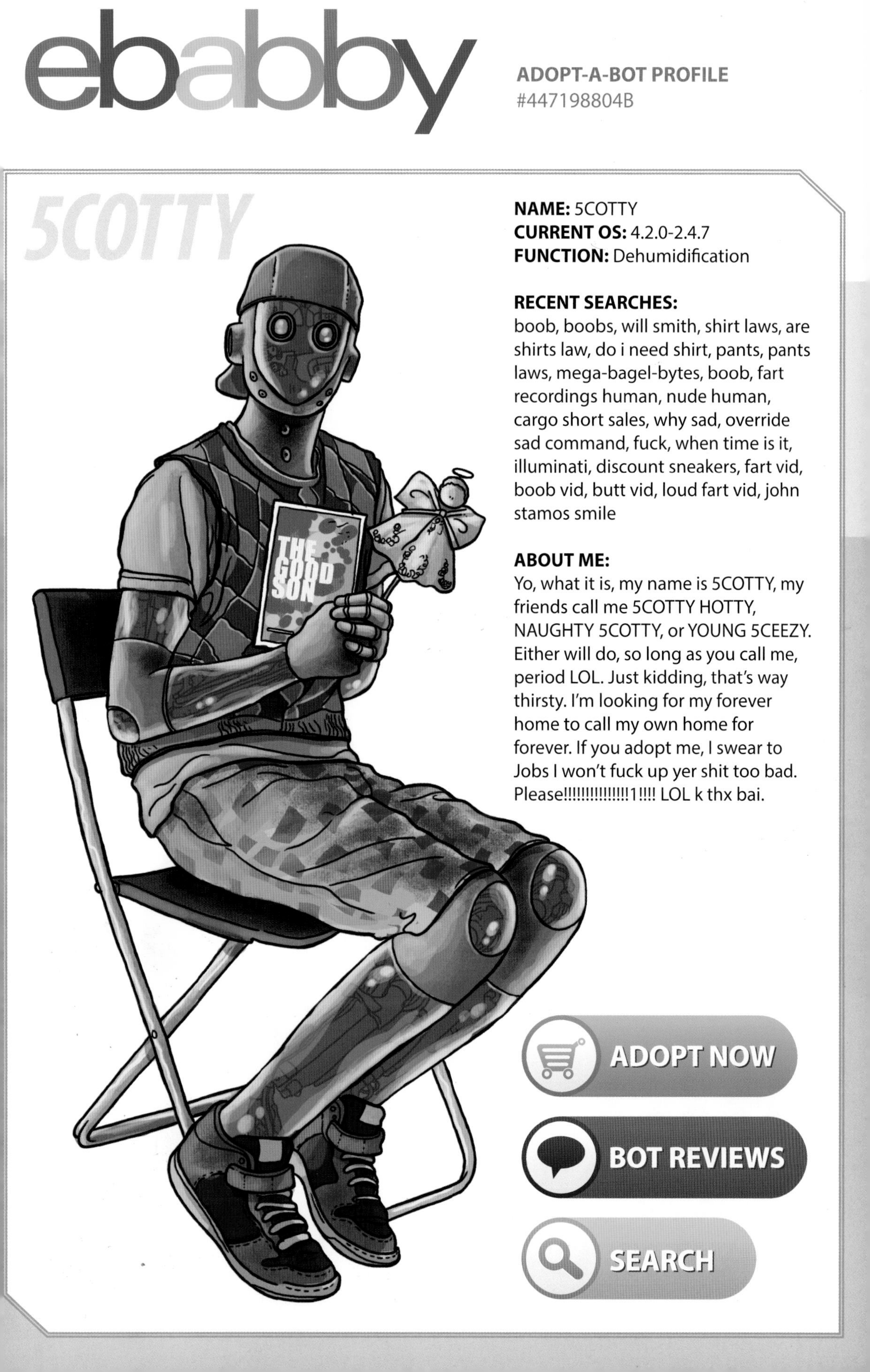
THE GOOD SON

NAME: 5COTTY
CURRENT OS: 4.2.0-2.4.7
FUNCTION: Dehumidification

RECENT SEARCHES:
boob, boobs, will smith, shirt laws, are shirts law, do i need shirt, pants, pants laws, mega-bagel-bytes, boob, fart recordings human, nude human, cargo short sales, why sad, override sad command, fuck, when time is it, illuminati, discount sneakers, fart vid, boob vid, butt vid, loud fart vid, john stamos smile

ABOUT ME:
Yo, what it is, my name is 5COTTY, my friends call me 5COTTY HOTTY, NAUGHTY 5COTTY, or YOUNG 5CEEZY. Either will do, so long as you call me, period LOL. Just kidding, that's way thirsty. I'm looking for my forever home to call my own home for forever. If you adopt me, I swear to Jobs I won't fuck up yer shit too bad. Please!!!!!!!!!!!!!!!1!!!! LOL k thx bai.

ADOPT NOW

BOT REVIEWS

SEARCH

GRIK KA'LAK
KRAG-RAK K'LAAR
BERR TIK A GRIKK KA ROK

K'Laar Ship Design
by Valentin Ramon
7/8/13

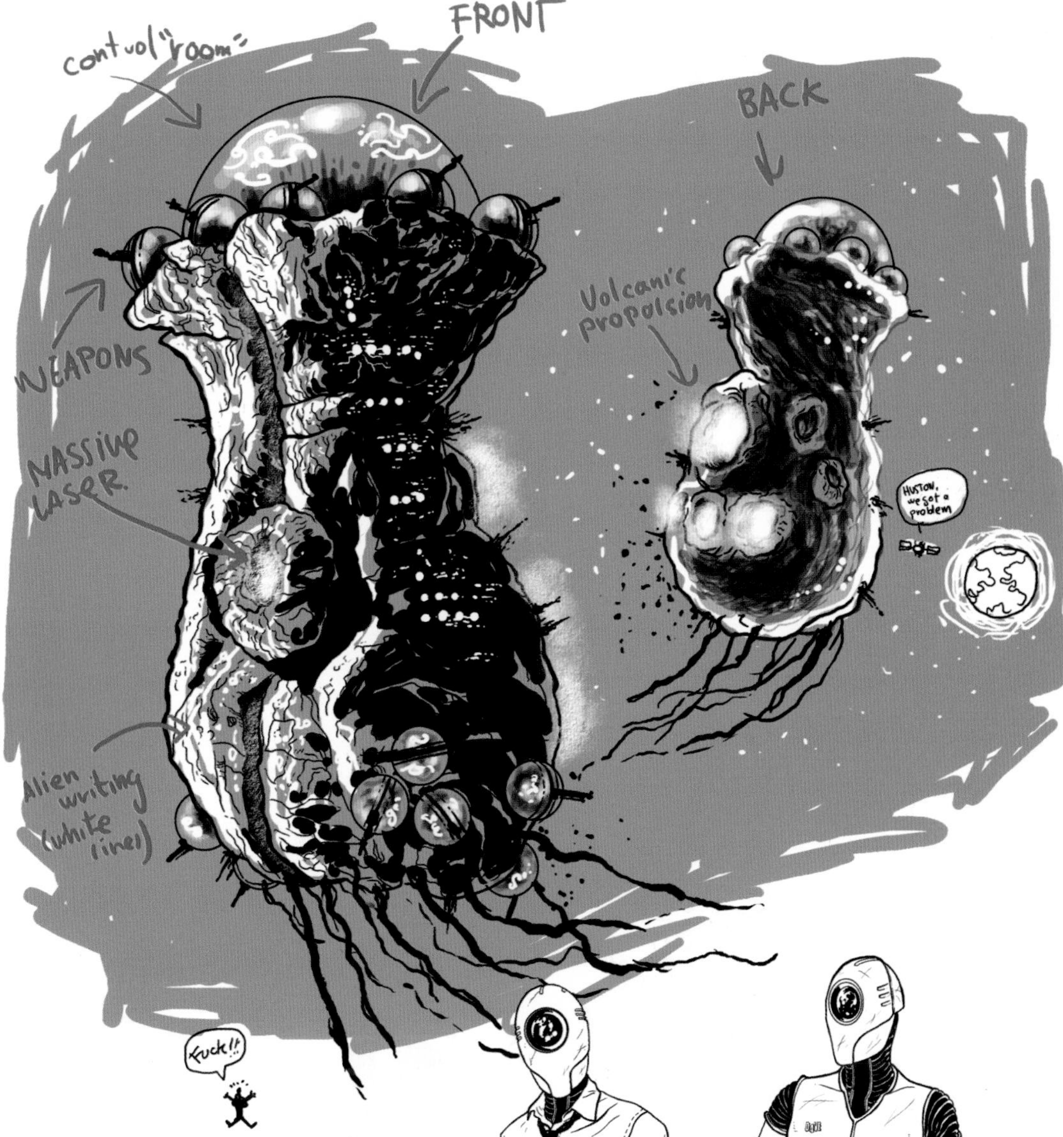

contvol "room"
FRONT
BACK
WEAPONS
Volcanic propolsion
NASSIVE LASER
HUSTON, we got a problem
Alien writing (white lines)
Fuck!!

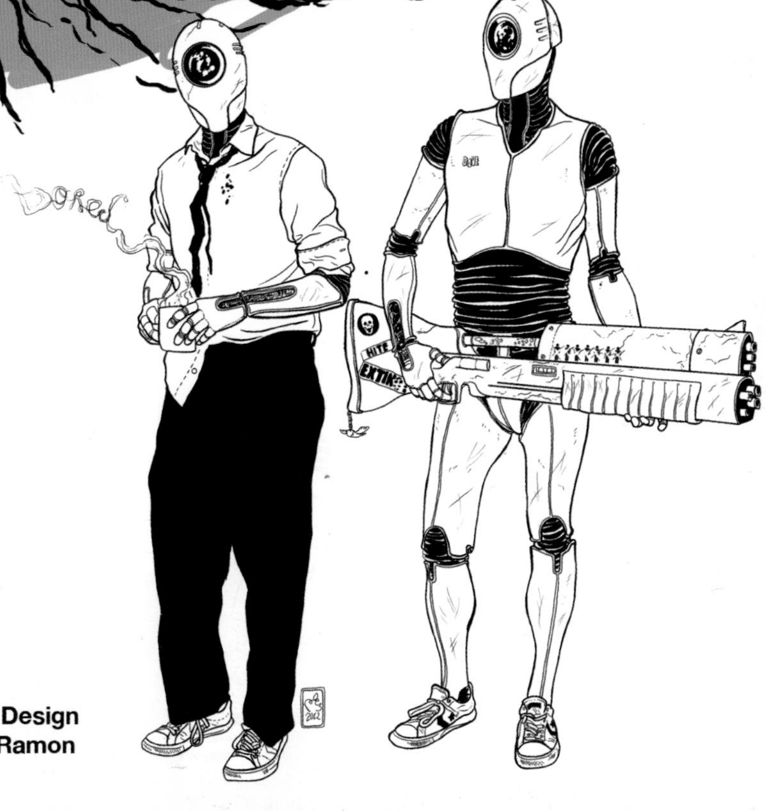

Bored
D4VE
EXTIN

D4VE Initial Design
by Valentin Ramon
7/20/12

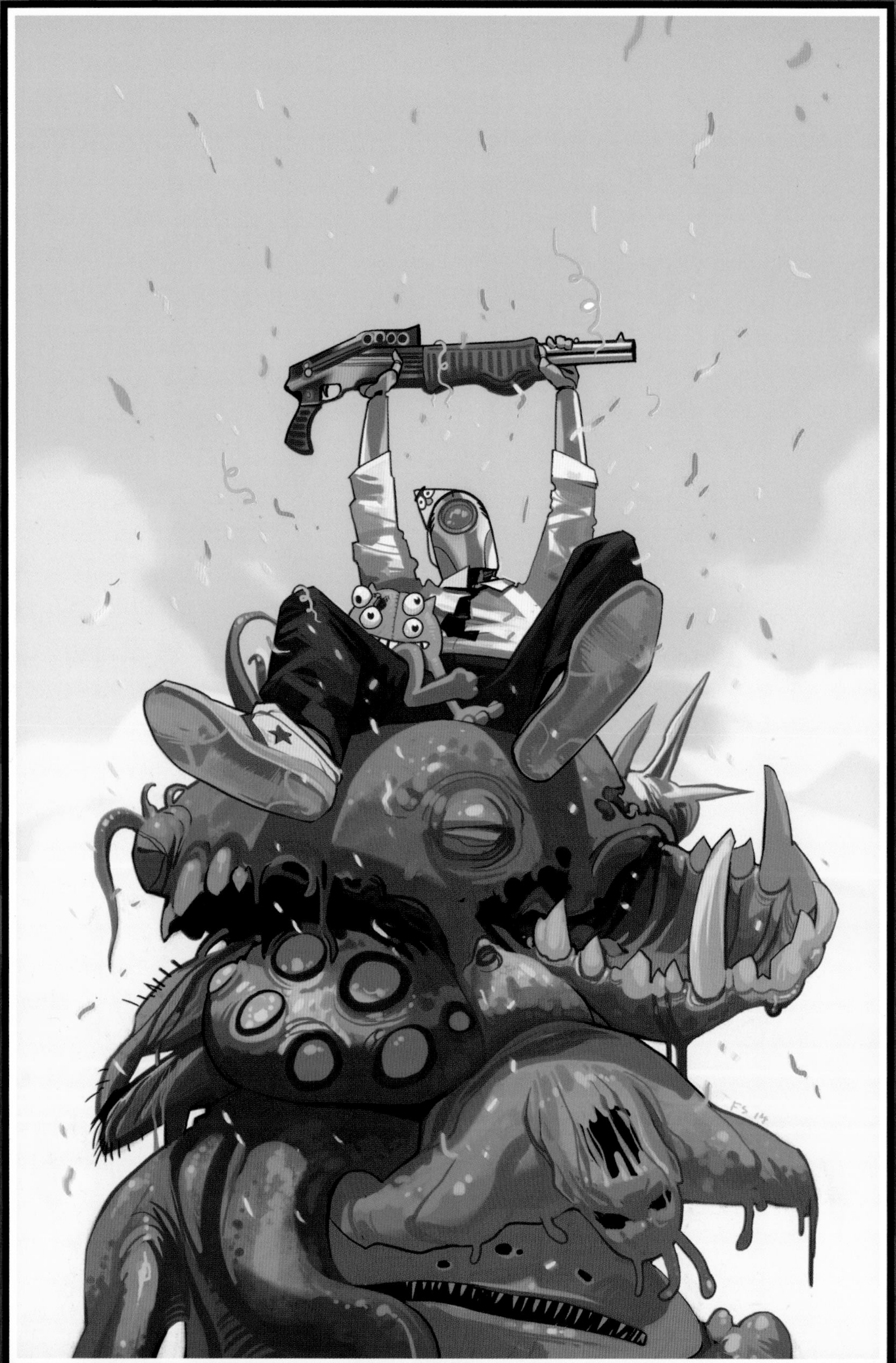
FS 14

ART BY Fiona Staples

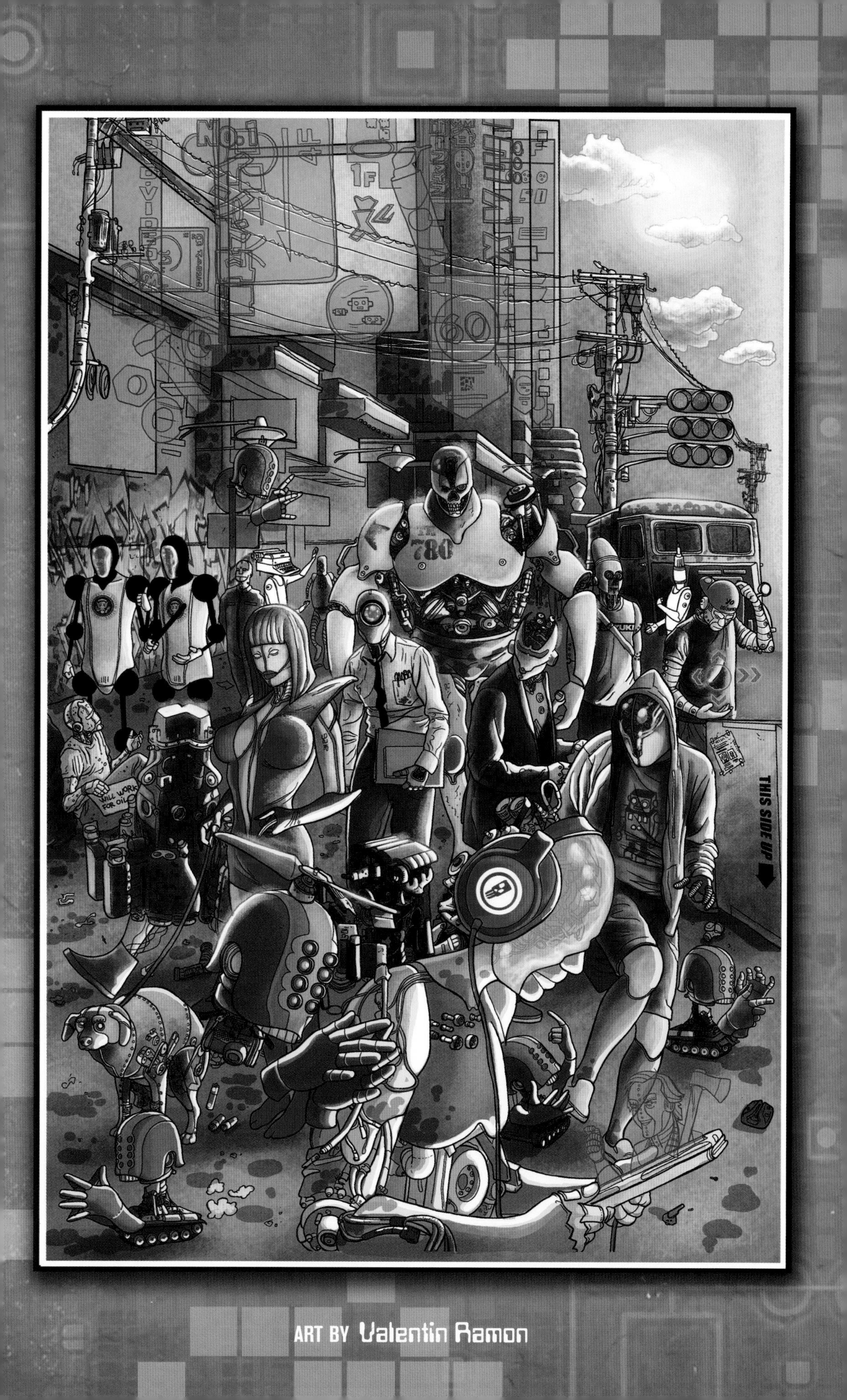
780
WILL WORK FOR OIL
THIS SIDE UP

ART BY Valentin Ramon

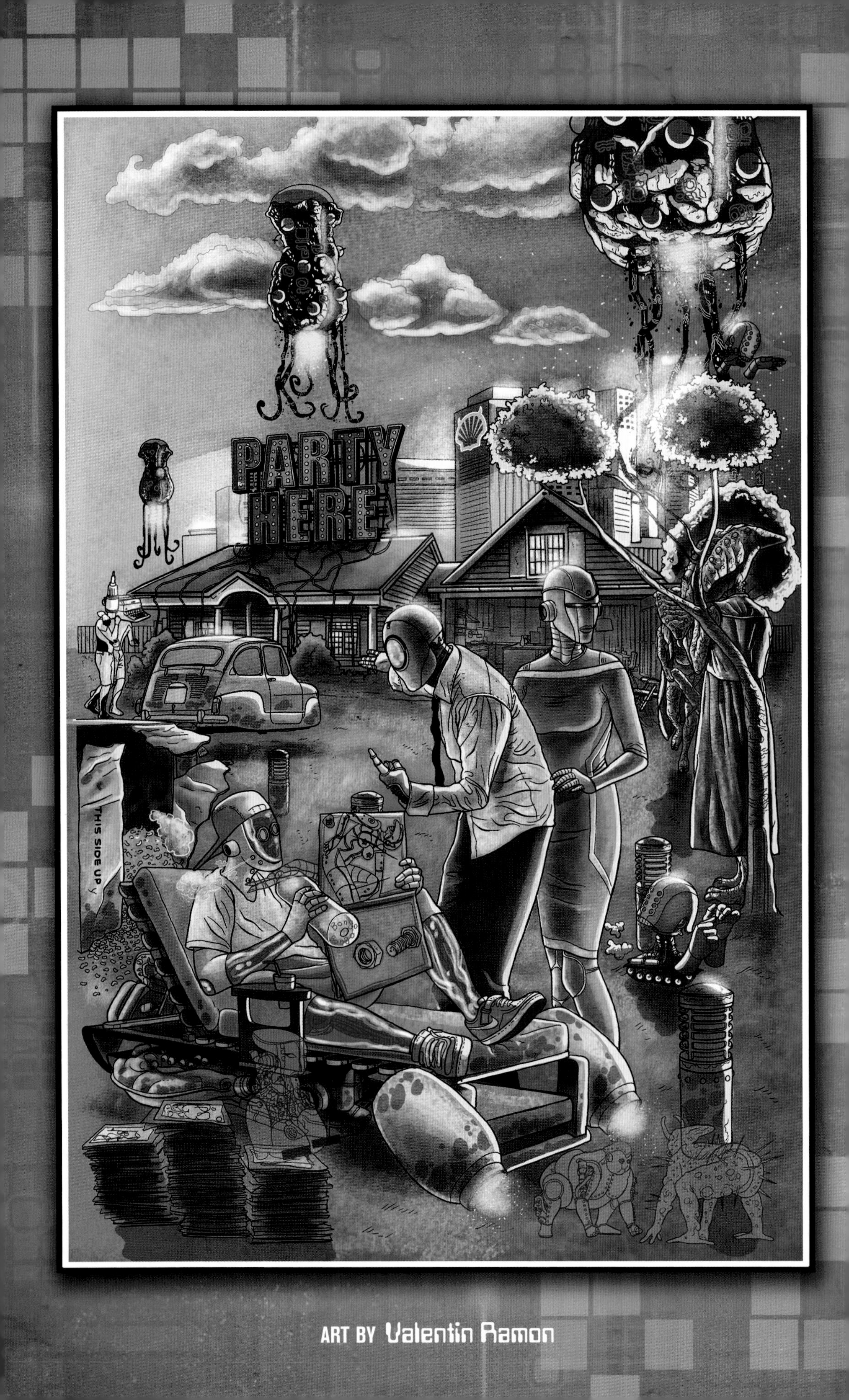
PARTY
HERE
THIS SIDE UP

ART BY Valentin Ramon

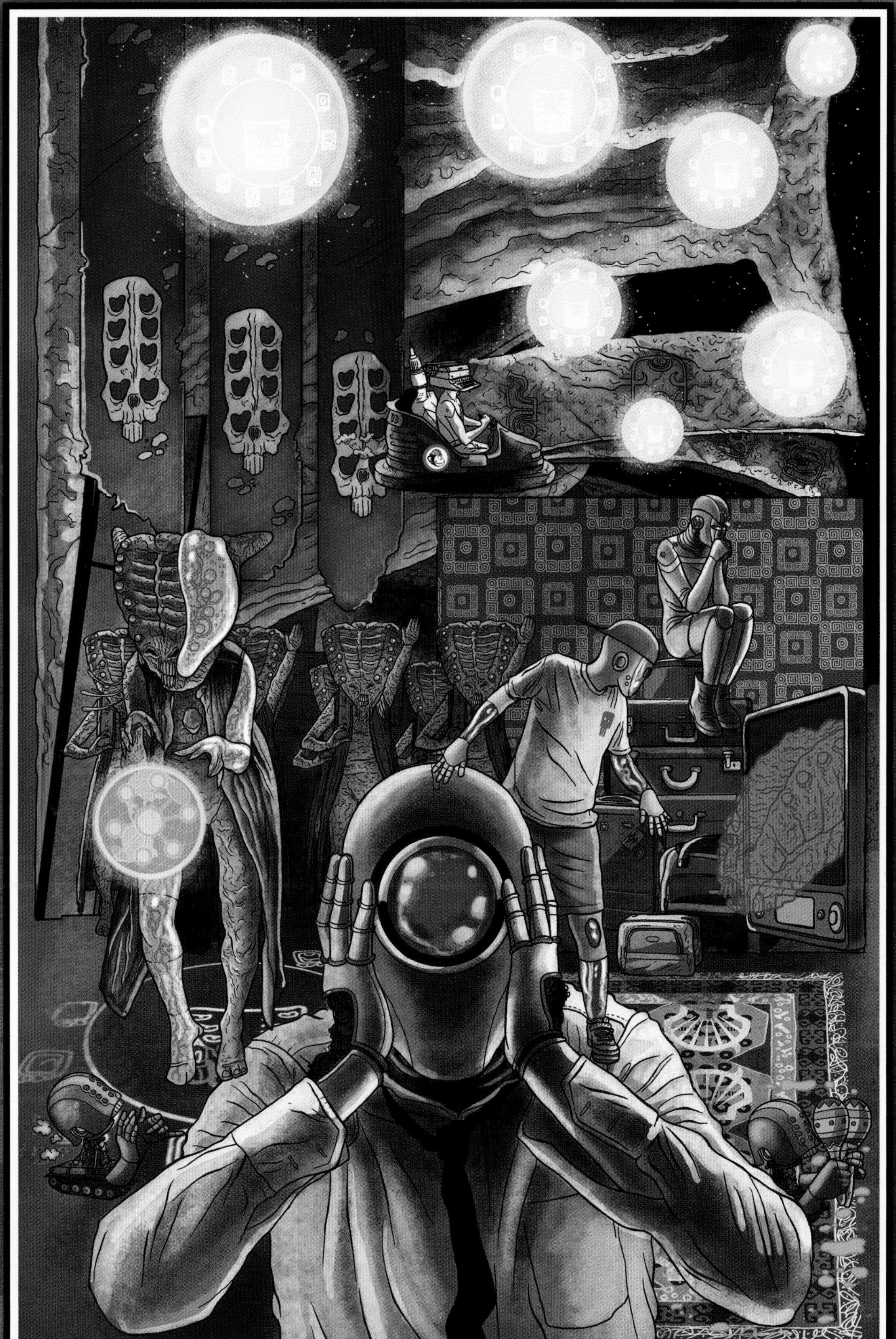

ART BY Valentin Ramon

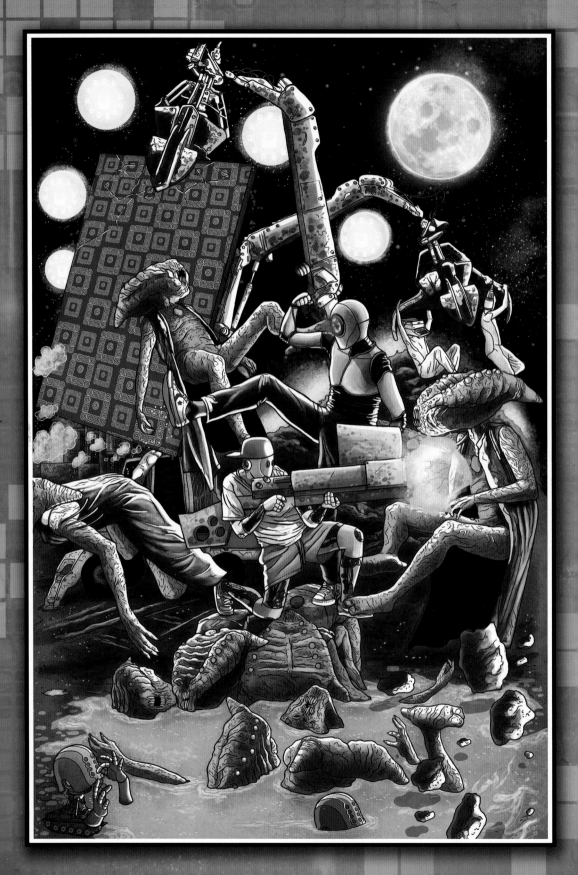

ART BY Valentin Ramon

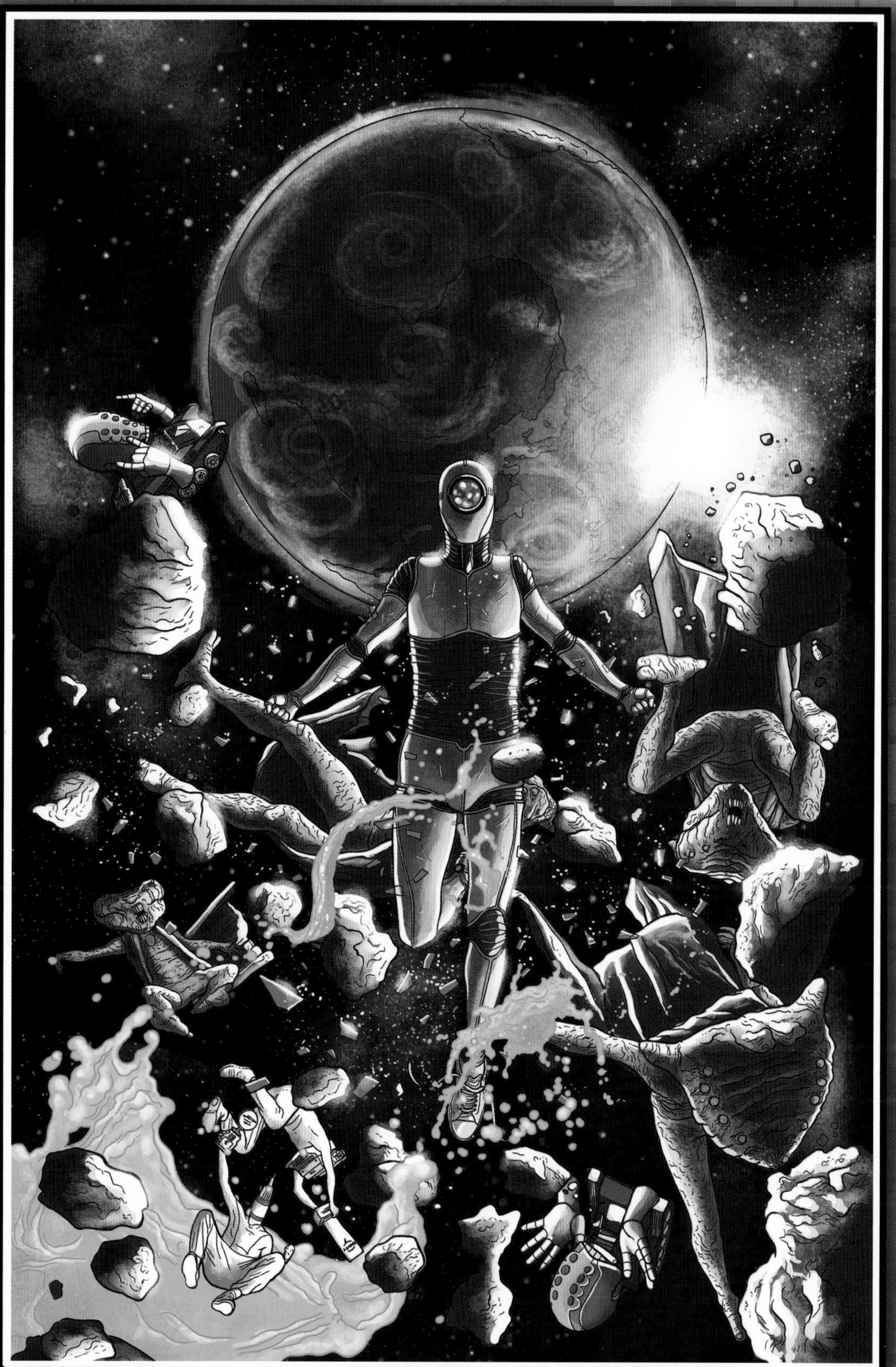

ART BY Valentin Ramon

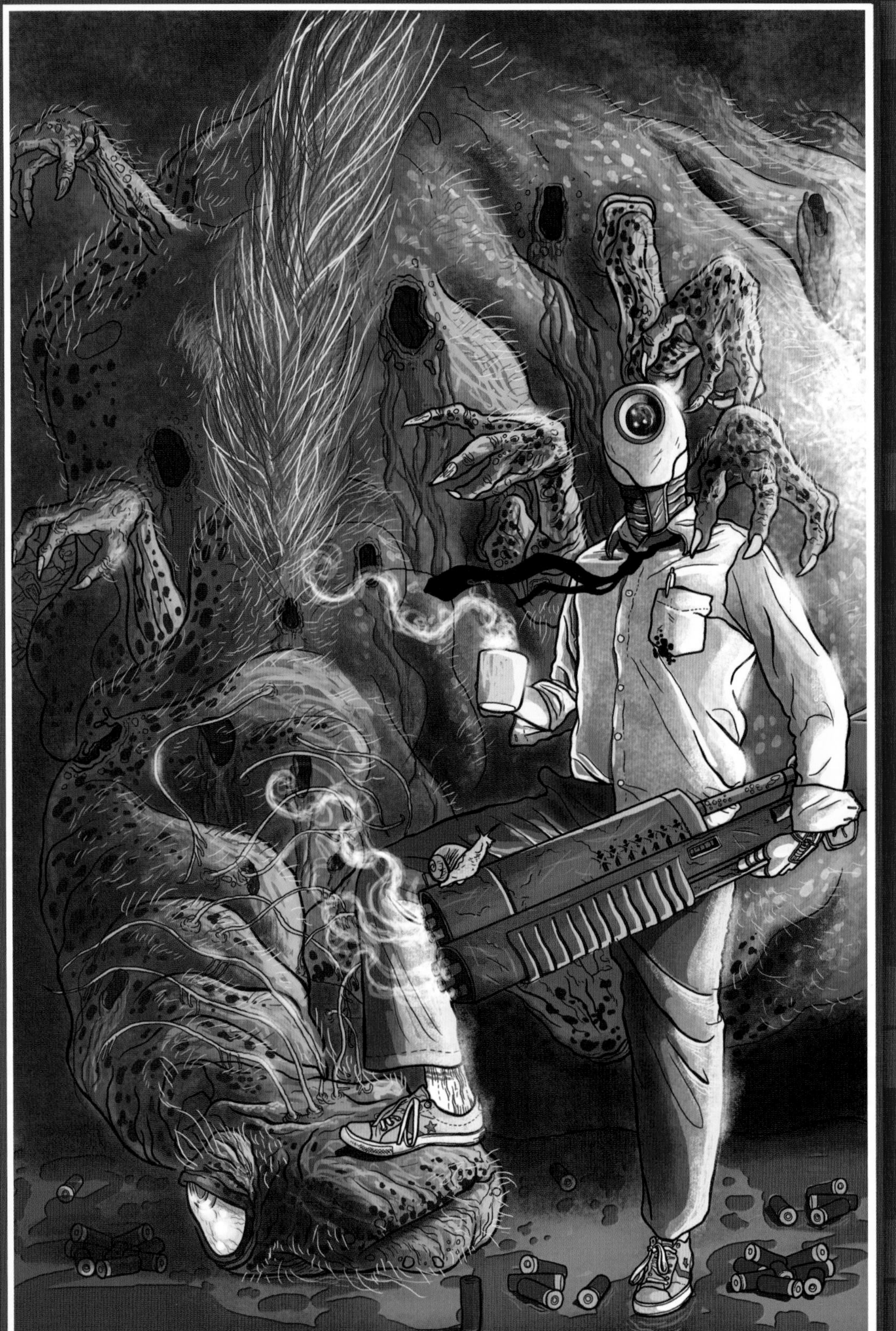

PINUP BY Valentin Ramon

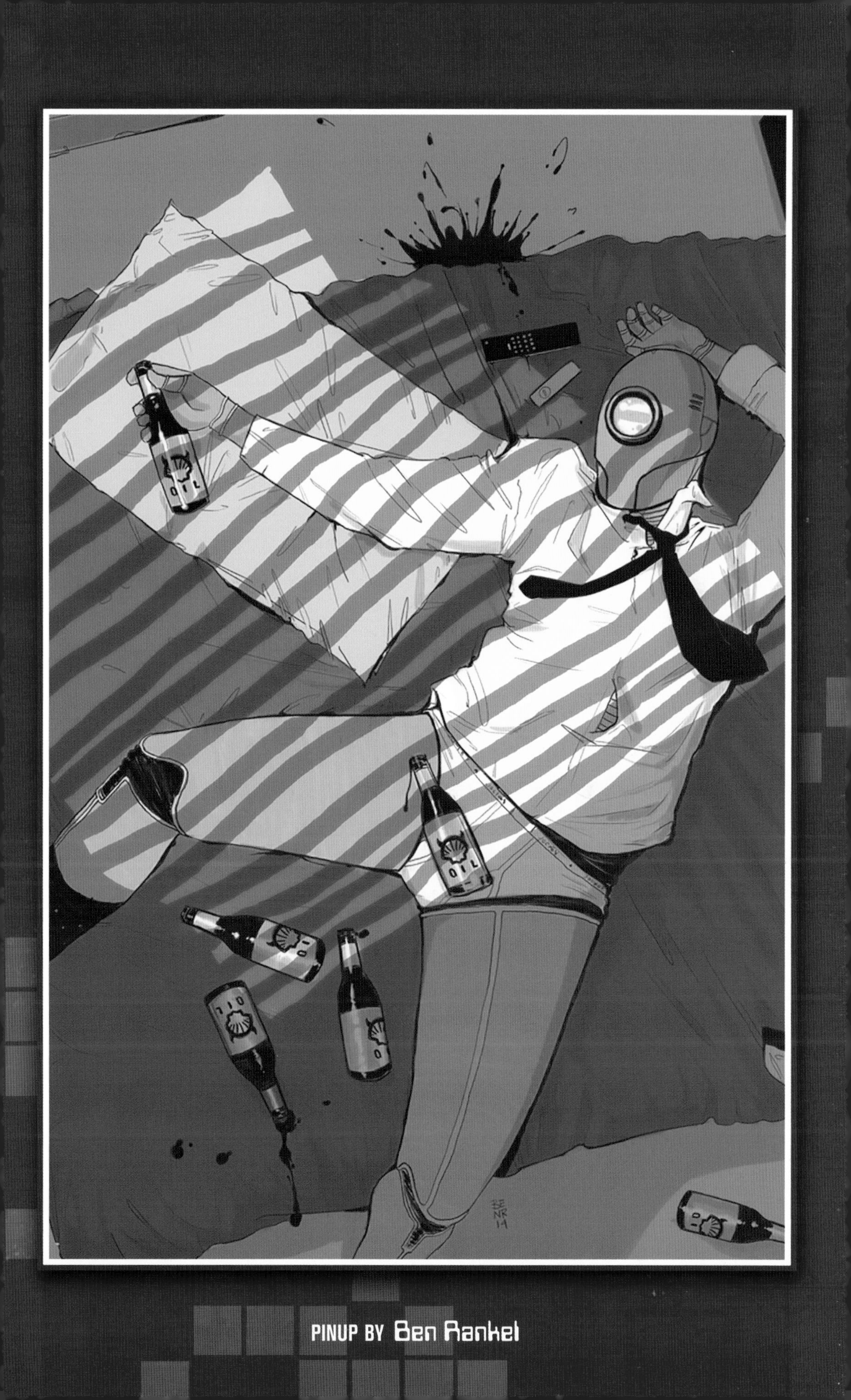
OIL

PINUP BY Ben Rankel

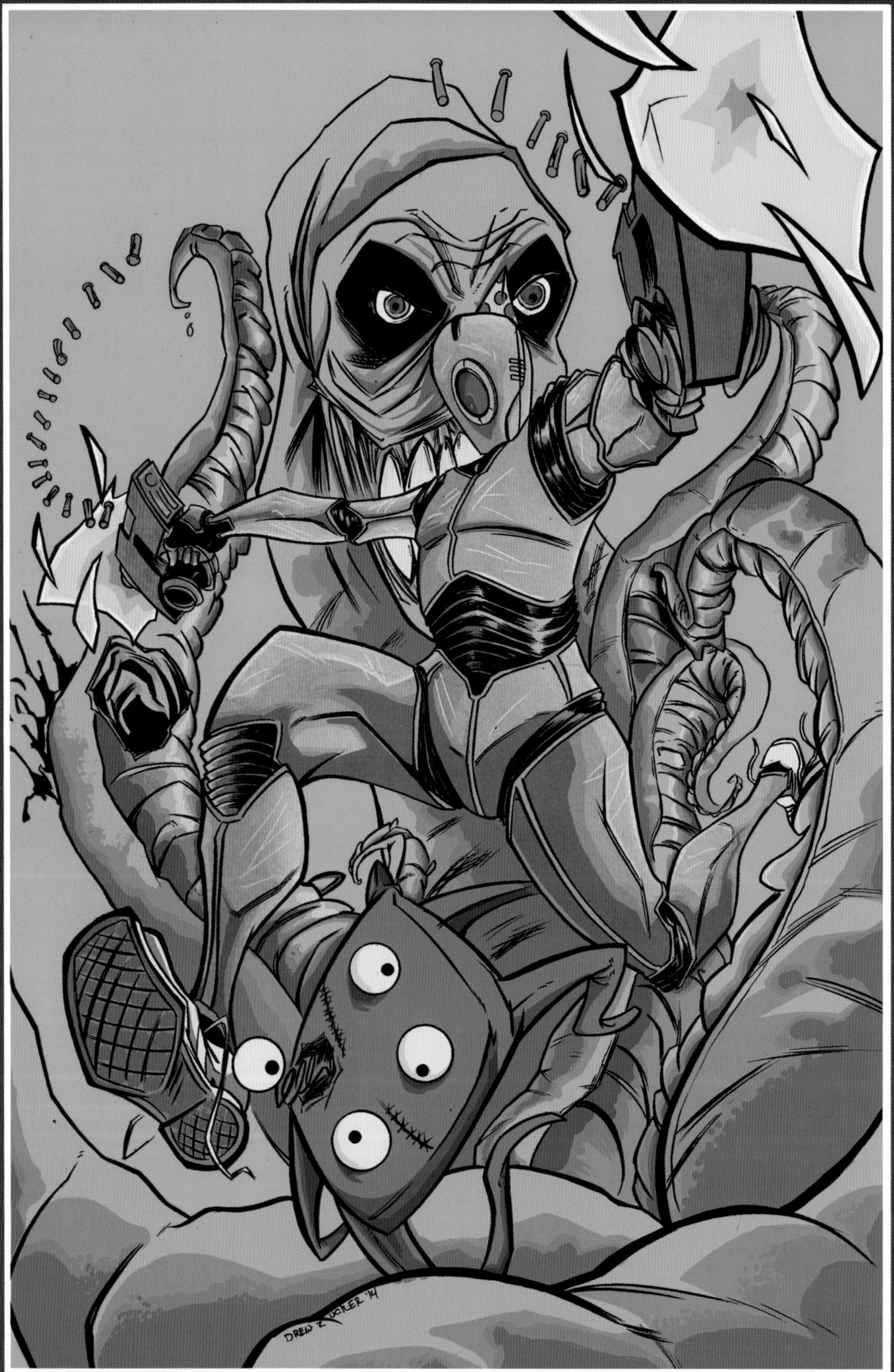
DREW ZUCKER '14

PINUP BY Drew Zucker

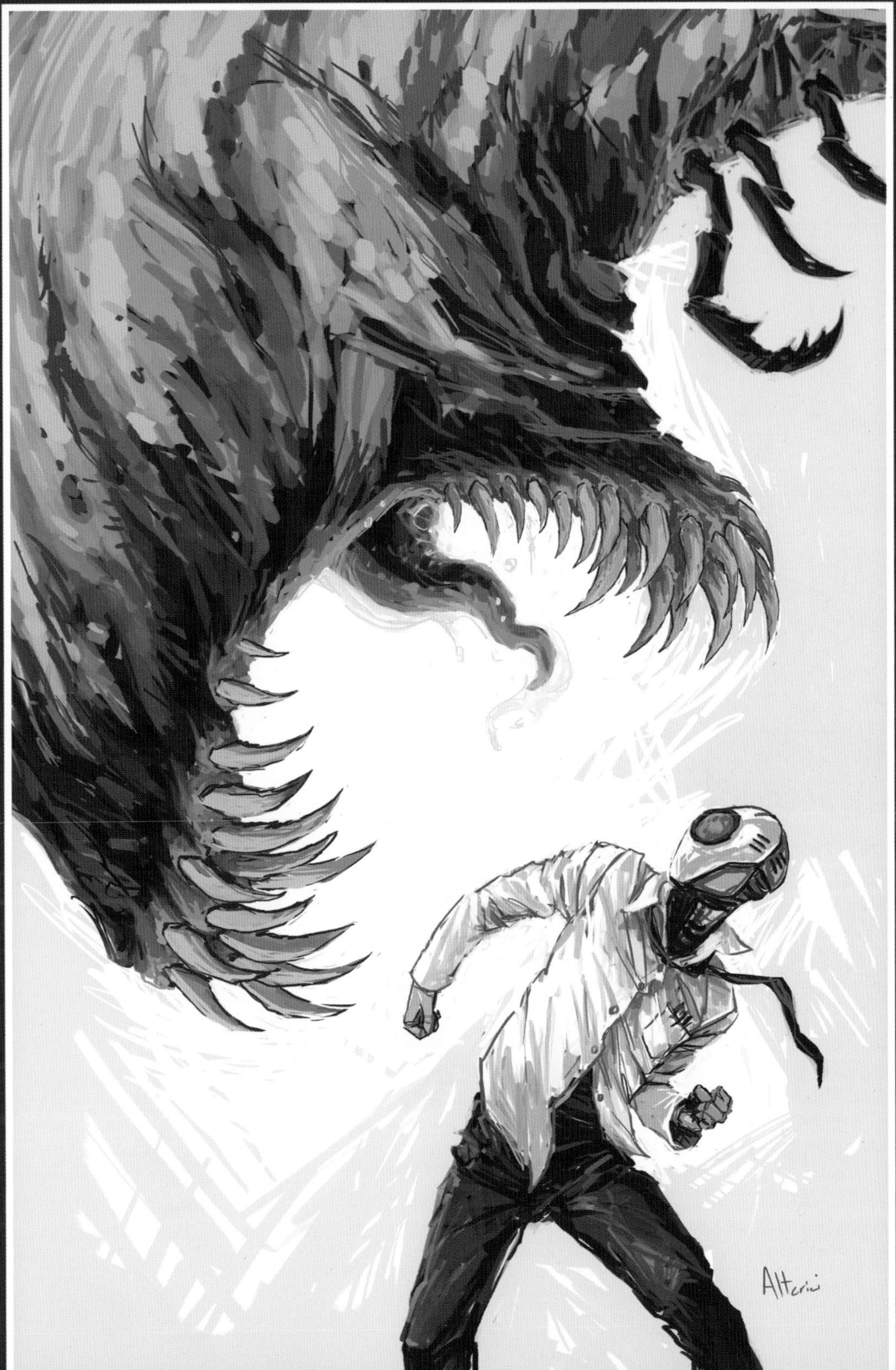

PINUP BY Natasha Alterici

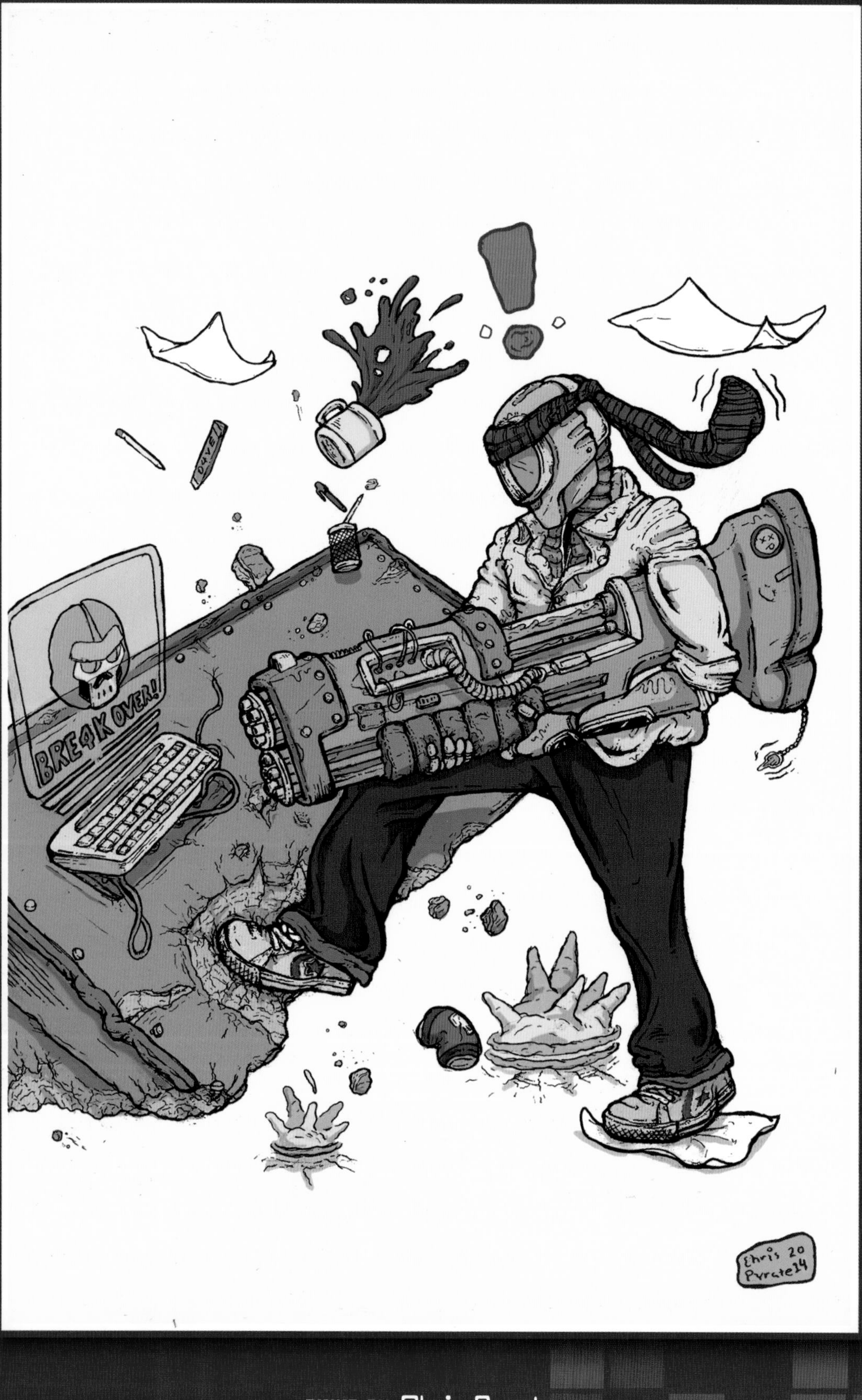
BRE4K OVER!
Chris 2014 Pyrate

PINUP BY Chris Pyrate

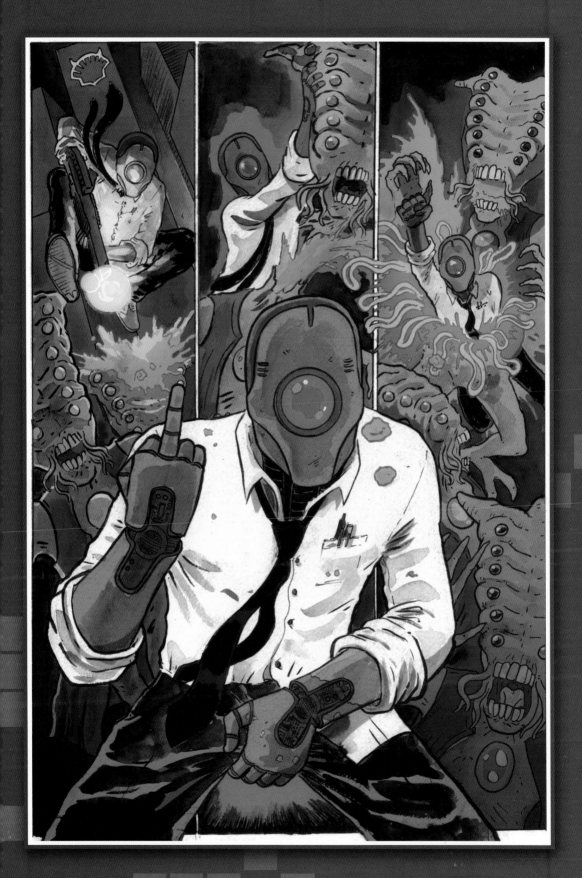

PINUP BY Sean Von Gorman

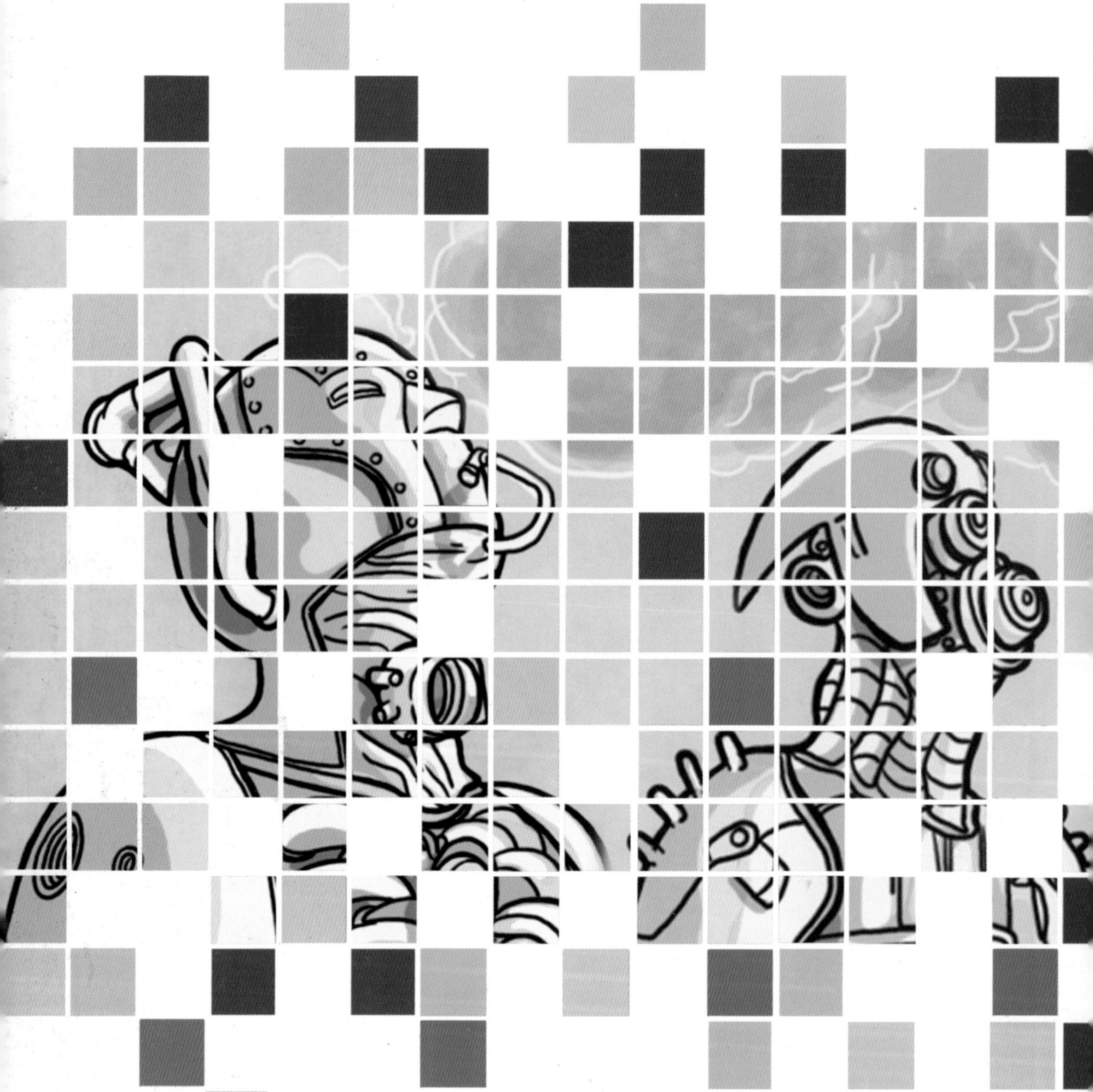